THE DEAD WALK THE EARTH

LUKE DUFFY

www.severedpress.com

ISBN: 978-1-925047-88-2

1

The rain continued to fall heavily, cascading down in sheets and saturating the muddy ground and the dark glistening wet figures that trampled through the thick mire. It seemed that it had been raining for a lifetime, tirelessly pouring from the heavens with a rhythmic drumbeat from the heavy droplets that splashed against every surface.

The two soldiers stood at the high wall, staring out into the dark wasteland, squinting through the squalls that blew in at them from all directions, waterlogging their clothing and soaking through to their bodies.

Pushing back his hood, hearing the material crinkle in his hands and feeling the biting cool air and rain sweep across his bare skin, the larger of the two threw his head back, blinking up at the night sky as the cold water streamed across his face and down his neck in rivulets. He watched the dense clouds as they drifted by above him, billowing in their multiple shades of grey.

"You have to love this country," he said loudly, in an attempt to be heard by the man standing next to him, over the loud pitter-patter of the downpour. He stuck out his tongue and savoured the icy water that splashed into his throat. "Even in the summer, it's as wet as a Tom Jones groupie's knickers."

"Does Tom Jones do many gigs these days?"

"I saw an old CD of him being used to scrape some mildew from the back of the stove in the kitchen the other day, does that count?"

"I suppose it will have to."

"Doesn't matter anyway," he said throwing his hood back over his head and looking out into the inky blackness. "You see anything out there?"

"Nothing, but I can still smell them," the smaller man sighed.

Far to the right, a sudden series of flashes erupted from one of the heavy machinegun positions stationed along the top of the wall, momentarily illuminating the long barrel and the men who sat behind it. A second later, the distant low rumble of the discharging rounds reached their ears. They watched as the bright red tracer bullets shot out from the parapet and glided gracefully through the air, far out into the dark landscape. They sailed for hundreds of metres in a gentle arc before finally arriving at their intended destinations.

In the distance, beyond the vision of the naked eye, they smashed their way through their targets, ripping their prey to pieces and ploughing on through to the other side. Some of the projectiles hit hard objects like rock, steel..., bone, ricocheting vertically into the air and soaring high like a glowing crimson rocket, far off in the distance.

The guns fell silent and the rain quickly picked up the same pattering beat again to keep the silent night at bay.

"There must be millions of them out there," the large man grunted and nodded thoughtfully, his eyes fixed on the blanket of darkness that stretched out far beyond the wall.

"When this thing began, there were seven-billion people on the planet. There aren't many places left with living people, so yeah, I'd imagine that we have quite a few of them on our doorstep."

The wall had been built early on in the days when anarchy reigned, using the same type of construction method that the American army had used in the early days of the Middle Eastern wars. Mass-produced T-walls, made from thick slabs of high-grade reinforced concrete, were slotted together like giant toy building blocks, creating a one kilometre square impenetrable ring around the base. A second, much higher wall was then built inside of the first, with towers and defensive positions placed at regular intervals along it and large heavy plate steel gates built into the thick six-metre high pillars.

Inside, a network of prefabricated cabins were placed into a strict floor plan, to act as laboratories, operations centres, offices, kitchens and living accommodation. Even during the early days of the chaos, when cities were being overrun and armies were wiped out, the plans had gone to the lengths to make arrangements for a recreation room and even a gym. It was a template taken directly from one of the many Forward Operating Bases that the allies had used in Iraq and Afghanistan.

Originally, it had been intended as an FOB, with soldiers and scientists continuing the fight against the armies of rotting bodies. When they realised that the war was lost, the scientists abandoned the base, but many of the soldiers stayed, keeping their families safe within the walls. During the first years, a steady stream of refugees arrived at the island of life that held out amidst an ocean of death, adding to the growing community.

Beyond the outer wall, for hundreds of metres, the barren wasteland was carpeted with barbed wire obstacles and deep ditches, saturated with anti-personnel mines and low wire entanglements that would snare anything that stumbled into the demarcation zone around the fortress.

The machine gunners and sharp shooters, stationed in the towers, knew the area and the exact range of each and every dip and fold of the terrain. They sat and watched, keeping a continuous vigil on their very own 'No-Man's-Land', chalking up their nightly kills and awarding extra rations of their toxic homemade vodka for the man with the most confirmed hits at the end of each day.

For a vast area around the stronghold, lay a desolate wilderness of death and destruction. Burnt and twisted vehicles, APCs, and even tanks, sat silently rotting away, their occupants still inside and entombed forever.

Countless bodies, dead and undead, mangled and twisted, lay ensnared within the barbed wire, or trapped at the bottom of the deep trenches, unable to work their way free from their eternal bondage while the bones of the thousands of fallen, their tattered clothing stubbornly clinging to their remains, slowly crumbled to dust as countless seasons passed them by. The place was a boneyard with the skeletons of men and machinery, all stirred together in a thick soup of churned mud and decay.

Over the years, there had been many attacks on the base. All had failed, but there were a few times when the brave defenders had believed that they were living through their final moments.

Raiders, rogue army units, and armed civilians wanting to seize what was not theirs from the men and women inside, launched countless assaults against the walls, only to be repelled by a ferocious defence, born from the desperation of the people manning the walls to hold on to what they still had.

Their most valued possession was their life and the lives of their families within the protection of their walls. They had all lost and suffered and were determined to cling on to what remained of their existence.

Their deaths came at a high price to their enemies.

Then there were the others, the dead. No matter how many of them were destroyed, they never retreated. Their sustained onslaught against the walls brought the men and women inside to the brink of defeat. Trapped for years, they watched and battled as the army of walking dead piled up around them, trampling over their fallen to launch themselves at the fortress walls. But the barrier held and when the fires came, the thousands of reanimated corpses were reduced to ash. The flames had almost engulfed the survivors too, but it had been a gamble they had to take, or risk being overrun.

Only the searing flames that consumed thousands of them, forced the dead back. Their mindless attacks thwarted, they had retreated to a safe distance, beyond the wire. Now, they remained at the outer edges of the defences, encircling the tiny island of humanity, watching and waiting, as though the years of innumerable failed attacks had taught them of their own mortality.

The air was thick with their stench. It drifted to the living like a creeping vapour, slowly crawling across the barren ground and permeating everything that it touched. Their sound, the low incessant hum of their voices, moaning and wailing in unison, covered the land like a pulsating blanket, haunting the survivors to their core.

They were always there, crowded together in a dense throng of rot. Their black and decaying tissue slowly fell from their emaciated bodies. Their ravenous, lifeless eyes, always gazed longingly at the high impenetrable walls that protected the living people beyond.

Since the dead ceased their mindless attacks, the people within the base had argued that the billions of corpses that now roamed the earth might possibly be gaining a degree of self-awareness. Many shuddered at the thought and refused to believe that the dead could be learning and remembering.

“Well, I suppose it’s time we got a move on.”

The two soldiers descended the steps, their boots squelching in the sucking sludge as they stepped down into the area in front of the large steel gate. Together, they began preparing themselves for what was ahead. They removed their thick nylon waterproof cloaks, filled with holes and tears and barely capable of withstanding the lightest of showers. They rolled them up tightly and stuffed them in to their small packs along with their supplies of food and water.

They were stripped for battle, ready to move with all unnecessary equipment stored away in their packs. Their weapons, equipped with silencers, were oiled against the elements and their ammunition tucked into the pouches of their armoured vests, accessible and easy to reach. Covering their bodies, they wore thick layers of clothing made from buckskin and denim, topped with greaves and vambraces made from hard moulded leather and ceramic armour plating to protect their arms and legs.

They inspected one another, ensuring that their straps were tight and secure, checking that nothing protruded that could be snagged, or cause them to become entangled.

"Have you two girls finished checking each other out?"

They turned to see a figure striding towards them from across the open space between the wall and the buildings that housed the survivors. They had already recognised the voice, but the dark silhouette and long strutting gait was also unmistakable.

"Shit," one of them grumbled under his breath, "here comes the *Fuhrer*."

She stood in front of them, indifferent to the cold water that ran through her hair and over her pale face. She was tall for a woman, with hard refined features and bright blue eyes. Even now, after all the suffering and horror that they had endured, her eyes sparkled with a brightness that seemed to radiate from deep within her. She was pretty once, and even now with endless hardships behind her, and no doubt, many more to come, she had a natural beauty about her. A beauty that came without effort and was as much to do with her bearing, as with her physical appearance.

"You come to see us off then, Captain?" The large man grinned at her as he began fastening the chinstrap of his helmet. "You're not going to get all misty on us, are you?"

"Chance would be a fine thing," the other retorted, nodding at the captain as he lit a cigarette and inhaled deeply. "She has nitrogen in her veins, not blood."

She smiled fleetingly, and watched the plumes of pale blue smoke from the burning cigarette drifting up into the drizzling rain. It had been years since she had given up smoking, but even after all this time, she still found herself craving for a smoke from time to time.

She eyed the two soldiers for a moment. Thoughts of days that had long since passed came racing to the forefront of her memory.

They were all that was left. These two men, the smiling mountain and his skinny friend with the crooked nose.

Over the years, one by one, the others had been consumed by the cruel new world, until only two of her original group remained. She loved them. They were her family and her men, and for years, they had fought side by side, watching their friends die around them and grieving together for their loss.

As hard and cold as she seemed, the men knew her well and never doubted her care for them. She was a true leader, willing to suffer and endure any hardship alongside them. Unafraid to do what was necessary, they had recognised her abilities very early on and against her own wishes, they had elevated her to the position of their leader.

"Just be careful out there, you two. No heroics."

The pair turned and tramped across the yard, the wet filth splashing up from their boots as they made their way towards the small concrete alcove that was set into the wall further along from the main gate.

To their right, the cooks busied themselves beneath the canvas roof of their open air kitchen. It was Friday, and despite the atrocious weather, that meant barbeque night. The head chef raised a hand and waved to them through the coils of steam and smoke that filled the area beneath the canopy.

The two soldiers returned the gesture, raising their rifles in salute to the men and women who continued to work their modern day miracles, providing a degree of morale in the form of tasty meals for the other survivors.

"Save us some of that crap that you palm off as chicken, will you? Even if it *is* a fucking mangy cat, it's better than nothing."

"Mangy cat?" The chef hollered back to them. "They're reserved for Royal visits. Where do you think we are? The fucking Ritz?"

They arrived at the alcove. It jutted out from the inner wall at an upward facing angle, rising out of the ground with a thick steel door set into it. The guard stepped forward from the shadowy recess beside the entrance and nodded to them as they approached.

"How's things, John?" They greeted him as they stopped and waited for him to let them through.

"Same shit, different day. Bring me back something nice," John replied as he slid back the heavy bolt in the locking mechanism.

The bolt fell into place with a loud clang that echoed around the compound, causing many heads to turn in their direction and watch with anticipation, knowing that their defences were about to be opened, only slightly, but opened nonetheless.

The door pulled outward with a loud metallic creak as the hinges sang in protest against the rust that attempted to hold them tight. Inside, a blackness so complete that it was impossible to see past the threshold, greeted them. A draft of stale air gust out from the dark passage and brushed at their faces as they peered inside.

The two men, gripping their weapons firmly in their hands, glanced at one another, feeling the hairs on the backs of their necks stand to attention.

"What's up?" John asked them with a sneer. "You two nervous?"

The large man stepped forward, his shoulders seeming twice as broad as normal due to his equipment and armour. With a cold expression, he stared down at the guard who had already began to retreat towards the comforting shadow of the recess, wishing he had said nothing and kept his mouth shut.

"It's been over ten years," the soldier began in a low menacing voice. "I've been out there more times than I can count. All my friends are dead, but I am still here. I have killed thousands of them, and never received a scratch. Am I nervous?"

He raised a questioning eyebrow at the cowering guard and suddenly grinned, bearing his white teeth that glowed in the darkness.

"Of course I'm fucking nervous. I'm terrified, John!"

He reached forward and slapped the man on the shoulder, almost knocking him over into the boggy water at his feet.

“Shhh,” the skinny soldier ordered silence, “the rain’s stopped.”

They paused and looked up into the sky. The clouds, still grey but less densely packed had begun to separate, revealing a blanket of stars twinkling high above the atmosphere against the blackness of space.

Suddenly, they realised that they no longer had to raise their voices in order to be heard over the hammering raindrops that drowned out all other sounds. The night was still and silent. Then they heard the distant low, electrifying murmur.

“It’s always there, isn’t it,” John whispered, as he stared up at the top of the wall that protected them and held back the tide of death.

Thousands upon thousands of woeful voices were joined together as one in their lament. The dead crowded the outer perimeter, their haunting chorus creeping across the land and assaulting the wall. It was a resonance that was the one constant the survivors could guarantee, but they could never become used to it. It haunted them, tearing at their nerves and perpetually fuelling their fears.

They knew that the dead would never leave them.

In the tunnel, the two men walked side by side down the gentle slope, headed deeper and deeper underground. It had taken nine years and the lives of over fifty men and women to construct. Now, with their fortress surrounded by the mass swarms of festering bodies, it was their only lifeline.

It had been seven years since the only helicopter they possessed had broken down, and the mechanics despite their skill and toil, had never been able to fix it. Now, it sat rusting away, watching the seasons pass as it slowly turned to yet another relic of mankind and the marvels of civilisation.

The three Challenger-II tanks had been vital to their survival, but they too had succumbed to the ravages of time and the hazards of the new world. One was stranded four-hundred metres beyond the walls, having thrown a track six years earlier.

The dead had quickly engulfed the machine, leaving the men trapped inside and unable to escape. For over two weeks, the people within the fortress still had communications with the tank crew, speaking to them, and promising that they were doing all they could to come up with a rescue plan. Eventually, when every attempt to relieve them had failed and the imprisoned men had run out of food and water, they took their own life, and there they remained.

The rusting tank was their eternal tomb.

The other tanks had been destroyed in the many clashes with living attackers, and now it was down to the tunnel to allow scavenger parties to move in and out from behind the walls.

Thankfully, there were no rogue armies of the living left to fight.

They continued along the gloomy passageway, dimly lit by the few bulbs that could be spared. Rats screeched and scurried along the walls, their claws scratching at the hard packed clay, and the water that seeped through the earth, fell from the thick wooden supports of the walls and ceiling in echoing drops that rang out in the narrow space.

The shaft, wide enough for a man to stand in with his arms stretched out on either side, continued for a long way. Two-point-nine kilometres to be exact. At every five-hundred metre interval, a gate of thick steel bars blocked their path, needing to be unbolted and slid back from the wall and then replaced behind them. At two points, the tunnel was rigged with explosives, ready to be detonated should the dead ever discover their secret passage.

They walked, and soon without realising it, both men found themselves staring up at the ceiling of the tunnel as they continued their journey through the dimness. Neither of them needed to say a word. They both knew what the other was thinking.

Just above us, there's an army of rotting feet.

At the far end, they reached the final door. It was a hatch that had been taken from a war ship. Made from four centimetre thick steel, and virtually impossible to force open, it was the final barrier that separated them from the danger of the outside.

The construction of the passage had been a work of genius, overseen by an engineer named Michael. He had spent months, years, surveying the area at huge risk to himself and his team, losing many of them along the way. With great skill and patience, he had studied and poured over every map, aerial photograph, and town plan. Anything that could help him with the task ahead. Under the circumstances, it had been a feat of engineering that the survivors considered to be more important than any architectural wonder from the old world.

He had plotted the tunnel so that it came up beneath the foundations of an old Victorian pumping station. The building had still been in use up until the days when the world had crumbled beneath the onslaught of the dead and the strong walls and heavy gates helped to ensure that the hidden passage would remain unseen and protected.

With absolute accuracy, the tunnel had been completed, emerging exactly where Michael had intended it.

Unfortunately, Michael had died the previous year from cancer. It had eaten him to the bone and there was nothing that anyone could do to help him. In the end, he had taken an overdose of morphine to ease his suffering.

At the door, the two soldiers paused and silently read the inscription that had been etched into the wall.

To Michael,

The man who, with a shovel and pick, fought for our survival but lost his own personal battle.

Always remembered.

Sleep well.

On the floor below it, laid a bouquet of wilted flowers and a candle that had burned down to nothing more than a solid puddle of melted wax.

Standing back from the door, they raised their rifles and pulled back on the cocking levers slightly. Just enough to see the shine of the brass case that was sitting snuggly in the breach. Happy that their weapons were ready to fire, they pushed the working parts forward again and conducted a final check of their equipment, weapons, and ammunition.

The larger man covered the door, while the other began slowly to lever the locking mechanism out from its recess in the thick stone wall. The lock was stiff and he winced as he pulled, afraid to put too much of his weight behind it and bring it crashing towards him, making a deafening racket that would alert everything on the surface.

The lock was painstakingly released and the door was free.

Holding the rifle firmly against his shoulder, the big soldier could hear his heart pounding against his chest, and feel the sweat that soaked his brow and running down into his face. He nodded to his friend who then pulled at the bulky hatch.

It fell open with a faint whine, and both men readied themselves to receive whatever happened to be on the opposite side, stepping back and taking up the first pressure on the triggers of their assault rifles.

Nothing but blackness greeted them and both released a sigh of relief.

"Why the fuck didn't old Mike put a peep-hole in this fucking door?" The skinny soldier hissed through the gloom.

They stepped through the hatch and sealed it shut behind them, locking themselves into a small chamber containing a number of large pipes and valves. Below their feet was a heavy iron grate, running into the sewers. The sound of trickling water echoed around them in the cramped space, mixing with the screech of the rats that scurried through the network of sewer tunnels beneath them.

In the low light, the steel staircase leading up to the surface was barely visible, but they had been here many times and knew it was there, and how careful they needed to be as they climbed the rickety steps.

Slowly and silently, they both began their ascent towards the dead world above.

2

Sierra Leone, West Africa. Twelve years earlier.

The rattle of automatic gunfire continued to echo throughout the lush green valley, carried along on the wind and rebounding from the low lying hills on either side of the river.

The attack was over.

The loud deafening concussions of high explosives, the rapid crack and thump of machinegun fire, and the lingering, agony filled cries of the dying had been replaced with cheers of triumph and celebratory volleys fired into the air from the Kalashnikov assault rifles.

Excited voices called out to one another and orders were barked as the rebels swept through the ruined village, ransacking the remaining homes that were still standing and had escaped the ravages of the short but brutal battle.

Dressed in a mix-match array of military uniform and civilian clothing, the confident rebels sauntered arrogantly amongst the devastation, sifting through the debris and searching for anything of use or value.

They were never concerned about why they attacked and their brutality never faltered. Their commanders would order them onto the offensive and they would obey without question. The reasons did not matter to them, but their lust for blood and loot did.

The rebels were not soldiers. They had no military skill or knowledge, and many had been snatched away from their villages and towns as children, forced to fight and commit acts of butchery. Controlled with drugs and the promise of reward by their warlord commanders, they had become brainwashed and savage, indifferent to the suffering that they caused and unconcerned with anything, other than plunder, rape, and murder.

Now, they were high on the euphoria of their success, believing themselves to be brave and noble warriors, fighting for a cause that warranted the total slaughter of anyone they considered to be their enemy.

They chanted and sang as they pillaged, firing their rifles into the air and claiming a glorious victory against their foe. Even in the aftermath, with the mixture of drugs and adrenalin in their veins subsiding, and the fear coursing through their bodies being replaced with pride, they remained oblivious and uncaring to the pain and grief that they had dealt out to the once peaceful village.

Their yellow tinged glistening eyes scoured the earth, searching for their rewards, apathetic to the mutilated bodies splayed out on the ground all around them. Men, women, and children, lying in pools of steaming blood, were butchered like cattle.

A loud horn blast from their commander's truck signalled that it was time for them to leave. With high spirits, the rebels returned to their vehicles, dragging their bootie and two beaten and bound white men with them. They kicked and screamed at the two prisoners as they were hoisted up on to the bed of the truck, raining down blows with their fists and rifle butts until the men collapsed into a heap of swollen flesh and gushing blood.

The engines rumbled and the heavy wheels sent up clouds of dust into the air, cloaking their withdrawal from the area and the echoing sound of their celebratory fire steadily receding into the distance, leaving a landscape of devastation in their wake.

The rebels left the village with their spoils of war.

Plumes of acrid black smoke swirled in the hot wind that gust through the remains of the huts and small farms, obscuring the blood soaked soil and concealing the destruction and horror that had taken place just moments before. The fading gunfire added to the sound of crackling flames as raging fires continued to spread and burn all in their path.

The air hissed with the thousands of scavenging insects that descended upon the shattered settlement, eager to feast on the remains of the villagers.

Every structure bore the scars of battle. The homes and communal buildings lay in ruins, their roofs caved inward and the licking flames steadily consuming everything that they came into contact with. The mud brick walls that were left standing, glowed and slowly crumbled from the intense heat.

An abandoned vehicle, one of the many that had brought the blood thirsty rebels to the unsuspecting village, lay smouldering at the outskirts. Its steel frame was twisted and pockmarked with bullet holes, having fallen victim to the ferocious firefight that had engulfed the small town.

In the driver's seat, still seated at the helm, was the charred and skeletal body of one of the attackers. His fingers still clutching at the wheel, and his blackened grinning skull, the eye sockets void, staring out at the tattered remnants of the village.

Countless bodies were scattered throughout the area. Some lay in heaps; families that had died together, their lifeless corpses hugging the earth while their cold hands continued to cling on to one another in their death grip. Others had fallen alone, with no one to hold on to in their final moments, cut down and slaughtered by the ruthless monsters that laughed and sang as they butchered everyone they found.

The scale of the massacre and the extent of the vicious wounds inflicted, were testament to the shared suffering of the unfortunate people.

No one had been spared.

The children of the village had suffered along with their parents. They had been ruthlessly shot, hacked with machetes, and bludgeoned with clubs. Their screams of terror and pain, and their pleas for mercy had fallen on deaf ears, as their attackers had swept through, raping and killing in an orgy of blood.

At the crossroads in the centre, four pale naked bodies lay in the dirt. Their headless carcasses baking in the midday sun as their blood seeped into the earth around them.

They were the remains of British soldiers.

They had fallen in the hailstorm of the battle, fighting hard to defend the helpless villagers from the onslaught. Many of their attackers had died during the assault, but the soldiers had eventually been overwhelmed. When their ammunition was expended, they had fought with fixed bayonets and hand-to-hand against the merciless rebels, but one by one, they had been cut down.

Now, they lay mutilated in an undignified heap, stripped of their equipment, clothing and personal possessions, the rebels carrying it all away as souvenirs of war.

The cries and whimpers of any remaining survivors had been quashed by the rebels before they had left, leaving only the hush of death.

Not even the birds dared to make a sound now. They sat in the trees, or circled above the blood soaked earth, quietly watching.

A ghostly silence slowly fell over the area as the sound of gunfire faded, leaving the insects unhindered to feast upon the dead.

Hours later, as the flames died and all that remained were the smashed and burned remains of humanity and village life, all churned together into the mud, there was movement in the village once again.

Dark shadows moved from within the wisps of smoke.

Rising up from the ashes, the eerie silhouettes, silent and lumbering, drifted through the rubble, driven forward by an unseen force.

A woman, her abdomen split open from her breasts down to her groin, her bloated and mottled intestines splayed out and mixed in with the dusty soil around her, began to move. Her heart did not beat from within her chest, and the remaining blood in her veins, coagulated and cold, did not flow through her body.

She was dead.

Her fingers twitched, barely detectable at first, but soon, they grasped at the black dirt, digging her broken nails deep into the soft earth.

With each passing minute, her body became more animated. Muscles that had stiffened with rigor mortis, twitched and jerked as her limbs struggled to regain their function. Her mouth opened, a gasp escaping from within her lungs as the last breath she had taken was expelled from her lifeless body. Her jaw snapped shut again, the teeth clashing together loudly from the force.

The woman's eyes flickered open. They were flat and dull from the lack of blood pressure, showing no spark of life. The pale film covering the iris showed no hint of a soul as her large black pupils stared, unseeing, at the pale blue sky above her.

More bodies began to move.

Dozens of mutilated and grotesque figures clumsily dragged themselves to their feet, ignorant to their injuries and the clouds of bloated black flies that had descended upon them, swarming through the air with an incessant buzz.

As the sun began to dip towards the tops of the trees, the shadowy remains of the massacred village stumbled through the wreckage and out on to the dusty track.

3

Syria.

The sky had turned to a bright blue, but it would be another hour before the sun was ready to rise above the horizon and begin warming the landscape with its radiance. It was still very early in the year, and the nights were bitter. The freezing February air would attack any exposed body parts like a sudden harsh slap.

A fine layer of frost coated the ground, its microscopic crystals sparkling like a blanket of stars stretched out over a hardened crust of black soil. In the severe cold, the rocky terrain seemed harder than ever, as though the low temperatures had sharpened the pointed edges of even the smallest of pebbles.

He remained still.

His breathing was slow and controlled, instantly freezing into a white mist that drifted up above his head and dissipated into the cold air. His bulky mass was pressed close to the ground, sinking into the earth and becoming part of the topography, while his attention stayed fixed on the target area in front of him.

His unblinking green eyes and hard expression betrayed his absolute disdain for their current situation. He let out a low sigh and shifted his position to give his stiff muscles and aching bones a moment's respite from the icy temperatures that they had been forced to endure for the entire night.

For four weeks, they had battled against the elements, suffering the extremes of the climate and the land, pushing their bodies and stamina to the limit. Methodically, they had collected all the information that they needed before putting their final phase into motion. Every aspect of the plan had been scrutinized down to the smallest detail. Nothing had been left to chance, and a number of back-ups and alternatives had been put into place, ready to be brought into play on the receipt of certain code words that would be given to them by their commander over the radio.

"I fucking hate this place, Marty," he grumbled to the man next to him. "Why can't they send us somewhere nice for a change?"

Marty shrugged, blinking his eyes rapidly to help with his focus as he pulled his face away from the thermal imaging sight. A wry smile spread across his lips.

"I don't think they have much call for the likes of us in Antigua right now, Bull," he replied in a voice that was little more than a whisper.

Bull grunted.

His real name was Manus, but the nickname 'Bull', had followed him throughout his adulthood. He remembered, even as a child, one of his many foster parents had referred to him as a *'Raging Bull'*. Being tactful or subtle could never be considered as one of his strong points, and his approach to anything in life was to take it head on, with brute force and maximum effort, mentally and physically, as though everything was a fight to the death.

Grace and diplomacy were not familiar words to him, and he was as quick with his fists as he was with his tongue.

However, contrary to his own beliefs, the nickname had not derived from his personality, or his large muscular frame. It had first been given to him during his time as a young soldier and no one, not even his closest friends, had ever plucked up the courage to inform him of the true origins of his bestowed title.

Early in his army career, based in the garrison town of Aldershot in the south of England, the rugged, good looking, Manus, soon drew the attentions of many of the local women. In the bars and clubs, his broad shoulders and piercing eyes turned the heads of many.

It was not long before one lucky girl managed to snare him, even if it was only for just one night. As it happened, she too had a nickname. *'Machinegun's Mary',* was a regular face in the barrack block belonging to the Heavy Weapons Platoon. On most weekends, she spent her afternoons and evenings flitting from one room to the next, enjoying the company of the soldiers there. Often, with more than one at a time.

After managing to seduce the inebriated Manus one evening, she convinced him to escort her back to camp. Something that Manus was more than happy to oblige her with.

The next week, when Mary took up her usual position at the bar in the Trafalgar Inn, she was asked how she had got along with the 'mighty' Manus.

"It was over before I realised it had even started. He went at it like a bull in a China shop, and then fell asleep," she replied.

From then on, he became 'The Bull'.

"I'm just sick of being in crap places," Bull continued to grumble as he lay in the cold beside his friend. "Everything is a pain in the arse. If I want a dump, I have to do it in a bag and keep it. Then, after a few days of walking about with a bag of shit in my pocket, we walk twenty miles just to go and bury it so no one can find it. I haven't had a hot meal for over a month or changed my fucking underpants. What kind of a life is that?"

Marty stole a quick glance to his left to look at his friend, and nearly erupted into laughter.

As always, Bull never failed to amuse him. His face, framed in a thick scarf and topped with a misshaped, overly large woolly hat, had taken on the appearance of a frozen slab of pork. His four-week-old beard was covered with frost, and mucus that had solidified into pale stalactites, dangled from his nostrils. His skin was a pale grey, except for his nose, which was a bright crimson, but it was not the pathetic dishevelled appearance that made Marty want to laugh, it was the expression in Bull's eyes.

He was miserable, and that made Marty feel better. Just knowing that someone else was there with him and sharing the discomfort, suffering just as much if not more than he was, was enough to raise his morale a notch.

They had known one another for a long time, even serving in the same parent regiment together and it was Marty who had told the others about the secret origins of his friend's name.

Marty was what they all referred to as, 'the Angry Jock'. He was originally from Glasgow, Scotland. Tall, dark haired, and with a thick Glaswegian accent, everything he said sounded as though it was spat with anger and venom. He could be trying to describe his opinion and appreciation of a great and beautiful piece of artwork, or opera, and it would still sound as though he hated it. His words were harsh and his expressions were even harsher, and it always seemed as though he was about to unleash a torrent of blows on to any unfortunate soul in close proximity to him.

However, anyone who made the effort to get to know Marty soon realised that under the frightening exterior of pale skin, crooked nose, and glaring eyes, the tall Scotsman was a witty and friendly man. Fiercely loyal and extremely intelligent, he was a close and trusted friend to everyone on the team.

Marty placed his eye back on to the rubber cushion surrounding the sight. Nothing moved in the target area, but a quick glance at his watch told him that within the next thirty minutes, all that would change.

Directly ahead of them, exactly three-hundred and twenty-three metres away, was a small one storey building made from a mixture of orange and grey bricks, topped with a heavy thatched roof. To the left and right of it, three smaller structures of mud brick and corrugated iron completed the tiny farm complex.

They knew the exact distance, because Bull and Marty had measured it with the range finder, and set the sights on their weapons accordingly.

The ground around the farm complex was open and flat, with a number of small enclosures fenced off with barbed wire, containing herds of scruffy goats and emaciated looking cows sifting through the filth at their feet.

The ducks and geese had been the hardest obstacle. Over the previous week, the team had infiltrated the area, planting listening devices, tiny cameras, and even explosives. Negotiating their way past the ever vigilant poultry had been an achievement in itself.

Geese were always considered as a good alternative to guard dogs or sophisticated and technologically advanced early warning systems.

They were cheap, and very easy to install.

The final phase of the operation was about to begin. All the hardship, painstaking accumulation of intelligence and meticulous planning, was about to reach its climactic end.

Marty glanced down at his watch again.

"Fifteen minutes," he murmured from the corner of his mouth.

Bull nodded and removed his woolly hat and scarf from around his head, and then stuffed them into the front of his jacket. Next, he pulled at his thick mittens, leaving his thin leather pilot's gloves as the only protection between the delicate skin of his hands and the harsh, ice cold steel of his machinegun.

He turned his attention to the weapon in front of him. He knew it was in perfect working order, and he had shown more care and attentiveness to the machinegun than he had to himself, yet, he would still check it. It was a maxim that had become part of his instincts.

First my weapon, then myself.

Next, he began to flex his muscles to ensure his limbs had the circulation they needed. The pain in his frozen feet was almost unbearable, as he forced his blood back down into his toes and he grimaced at the sharp pins and needles that began to stab at his fingertips.

He had performed the same routine, *ritual*, a thousand times before, but it never got any easier. Bull had been a soldier for as long as he cared to remember, but there were certain hardships that his body could never get used to. Nevertheless, he never let them hamper his ability to perform his duties, and even more importantly, he never allowed *anyone* to see his discomfort.

Satisfied that everything was ready, he raised the butt of the gun and placed it against his shoulder, pushing forward against the bipod legs slightly to strengthen his firing position. Next, he set about ensuring that the long belt of ammunition entering into the left hand side of the weapon remained unobstructed so that it could flow freely through the feed-tray without stoppages.

With his thumb resting against the protruding safety catch that was built into the pistol grip, Bull settled himself into his fire-support position, and waited.

Marty could almost hear the seconds ticking by. It was the final moments before H-Hour that were always the worst. As the adrenalin would begin to pump through his body, and his mind would race, time would seem to stand still. The inevitable knots would form in his stomach and his senses would become more acute. His eyes would notice the smallest of details, and even the slightest noise would echo in his ears.

He was never afraid of dying. That was a risk that they had all faced on countless occasions and if it was to happen, he just hoped that it would be quick and painless.

His biggest worry, as with every other member of the team, was always that something may have been missed. He went through his mental checklist, ticking off each item as he confirmed to himself that everything was in place. If anything *had* been overlooked, there was nothing they could do about it now.

"Five minutes," a raspy voice informed them through their earpieces.

It was their commander, Stan.

Neither of them needed to see him, but they knew that Stan was off to their right, just fifty metres away with an over-watch on the entire area from where he could command and control the operation.

Stan was a much older man, but his appearance was deceptive. He was immensely strong and fit, and many believed that he had absolutely no weaknesses. No one knew his exact age, but from his greying hair and hard weathered features, most people guessed that he was in his early fifties. Regardless, his agility and strength defied his years, and his watchful eyes and sharp mind never missed the slightest detail.

Legend had it that he could smell lies and that he had once worked as an interrogator for MI5, but getting the true account of Stan's life from him was almost as impossible as getting blood from a stone. Instead, the men of the team had to amuse themselves with making up their own stories and tales about their leader's past.

Of average height, but powerfully built, Stan cut a figure that many a man would side step if they saw him approaching in the street. He walked with purpose, and his unblinking eyes always seemed completely focussed on what was ahead of him.

His face was perfect for playing Poker, because his expression never changed and most people struggled to tell whether he was happy or sad, and instead, judged him as apathetic to everything around him.

To the left of their position, another two of their men, Nick and Brian, lay still and silent in the cold morning air, waiting for the final words of command to be given. They were a sniper team, and Marty knew that at that very moment, they would be going through their final checks, calculating the wind strength and direction, and confirming the range to their target.

Far off to the right, another sniper pair lay in wait, watching the minutes slowly tick by and preparing themselves, mentally and physically.

Their prey was a Syrian terrorist named, Ali Hussein Bassim.

Believed to be a high-ranking member of Al-Qaida, Bassim had launched his own campaign of terror throughout the region, attacking rebel factions and the Syrian army alike. His brutality knew no bounds and he never distinguished between military and civilian targets.

His attacks were completely without prejudice, and in a video sent to Al-Jazeera television, he once stated, *"It is not for me to decide who lives and who dies. It is the will of God. I am just a weapon of Islam. It is for the mighty Allah to pass judgement, and I will continue to send the infidel and the faithful to him until he tells me to stop."*

Whether he was planting explosives in busy market places, or launching ground attacks against armed militia and soldiers, the aftermath would always be a scene of destruction and slaughter, the like of which had not been seen since the days of Al-Zarqawi in Iraq.

Prisoners were always executed. Every week, there was fresh footage circulating through the internet of captured soldiers, Red Cross workers, Christians, and suspected collaborators, being beheaded by Bassim and his men.

For a long time, the western governments failed to act, but when the peace talks began, and Bassim increased the ferocity of his attacks in order to disrupt the negotiations, it was decided that something needed to be done.

However, the west was reluctant to be dragged into another Middle Eastern war, but despite numerous attempts, Bassim always seemed to survive the ambushes and strikes that were launched against him by Syrian forces and rebel groups.

The war against Iran and North Korea had already stretched the western armies to their limits. When China entered into the war, the western allies had suffered a number of setbacks and defeats, only recently managing to retake the initiative and go back on to the offensive, and then, being halted once again.

Overtly intervening in Syria could have catastrophic consequences, destroying the already fragile peace agreements with Saudi, Lebanon and Jordan, not to mention the Russians, and opening up a completely new front for the western allies to fight on.

Instead, the British government had sent in their most deniable operatives to *'take care'* of the Bassim problem.

The team, which they were a part of, was a clandestine and completely deniable branch of the British military. The only reason the team and their operations had never been classed as illegal was as one senior member of the army had once considered,

'For something to be illegal, it first needs to be acknowledged.'

Very few people knew about them and their operations, and those who did, wished that they knew nothing at all. At the mere mention of their unit, politicians and high-ranking military personnel in Whitehall would become intensely uncomfortable.

They were completely below the radar and used in the most politically sensitive theatres around the world. When a job was far too delicate for even the conventional Special Forces, such as the SAS or Delta Force, 'the team' would be sent in to do the job.

Since the turn of the millennium, governments in the west had found themselves in constant need of soldiers to do their dirty work, but at the same time, deny any knowledge of them. Stan and his men, and other units like them, were ideal for the sensitive feelings of the various western powers and were used in many different roles, from assassinations to intelligence gathering.

Even stealing foreign government secrets was nothing new to the men.

On one particular mission, they had been sent to Brussels to retrieve a dossier containing diplomatic information about a meeting between the American and French Presidents on the subject of Iran on the eve of the invasion. The operation had lasted for two months and Stan had discovered much more than was expected. On his return, as it was rumoured, he was treated very handsomely by the British government in order to prevent a scandal.

No one ever knew what it was that was found along with the dossier, but Bull always claimed, *'it was a pile of photographs of*

Tony Blair, wearing a gimp suit and playing hide the sausage with Osama Bin Laden.'

Their earpieces crackled again.

'One minute. Stand by, stand by...,'

With precision timing, the door to the small farm house was pushed open. A number of men emerged from the dark interior of the building, each carrying a bundle under his arm and moving towards the open area at the front.

Leading the way was a short, rounded man with a thick beard and shaved head. He moved with short rapid steps, as though his shoes were tied together and he was struggling to remain upright. To the unknowing eye, there was nothing much to him.

He raised his hand and gestured to the other four men to follow him. They hurried after him, falling into line behind the short fat man as he led them to the dusty courtyard.

Bassim stopped and the others fanned out to his left and right, positioning themselves on his flanks. He issued another set of commands to his men and together, they pulled out their bundles and began to unroll their prayer mats.

"Brilliant," Marty whispered with glee, clicking off his safety catch. "One thing you can always rely on when fighting Islamic extremists..., they *never* fail to say their morning prayers. You can set your fucking watch by them."

The terrorist leader positioned himself at the foot of his rug, glancing up at the horizon and checking that his angle to the rising sun was correct and that he was facing towards Mecca. Underneath his thick coat, he wore a green canvass vest with a row of pouches containing magazines for the AK-47 that he unslung from across his back and placed down onto the dusty ground by his feet.

They were ready to begin their morning prayers.

Bull tightened his grip on the gun and pushed his thumb against the safety catch, hearing and feeling the light, barely audible click, as it was set to 'fire'.

Everything faded into the distance.

The cold seemed to lift itself away from him, no longer biting at his hands and feet. The songs of early morning birds evaporated from the sky, and the only noise in his ears was the sound of his own breathing and the rhythmic thud of his beating heart. Nothing else mattered now, except the foresight of his machinegun and the five figures in the distance, lined up, ready to say their final words before he helped to send them off to Paradise.

'Target confirmed...,'

At that moment, Marty knew that Stan would be sitting in his position, staring at a small LED screen in front of him. On the readout would be three boxes and they would be lit with either green or red lights.

Each box represented a sniper and on their rifles, each of the shooters had a small button where their thumb rested on the grip. If the box was green, it meant that particular sniper had a clear shot on the target. If it was red, then they had no shot.

Only when two or more of the boxes were green, Stan would give the order to fire.

Bull made a final check for 'windage'. He watched the long blades of grass swaying beside the farm buildings and the length of cloth they had fastened to the fence post of the animal pen, confirming the strength and direction of the wind.

"Left, three," he whispered from the corner of his mouth.

Marty made a slight adjustment and slowly released a breath until his lungs were half deflated, then paused. The telescopic sight of his rifle stabilised and the crosshairs remained fixed in the centre of his target. His aiming mark; the lower part of Bassim's face. A shot placed into that area would, in less than a microsecond, destroy the brain stem, dropping him instantly, with no chance to scream, let alone survive.

Far off to the north and south of their position, the other snipers would be aiming at the target's earlobes. Bobby and Taff were on the right, with Brian and Nick taking up positions on the left flank.

Ali Hussein Bassim was about to be taken out from three directions, simultaneously.

There would be no need for any further talk or instruction from Stan. The three snipers would sit and wait until he gave the word, 'fire', once he received the green lights.

Bassim and his men continued their prayers. They raised their hands, muttering their holy words and then bowed to their rugs, making their promises to God and offering Him their complete devotion.

A final bow and Bassim raised himself to his feet, crossing his hands in front of him and lowering his head.

4

The Operation's Room was silent. Literally, quiet enough to hear a pin drop.

Samantha crouched down and run her fingers across the smooth linoleum floor, searching for the hairclip she had been nervously playing with in the dimly lit command centre, as she stood, staring at the huge monitors attached to the wall in front of her.

The room was a large oval shape, crammed with sophisticated communications and surveillance equipment that enabled them to have a real-time insight into whatever was happening with their operations and the men on the ground from all over the globe.

From that one room, they could gain high level intelligence on anyone, anywhere in the world. CCTV cameras from all over the planet, police radio and computer data, and diplomatic information could be tapped into without anyone knowing.

Phone records could easily be retrieved, bank accounts accessed and scrutinized. Personal computers and online data, even with the most up to date firewalls and anti-intrusion programmes, were no match for the skilled technicians that sat in the semi-darkness, drinking their body's weight in coffee and suffering from a severe deficiency of vitamin-D.

"How's it going, Sam?"

She did not notice him arrive at her side, and his sudden deep rasping voice almost made her jump.

"I think we're about to get an answer on that, sir," she said, rising to her feet, having found her clip and nodding towards the large screens. "I picked the wrong time to give up smoking, I'll tell you that much for sure."

The General smiled faintly, acknowledging that he understood and sympathised with her tenseness.

"How are the boys?" he asked, his glaring eyes narrowing as he studied the monitors.

In the centre, the main screen showed a high definition colour image of a landscape, taken from one of the many satellites orbiting above the Earth. On either side, smaller screens displayed the same patch of ground, but from different sources.

The left hand screen showed a grainy black and white flickering image that changed constantly. It was the live feed from the unmanned stealth drone aircraft that they had circling at high altitude. The land showed as different shades of grey and black and anything living, radiating body heat, showed up as white through the thermal imaging.

On the right, the screen that the General was focussed on, a digital overlay map, showing the main roads, rivers, and urban areas of the operational area. In the centre of the screen, a cluster of eight red dots sat grouped together in pairs, forming a rough triangular shape.

"See for yourself, sir," Samantha nodded. "They've been in position all night. According to their bio-readouts," she indicated a pile of paper stacked on a table to her right, "two of them were close to the early stages of hypothermia a couple of hours ago. The temperature dropped to zero during the night."

The General did not bother to check the readouts. He knew the men and what they were capable of enduring. At that moment, he was more concerned with what was about to happen. He grunted his appreciation of the fact that the team was uncomfortable.

"What about video feed, do we still have it real time from the ground?"

Samantha shook her head.

"No, sir. The blokes pulled their cameras in last night. We have a lot of footage from the last five days, if you're interested in reviewing it?"

She unfolded her hands from in front of her chest and indicated the hard drives containing all the camera data that had been collected.

"I need to talk to you after this, Sam," he said without taking his eyes from the screens in front of him.

"About...?" Samantha was just as transfixed with the unfolding events and the digital clock that was ticking away in the top right corner of the satellite imagery.

"The Africa thing."

This time, Samantha tore her eyes away from the live feed and glared at the tall pale man with burning eyes standing next to her.

"What's happened?"

The General looked at her and shrugged, a faint smile creasing his thin lips.

"We don't know. The MoD has only just been kind enough to inform us that they have lost comms with the section that was sent in."

"And the doctor?"

He shook his head.

"How long has it been since they last heard from them?" She asked, searching his face for any indication of whether he was holding anything back from her. In the gloom, it was hard to tell what he was thinking.

"Nine days."

"Bollocks," she hissed, "does the WHO know about this?"

He nodded.

"They're coming in to brief us. With the doctor missing, they're presuming the worst."

"Are they going public yet?"

He shook his head and shrugged his shoulders.

"With what? Without the doctor's research, all they have is rumour and theory," he replied dismissively.

"There's the reports and footage from Belize and Haiti, what about that? You've seen it all yourself, sir."

He shook his head again.

"Unreliable, I'm afraid. They can't announce this thing to the world without having it all nailed down."

"Well, they need..."

"Movement in the target area, ma'am," a voice called to her from across the room.

She looked over to see the sergeant staring back at her from behind his computer, the light from the screen casting an eerie glow over his features.

On the large monitor, she saw the glowing white shapes of men moving away from the farmhouse.

"Right on time," she murmured and turned to the man beside her. "Time spent on reconnaissance is seldom wasted, General Thompson."

"Stan's confirmed the target, Captain Tyler," the communications officer reported to Samantha from the table behind her.

She made to turn away from the General and begin dealing with the immediate matters of the operation.

He placed his hand on her forearm, stalling her for a moment and leaned across so that his lips were close to her ear.

"As soon as they're clear of the area, get them out of there. Don't wait for them to be at the RV, pull them out."

He stepped back from her and fixed her with a hard look.

"You know this is going bad, don't you, Sam? We have to get them back and ready as soon as possible. I think we will be needing them again before the week is out."

5

'Fire...'

Before the order was completed, three rifles released their shots together.

Marty felt the recoil buff against his shoulder and his ears pop, as the round, almost silently, erupted from the barrel of his rifle. The suppressor did its jobs well, keeping any signature and sound to a minimum as the copper plated bullet sprang from the breach and raced towards its mark.

A split second later, Bassim's head disappeared in a swirl of red mist and splintered bone as the three bullets ploughed through his skull, his body remaining upright for a moment before the muscles and nerves ceased to receive the signals from his obliterated brain. The headless carcass dropped like water, crashing to the dirt in a heap.

The men to the left and right of his body instinctively ducked as they heard the supersonic crack of the rounds that snapped by, displacing the air and smashing through the head of the terrorist commander. Dumbstruck for a second, they hesitated and stared at the body of their fallen leader, and then at one another.

That was all the time that the snipers needed before more high velocity rounds were sent down the range towards their next victims. Three more men fell, blood spouting from their wounds and silent screams becoming lodged in their throats as the life was snatched from their bodies in an instant.

Finally, the remaining man realised what was happening. With a quick glance over his shoulder, his eyes blazing with fear, he turned on his heel and ran for the house. He had only moved a couple of metres when the ground around the dilapidated farm building exploded in a deafening roar, throwing debris and speeding shrapnel through the air, mixing metal, rock, and bone together in a fountain of annihilation.

Bull increased the pressure on the trigger and the machinegun barked loudly and juddered against his muscular shoulders. The long belt of ammunition twitched as it began feeding through the weapon's chamber and the empty cases sprang from the other side, clattering on to one another and forming a small, ever growing, pile of brass.

Each time he squeezed, he silently whispered to himself, *'I can fuck you before you can fuck me,'* the phrase he was taught all those years ago to help control the rate of fire for a belt-fed weapon. Then he would release his finger for a moment, adjust his aim, and then begin the process again.

The loud rattle of the gun was always comforting. To him, it sounded comparable to sheet metal being torn apart by giant hands like a piece of flimsy cloth.

He watched his fall of shot, seeing the bright tracer bullets sail through the air and smash their way through the rickety walls of the outbuildings around the farm complex. Even the goats and cows had not been spared. Hundreds of rounds punched through their bodies, chewing the flesh and bone to pulp and scattering them across the ground.

The column of debris and dust from the explosion fell back to earth. Large clumps of brick and steel crashed to the ground with heavy dull thuds, mixing with the organic material of the dead and dying.

The team had been well aware that women and children, the families of Bassim and his men, were inside the buildings. They had planted the explosives five days before, when the area had been empty, and two days later when Bassim arrived with his wife and five young children in tow, they had been caught in a dilemma.

"It's collateral damage," Nick suggested in his thick, almost unintelligible, Newcastle accent. "*Why should we let those little bastards grow up to avenge their old man?"*

"That reminds me," Bull added with an indifferent grin, *"I need to get my 'collateral' checked by the Doc when I get home. I love takeaway, you see."*

Although it was a rather callous outlook, Nick's opinion had been the general consensus. In the end, it was decided that they would stick to the plan, and the plan was to make it appear that Bassim and his group had been attacked by Syrian forces, or another rebel cell, who would not care for a minute that they killed women and children, as long as they got the terrorist leader with them.

Using a drone strike or smart bomb was never an option. They were not certain to kill the intended targets and they always left debris that could be identified. Finding a piece of circuitry or tail fin with traceable serial numbers on it would be difficult for western governments to explain.

"Close in, close in...," Stan ordered, prompting the sniper teams on the flanks to collapse their positions and begin pulling back into the rendezvous with the rest of the team.

As they began to move, Bull continued to pour his long bursts of machinegun fire into the farm complex, covering their withdrawal and ensuring that nothing would be left alive amongst the ruined buildings.

Two more explosions detonated to the left and right. Much smaller than the first, they were the sniper teams sanitising their areas, leaving no trace behind of the positions that they had occupied.

Marty brought himself up into a kneeling position and began stuffing his thermal imaging sight and the spare ammunition for the machinegun into his small pack.

"Okay, Bull, good to go," he said as he patted him on the shoulder, making sure that his friend knew that it was almost time for them to leave.

"Roger that."

Bull fired one final long burst, the streaks of glowing tracer zipping through the air and demolishing the one remaining wall of the building to the left of the courtyard. Satisfied that there was nothing left, he jumped up into a crouched position and scooped up the heavy weapon in his arms, cradling it like a small child. He remained where he was, watching the ground to his front while he and Marty waited for the final call from Stan to close in.

"Marty, Bull, move to the RV."

Together, they jumped to their feet and ploughed their way through the small bushes that had obscured them from view. Behind their position, they turned onto a small goat track and sprinted along it, headed for the rally point with the rest of the group.

As they approached the rendezvous, a small dip in the ground roughly two-hundred metres from their fire-support position, Marty slowed his pace, allowing them to get a view of the area and ensuring that they did not run blindly into an ambush.

"Marty coming in," he repeatedly called in a hushed voice as he drew near.

A face appeared just a few metres ahead and grinned at him. It was Bobby, the medic for the team. He had been part of the sniper group on the right flank and it had been their job to secure the rally point once they were given the order to pull back.

Bull and Marty crashed through the underbrush and into the dip. The rest of their men were already there, spread out in a circle, covering their arcs and providing all around defence.

Stan was in the centre, kneeling on the frozen ground and adjusting his equipment, tightening his belt and checking that all his pouches were secure and that he had a fresh magazine on his rifle. His eyes locked with Bull, who bared his teeth in a rueful grimace.

As always, Stan's expression showed no emotion at all, as he acknowledged him with a slight nod of his head. To Bull, it was as if their commander was incapable of feeling anything and was in a perpetual state of concentration on the job at hand. Even when they were back in the UK, the man never seemed to smile.

Bull moved to the far side of the dip and placed his machinegun down so that it was covering the direction they were about to head in. He knew that they had a hard slog ahead of them, through a narrow rocky pass and over a steep feature. It would be a tough few hours, but every one of them were well aware that they needed to put as much distance between them and the target area as possible, and quickly.

Inevitably, there would be a follow up. They had made enough noise to alert every rebel and Syrian soldier in the district, so it was paramount that they get away from the area. Now, their fitness and endurance would be the most important factor.

"One minute and we're out of here," Stan announced as he stood up and moved into position beside Bull, ready to lead the way and set the pace for their withdrawal. It was fifty kilometres to their extraction point, and he intended for them to be there before nightfall.

At a pace that defied their appearance and loads, they raced off through the gorge and towards the high ground.

Thirty minutes later, as the men approached the top of the ridge, a resounding boom echoed up to them from the valley floor. They turned to see a large column of smoke and dust reaching high in to the air, a kilometre to the north of the wrecked farm buildings.

"That's the follow up, boys," Stan grunted as he increased his stride towards the summit.

Along the road, leading into the complex where Bassim and his men had been hiding out, Stan and Danny, the youngest member of the team, had planted a surprise for anyone who came to investigate.

An Improvised Explosive Device, IED, made from three 105mm artillery shells, attached to a pressure release pad, would be enough to destroy any vehicle that triggered it. Anyone else wishing to follow would be more cautious on their approach, slowing them down and allowing Stan and his men to gain as much ground as possible.

Once they were clear of the high ground, Stan turned south, contouring the feature as they continued at top speed towards their anticipated extraction. They were making good progress and they now had a gigantic pile of rock and dirt between them and the scene of their crime, the hill acting as a physical and psychologically comforting buffer from any potential danger and prying eyes.

The sweat was pouring from Bull's head, running down his back in rivulets and accumulating at his waist. His soaking belt was already starting to chafe his skin and he knew that he would have a few uncomfortable nights ahead as a result. His heavy feet pounded at the dusty slope as he forced himself forward with the agility of a mountain goat, bounding from one rocky outcrop to the next.

All of them puffed and panted as they drove themselves onward, carrying their heavy equipment and weapons, never letting up on the tempo. The terrain was extremely uneven, with sharp rocks jutting up from the ground that threatened to trip them at any moment, but no one could afford to fall. An injury would slow them all down and hinder their ability to react to a threat that could spring at them from any direction.

Stan adjusted their direction and steered them towards the foot of the hill, paralleling the fast flowing river that coursed along below them. Once they were on flatter ground, he pushed a few hundred metres further on and then led them into a small re-entrant that was surrounded by thorny scrub.

"Go firm here," he panted as the others followed him in and took up defensive positions. "We'll do a quick map check, and then crack on. One minute…,"

As Stan and Danny began confirming their location with their compasses, maps, and GPS, the remainder took in some much needed water. Despite the freezing morning temperature, they were all soaked to the bone with sweat from the hard and fast climb over the steep feature and they needed to quickly replace the fluids that they had lost.

Bobby reached across, and without a word, stuffed a large piece of chocolate into the mouth of Stan, knowing that their leader did not have time to see to himself, as well as checking their bearings.

"Get that down you, old man. You look like you're on your chin-strap, mate," Bobby grinned at him.

Stan grunted his thanks and continued his confirmation with Danny.

Bobby, slightly built but as strong and determined as any other member of the team, was always quick with a smile. Regardless of the situation, he had a natural ability to lighten the mood with just a few flippant remarks. He had spent most of his army career as a medic in an infantry unit, but with just a few years to push before his retirement date, he had grown bored and developed a severe case of itchy feet, feeling unfulfilled with the career he had led. After being approached by Stan, he had jumped at the chance to be recruited into the newly formed unit, providing that he passed the rigorous selection course first.

He had first met their commander in Afghanistan, when Bobby's battalion had been attached to the same SAS squadron as Stan as a support group. His knowledge, strength, and ability had not gone unnoticed by the attentive veteran, and when the team was put together, Stan wanted Bobby on board as the medic.

Since then, they had been close friends and reliant on one another.

Twenty kilometres further on, and Stan was satisfied that they had gained enough distance. No one would be looking for them so far away in such a short space of time. If there were a search, it would probably be localised to the area around the farm complex and the roads leading in and out of the valley to the west of the ridgeline that they had crossed. It would take some time before their firing positions were discovered and the team hoped to be long gone and back in the UK by then.

They slowed their pace a little, patrolling and using the ground to their advantage for both cover from view and fire. The men knew that they were still not out of danger, and complacency in the last leg of an operation had been the downfall of many soldiers throughout history. It was now that they had to be on their guard, more than ever.

The hours passed and the team pushed on, the sun making its slow journey across the sky, remaining close to the horizon in its winter track.

The village was just a kilometre away.

Using a dried up riverbed to conceal them, the men spread out, watching the area and searching the ground for any sign of a waiting ambush. Everything was quiet, and nothing moved. Even amongst the buildings, nothing stirred and Stan felt unsettled by the unnatural calm.

Their intention had been to follow the riverbed between two small settlements, using the steep banks as cover as they pushed through and towards the north. From there, close to the border, they would be picked up by helicopter and taken out through Turkey.

However, something was wrong.

The village to the west of them was too far away for them to see anything, even with the binoculars, but to the east, an eerie scene greeted them and forced them to hesitate before pushing further on.

Through the binoculars, Stan could see vehicles abandoned in the streets, their doors lying open and their windows smashed. Houses were full of pockmarks from bullets that had ripped their way through the thin brick walls. Doors hung from their hinges, caved inward as though a rampaging mob had been through, ransacking the homes of the town. Windows sat like gaping black maws, revealing nothing of their interiors, their glass broken and their frames in tatters.

Here and there, from behind the buildings, faint columns of smoke could be seen rising up into the air, and soon, Stan began to notice the bundles that littered the ground around the buildings and vehicles.

Motionless bodies were scattered in every street. There had been a massacre.

"What do you think, Stan?" Marty asked as he pulled his eye away from the scope on his rifle and glanced at the blank face of his commander.

Stan squinted, his eyes fixed on the buildings and the streets of the ghost town.

"Could've been rebels, or even Syrian troops," he shrugged. "Looks like they wiped out the whole town."

Nick, the large bulky northerner, closed in from the flank, eyes alert and a look of concern etched across his rounded face. He held his sniper rifle close to his chest while he approached, as though hugging it for comfort.

"We've got movement," he hissed.

The rest of them turned in the direction that Nick indicated and saw a gaggle of distant figures, clambering around a house on the east side of the built up area. It looked as though they were attempting to gain entry through one of the doors.

Marty raised his rifle and peered through his telescopic sight, focussing on the group. There was something clearly wrong with them. They moved in a strange way, slow and clumsily. Even from that distance, they looked pale and dishevelled.

The cluster of men, women, and children, were gathered around the building, but their efforts to get inside seemed half hearted, until the door collapsed. Then, the small clutch of people exploded into a frenzy, pulling at one another and forcing their way inside.

Marty looked at Bull, who was standing beside Nick, his machinegun resting on the edge of the bank and aimed at the ravaged town.

Nick shrugged and began to speak, his words flowing from his mouth in his distinct 'Geordie' accent that took a lot of effort to understand.

"Maybe the people who attacked the village are in that building and the survivors are after payback?"

"Do we crack on with the intended route?" Danny asked, turning to Stan.

Stan shook his head, and then shrugged his shoulders. He paused for a moment, glancing to the north, in the direction they wanted to go.

"The people who took out this village could have headed in that direction. Maybe even have an ambush waiting for anyone who comes along after them."

He turned to Danny and nodded.

"It's what we'd do."

"Shit," Nick suddenly hissed, drawing the attention of the others, "aircraft coming in from the north."

Everybody turned and squinted up at the bright sky.

Low to the ground and far off in the distance, a black dot, a helicopter, was headed towards them, but its engines and rotors could not be heard due to the range and its low altitude. All the noise of its roaring motors was being forced down by the swirling blades above it and soaked up by the desert floor.

"Bollocks," Bobby snapped as he ensured he had a full magazine on his rifle and checked his equipment in anticipation of a hard fight, "and everything was going so well. Now we have a gunship coming at us."

Immediately, the team took up defensive positions, keeping themselves low and readying their weapons and ammunition to fend off the approaching menace. The helicopter was on a direct intercept course with them, its nose aimed at the riverbed and tilted downward as it increased its speed, leaving no doubt in the minds of the men that the aircraft knew where they were and was coming for them.

"Ready boys," Stan called to his left and right as they all tensed and prepared for the coming battle. "Wait till he pulls up, and then nail the fucker."

Every man removed their safety catches and adjusted their aims, pulling their weapons tightly into their shoulders.

Danny could feel his teeth grinding, a habit that had followed him from his days of wearing a gum shield when he was a boxer in the army. He could see the aircraft more clearly now, and the sound of its engines had reached their ears. The steady thump of its rotors echoed along the ground like the beating of Zulu drums.

He smiled to himself, almost tempted to call out a joke about the similarity to their situation and the British Army outpost at Rorke's Drift.

Bull took up the first pressure on the trigger of his machinegun, ready to send a torrent of whizzing projectiles towards the attacking aircraft. He closed his left eye and focussed his foresight on the dark shape of the helicopter's cockpit.

"Come on, you fucker...," he growled under his breath.

Stan looked back to the village to check on the gaggle of people they had seen and what they were doing. They poured out from the house and more of them began to appear from amongst the other buildings. Glaring up into the sky and seeing the helicopter, they began sprinting through the streets and towards the riverbed where the men waited.

The helicopter was close now, just a few hundred metres away and headed straight for them, its heavy mini-guns and rockets clearly visible on either side of the fuselage.

The bulky shape of the aircraft, a Black Hawk, suddenly slowed and yawed to the right, as though about to fire its weapons into the riverbed while avoiding incoming fire.

"Hold your fire," a voice suddenly rang out from the far end of the line.

It was Bobby. He had seen something that the others had not.

"Don't shoot," he shouted, waving his arms, and at the same time, gesturing towards the helicopter. "It's one of ours."

They all soon realised that Bobby was right. It was the aircraft that was supposed to pick them up, twenty kilometres further north.

The Black Hawk pulled its nose upwards and pivoted, so that it approached the dried up riverbed side on, its downwash kicking up a tornado of dust around it as the skilful pilot hovered just a few metres above the desert floor.

Stan made eye contact with the man in the cockpit, who waved back at him and pointed over his shoulder, instructing him to move towards the side doors.

All eight men jumped from their positions, moved towards the aircraft, and began climbing into the passenger compartment.

"What the fuck is going on?" Stan screamed over the shoulder of the pilot so that he could be heard over the engine. "You were supposed to meet us further north, in three hours. Why are you this far across the border?"

The pilot shrugged and pointed to a screen mounted on the console in front of him. Stan looked and saw a digital map of the area and a number of glowing red dots.

"We tracked you to this location," the pilot called back to him as he began to lift the aircraft from the ground. "We had orders to come and extract you immediately, regardless of whether we had to cross the border in daylight."

He glanced back at Stan, an apologetic expression on his face.

"I can't tell you any more than that, because that's all I know, mate."

Stan sat back in confusion and realised that Bobby and Nick were fixated with something that they had seen through the window.

Leaning over their shoulders, he could see the gaggle of people they had been watching earlier, clustered on the ground below them. They all converged towards the helicopter, staring up as it passed low over their heads. They scrambled and jostled against one another, reaching out towards the undercarriage of the Black Hawk. They did not look as though they were asking for help, but more like they were angry and wanted to attack the helicopter.

Did they blame us for their village being attacked? Stan wondered to himself.

Their faces, gaunt and pale, and spattered with blood, stared back at him, their mouths stretching wide and their teeth snapping shut again. All around the strange people, a multitude of mangled bodies lay motionless in large pools of blood, dismembered and torn to pieces.

The people below looked wrong. He had seen the sick and the dying on countless occasions, but he had never seen people who looked the way the villagers did. Though they moved and walked, they did not look real.

They looked, *dead.*

The helicopter soared upward, the pitch of the engine changed, and the battered village and the remnants of its people were left behind.

Stan sat back, his mind trying to make sense of what he had just witnessed.

6

He lay there, still breathing heavily, his chest rising and falling rhythmically while his heart continued to pound away at a rapid rate, beating like a base drum in his ears. His naked body, worn out and exhausted, was coated in a fine layer of sweat that seeped into the sheets beneath him.

His eyes had closed, unable to summon the strength to lift their disproportiately heavy lids anymore, and he was barely aware of his surroundings as sleep tugged at him, threatening to pull him over the precipice of the deep black chasm that had been created from the euphoria of orgasm.

Her hands brushed over the moist skin of his chest, caressing him as he slowly began to drift away. She twined the black hairs of his torso between her long slender fingers, gently pulling at them with just enough force to keep him from slipping into complete unconsciousness. She watched the glistening chest hairs, coiled around her fingers and tweaked them, just enough to raise the skin a little and prevent him from falling asleep.

Her face was close to the crook of his neck, and he could feel her sweet breath against his warm flesh. She giggled at the sight of him twitching against the slight discomfort she inflicted upon him, but he did not attempt to bat her hand away. He liked the feeling, bordering on pleasure and pain.

"Matthew," she whispered.

"Hmm…?" He did not have the energy, or desire to speak.

"Your phone is ringing."

In his dreamy state, he had become oblivious to everything around him, hypnotised by the sound of his own heart and the endorphins that raced around inside his numbed brain. The sound of traffic outside in the street below the hotel room, seemed a million miles away. The TV, the volume having been turned down to little more than a whisper, did not register in his floating mind.

He was far away, being carried along on the billowy pillows of sexual exhaustion.

His phone, switched to silent, throbbed in the pocket of his trousers that had been hastily removed and discarded on the floor. The hectic movements of the device's vibrations caused a light hum that he could barely hear, even when he concentrated on listening for the sound.

"Fuck it," he slurred, refusing to put himself through the effort of moving to retrieve it. "It'll be the wife."

Michelle, the woman beside him who was as equally naked and coated with perspiration, was not his wife. They had first met ten years earlier, when he was an office manager and she had applied for a job as a receptionist.

Due to her looks and flirtatious ways, he had instantly hired her as his Personal Assistant, justifying it to himself as, '*a bit of eye-candy to look at while I'm at work wouldn't do any harm.*'

However, with Michelle's ambition to advance within the business, doing whatever it took to get to where she wanted to be, becoming part of the temptation, Matthew had soon seen an opportunity presented to him that was too good to pass. He knew that he was taking advantage of her drive for success, but he could also see that it was how she operated, using her looks and charm to carry her forward rather than having to begin at the bottom, fighting hard for every inch of ground.

As her teasing style of dress and innuendos became more and more alluring, he found himself encouraging her behaviour, even actively taking part.

He knew that she was a businesswoman and that she was doing what she felt would help herself, but he did not care. He liked what he saw, and with the relationship with his wife waning and becoming bogged down in the bedroom department, Michelle's advances ignited a new fire within him.

From the very start, he was drawn to her, seduced by her sexual powers and he knew, that it was only a matter of time before someone would make a move on her. Finally, he decided that it should be him.

After their first drunken sexual encounter at the company's annual Christmas party, their relationship grew into an unspoken mutual understanding. A partnership that he was more than happy to be part of. She would fulfil his sexual desires and needs, and in return, he looked after her from a career sense.

As he was elevated to the dizzying heights of company director, she too received promotion, but as Matthew scaled the corporate ladder, he always made sure that she stayed a number of rungs below him. He was well aware that if the day ever came where the tables turned and the power and dependence changed hands, he would find himself cast out and forgotten, maybe even ruined and disgraced to keep Michelle free from any rivals.

She had never shown him any evidence of a darker side. Quite the contrary. She had never appeared as anything but caring, affectionate and charming, but in her eyes, he saw something, lurking just below the surface. Each time he gazed into her beautiful face, he caught a glimpse of a ruthlessness, born from her high ambition, and he knew that she would bring it to bear if the situation called for it.

It scared him, but equally excited him.

For the past ten years, they had played a silent and subtle game of cat and mouse against one another, vying for position. However, Matthew had always outmanoeuvred her, using his position as leverage and always keeping a firm grasp on the advantage.

He was more than pleased with himself and especially happy with the status quo. He got what he wanted, and *she* seemed content to continue the game.

Michelle moved her hands away from his chest and glided her fingers, delicately dragging her manicured nails along his stomach and down towards his groin area. Suddenly, she cupped his genitals and gave a gentle squeeze, just enough to get his attention and tear him away from the slumber that beckoned him.

"Well, my dear, Matty," she breathed into his ear seductively, relaxing her grip on his testicles, slightly, "you had better answer it. We don't want your lovely wife ever having reason to become suspicious, do we?"

He grunted and sat up, swinging his legs over the edge of the bed and running his hands through the sweat sodden black hair of his head. He reached down to his trousers and pulled out his shuddering phone, checking the name on the screen.

"Yeah, it's her," he croaked, holding a finger to his lips to remind Michelle to stay silent while he answered.

She rolled her eyes at him, feeling slightly annoyed and insulted that he would even need to tell her something so obvious.

He thumbed the green button.

"Hey, darling," he answered with an air of enthusiasm and affection that he found difficult to muster.

He fell silent for a moment, obviously listening to what his wife was saying on the other end of the line.

"Yeah," he began again, thinking his way through the lies he was about to tell, "I've only just got out of a meeting with the partners. Clive was harping on about production and giving us a hard time, as though it's our fault."

He stood up and began to pace the room, the perspiration on his body glistening in the light that filtered through the gaps in the curtains covering the large floor to ceiling windows. He nodded and hummed, throwing in the occasional *'yes'* and *'really?'* as he continued the conversation as best he could.

He stopped and stared down at Michelle, still naked and sprawled on the bed, looking back at him with a wry smile.

As the voice of his wife drifted away, becoming barely audible in his lustful mind, he eyed the exposed body of the woman in front of him.

His eyes burned with desire and his tongue hungrily licked at his blood filled lips.

Her long brown wavy hair cascaded down over the nape of her neck and towards her breasts like a dark waterfall that had been frozen in mid flow. Her seductive green eyes gazed back at him, silently telling him a countless amount of forbidden secrets and enticing him to experience them for himself.

Even after ten years, and now in her late thirties, she had a figure that drove him to burst with desire and would put most girls of twenty years old to shame. Her skin was as soft as a baby's and free of any imperfections, and her legs, to him, they were something from a dream about what paradise should look like.

With her appearance, intellect, and physical skills, it was impossible for him ever to become bored, or even want to resist her.

Finally, with a great deal of effort that almost made him feel faint, he was able to drag himself back from the erotic daydream he had slipped into and focus his attention, fleetingly, on the grating voice of his wife in his ear.

"Listen, love," he began, apologetically, "I have to go. Clive is waving to me and calling me back into his office for something. That bastard isn't happy unless he's busy whipping someone half to death."

His wife said something and he began to nod.

"Yep, I haven't forgotten. I'll be home in time."

Again, he dipped and raised his head vigorously, acknowledging what his wife was telling him from the other end of the phone and willing the conversation to be over.

"Will do, darling. I'll pick it up on the way home. I know the one you like. It's the Italian Rose that we had the other weekend, isn't it?"

More nods.

"Yep, got it. Love you too."

He hung up and shook his head.

"Fucking pain in the arse," he grumbled as he turned to Michelle and seeing her knees part slightly, deliberately giving him a glimpse of what lay beyond, felt his carnal yearnings return.

"She organised a dinner party with the neighbours and wants me to pick up the wine. I really can't be arsed with it."

Michelle said nothing.

"I'd rather stable my balls to a race horse at the Grand National," he continued.

She sat there, watching him with an impious animalistic look in her eyes that made him feel like she was contemplating ripping him apart. He was more than willing to let her too.

She was breathing heavily, her chest rising with each intake of air and forcing her perfectly formed breasts to lift and fall, jiggling slightly as they came to rest after each exhalation. She placed her hands on her knees, and then gently began to run her fingers down along her smooth inner thighs.

All the time, her sultry gaze remained locked on the visibly excited man standing at the foot of the bed, leering over her.

He grinned ruefully, grabbing his penis and taking a step closer to the bed and dropping his phone to the floor.

"Fuck dinner parties. Do you mind if I wear your arse as a hat for a while?"

Three hours later, Matthew pulled up on his driveway, bringing his expensive sport's car to a halt. As he pulled his keys from the ignition, he stared up at his home.

He had it all.

A big house, lots of friends, lavish holidays three times a year, two beautiful kids, Paula and William, and a loving wife.

Paula was twelve and William was ten, and he knew that he would lose them if his affair was ever uncovered.

So why am I risking it all for the baser pleasures that my assistant plies me with?

He paused and thought for a moment, and then his pangs of guilt turned to fiery resentment that seethed from deep within him.

"If she put out more often, and with a little more enthusiasm, I would never have gone looking elsewhere for it," he growled to himself through gritted teeth as he opened the door and stepped out into the frosty air.

"Fucking bitch."

Satisfied that he had checked his feelings of shame, he locked his car door and admiringly run his hand along the gun metal coloured paintwork.

With a smile of satisfaction and contentment, he turned and began to walk up towards his family home, whistling the tune to the Beatles song, *Please Please Me.*

His smile grew broader as he sang the lyrics in his head.

How apt, he mused to himself.

Halfway to the door, as he fumbled for the keys in his pocket, he stopped, the tune rapidly fading from his lips. He slowly turned around, raising his face up to the stars in the clear night sky and grumbled to himself with annoyance.

"Bollocks. I forgot the fucking wine."

7

The debriefing had not taken long. The outline of the operation and the summary were given to the Secretary of Defence by Stan, and that had been all the assembled senior officers and politicians had wanted to know. The Top Brass did not seem overly interested in the details, and appeared uncomfortable with being informed of anything at all to do with the mission in the first place.

They wanted the bare minimum from the gruff and experienced soldier who stood before them.

As Stan realised that his audience were checking their watches and shifting in their seats, he rounded up his after action report with the conclusion that the task had been accomplished with minimal collateral damage.

He had wanted to question them about why the helicopter had ventured so far into Syrian airspace, and brief them on the destroyed village and the strange behaviour of the locals, but he knew that he would receive no answers.

The Defence Secretary, sitting with his legs crossed and a leather folder on his lap cleared his throat in an attempt to command the attention of everyone in the room. He sat upright and adjusted his tie, then swept his grey hair to the side before gently patting it down into place with his perfectly manicured hands.

"After the mission was, *completed*," he began in a patronising voice that held a certain degree of suspicion, "did you consider confirming that the target was dead, and maybe collecting DNA evidence to back it up?"

Stan felt his blood begin to heat up in his veins. His jaw flexed and the hairs on the back of his neck stood to attention. As usual, he showed no outward emotion, but he locked eyes with the immaculately suited politician, fixing him with a cold stare.

"I can give you the directions to where it all happened, if you like, Mr Secretary?" Stan replied, his eyes unblinking and remaining fixed on the pompous government official. "You'll find plenty of DNA splattered all around that grid-square."

Gerry, the official commanding officer of Stan's unit almost choked. The coffee he had been sipping at had been inhaled along with the gasp of air he had taken in as a reaction to the overtly hostile sarcasm that Stan had showed to the Secretary of Defence.

As he sputtered and attempted to regain his self-control, the eyes of everyone in the room became focussed on him. He patted at his chest as his vision blurred and his eyes began to fill with tears. He raised his hand towards Stan, struggling to speak, and gestured to the door dismissively, ushering him from the room before he could do more damage.

"That'll be all for now, Stan, thank you," he wheezed.

Stan nodded and turned to leave, relieved that he did not have to stay there any longer and be subjected to more ridiculous questions from people who spent all their time tucked safely behind a desk.

As he passed by, he caught the eye of the senior military advisor to the Prime Minister, General Thompson. His nickname amongst the troops had always been 'The Prince of Darkness', due to his constantly bloodshot eyes and extremely pale skin and gaunt features. Many believed that if he had not joined the army, he would have made a good career for himself playing Dracula.

The General's lips curled slightly at the corners, giving a hint of a smile and Stan saw what he interpreted as a glint of an applause in the his eyes for the retort he had thrown at the Secretary of Defence.

Stan left the spacious briefing room, the sound of Gerry's coughing fading into the background as he closed the large heavy door behind him.

They were deep below the city of London, the command centre having once been part of Winston Churchill's bunker during the Second World War. From what he could see, structurally, very little had probably changed since the cigar chomping Prime Minister had occupied the catacombs, conducting the war effort safely out of reach from the bombs of the Luftwaffe. The tunnels and vast collection of chambers were solidly built, but inevitably, due to it being subterranean, a degree of damp made its way through, giving the underground lair a faint musty odour.

The sound of his footsteps echoed along the dark narrow corridors, but they barely registered. The low voices, squawking radios and ringing telephones of the operation's staff seemed a million miles away, as he continued to make his way through the rabbit's warren of the underground command centre, his mind drifting back to the strange events in Syria.

It had been confirmed through the Syrian government announcements and news reports that the Al-Qaeda terrorist, Ali Hussein Bassim, was dead, and of course, the Syrian army stole all credit for the kill.

Stan and his men had expected and hoped for that. With the Syrian commanders claiming responsibility, there would be no comebacks to him, his team, or the British government. The operation had been a great success, militarily, and politically.

However, his confusion continued to grow.

Seeing massacred towns was nothing new to any of them. Witnessing the toll that the horrors of war, poverty and disease had on local populations, were not likely to cause him to lose any sleep. He had seen it a thousand times, on every continent and in the name of every regime and religion. He was numb to it, but it was not the suffering of the innocent that played on his mind. It was what he had seen in the eyes of the Syrian town's surviving population. He could not make sense of what he saw, and a feeling of impending doom and foreboding, on an epic scale, pushed down heavily on his shoulders.

They had been extracted ahead of schedule, and while they were still deep in Syria. Politically, the government and military high command would never have risked such a move unless it was completely unavoidable. Stan's experience told him that, if the original concept of operations had been followed and the helicopter had only gone to the planned extraction point, and the team failed to arrive, then they would have been left, written off and covered over, with all knowledge of them denied by their government.

They were, regardless of their abilities, expendable.

Instead, the top brass had risked an international crisis by sending one of their aircraft into a country that they were not supposed to be in.

Something big was on the horizon. Stan could feel it in his bones.

Gerry came bounding down the corridor behind him, hailing for him to stop and wait. Stan turned and prepared himself to receive an attempted dressing down from the officer.

"Good work out there," Gerry smiled as he reached out and shook hands with him. "How are the boys, good I hope?"

Gerry was a tall and gangly man with elongated, almost rodent like features. His narrowed eyes gave the impression that he was always trying to find an angle, a way through a person's defences in order to gain a glimpse at any weakness that could be exploited and used at a later date to his own advantage.

However, his character did not match his appearance.

On paper, he was listed as the commanding officer for the unit, but in reality, he was nothing more than a front man. An officer that could take the heat for them when things went wrong and alternatively, receive the pat on the back when things went right. He had been a battalion commander in the infantry and had also served a two-year posting with the SAS. Since then, he had held a number of staff positions and now, because of his influence and maturity, acted as the Operation's Officer for all the problems that the government needed taking care of, secretly.

The men liked Gerry. He was a caring man and always kept the best interests of the team at heart. Although he knew that he would never be accepted as one of them, he endeavoured to make it perfectly clear to them that he would always support them, no matter what.

He was never one to interfere with how they run things and he acted more as a Quarter Master than anything else, procuring kit and equipment, providing them with the most up to date intelligence for their tasks and seeing to it that the team's ability to function was unhindered. Most importantly, he was the one that soaked up all of the flak for them.

Sometimes, the men took liberties and before he knew it, Gerry would find himself acting as their fixer and even their nursemaid. The day when he arrived at their accommodation for the first time, he was greeted by Bull's dirty underpants being thrown at him and told to get them washed. Gerry knew that he had to dig his heels in, stand his ground and don his stiff upper lip, which had been an integral part of his higher class breeding.

It was the team's way of testing him, and they never failed to get a kick from watching him attempt to pull rank on them or instil discipline.

"This isn't the army, Gerry, and you're lucky if you get a fucking handshake, never mind a salute."

In the end, Gerry, a full Colonel in the British Army, realised that the men he was supposedly commanding were a different breed, and as a result, would need to be handled differently. They were not listed on any records. Their regimental numbers no longer existed and they were not subject to military law. Even their Oath of Allegiance to the Queen had been stricken from any database.

"Listen, if you're going to get all uptight over that prick in there," Stan growled and nodded back in the direction they had come, indicating the Secretary of Defence, "then I suggest you take…"

Gerry was shaking his head and smiling.

"Not at all, Stan. It was a good way of rounding it all up and gave me an excuse to get you out of there. You looked bored and frustrated and keen to get some down time. Anyway, everyone knows that the secretary is a prick."

Stan relaxed and nodded his appreciation.

"Did you read my report?"

"Yeah, I did," Gerry nodded, a little too enthusiastically for Stan's taste.

They both turned and began to walk along the gloomy passage.

"I know you have questions, but at the moment, I have no answers for you. Something is going on, and that is about all I know. The Op's Room has been a hive of activity for the last forty-eight hours and there's something big on the horizon. That's why they pulled you all out and risked such a stunt."

Stan nodded, accepting that Gerry was either in the dark, or being evasive for the sake of operational security.

"Did you read the bit about the village? Something wasn't right and personally, I don't think it was anything to do with rebels or Syrian soldiers. They were fucked!"

Gerry's expression changed and his eyes glanced to his left and right, as though he was about to reveal a dark and deadly secret.

"When I presented your report to the Prince of Darkness, his face went pale, more than it usually is. Almost transparent, even. After reading that, the head-shed didn't care about the Bassim part of the op. They were more interested in the village, even though it was just a tiny paragraph of your report."

Stan bit his lip and nodded, his mind ticking over.

"Anyway," Gerry continued, his words taking on a more cheerful tone, "where's the men, they all okay? I have their pay and new identities in my office. A good bottle of whisky too, so if you give me a minute, I will tag along with you and show my face to the guys. I'm sure they would appreciate my gifts."

The accommodation for the team was not the average army barracks. Of course, they referred to it as 'the barrack block' out of habit, but it was anything but. It was actually an entire floor of luxury flats on the eighteenth storey of a high-class apartment building in the heart of London, courtesy of the Ministry of Defence.

The team had their leader, Stan, to thank for their lavish surroundings. After they had come back from the Brussels job, they had all suddenly been moved out from the three bedroomed flat on the outskirts of Peckham that they were crammed into, and elevated to the higher echelons of society, literally.

As Stan handed them their envelopes containing money and fresh identities, Gerry poured the whisky and continued with his over excited tirade about how good it was to see them back, safe and sound, after a job well done.

Every month, the men were paid handsomely, and in cash. They had no bank accounts in the UK, their money being secretly dropped into deposit boxes and then transferred to foreign banks.

As with their operations, their pay was also kept off the books.

There was no trace of them with the MoD. They never wore military issued clothing or equipment and dressed as they pleased. Everything that they used, including radios, night vision and navigation equipment, was available on any black market, and even through the internet. Serial numbers were meticulously removed, leaving no traceable link between the men, their equipment, and their origins.

Weapons were different and more difficult to arrange, but with the contacts that Gerry and the men had throughout the world, they were always able to purchase something locally to suit their needs.

Back in England, they came across more as being anything but soldiers, living in comfort and always flush with money. Being accommodated in the apartments suited them because they did not draw any attention. Everybody else that lived in the building was rich and lived with a degree of discretion, so the eight burly men, coming and going on a regular basis, did not turn many heads.

There was always one exception to the rule though.

A couple of floors above them lived an extravagant hell-raiser named Roland. He had been a bit of a gangster at one point, so the story went, but now owned a chain of magazines and newspapers, and had a tendency to upset politicians and celebrities with complete indiscrimination. If he had dirt on someone, he rarely hesitated to dish it out. He had a lot of highly situated friends and just as many enemies, equally as important.

The team had become very friendly with Roland, attending many of his parties and enjoying the delights on offer. He was no fool and he knew that the mysterious men that lived below him were a surreptitious part of the British military. To Roland, with his ever watchful eyes, it was obvious and he laughed when Bobby introduced himself for the first time, claiming to be a rock and roll music producer.

Bull especially indulged in the wild goings on due to the fact that there was always an abundance of beautiful women, ready to do anything necessary to become a part of Roland's inner circle of friends. Naturally, Bull was always ready to pick them off, like a shark prowling through the aftermath of a shipwreck.

As they counted their money, the men of the team sat back and began to sip at the whisky that Gerry had provided. It had been their first drink in a long time, and many savoured the warm smooth taste of the expensive brand. Everyone except Brian that is, who slugged his drink back in one gulp and demanded a refill.

He raised his glass and in his thick Belfast accent, proposed his toast.

"Here's to Ali Hussein Bassim. Gone to Paradise in a million pieces and I hope his seventy-two virgins can't find his dick."

Brian, having grown up in Northern Ireland during the height of the troubles, was as tough as they came. His words were spoken with aggression and every sentence contained at least four or five profanities.

His shaved head and staring eyes, coupled with his overtly hostile speech and body language made him appear like a football hooligan. He could never hold his tongue, and if he had an opinion on something, he gave it without thinking through on the consequences. He considered this to be a good trait of his, but his four ex-wives begged to differ.

Next, they all turned their attention to the envelopes containing their new identities and documents. Each month, new passports, driver's licences, credit cards and even gym memberships were produced for them. Their photographs matched and even their personal details and records were changed on the international databases. For instance, if any of them were ever arrested, their fingerprints would match perfectly to the name and description on the police system.

"For fuck sake...," Bobby suddenly burst out with anger, "is this some kind of joke, Gerry? Are you taking the piss?"

Gerry looked back at him vacantly then glanced towards Stan for support.

"What's up, Bobby?"

"This fucking I.D, is what's fucking up," he growled, slinging the documents across the table and reaching for a fresh glass of the strong vintage whisky.

Marty snatched up the package and pulled out the passport from inside. He began reading and then erupted with a howl of laughter. Everyone in the room turned to him, expectantly waiting for him to share the joke.

Stan snatched the passport and read the name aloud.

"Sharon Clements."

The room resounded with the ridiculing guffaws that were aimed at Bobby. He sat there, glowering and threatening each one of them with his wrath.

It was not so much the name that bothered him, but the fact that he was unable to leave the apartment until the matter was cleared up. If the worst happened and he found himself in trouble with the law, or in an accident, the inevitable questions about his identity would be asked. The name, Sharon Clements, clearly did not match the man, his description or his biometrics, and it would not be long until the problem was dropped into the lap of the MoD and followed by a torrent of awkward questions.

Drawing unnecessary attention to themselves was not a habit that the team could afford to get in to.

Bobby sat back and crossed his arms, a deep series of creases spreading across his forehead, as he stared through the large bay windows that expanded the length of the room in front of them. He had been away for almost five weeks and the city awaited, but instead, he would need to remain in the building until the mistake was corrected.

"Get this sorted out, Gerry, and do it quick," he growled.

"Hey, Bobby, have a guess what my name is this month," Marty teased him.

Bobby did not answer and continued to sulk.

"Steve Rockwell," Marty gloated. "Oh, you know I'm going to have some fun with a name like that. I should be a porn star."

Within an hour, the men had dispersed. Gone to indulge themselves in the things they liked to do during their time off.

Danny, Nick, Marty and Brian, as usual, headed into town to get drunk and party hard.

Stan and Taff, being the older and more mature of the group decided to pass on the bars and clubs, opting for some decent food and a few quiet drinks in one of the local pubs and then the hotel bar.

"Right then," Bobby announced, finally snapping out of his foul mood. "Looks like I'll go up and see Roland. There's always something going on at his place."

"Yeah, you do that," Stan replied with a stern look. "Keep away from that white stuff he's always shoving up his nose."

"Yes, dad," Bobby retorted with a dismissive wave of his hand as he headed for the door. "You know me, I'm not into that shit. Anyway, I prefer to sniff glue."

Bull, as always, made his excuses and waited until he thought no one was paying him any attention before slipping away. His cunning was as subtle as a brass band. His secret was not even remotely secret to the rest of the team, at least. They all knew where he went and what he got up to.

Each one of them had been handpicked for their lack of ties. None of them were married or had children, or siblings. Their parents were either dead or unknown, and every member of the team was legally dead. They had been listed as Killed in Action or died due to accidents and illness.

According to the database, Nick Roberts had died of AIDS and still received a hard time over it from his teammates.

However, three years earlier, Bull had somehow tracked down his mother.

As a baby, he had been dumped outside his local Post Office in a carrier bag with a note asking for *anyone* to take care of him. He grew up in foster homes and approved schools, bouncing from one town to the next, forever getting into fights and trouble with the police, and never really felt at home anywhere, until he joined the army.

When Bull began disappearing for days on end, then showing up *without* bruises or stories of wild parties and orgies, Stan and Marty grew suspicious.

It had not taken long for them to discover the truth.

The hedonistic Bull, who usually wanted nothing better than to tear up the town, causing mayhem and living like a 'Rock Star', was going for walks in the country and having picnics with his *'Dear Old Mum.'*

Stan and Marty felt no need to confront him over it, and allowed their friend to feel what it was like finally to have a mother.

They could not help sniggering though, as they sat three hundred metres away, binoculars glued to their faces and a beer in their hands, watching the mighty Bull, eating French Fancies and picking wild flowers with his aging mother.

Morning arrived with a multitude of aching heads and blurry minds.

Stan, having been woken early by a phone call from Gerry, was kept busy going from one apartment to the next, dragging his men from their beds, screaming at them like stubborn children in an attempt to get them coherent.

Nick and Brian had obviously struck it lucky and had not gone back to their apartments and Stan's numerous attempts to reach them on their phones, was an exercise in futility.

Bobby, his head thumping from the hammers that seemed to be pounding away at his skull, forced himself up from his bed when he heard the door to his apartment reverberating from Stan's assault.

"Alright, alright," he shouted back towards the doorway, the sound of his own voice echoing through his mind and causing him to wince. "I heard you. Just give me five-fucking-minutes, will you?"

The banging stopped, Stan obviously moving on to the next door.

Bobby slumped on the edge of his bed, his hair standing on end and his eyes bloodshot and unable to focus. He grimaced at the taste in his bone-dry mouth and glanced around the room, looking for his clothes but unable to see or remember where he had left them.

In fact, there was nothing he *could* remember from the previous evening.

From behind him, he heard a low rumbling groan.

Startled, he spun around, his drunken vision taking a second longer to catch up with the rapid movements of his head and almost causing him to black out as his eyes seemed to rattle within their sockets.

He looked for the origin of the noise and noticed a large mound in the middle of his bed, covered with the thick white duvet. He blinked hard and pinched at the top of his nose in an attempt to focus.

"Sorry, love," he croaked, "but I'll be honest with you. I don't remember your name, and I think it's pointless you telling me, because I'll be asking for it again in about five minutes."

The covers moved and a tangle of blonde hair appeared from underneath. A pretty face, though smeared with lipstick and mascara, turned to him with just one eye open, struggling to focus in the same way he had.

"It's okay, I don't remember yours either, and I can't remember anything that we did. So it couldn't have been all that great. You can make it up to me by getting some coffee though, if you really want to."

Bobby nodded and smiled.

"Touché..."

It took Stan and Taff the better part of two hours to locate and round up their team. They were all a little worse for wear, all except Bull.

He was as sober as a judge and grumbling about being dragged to HQ before having had the opportunity to spend some money and raise hell.

They walked and staggered along the dimly lit corridors of the bunker, turning corners and cutting through rooms. The intoxicated members of the team were struggling to keep their bearings and some were beginning to feel dizzy.

"What's going on, Stan?" Brian asked as he drained the last of his coffee from his thermos mug.

Stan was getting annoyed with being continually asked the same question.

"I haven't a clue," he said dismissively. "We've been dragged in for something and that's all I know."

He turned to Brian and looked him up and down.

"Look at the fucking state of you lot. You're like a bunch of teenage kids on your first holiday to Tenerife."

"I wish I *was* in Tenerife," Bobby grumbled.

They arrived at the briefing room and immediately, they realised that something big was going on. The space was crammed with people, all in a hurry and rushing about. It was a hive of activity. More so than usual.

The men in lab coats were particularly interesting, a rarity in the bunker and especially, in the tactical briefing rooms. They stood in a huddle, talking quietly amongst themselves and comparing their notes from the stacks of paper and files that they held in their hands.

Taff looked across at Stan and raised a questioning eyebrow.

Gerry was at the far end, speaking with a couple of Intelligence Officers and he made his way over to Stan and his men when he saw them arrive. Normally, he would smile and make small talk, but this time, his expression was complete seriousness and clearly, there was no time for formalities and trivial chitchat.

Samantha was also there, and began to cross the room, making a beeline for them.

"The briefing will start in about ten minutes," she informed them. Then she noticed their condition and her face formed a look of frustration and impatience.

"Oh, I see the children have been allowed out to play again?"

Her statement was aimed at the whole group, but her attention was focussed solely on Bobby as he stood swaying.

"Fuck off, Sam," he spat, rubbing his hand against the side of his head. "I've got a hangover that could put a rhino on its arse and I don't need you adding to it."

The history between Bobby and Samantha was still recent and the rawness between the two had still not subsided enough for them to deal with one another without one having to make the other feel uncomfortable.

"Sorry, I didn't mean to upset you. Please accept my apology…, Sharon."

Marty snickered and nudged Bobby in the ribs.

"Shit and fall in it, Samantha."

She turned to Stan, satisfied that she had accomplished her mission in ruining Bobby's day.

"I suggest you all go and get more coffee, and quick."

8

Danny peered down from the open door and watched the jungle rapidly sweeping by below. A blanket of endless shades of green drifted along beneath his feet, looking like a patchwork quilt of lush foliage. The trees were so closely packed that it was impossible to see the forest floor. Only when the continuous mantle of high reaching glistening wet leafs and branches were broken by fast flowing rivers and sheer cliff faces, did he see any ground detail.

It had been many years since he had dressed like a soldier, but now, wearing jungle uniform and boots, and carrying an M4 ArmaLite, he once again felt like he was on operations with a regular army unit.

Although Danny was the newest member of the team, he was no stranger to war. He had served his share of operational tours with his parent unit and even been a member of the Pathfinder Platoon of the UK Airborne Forces. Strong and extremely fit, there was no physical challenge that he would not face, including a hard fight with the odds stacked against him. Tall and dark haired, with long arms, he had been a talented boxer in his time, even representing the British Army overseas.

Everyone had instantly warmed to Danny when he first arrived, making him the butt of all their jokes, testing his character and level of retaliation. Bull had learned the hard way. After subjecting Danny to a horrendous night of taunts and practical jokes, he fell asleep in a drunken stupor and as a result, lost both of his eyebrows to Danny.

The helicopter transported the team eastwards, banking and twisting as it followed the contours of the landscape. On occasion, its rotors were just inches away from the treetops, an indication of the skill of the pilot.

The noise was deafening.

The open doors on either side of the fuselage created a storm of wind that howled through the interior, making it impossible to hear anything other than the ear-splitting thump of the whirling blades and the growl of the engines.

Danny had nothing to say anyway.

He did not feel like engaging in conversation with anyone. Just a brief glimpse around the interior of the aircraft at the others, dressed in multi shades of green, told him that the rest of them felt the same way.

Instead, he leaned back, ignoring the powerful stench of aviation fuel and rested his head against the helicopter's interior. As he continued to stare out at the wild tropical landscape, the vibrations from the motors, travelling through the aircraft's structure, sent him into a mild trance.

They had a job to do now and they were all busy tuning themselves into their environment, lost in their own thoughts and preparing themselves in their own private ways. Some were trying to sleep, while others, like Danny, remained locked in their own little world.

Brian was fruitlessly attempting to get through a chapter in the book he was reading, fighting a losing battle against the gale that tore at the pages. In the end, he gave up and angrily stuffed the novel into the space beneath his seat, wedging it between two heavy steel boxes of ammunition.

Stan was busy staring at a map and a number of photographs, glancing out of the doors on either side as he orientated himself to the ground while speaking with the pilot through the headset at the same time.

Danny caught his eye and Stan nodded at him, holding up five fingers, informing him that they were almost at the Landing Zone.

The mission brief had revealed nothing new, at first. As usual, they were given a summary of the global situation.

Military reverses in the wars against Korea and Iran were forcing the western governments to rethink their strategy. China had managed to sink the aircraft carrier, USS George Washington, creating a severe dent in the ability to provide air operations and close support for the land based units engaged in South Korea, having already been pushed back during the massive Korean counter offensive from the north.

The Iran front had become bogged down in a stalemate. The war had lost its momentum and had begun to resemble something from the First World War, with both sides digging in and occupying heavily fortified positions and launching small-scale assaults that yielded very little in the strategic sense, and neither side gaining the upper hand.

The technologically advanced west did not have the resources to sustain a prolonged war in the Middle East. To begin with, things had gone well and it looked as though the American and British armies, along with limited supporting units from France and Germany, would secure another easy, *initial*, victory against the conventional troops of Iran. Then, as had happened in Iraq, an anticipated insurgency would need to be dealt with, but Britain and the US believed that they had adequately prepared for that eventuality.

When Iranian resistance proved to be much stronger than what their neighbours, Iraq, had been able to muster, the western armies immediately run into problems. The enemy hit back with similar, state-of-the-art weapons, provided to them from Eastern Europe and China, and wielded them with a skill and strategy that matched the invading troops.

Iraq had been a relatively easy invasion, with the Iraqi commanders unable to think in a completely three-dimensional perspective and adjust for their lacking of sophisticated weaponry. Their infrastructure had been severely damaged through years of sanctions and their army was already demoralised.

Iran was a different beast.

Their soldiers proved to be of a much higher calibre and the Iranian commanders were extremely well trained and practiced in the arts of warfare. They had better tanks, weaponry and even their pilots were better skilled than the Iraqis had been. When the invasion began, the allied airstrikes proved ineffectual. Due to the concentrated and extremely effective anti-air defences of the enemy, many of the guided missiles and manned aircraft were shot down before reaching their targets.

In the end, the allies had to push on without having gained complete air superiority.

Soon, all the stocks of the technologically superior weapons that the British and American forces relied upon so heavily, began to dwindle and the troops on the ground had to rely solely on their skills as soldiers. It had become a war of attrition and a political disaster, as more and more body-bags were sent home, containing the remains of fallen sons, fathers and brothers, fighting in wars that the majority of the public did not agree with.

The allies were fighting multiple wars, on multiple fronts and things were not going the way they had wanted. The words *'Nuclear Strikes'* were often thrown around in the media, and to many people, it seemed that the world was on the brink of an apocalypse.

None of this had been revealing news to the men of the team, but when the men dressed in lab coats stepped forward and began to explain the situation through the eyes of the World Health Organization, WHO, Stan and his teammates were enlightened to a much larger and potentially more devastating threat.

One that none of them had realised even existed.

They had all seen the news footage of South America and Africa, in the grip of famine and disease, but that was nothing new. The Third World was always suffering while the First World got fat and happy. What really caught their attention was the epic scale of it all, and the distinct similarities of the suffering and the effects it was having on them, socially and economically. Considering that both continents were separated by a vast ocean, their symptoms were very similar, almost identical.

Entire towns and cities had been wiped out by a mysterious virus and the authorities were battling hard to keep it out of the limelight, for now.

Described as an extremely lethal strain of flu by the *'nerds in white'*, as Bull referred to them, was all the detail that was given to them.

A doctor, named Joseph Warren, had been searching through the villages of Sierra Leone, east of Freetown, where he believed that the virus had originated. He had been hoping to find *patient zero*, dead or alive, but no one as yet could explain how the illness could have crossed the Atlantic and seized South America in the same vice like grip.

The doctor, along with a group of British soldiers assigned to protect him, had gone missing nearly two weeks earlier, and no trace had been seen since. A report containing pictures of a massacred village arrived from the Sierra Leone government, but it was unclear if the doctor was amongst the dead.

"So, why are you sending us?" Stan had asked. *"Surely this is a simple search and rescue op' that could be carried out by a regular army unit, even the SAS if you want to give them the VIP treatment?"*

"Doctor Warren is the leading expert on this right now and it is vital that we recover him, or at least, his notes," Gerry replied. *"Besides, there isn't anyone else. In case you haven't noticed, our army is pretty stretched at the moment."*

One of the 'nerds' had stepped forward.

"We believe that the doctor was close to something, and we need his ground knowledge and research."

"Does this have anything to do with the village in Syria? Has the virus spread from Africa to the Middle East?" Stan asked, finally able to put someone on the spot and maybe receive some answers.

At the very least, he was hoping to see their reaction and judge things for himself, forming his own conclusions on the scale of the problem.

The 'nerds' glanced nervously at one another, none of them wanting to continue the line of questioning that Stan was steering them towards.

They turned towards Gerry for support.

"It's strictly on need to know at the moment, Stan. When you get back, and if you've recovered the doc', then hopefully, more information will be made available," Gerry replied, coming to the rescue of the uncomfortable scientists.

Stan nodded. He had heard that same phrase a thousand times.

"You and the guys will be going in as conventional soldiers on this one, Stan," Gerry informed him as they came to the end of the briefing. *"Weapons and equipment will be arranged and issued. We're using the Quarter Master for Hereford. They've been kind enough to let us do a 'supermarket sweep' of their stores."*

From there, they had gone into detailed mission planning, collating all the intelligence they could get their hands on, scrutinising maps and aerial photography and studying the political situation and the likely rebel groups who may have been responsible for the disappearance of the doctor and the soldiers.

Four of the bodies from the village had been listed as being western and it was assumed that they were part of the British unit attached to the doctor. Other bodies were so badly burned, or already decomposing so rapidly, that their DNA was having to be checked before any identification could be made.

At the very least, the team had a potential starting point for their search…

“Two minutes,” Stan shouted at the top of his lungs, trying to be heard over the din of the aircraft. He held out his hand, showing two fingers to each of the others to ensure that they had all understood.

They nodded back at him, confirming that they had received the message, and began preparing themselves to move. They unbuckled their harnesses, checked their pouches were secure and then, pulled the cocking levers back on their rifles and machineguns, chambering a round, ready for action should they happen to arrive at a hot Landing Zone.

The men moved towards the doors on either side, ready to jump down and fan out on the ground as soon as the aircraft touched down.

As the Black Hawk slowed, it banked to the left and began a three-hundred and sixty-degree sweep of the area.

Below, the remains of the village came into view.

The river to the west, twisted its way through the grassy plains, snuggled close to the tree-covered foothills. A road, little more than a red dust covered track, ran out from the jungle, dissecting the small community in two. On either side, the crushed and scorched mud brick huts, once the homes of the families that had worked the land, now sat empty and dead, their roofs caved in or burned away, and their owners butchered.

Animal carcasses, their bodies bloated and swarming with insects, littered the sides of the road, gradually being consumed until only bones remained.

Danny immediately recognised the signs of a battle, not just a massacre. A number of trucks, mangled and burned to their frames, lay discarded on the outskirts. They had been destroyed as they had made their way along the track during the rebel advance on the village. The earth around the vehicle remains was scorched and splinters of metal and piles of fragmented glass were scattered in a wide arc around them.

He knew that, the only thing that could have caused the widespread shrapnel, were detonations from High Explosives. The fuel tanks igniting would not cause the metal frames to twist and shatter, and the windows to blast outwards. They had probably been hit by the 40mm grenade launchers attached to the weapons of the British soldiers.

As the helicopter completed its circle and moved closer, the evidence of battle became even more apparent. Piles of empty brass cases, strewn in the dirt and scattered between the small huts could be seen twinkling in the bright sunlight. Disintegrated masonry and small craters marked the spots where grenades had exploded. Pockmarks, where machinegun and rifle fire had punched through brick and steel sheeting, scarred the walls that had escaped complete destruction.

The Black Hawk slowed to a hover and began decreasing altitude. The downwash from the rotors flattened the long grass in a large circle below the aircraft, and as it settled to just two metres from the ground, Stan gave the order to jump.

Together, they dropped from the doors on either side, landing on the soft soil then pushing forward to create a defensive perimeter around the landing site. As the pilot adjusted the angle of the rotor blades, the machine lifted back into the air, the squeal of its engines rising as it increased power and gained altitude, leaving the eight men on the ground to fend for themselves.

As the sound of the aircraft faded, Stan and his team remained still and silent, maintaining their defensive perimeter as their senses adjusted to their new environment. As always, they waited a few minutes, allowing their hearing to acclimatise to the silence of the open landscape, as averse to the harsh mechanical noise of the interior of the helicopter.

With a nod of his head, Stan signalled for Danny to lead them off towards the centre of the devastated village.

Everywhere they looked, the team saw traces of the horror that had befell the locals.

They split into pairs and fanned out through the wreckage, looking for any sign of the doctor and the soldiers.

"Nothing," Marty finally reported to Stan after they had swept the area. "There's no trace of them. Plenty of blood and a few positions where the troops may have held their ground, but nothing to confirm where they went afterwards."

Danny stooped and picked up a brass casing from the dusty ground, holding it up to the sun as he inspected it. He recognised the calibre immediately.

"I think we're in the right place to start, Stan," he said as he turned and handed the expended round to his commander.

"Five-point-five-six," Stan said to himself as he studied it.

The rebels, like most other armies and militias of the world, used mainly Kalashnikov assault rifles and other Eastern European made weapons, firing 7.62mm rounds. Only the western armies used 5.56mm.

"There's a lot of tracks leading out of the village to the east, both vehicle, *and* people on foot," Taff reported as he joined the rest of the team. "The rebels either marched them out, as prisoners, or for some strange reason, they followed the trucks when they left."

Bull shook his head.

"That makes no sense, Taff. Why would the villagers follow the cunts that had just attacked them?"

Taff shrugged.

"Don't ask me, mate. I just work here."

As well as being the second-in-command, 2ic, of the team, Taff was also their expert tracker. He could gain all kinds of wonderful knowledge just from the smallest of tracks. He was able to scour the terrain in a way that no one else could, searching for *'ground sign'* and *'top sign'*, and gaining a great deal of information from something as simple as a single footprint or broken branch.

Short and broad, he had been an excellent rugby player for the army, and coming from Wales, he loved to sing the songs about the green valleys and high mountains of his homeland. The only problem was that he could not hold a note.

They headed eastwards, remaining within the trees for concealment and paralleling the road. Through the whole of the day, they patrolled towards the rebel camp that they had seen on the satellite photography.

It was tucked away in a large depression in the ground, surrounded by thick jungle that obscured them from prying eyes. However, nothing could be hidden from the air, especially when they were the centre of the search.

They had estimated that the camp held between forty and sixty rebels. On the imagery, they had identified a number of guard towers, but they could not be sure of further defences. The team would have to conduct a Close Target Reconnaissance, CTR, to confirm enemy numbers, defences, routine and whether or not they were holding the doctor, before they could make their plan. It could take a number of days before the CTR was completed and the team would need to establish a Lying up Position, LUP, to operate from.

They pushed on, their bodies soaked with sweat and their flesh being savaged by the thousands of mosquitos that buzzed around them incessantly. The humidity was at seventy-five percent and to the men, it felt like they were patrolling through a steam room.

Going from the cold of Syria, to the intense heat of the jungle, without acclimatising beforehand, was taking its toll on the team.

Every few hundred metres, they would stop and check the road, confirming that they were still on the right track and taking the opportunity to catch their breath and take in the much-needed fluids that their bodies rapidly sweated out in the African heat.

During one such stop, Taff came back after checking the track, shaking his head with a perplexed look on his face.

"It makes no sense," he said in confusion. "The tracks are weird, Stan. It looks like there were dozens of them, moving along the road, together."

"What's so weird about that?"

Taff shrugged.

"Well, either I need to brush up on my tracking skills or…, the people we're following are all shit-faced," he said, scratching his head. "Judging by their footprints, it looks like they've all been hammering the vodka."

With three hours left before darkness arrived, they moved into an area just a kilometre away from where they believed the rebel camp to be. Stan led them into the LUP, checking their ability to defend the area should they come under attack and confirming their exact location. The others conducted clearance patrols, pushing out one-hundred metres, ensuring that they were not being observed or in a location close to tracks or natural walkways that people may travel along.

Next, it was important to get visual confirmation of the enemy position. At least then, they could begin their reconnaissance once first light arrived.

Movement at night in the jungle was out of the question. The darkness was as black as the heart of a witch and they were more likely to get lost or suffer an accident than anything else during the dark hours.

Taff and Brian were tasked to push forward and conduct an initial recce of the area.

In the meantime, the rest of them began to organise themselves, checking their equipment, weapons and taking in some food.

"Fucking hell," Bull remarked as he stuffed some cold Lancashire Hot-Pot from his rations into his mouth. "It's like being back in the army this."

Nick grinned back at him from behind his machinegun, seated in his sentry position.

"Nah, it's more like camping. It's all good fun, mate."

9

The crunching footfalls and gasping breaths of the two men could be heard echoing through the jungle as they approached the LUP, returning from their reconnaissance. The remainder, alerted to the sound of them running and ploughing through the jungle, uncaring of the noise they were making, immediately took up defensive positions, believing that danger was advancing towards them.

Stan watched as Brian and Taff closed in, their faces soaked with glistening beads of moisture as their exertion caused them to sweat profusely. They were moving fast, indifferent to any tactical requirements, or the sign that they were leaving behind as they crushed the jungle foliage beneath their heavy boots and bashed against trees with their equipment.

Stan began to feel angry at their reckless behaviour, but he knew that they would not be acting in such a way if the situation did not warrant it.

They crashed into the LUP and fell into a heap, cursing and panting for breath. Their faces were pale and their startled eyes darted from Stan to one another, continually glancing over their shoulder in the direction they had come from.

Everyone turned to them, waiting for an explanation to why they were behaving in such a way and what they had seen.

"You need to see this for yourself, Stan," Brian gasped, visibly shaken.

"See what?"

Taff looked at Brian, and then turned to their commander.

"The camp. It looks like they were attacked."

"Saves us the job then," Bobby remarked with a shrug.

Taff shook his head as he regained control of his breathing and wiped his brow with the back of his hand.

"Whoever did this," he panted, "was severely pissed off over something. There are bits of them all over the fucking place."

Brian nodded.

"Weapons, ammunition, equipment, supplies…it's all still there, so I don't think it was a raid of any sort."

"Bits of them all over the place?" Danny repeated, unsure if he had heard correctly.

Taff nodded.

"Yeah, the rebels. Looks like they were fed through a fucking meat-grinder, mate. Proper butchery style stuff."

The light was steadily growing fainter, but they needed to move forward. It would soon be pitch black, and Stan did not savour the idea of a night under the trees without knowing what was happening in their immediate area.

Quickly, they covered the ground to their target and arrived at the outer perimeter of the rebel camp. As they drew near, they began to see an abundance of ground sign. Footprints swathed the whole area, leading in all directions. Strike marks covered the trees from bullets that had smashed into them, their bark stripped away and the white pulp shining brightly in the fading light.

Blood spatter was clearly visible and ground into the thick mud at their feet, they began to see dozens of bodies.

"Looks like they've been trampled," Danny whispered.

He continued forward, glancing down at the lifeless corpses leading up to the outer perimeter of the rebel base. They were twisted, with arms and legs splayed at strange angles, and ribcages crushed and flattened.

Barbed wire had been erected, strung from one tree to the next as a barrier against anyone attempting to penetrate the defences. In a number of places, it had been levelled and pushed to the side. Scraps of clothing hung from the barbs and below, numerous feet had churned the ground to squelching mire.

They could see bullet casings littering the ground all around them as they carefully stepped through the dismantled defences. Weapons, their magazines empty, were everywhere, discarded by their owners as they ran out of ammunition and fled from whoever was attacking them.

Inside the perimeter, rows of canvas tents and huts lay in tatters, tables and chairs overturned and boxes containing equipment scattered far and wide.

Then, there were the bodies, dozens of them.

It was hard to estimate the number of dead due to the condition of the corpses that lay in piles all around. The one thing that they all had in common was that they had all suffered head wounds. Skulls lay open to the air, congealed blood and mashed brains oozing from the gaping holes. Dismembered limbs and crushed ribcages littered the muddy jungle floor, buzzing with flies and already crawling with tiny white maggots.

The stench was overpowering. It hung in the air, trapped beneath the canopy of trees, as though it had a physical form and clung to anything that it came into contact with.

Danny gagged and had to step to the side to avoid vomiting over the man in front of him. His stomach churned and he swallowed hard to keep his last meal within the confines of his stomach.

"Jesus," Nick grunted, holding his hand over his mouth and nose. "What the fuck happened here?"

"These don't look like rebels to me, boss," Bobby commented.

He squatted beside the body of a woman that had been torn open from her neck, down to her genitals. He leaned in closer and inspected the ghastly wound then, looked up at Taff who was standing close by.

"She's completely empty."

"Empty?" Taff questioned, looking down at the mangled corpse.

Bobby nodded, poking at the woman's ribcage with the muzzle of his rifle.

"Yeah, *empty*, as in, there's nothing inside her. Fucking weird, mate."

None of the dead looked like rebels, Stan suddenly realised. They were all dressed completely in civilian clothing; men, women, and children alike. There were young and old, all mixed together, all with gunshot wounds to their heads.

That was the one thing that was consistent throughout the rebel camp and the countless bodies strewn in the mud.

"What about the rebels?" Bull asked to no one in particular.

"All over the fucking place," Danny replied with disgust, nudging a headless torso with the toe of his boot.

Its arms were also missing and its flesh looked as though it had been flayed from its bones. Where the genitals had once been, there was a gaping hole, the damage to the skin and sinew around the wound indicating that the testicles and penis had been violently ripped from the body.

Bull looked around at his immediate surroundings. He noticed the limbs and other body parts that still had the unmistakable rebel style clothing and regalia that the militias always liked to adorn themselves with, still clinging to them. Bangles and necklaces with the usual symbols of witchcraft, given to them by their tribal witch doctors to protect them from bullets and harm. T-shirts, with western rock groups and diamante encrusted skull designs. Aviator sunglasses and bandanas…

They were all there.

The rebels were all around them, torn to pieces and scattered through the camp and the surrounding jungle.

None of it made sense. Rebels dismembered and civilians with festering wounds and gunshots to the head.

All around the perimeter fence, countless footprints could be seen, all headed into the camp from every angle. It appeared that the civilians, possibly from a local village, had decided to neutralise the threat that had taken up camp on their doorstep. It was the only explanation, as far as Stan could see, and he suddenly felt a great deal of admiration for their bravery, but he had never heard of anything like that happening before.

He heard a clicking noise, he turned to see Bull, and Marty, walking in a crouch with their weapons at the ready, both headed towards a collapsed tent connected to a structure made from bamboo. Bull was holding out his hand, snapping his fingers to get the attention of the rest of the team, while he kept his eyes to his front, taking careful steps as he drew closer.

Stan and the remainder did not need an explanation, and immediately raised their rifles, covering their arcs and their friends as they closed in on potential danger. Bull had seen or heard something, and that was all that they needed to know for the moment.

Bobby and Taff pushed out to the left, ensuring that their flank was protected, while Danny and Brian pushed to the right. The team was now fanned out into a base line, ready to send a devastating amount of firepower into anything they perceived as a threat.

Bull, just a couple of metres away from his objective, paused for a moment and nodded to Marty, signalling him to be ready and to cover him.

They had both heard the noise; a low groan and the sound of a body moving in the sucking mud beneath the canvas sheeting. It was unmistakable and they knew that someone was in there.

He stepped closer, the barrel of his Belgian made Minimi machinegun pointed at the centre of the collapsed structure and his finger taking up the first pressure on the trigger. His body was tense, ready to jump into action, or away from harm. Every muscle was taut, filled with oxygenated blood as his heart rate increased his circulation and the adrenalin pumped through his veins.

From the corner of his eye, he glanced across to Marty and saw the M4 rifle pulled tightly into his friend's shoulder. His finger was resting on the trigger, and Bull knew that the safety would already have been switched to 'fire', with the barrel aimed at the area where Bull's hand gripped the thick canvas material.

With a heave, the sheet was ripped back and tossed to the side. Bull released it and grabbed his gun with both hands, ready to open up with a long burst of 5.56mm rounds into whoever was beneath, waiting for him.

It was a cage.

Held together with wire and cord, the bamboo structure was no bigger than a metre square. At the bottom of the cage, a dark mound quivered and whimpered in the mire.

Bull nervously glanced at Marty before taking a step forward and tapping the bars of the enclosure with the barrel of his weapon to gain the attention of the person inside.

Nothing happened. The shivering form did not react.

"Hey, you," he hissed, this time nudging at the bamboo prison with his foot, "can you hear me?"

The body inside suddenly became still.

The jerky movements stopped and it paused for a moment. Then slowly, it turned around to face Bull.

The man's face was ghostly pale. His sunken eyes seemed to disappear into the depths of his skull and his hair, covered with filth and grease, was matted to his grime-covered forehead. He saw Bull standing just beyond the bars, peering down at him.

With lightning speed, he lunged, his eyes blazing wildly and his hands thrusting through the gaps in the bars and out towards the burly soldier in front of him, his fingers snapping shut on thin air as his prey avoided his grasp.

Bull's reactions were fast. He stepped backward slightly, just enough to keep him beyond the reach of the man's fingers, his weapon remaining trained on the feral grunting form inside the cage.

"What the fuck?" Marty exclaimed.

The imprisoned man turned to look at him. Their eyes locked as Marty tightened his grip on his rifle, judging whether he should put a bullet into the wretched man or not.

"Please," the prisoner suddenly pleaded with them, his voice weak and filled with terror and desperation, sounding like he was on the brink of madness.

"Please, don't leave me here," he said hoarsely. "They might come back. You can't leave me, you can't."

He was shaking uncontrollably and his wild, bloodshot eyes bulged as they darted from one man to the next, giving him the appearance of a wild animal, trapped in a hunter's snare and desperate to be set free.

"It's the doc…I think," Bull called over to Stan.

"Doctor Joseph Warren?" Stan asked slowly, speaking to the bedraggled and terrified man as he made his way towards the cage. "Is that your name, Joseph Warren, from the World Health Organisation?"

The doctor turned to him, recognising his name and seeming to settle slightly, regaining control of his racing mind and clearly jumbled nerves.

He nodded.

"Get him out of there, Bull," Stan ordered.

Bull pulled his knife from his belt and began cutting at the tightly bound cord that held the cage together. The doctor, still looking terrified, coward in the corner, continuously looking around him with jerky head movements, like a threatened animal.

Stan reached in and dragged the doctor out, grabbing him by the scruff of his filth-ridden shirt and pulling him upward so that their faces were just inches apart. The man struggled and twisted against Stan's grip, trying to free himself and run for the woods.

"Doctor," Stan said in a growling voice as the man squirmed and whimpered in his grasp. "Doctor, I need to know what happened here. The soldiers that were with you, where are they, do you know where they are?"

Doctor Warren, still shaking and with a wild expression on his face, nodded again and turned his head in the direction of the far side of the enclosure. Stan followed his gaze and watched as Bobby and Taff began to head to the area where the doctor had indicated.

Discarded in the mud like an unwanted heap of rotted meat, they discovered the bound and headless body of the last remaining British soldier. It looked as though he had been beaten and tortured, tied to a tree and subjected to an untold amount of suffering.

"Cunts…," Bobby spat as he turned to Stan and shook his head.

Without needing to be told, Taff began carefully wrapping the soldier's remains in a canvas sheet, ready to be carried out with them and taken home for burial. They looked around their immediate surroundings, searching for the head of the unfortunate man, but it was nowhere to be seen.

Stan sat the doctor down.

"It's alright, Doc. We've got you now and we're taking you home," he said, trying hard to reassure him and bring his mind back to reality from the terrifying and chaotic place that it seemed to be lost in.

"Nick," Stan called. "Get on to Gerry and tell him we've found the doctor. We need the heli to come in for immediate extraction."

He looked up at the darkening sky and then at the trees around the perimeter, judging the amount of light that they had remaining and the size of the open area and whether it could be suitable as a Landing Zone.

"This location will do as the pick-up-point, Nick. Tell the pilot that we'll bring him in on infrared."

"Roger that," Nick replied.

"What happened here, Doc?" Stan asked again while Nick worked on getting their communications up and running with the satellite phone.

The doctor stared back at him blankly.

Stan decided to try from another angle, pulling a bottle from one of his pouches, and offering it to the traumatised bundle of rags in front of him. The doctor snatched it from his hand and noisily gulped at the refreshing fluid.

For the next ten minutes, Stan allowed the doctor some time to recover as he continued to drink and eat, as though he had not had sustenance in a long time. He sat there, growling and slurping, as he stuffed chocolate into his mouth and poured water down his throat.

"What do you think happened?" Nick asked, staring down at the wild man.

Stan shrugged.

"I haven't a clue. I can't get any sense out of him at the minute. How we doing on comms and the pick-up?"

"HQ is informed and the heli will pick us up here. They should be inbound in about ten minutes or so."

Stan nodded, and then stepped forward towards the doctor again. He squatted down into the mud in front of the deranged man, and stared into his unblinking vacant eyes.

"What happened here?" This time, Stan's voice held a hint of menace, his patience wearing thin as he and his men tried to make sense of what had occurred at the rebel camp.

Finally, the doctor wiped his mouth with the back of his grimy hand, his eyes remaining fixed on the harsh face of his rescuer. Stan's dark brown eyes, almost black like a shark's, burned into him.

"They were dead," the doctor replied in a hushed voice, glancing to his left and right, seemingly worried that someone may overhear what he had to say.

"The rebels?" Stan replied. "You mean the rebels are all dead, or do you mean the soldiers that were with you?"

Doctor Warren shook his head.

"I mean *everyone*. They…were…all…*dead*," he repeated slowly, emphasising his words and leaning in towards Stan as he spoke them. "They came and killed everyone. No one could stop them. They just kept coming."

Before Stan could question him further, alarmed voices to his right grabbed his attention. Danny and Brian both had their weapons up, pointing them at the treeline and taking up fire positions behind nearby overturned crates and boxes.

"Stand-to," they called over their shoulders, warning the rest of their teammates of possible approaching enemy. "We've got movement to the right, in the trees."

Everyone reacted immediately, turning to face the potential threat and checking their fields of fire. They all pushed out to the left and right, creating a baseline where they could send up a wall of fire from. Stan remained in the centre, the doctor close by and back to being a quivering wreck, jabbering on in a hushed panic-stricken voice as he rocked back and forth, staring at the ground.

"They're coming, they're coming back," he whispered repeatedly.

"What have we got, Brian?" Stan urgently called through his radio, looking over towards the right flank.

Brian was about to reply when, a long hollow wail echoed through the trees towards them, quickly joined by more haunting voices that moaned from deep within the shadows of the jungle canopy.

The men squinted into the gloom, trying to penetrate the dark shadows cast by the foliage to see what was happening.

"They're coming," the doctor whimpered again, dropping to the floor and curling himself into a ball as he trembled uncontrollably.

The noise grew louder as more woeful voices rang out from the darkness. It sounded like there were hundreds of them, closing in on the rebel camp and howling like demons. The men glanced at one another, their eyes flashing with uncertainty as the din reached fever pitch and the voices were joined by the sounds of snapping branches and heavy footfalls, getting louder and headed towards them. Growls, shrieks and screeches came to them through the trees, rising in volume and number, as whatever it was that was approaching, closed the distance, fast.

The team was tensed, feeling the imminent fight advancing upon them. They tightened their grips on their weapons and focussed their eyes and ears on the rainforest that surrounded them on all sides.

"You see anything?" Bobby called from the far left.

"Nothing," Danny replied from the right of the line.

The jungle continued to echo with the eerie resonance and the thumping of running feet.

"Here they come," Bull shouted, squirming behind his machinegun as he adjusted and reinforced his fire position, his eyes locked on the treeline. *"Stand-by, stand-by."*

Stan, taking his eyes away from the wall of green in front of them for a moment, turned to the almost incapacitated doctor at his feet.

"Who," he growled over the rising wails, "who the fuck is coming?"

Doctor Warren, his eyes growing impossibly wide and filled with fright as he looked up at Stan and then at the jungle, raised his pallid hand and his grimy finger pointed towards the trees to their left.

"Them..."

Stan turned to look in the direction that the doctor pointed and saw a dark figure emerge from the gloomy shadow of the forest canopy. It burst forth, ignoring the branches that whipped at its face and arms. It broke into a sprint, crashing through the foliage and over the tangles of barbed wire, its hands reaching out ahead of it as it caught sight of the men.

A groan of anticipation, rising into a howl, erupted from the figure's throat, rasping and gurgling.

Bobby turned, bringing his rifle around and aiming it at the approaching man. Without a word, he fired a round into the centre of mass as the rampaging individual closed in on him. The bullet punched through his chest, smashing ribs and tearing flesh and organs alike before exiting through the back in a cloud of blood and splintered bone.

The man did not fall.

As the echo of the first gunshot continued to ring out around the camp, Bobby fired again and again, hitting the advancing figure with numerous shots and reducing his chest to a bloody pulp.

Bobby felt panic rising inside him as he watched his rounds hit, but have no effect on the advancing wild man who had closed the gap quickly, still howling and showing no sign of slowing.

He fired again, feeling the weapon jerk in his hands and the recoil push against his shoulder. Again, he squeezed the trigger, the round exploding in a bright fountain from the muzzle of his rifle. Again, the bullet hit its mark, ripping another hole through the torso of the approaching person who continued to snarl, snapping his teeth, as he drew near.

With just a few metres to go, the man threw his head up, his gaping maw stretching to the point where all of his teeth could be seen in his black cavernous mouth, a moan of excited expectancy emitting from his ruined and perforated lungs.

Bobby squeezed the trigger again.

The bullet erupted from his M4 and smashed a hole through the man's skull. His body buckled and lost its momentum and veered to the right before dropping to the ground with a heavy thud. The dead man skidded through the mud, the devastated head coming to rest just inches away from Bobby's boot.

"Fuck," Brian exclaimed as he saw more of the screaming and flailing people emerge from the trees.

"Contact front," he bellowed.

As one, all their guns fired in a deafening roar.

Speeding projectiles of copper and lead, snapped through the air, piercing bodies and trees alike. Everybody opened up with their machineguns and rifles, cutting down the numerous figures that burst forth, indifferent to the deadly wall of fire that they run in to and the countless hits they received.

Limbs were ripped away, abdomens split open and heads exploded, but still, the fanatical attackers surged onward, smashing their way through the trees and charging towards the men as they continued to cut them down in their droves.

Dozens of them had fallen as the jungle rang with the crescendo of gunfire. They tumbled through the mud, their arms whirling and paying no interest to the wounds they had sustained. Many, having been shot, fought to regain their footing and continue the assault, dragging themselves through the mire and snarling at the men in front of them.

The inferno continued.

"Magazine," someone screamed out.

"Contact left," another hollered.

The bodies continued to drop, but more of them emerged from the trees, taking up the places of their fallen comrades. Despite their casualties and the futility of their attack, Stan soon realised that the crazed people were not going to yield.

Khat, they must be high on Khat, he thought to himself.

He squeezed his trigger and saw another person, an incensed child, collapse in front of him, the round smashing through her delicate head and creating a gaping hole at the back of her skull.

"We can't hold them," Brian cried out from the right flank as he and Danny began to step backwards, still firing their rifles into the advancing crowd.

Stan glanced to his left and saw Bobby and Taff doing the same, slowly retreating under the pressure as more of their attackers launched themselves at the line. They were being overwhelmed, *by unarmed madmen,* he thought.

His mind raced and struggled to understand what was happening. He had never seen anything like it in his life, but here they were, pouring a devastating amount of fire into a mob of defenceless and enraged civilians, and unable to halt their advance.

In the centre, the progress of the assault was held, but their flanks were collapsing.

He glanced down to his right.

"Bull, switch left. Nick, switch right," he ordered, slapping them on their backs to grab their attention over the din of battle.

The two men complied, twisting in their positions and firing their machineguns across the front of their respective flanks, creating a wall of enfilading fire and giving their own men the time they needed to take up new positions.

Their perimeter was shrinking.

"Grenade," a voice warned from the left.

A second later, a deafening thud rang out from in front of Bobby's position as the High Explosives detonated, sending out a wave of pressure and flinging twisted bodies in all directions, mixed with mud, debris and shrapnel.

Another loud bang to the right, and a flash, followed by a cloud of smoke denoted the deaths of more of the attackers, but still, they came.

"Hotel-One-Zero, Hotel-One-Zero," Marty was screaming into his radio from behind Stan as he attempted to warn the helicopter of their situation.

"*Be aware, the LZ is hot. I say again, the LZ is hot. Approach from the south and give fire support. Enemy positions will be marked with infrared."*

Over the thundering machineguns, rifles and exploding hand grenades, Stan could hear the distant rapid thump of the approaching helicopter. They were on their way, but he could not afford to let up on their weight of fire.

"Stoppage," Bull hollered as his weapon ceased firing.

Immediately, he pulled back the cocking lever and began carrying out the drill to clear the misfired round, his hands a blur as he expertly worked his gun.

The area was awash with the bodies and blood of mangled people. The smoke from the rifles and detonations filled the air, stinging at the eyes of Stan as he fought to keep control of the battle and his men. The flanks were still retreating, firing and manoeuvring their way back towards the centre as they yielded under the enormous pressure of the assault.

Although they were not receiving any incoming fire, the men knew instinctively that something was seriously wrong and that they could not allow their attackers to come close. Everywhere they looked, more twisted and hideous faces sprang towards them, howling and wailing as they pressed forward through the hailstorm.

The sound of the approaching aircraft grew louder.

Stan reached into his vest and pulled out a red plastic object, roughly the size of a cigarette packet. He pressed a button on the side, and then tossed it high into the air. It landed close to the treeline, where the attack was coming from.

A couple of seconds later, a high pitched tearing noise rang out from behind them as the guns of the Black Hawk opened up, firing thousands of rounds into the jungle from its spinning barrels. Mixed in with the rumble of the guns, Stan could hear the clinking sound of thousands of empty bullet cases being expended from the mini-guns, landing in piles on the forest floor. The cannons roared, cutting trees in half, churning up the muddy ground, and disintegrating the wall of maddened human beings who continued to converge on the team.

The brightly lit tracers zipped through the air over the heads of the men, fanning out in a wide arc to their front as the skilled gunners created an impenetrable wall of fire.

Through the chaos, Stan could see bodies exploding and being scattered into the mud as the guns reduced them to nothing but organic smears or bone and tissue.

The men slowed their rate of fire as the helicopter's guns helped to ease the pressure on them and continued to slow the enemy advance. They changed out their magazines and took precision shots at the figures that managed to fight their way through, quickly realising that only headshots were affective and capable of stopping them in their tracks.

The attack was halted, and the pilot ceased firing, the echo of its guns slowly receding through the jungle. He kept the Black Hawk in a hover, remaining close to the treetops and his weapons trained on the perimeter as the men below began preparing themselves for extraction.

Down on the ground, the team stared around them at the carnage they had created. The ground was thick with the dead. Body parts of men, women, and children were scattered in a wide area, piled up on top of one another, like macabre pyramids.

Bull stepped back, his face black with the carbon from his machinegun while pale grey wisps of smoke drifted up from the glowing hot barrel.

"Fuck me," he said hoarsely, his mouth dry from shouting and fear. "I've never seen anything like it."

The team closed in, checking their ammunition while keeping their eyes on the perimeter, expectant of another fight.

"Let's get the fuck out of here," Stan shouted to his men over the whirl of the Black Hawk's engines.

They did not need to be told twice.

In the flat area, in the centre of the camp, the team fanned out to protect the Landing Zone, their weapons held at the ready and aimed at the treeline.

Stan signalled the pilot and the helicopter began to lower, its downwash kicking up a storm and sending debris in all directions around the rebel camp. Slowly, it descended and Stan was able to see the bewildered expressions on the faces of the pilots. He understood that they must have been pretty shocked and confused about what had happened but all he could do, was give them a slight shake of his head and shrug his shoulders.

The aircraft settled into a hover, just one metre from the ground.

Stan moved forward, dragging the unresponsive doctor with him and bundled him through the side door and into the passenger area.

Next, Bobby and Taff scooped up the body of the dead soldier and carefully lifted him into the helicopter.

The cordon moved back and the men, still covering one another, began to board the Black Hawk.

Through the pounding of the blades and the scream of the engine, Stan heard a howl and spun to see Nick, jumping backwards and falling into the sucking quagmire below the aircraft. A black figure, its body cut in two at the waist, was dragging itself through the mud, clawing at Nick's legs as he kicked at its face.

Stan jumped from the door, landing heavily in the sludge and almost losing his balance. Without hesitation, he grabbed Nick by the webbing straps of his vest and pulled him back, away from the mutilated man who defied all laws of nature and continued to pull himself along the ground.

The thing crawling towards them stared up at him. Stan looked into its eyes and saw no sign of life. They were devoid of anything.

His blood froze in his veins as he stared back at the monstrous face, its gnashing teeth snapping shut as it snarled at him. Stan knew what he was seeing. At that moment, he realised that he had seen it before, in Syria.

The man at his feet was already dead.

The noise of the gunshot was subdued beneath the clatter of the helicopter's motors as the bullet from Stan's pistol drilled a hole through the man's head. The body went limp and sank into the mud, his brains ruined and seeping from a fist sized hole above his ear.

Stan looked down into the shocked face of Nick and began pulling him to his feet, dragging him to the waiting helicopter where Bull leaned out, stretching his arms so that he could pull his friends to safety.

Nick groaned and hobbled towards the door, reaching down to a dark stain on the leg of his trousers and grimacing.

"The fucker bit me," he shouted over the thumping blades and howling downwash. "He bit me, Stan. Why the fuck would he bite me?"

"You're lucky that's all he bit, mate," Stan screamed back as he pushed him up into the powerful arms of Bull.

Stan climbed in after him and patted the pilot on the shoulder, informing him that they were all on board. The pilot nodded and took the aircraft up, above the trees and headed away from the camp.

Stan turned and eyed each of his men. They were veteran soldiers, hard and steadfast, but they looked traumatised and exhausted.

He told no one of what he had realised on the ground and he wondered if he had really seen it, but he knew that he had. There was no mistaking what he saw in those eyes.

The words of the doctor echoed through his mind;

"They were all dead..."

Now, he understood.

Turning to look back at the slaughter in the devastated rebel camp below them, Stan silently thanked the Gods that his men had all made it out alive.

10

Marty paced the room, alternately flexing his fingers then screwing them into a fist. He was beginning to feel cooped up and ready to lose his temper. He glanced about at the others who slouched and slept around him, sprawled out on the uncomfortable army issued cots that they were expected to rest upon.

It seemed that only Brian and Danny were truly asleep, while the others sat staring into space or attempting to nap.

The incessant thumping continued at one-second intervals and Marty could sense that his nerves were beginning to fray.

"For fuck's sake, Bull," he growled, "will you give it a rest?"

The thuds ceased and Bull turned to look at him, blinking heavily as though bringing himself out from a daze and rubbing his forehead as he stepped back from the large two-way mirror that was set into the wall. He had been steadily pounding his head against his reflection for the past forty-minutes, hardly noticing what he was doing or the effect it could be having on the others.

He looked back at the angered face of Marty and then around at the others. He shrugged his shoulders.

"Sorry, mate," he offered.

Since they were extracted from Sierra Leone, they had spent the last four days in quarantine. From the moment their helicopter touched down, they were swept away, with no explanation or debriefing and bundled into the secure room. The brilliant white of the walls and the bright lights above them that burned endlessly, added to the total frustration of the men. Even their watches had been removed, leaving them without the slightest sense of time and how long they had been there.

It could have been days, even weeks, for all they knew.

They had landed in an old army base somewhere in the south of England, they had guessed, and were immediately stripped of their clothing and equipment. From there, they had been sent through a series of decontamination chambers, being sprayed with chemicals that left their skin burning and their eyes stinging.

They recognised none of the men around them, clad in thick white rubber suits with independent air supplies and barking their orders through the integrated communications link in their face masks.

All their questions went unanswered and they soon realised that it was pointless to struggle. When Bull, standing his ground and demanding answers, received a shock that dropped him to the floor and completely incapacitated him, the team, at the sight of the cattle prods that their friend was disabled by, thought twice about any further resistance and complied with the orders of their guards.

Now, they sat waiting beneath the hot lights, cramped together in the immaculate quarantine chamber.

Bobby suddenly sat up, resting his elbows on his knees and leaning forward, letting out a long sigh as he did so.

"What do you think all this is about, Stan?"

Their commander had been doing his best to try to sleep, but was finding it impossible. Despite his experience and usually cool and calm appearance, he too was beginning to feel the strain. The total isolation and lack of information left them all feeling vulnerable and unsure of what was going to happen.

"How many more times do you want to go over this, Bobby?" He huffed from his cot, as he remained lying on his back, shielding his eyes from the bright lights with his forearm. "I know as much as you do. I told you what I saw and all I can think is that it's something to do with that dead bloke in the jungle."

Bobby shook his head, still unable to grasp what Stan was telling them. They had gone over this before, but the men still had trouble taking it in

"Personally, Stan, I think you're waffling shit." Bull stated from the other side of the room. "How can a dead man still be walking around, and what the fuck have they done with Nick? Why did they take him away, instead of putting him in here with us? I tell you, if that fucker is sat living it up in some plush hospital bed because he has a sore leg, I'll tear his balls off and feed them to him."

"That guy wasn't walking around. The fucker had no legs. Think what you want," Stan growled in frustration.

He sat up and looked at each of them in turn.

"Whatever it was that the doctor was doing out there, it's nothing to do with some weird strain of flu. That man, the one who took a bite out of Nick, was *dead*."

They all stared back at him in silence, seeing that their leader truly believed what he was saying. They had never felt any reason to doubt him over anything in the past, but what Stan was telling them, seemed completely absurd.

Bull was pacing now, shaking his head and growling under his breath. Stan looked up at the bulky man and then across to Taff who sat with his back to the wall.

"You know me, mate," Taff shrugged. "And I know you, Stan. We've worked together for a long time and I've never questioned you before, so I don't plan on starting now. I'm willing to have a little faith on this one, until proven wrong, that is."

Bull stopped mid stride and looked down at the rugged face of the Welshman. He could see that Taff was tired but despite his expression of disinterest, his eyes remained clear and focussed.

"So you're saying that you believe this bullshit?"

Taff remained indifferent and continued to wrap one of the ties from his hospital robe around his finger.

"Stan could well be right, Bull. Those people who charged at us in the jungle, they definitely weren't normal and if Stan says that they were dead, then I believe they were dead, or at least something like it."

He turned and nodded towards Bobby.

"How many rounds did you put into that guy that came at you out of the woods?"

Bobby shrugged, unable to remember the exact number.

"Not sure. About five or six, I think. All I know is that he didn't go down until I put one through his head."

Taff turned back to Bull.

"I've never heard of a man taking five or six hits to the chest without so much as a flinch, have you?"

Bull said nothing.

"From the minute we landed, they've stuck all sorts of needles in us, taking blood and doing tests. We've had no comms with Gerry and no one is telling us anything. Nick was swept away to, *Christ* knows where, and now we're sat in here, while they watch us from the other side of that window."

"Do the math yourself, mate. Something has them scared and I think we came into close contact with it in Sierra Leone."

Bull turned to look at his reflection and thought as he panned his eyes along the length of the glass. With a grunt and a nod to himself, he swept his flimsy hospital gown to the side and tore it from his shoulders, exposing his naked body.

Staring at the mirror, he grabbed hold of his penis.

"Well then," he roared, "I hope there are some pretty women doctors watching this."

He approached the glass, and standing on his tiptoes, began to press his testicles against the two-way mirror, glaring at his reflection and allowing his tongue to flop from his mouth and his eyes to roll upward, simulating the appearance of sexual ecstasy.

"How do you like that?" He hollered at the glass. "Come on then, don't be shy, it isn't *that* big. Come on, come and fucking get it."

The rest just sat and watched while Bull vented. They knew it would be a waste of time to try to encourage him to just sit and wait, patiently, and having him behaving in a lewd way was better than having to watch him lose his temper and begin trying to break down the door with his head, or worse, someone else's head.

After twenty minutes of smearing his genitalia against the glass and unleashing a torrent of profanities and insults, Bull lost interest and collapsed back on to his cot with a loud sigh.

"Alright, Stan, now that's out of my system, what do you think will happen next?"

A metallic clunk interrupted them before Stan was able to give his opinion. They all turned towards the door as a hiss of air announced the release of the locking mechanism. Immediately, they felt the air pressure within the chamber change, causing their ears to pop.

As one, they jumped to their feet, unsure of what to expect to come from the other side of the heavy steel hatch. They stood, shoulder to shoulder, in the centre of the room, ready to attack anyone that they saw approaching them with one of the hated cattle prods.

With a whirr and a heavy click, the door slowly separated from its frame, and then stopped, revealing only darkness on the other side through the small gap.

Barely visible, a pale hand appeared and pushed against it from the room beyond.

The men tensed and prepared themselves.

Gerry's face appeared from the gloom.

His expression was one of uncertainty and he hesitated as he stepped through the airlock, immediately locking eyes with Stan, desperately needing his support and hoping that he had control of the men after their frustrating time in quarantine.

Stan stared back at him, and as usual, showed no sign of anger or affability. He glanced down from the wary expression of Gerry and at the bundle that the officer carried in his hands. He was laden with luxuries and it was clear, Gerry was trying to pacify them and sway them from lynching him.

"Guys," he began in a faltering voice but fighting hard to keep the friendly smile on his face as he looked back at the glaring eyes of each of the men in front of him.

Bull looked especially fearsome. Completely naked and still holding his genitals in his hand, he glowered back at their officer.

"I'm really sorry about all this," Gerry continued. "I tried my best to speak with you, but they wouldn't let me. Believe me, I had no part in this, and I have reported it all up to The Prince of Darkness."

His eyes remained fixed on Bull as he spoke, expecting the enraged mountain to erupt with his fury upon him.

"It was the General who sent me and the quarantine is over."

Bull took a small step forward and glanced down at the bundle in the officer's arms.

Gerry looked back at him tentatively.

"Peace?"

He offered one of the many bottles of beer to the towering man in front of him. Bull snatched it from his hand and turned away with a snort.

"What's going on, Gerry?" Stan asked as the other men began noisily grabbing at the chocolate, cigarettes and alcohol.

"Yeah, Gerry, what the fuck is all this about?" Taff demanded as he tore at the plastic wrapper from a pack of cigarettes, threw one into his mouth and fumbled with the lighter, anxious to get his nicotine fix. "We're being treated like mushrooms here."

Gerry stared back at him blankly, unsure of Taff's meaning.

"Kept in the dark and fed on shit," the stocky Welshman informed him as he inhaled a lung full of smoke and exhaled it with a sigh of satisfaction, blowing a thick billowing blue/grey plume up towards the bright ceiling lights.

Marty snatched the pack from Taff and lit one for himself. He was not a full-time smoker, but at that moment, he felt the urge to have one.

Gerry placed his burden down onto the small white table in the centre of the room and looked back at each of the others who watched him, expectantly.

It was clear that Gerry did not know where to start, or how to explain the reasons for their incarceration. He looked nervous and unsure of himself.

Stan decided to help.

"Gerry," he began in a calm voice, instantly putting the officer at ease and gaining the attention of everyone in the room. "We know that the people who attacked us in Sierra Leone were dead…"

"Bollocks," Bull growled from a mouth filled with chocolate.

Stan turned and fixed the large naked man with a glare. Bull instantly fell silent and went back to devouring the Snickers bar that he had barely bothered to unwrap.

"They were dead, Gerry. Now, do you want to give us a truthful heads up on this and what is going on, or do we have to listen to a pile of shit first?"

Gerry sighed and the men saw his shoulders sag. They were not sure whether it was due to him feeling deflated because he was backed into a corner with no one to support him, or relieved that he did not need to lie to the men or skirt around the truth. They could see that he was exhausted and their feelings towards him softened a little as they realised that he most probably had *indeed* been doing all he could to get them out of the quarantine chamber.

He nodded.

"Yes, Stan, they were dead."

The room became silent and everyone glanced at one another before turning their attention back to their official commanding officer who stood leaning with his back against the table and staring at the floor.

Stan nodded, satisfied that Gerry was not going to begin by lying to them or holding anything back.

"Okay, you can explain the ins and outs of this to us later, but in the meantime, get us out of here and… where's Nick?"

Gerry's face lost all expression as he raised his head to look Stan in the eyes.

11

His eyes saw nothing. They stared blankly ahead of him, unfocussed and paying no attention to himself or his surroundings. An opaque milky film coated the once sparkling blue iris' that were now nothing more than dull and flat expanded black dots. A thick strand of congealed blood and saliva hung from his pale and crinkled lips, swaying from side to side as he stumbled about the small enclosure.

His body suddenly stopped and his gaunt face slowly raised as he detected movement close by. He became alert, peeling back his lips and baring his teeth as he caught site of another figure in the room.

With a long groan, he reached out for the man in front of him and launched himself forward. The figure also approached, racing towards him.

As they closed on one another, a resounding thump echoed around the chamber and he was rebuffed and sent sprawling to the floor.

Quickly, he regained his feet and resumed his assault against his reflection in the mirror. Again, his head smashed hard against the barrier, leaving a thick smear of blood and grease where his cranium clashed with the three centimetre thick armoured glass.

In frustration, he snarled, gnashing his teeth, and pounding his fists, clawing with his broken nails at the two-way mirror in a futile attempt to bore his way through. Finally, as though something had spoken to him from within his faltering mind, he calmed and no longer attempted to reach the man he saw staring back at him. Instead, he just stood and gaped, swaying and grunting and eventually, losing interest.

Bobby remained close to the glass, staring at the vision in the room beyond. It looked like Nick, but at the same time, he was unable to recognise the figure before him. His grey skin and sunken features resembled nothing of the perpetually grinning rounded face of the loud and charismatic man from Newcastle.

His body looked as though he had been ravaged by some terrible affliction that had eaten him down to the bone, leaving him as nothing but a wasted shambling carcass. However, it was the eyes that haunted Bobby. When he looked into them, he saw nothing of the man who had been his friend.

"How long has he been like this?"

"He died on the second day and has been like this ever since," one of the scientists informed them from behind in a matter-of-fact tone.

Bobby felt a hard slab of emotion slide down his throat. It was a mixture of sadness and sympathy for his comrade, mindlessly stumbling about in the room beyond the glass, and anger towards the doctors for leaving him in that state.

He struggled with his fury, keeping his eyes locked on the abomination in front of him and avoiding the urge to turn and tear into the man who had spoken so casually about the condition of his friend.

The rest of the men watched in silence, unable to comprehend or accept that Nick was actually dead, yet still moving about. They had all known Nick well and considered him as a brother, as they did one another. As far as they were concerned, they were the closest that each of them had to a family.

Now, seeing one of their own in this way sickened them to the core.

"Can he talk?" Bobby asked, keeping his eyes on Nick.

"No," a reply came from the doctors congregated behind him.

"Does he understand what has happened to him?"

Bobby turned and caught sight of Gerry who remained near the back of the assembled men and women, watching the team and their reactions. Bobby's glistening and emotion filled eyes locked with him.

"Is there anything we can do to help him? We can't leave him like this."

A tall man of middle age, wearing a grey fleece jacket, pushed his way through to the front and approached Bobby. His face, though weathered and extremely lean, making his features protrude, seemed to be the face of a warm man. It was his eyes, filled with sympathy and understanding for Bobby's feelings.

"I'm sorry, but when he was bitten," the doctor began. "The virus spread through his system at an extremely rapid rate. There is no cure and once the host dies, everything that made them what they were, dies with them. What comes back is nothing more than pure motorised instinct. They understand very little and don't seem to remember or recognise anything from their former lives."

Bobby looked back at the body of his friend, standing motionless in the room beyond the viewing pane.

The doctor placed a hand on his shoulder and initially, Bobby felt the urge to shrug it away, even twist his body around and grab the man's forearm and pull his shoulder from the socket, but the feeling passed immediately.

"I truly am sorry," the tall doctor continued. "Nick is dead, and that…what you see in there, is not your friend. He will attack you in the same way that you saw him attack his reflection just a moment ago, and if he can, he will kill you."

The doctor stepped back and looked along the line of men standing in front of the window as Stan and his team stared back at Nick's body.

"Make no mistake, gentlemen, a bite from one of the infected is one-hundred percent fatal, regardless of how deep the bite or where on the body it is received. There is no cure, *yet*, and even a graze will be enough to pass on the virus."

He stepped towards the glass, eyeing the reanimated corpse with interest for a moment and then turned to address them again.

"Nick was strong, fit, and healthy, but the infection burned through him, despite our efforts to stop it. He lasted two days from the initial bite until his body lost the battle. Four-hours later, his basal ganglia…," he paused and looked about, realising that he was about to begin bombarding them with information that they would not understand. He coughed slightly, then continued, "…and certain other parts of his brainstem began to show signs of activity. Over a period of five minutes, he became more animated and eventually, became this."

"So, they die, and then the virus brings them back?" Stan asked.

"Correct," the doctor nodded.

"And the only way to kill them is a shot to the head," Brian grunted.

It was a statement, not a question as he remembered seeing their commander put a final bullet through the brain of the creature that attacked Nick.

"Yes, that is right."

"Is he contagious?" Brian asked.

"No," the doctor replied, staring through the glass at his subject. "This strain of the virus passes only through the bites and the exchange of bodily fluids."

Before anyone knew what was happening, or could react, Brian had drawn his pistol and pointed it at the doctor's head.

The room resonated with gasps and whimpers as the doctors and technicians watched and expected Brian to pull the trigger.

The rest of the team, Stan and the others, did not bat an eyelid as the angry Irishman stood, staring along the sight of his weapon and looking directly into the eyes of the tall gaunt faced doctor.

"Good," Brian said with an air of satisfaction that his assumption was correct.

He glared at the doctor, his eyes narrowing as a number of metallic clicks broke the shocked silence as he pulled back the hammer on the gun in his hand.

"Now open the fucking door."

The doctor saw in the eyes of the man in front of him that he was more than willing to kill him. They were not the eyes of a crazy man, but the eyes of a loyal friend, of a brother to the thing that now occupied the room next to them.

No matter what he said or did, one way or another, the doctor knew that the door to the isolation chamber would be opened, whether he was dead or alive.

"You'll gain nothing from this, you know," he said calmly as he took a step back towards the panel at the side of the airlock.

"I'll get plenty and most importantly, I'll know that my friend isn't walking about like one of those fucking things we saw in Sierra Leone," Brian snapped back at him.

Gerry took a tentative step forward, his eyes darting from the doctor, to the gun in Brian's hand and then to Stan.

"Stan," he hissed, "the General will…"

"Shut up, Gerry," Stan growled back at him without even looking in his direction.

Gerry fell silent and realised that Taff and Bobby had stepped in behind him, blocking the entrance and preventing anyone from exiting the room.

Everyone remained silent, holding their breath with anticipation as the assembled group of scientists, their faces pale with fear and their bulging eyes glowing in the semi-darkness, watched Brian and waited to see what he and the doctor would do next.

"Open the door, Doc," Brian encouraged the tall man as he continued to keep his pistol trained on him.

The doctor made a half turn and faced the electronic key panel beside the airlock door. He glanced back at Brian nervously and then began to type in his access code.

"Please," he spoke as he kept his attention fixed on the electronic panel, "I know what you intend to do, and to be honest, I understand why you're doing it. I would want to do the same if it was my friend in there. But please, we need to be rational about this."

"Rational?" Brian repeated mockingly. "I'll rationally drill a hole through your fucking head, and then stick my dick through it if you don't open that door within the next five seconds."

The doctor stared back at him and blinked. He knew that the man meant every word and turned back to the panel to press the final key.

He nodded.

"Okay, I'm opening it, but please, remember what I said and don't let *it* near you."

The lock thudded as the hydraulics released the heavy dead bolts and the doctor stepped back, his face glistening with sweat.

He turned and looked at Brian.

"It's open."

Danny stepped forward and gently guided the doctor away from the door as Bull stepped up and positioned himself, ready to push it open and allow Brian inside.

With a heave, Bull forced the thick steel barrier away from the frame. A hiss of air sounded and the smell of decaying flesh instantly assaulted the senses of everyone in the room. Without hesitation, Brian stepped through and over the threshold, the pistol still raised and immediately aimed at the body of his comrade.

Nick saw him immediately and turned in his direction, his pale eyes locking on to the living being that entered into the room. For a fraction of a second, there was a pause as their eyes met.

In that instant, as Brian aimed his pistol, he hoped that Nick would recognise him.

The soulless body of Nick showed no sign of familiarity and sprang forward, reaching out for the man he had once knew in his former life.

"Sorry, Nick."

The shot boomed in the airtight room and the recoil forced Brian's hand to rock back as the nine-millimetre Parabellum round burst from the barrel.

The bullet struck squarely between the eyes and Nick's body fell to the floor, spilling thick dark blood across the immaculate white tiles.

Nick was finally dead.

12

As the seasons changed from winter to early spring, so did the global situation.

The virus was spreading at a phenomenal rate, enveloping the southern hemisphere and quickly spreading into the north.

While the World Health Organisation and government scientists struggled to find a solution to the outbreak, thousands of people were succumbing to the deadly plague. Those who contracted the airborne virus, soon found themselves fighting for their lives and with a high mortality rate, many of the victims were losing the battle.

It took two weeks from when the infection first hit Europe and America for the governments to acknowledge the problem and go public, informing the populations of the effects. Even then, many people refused to believe what they were being told by the various and conflicting experts and their statements.

"The effects of the flu strain are varied from one person to the next, but it has been noted that some of the sick develop heightened aggression, attacking the people around them, while others suffering from the infection, remain immobilised and eventually, die from the disease.

"As yet, we have found no cause for why people are reacting in different ways, but it has been proven that the bites from the aggressive strain carry the infection and is one-hundred percent lethal. Anyone coming into contact with the infected through bodily fluids, will contract the virus. As yet, we have found no viable vaccine or cure and it is recommended that the victims of this outbreak be avoided at all costs."

Riots were widespread throughout the cities of Europe and America. Looting had become a problem very early on, as people panicked and began to fend for themselves. Supermarkets were ransacked and in a short space of time, their shelves sat empty as more and more people failed to turn up for work and deliveries ceased to arrive.

Areas were cordoned off and placed under quarantine. The infected within the closed off areas then attacked the people guarding them at the blockades and it was soon realised that any attempt at quarantine would fail.

The police, having lost many from their ranks, were close to breaking point, having to cope with a massive strain on their limited resources, and before long, entire regions were left to their own devices, becoming lawless and off limits to anyone wearing a uniform.

It was not long before soldiers and volunteers, wearing bright bio hazard suits, began turning up to collect the dead. The streets were becoming littered with corpses and people dying from the plague. As the body collection parties moved from house to house, the landfill sites of every urban area were quickly filled with the bodies of the deceased.

The stench of burning flesh became a part of the atmosphere as the dead were hastily cremated and then buried beneath thin layers of soil, ready for the next layer of victims, and it was not long before reports were being circulated through the media of people still being alive when they were carted off for disposal. Naturally, this information caused more panic and many families barricaded themselves into their homes, fearing that the army would kill them, regardless of whether or not they were suffering from symptoms.

The countries of the so called civilised world were rapidly spiralling out of control.

Soon, within just two days of the acknowledgement of the spread into the northern hemisphere, further televised announcements were made, but this time, they came directly from the British Prime Minister and US President.

"Ladies and gentlemen, in the last hour, I have received a number of reports on the situation as it stands at this very moment. Though shocking and hard to believe, we have had confirmation from a number of government sources that those who have died recently are returning to life.

"At the moment we have no solid evidence on the cause of this, but it is widely speculated that the flu virus, which has now swept the entire globe, has again mutated. I am informed that whether death is from the flu, natural causes, or even a bite from an infected person, anyone who passes away will reanimate and then attack the living.

"I have been in contact with the presidents of America, Russia, China, and France, as well as the German Chancellor and many other country leaders. They have all confirmed the same facts. Every country in the world is being stretched to its breaking point and resources have become minimal.

"I am in negotiations with the Chinese and North Korean governments to come to an agreement to end the hostilities and to focus on the more urgent matters on our home soils, and to work together to come up with a solution.

"At this moment, I have no further information to give you and I'll now pass you over to Dr. Joseph Cox of the Department of Health."

A grey haired man appeared on the screen.

"Over the past five days, we have taken samples from numerous flu and attack victims. The findings were the same, but at different levels.

"While most of the flu victims, except for the aggressive strain, became lethargic and sick for up to a week with some making a full recovery, the bite victims became feverous and incapacitated within twenty four hours. So far, at the most, we have seen a bite victim continue to fight the virus for up to four days, before they succumbed and died.

"On reanimating, they show no vital signs. Heart rate, blood pressure, and core temperature are exactly what you would expect from any cadaver. They do not react to stimuli, or even recognise the people around them, and will attack on sight any living organism they encounter, including humans.

"The bite victims of the aggressive strain die, on average, within seventy two hours, and then revive and attack the living within a few hours after death. The time period has been recorded from as little as two hours, to as long as eight.

"Now, we have found that all recently dead, reanimate. Whether they die from the flu, a bite or even a car crash, every dead body will rise and attack the living. The virus seems to have mutated once again and is now a part the atmosphere, causing the recently deceased to revive. From what we know, the mutation to airborne does not mean that the living will be affected any further. It only causes the dead to reanimate.

"The bite victims develop a high fever, vomiting, headaches and eventually death. The results on revival vary. We have discovered that the fitter and more active the patient before death, the more mobile they are once they reanimate. Some of the cadavers on revival have been known to run, albeit at a slower and more uncoordinated pace than their living counterparts, and some can even problem solve with the likes of opening doors and using stairs.

"They do not recognise authority or even family members and will not react to emotional or sentimental encouragement. Their instincts are rudimentary and so far, we have discovered that they cannot be reasoned, or bargained with. They recognise nothing of their old lives and all emotional attachment should be disconnected from family members who become infected.

"We have discovered that the brain is the key to their revival and continued existence. Without the brain intact, the body cannot reanimate.

"We must remember that these are no longer our family and friends. Regardless of what we say or do, they will not react to their past lives, names, places, emotions or trinkets. They are nothing more than reanimated corpses that are, for some unknown reason, intent on killing and eating anything living that crosses their path."

Regardless of the situation and the attacks, many people still refused to believe that their friends and family would want to hurt them. Entire households became infected and that led to whole streets, districts, and before long, towns and cities.

The governments, in their haste to explain the situation had forgotten to pass new emergency laws on how to treat and deal with the infected. So when confronted with a walking corpse or violent strain of flu, people feared prosecution should they hurt or even kill their attacker.

To add to the problem, many people had friends or family who became infected, or even died through natural causes at home. Once revived, they could not reason that the thing that had just sat up and now walked towards them was anything other than their wife, husband, son, daughter, or even best friend.

Emotion and sentimentality became one of the deciding factors for humanity losing the war against the dead plague.

Whole cities and towns were lost throughout the world, as the authorities tried to stem the spread and regain control. What many did not know until it was too late was that the dead and infected could not feel pain on the same level as living people, or feel fear or consider consequences of their actions. Entire police and army units were sent in to secure this street or that square, only to be swallowed up and never seen again.

Some countries took a more extreme approach. Having lost cities and large areas to the infection, they tried reclaiming them with air strikes.

Many of the infected were blown apart in the attacks.

However, the air strikes created more dead than they destroyed. Most cities were still heavily populated by the living, holed up and trying to survive. Once the bombing started, they were either killed in the blasts and the fires, or their defences were destroyed and left open to the dead. For all the reanimated they killed, the ranks of the infected were replenished by the collateral casualties of war.

The Third World countries were written off by the West and Europe. Africa and Asia were left to die, and America closed its borders and waterways along Mexico and the Gulf area. Whole army divisions were sent to those areas to shoot anyone attempting to cross onto US soil. In the meantime, the other states fell to pieces with the spread of the infection within their own borders.

Worldwide communications began slowly to deteriorate. Mobile networks became temperamental and even the internet showed signs of failure. With people dying or abandoning their posts, the daily maintenance that was vital to the upkeep of the smooth running global communications network was not being carried out, and the more delicate systems were beginning to suffer.

City after city across the world fell silent, except for the moans and wails of the dead who shuffled aimlessly, en masse through the streets.

Any survivors were left to fend for themselves.

13

Matthew, returning from a long weekend away from work with his family, made his way through the office building. He strutted with vigour, whistling cheerfully as he sauntered along the corridor, gently swinging his briefcase in step with his feet.

He was wearing his favourite suit, a deep blue Italian cut three piece with white pinstripes. It fit like a glove and always made him glow with confidence. He felt fresh and re-energised, ready to meet the day head on.

The break had been seriously needed, for all of them. It had been a while since the family had the chance to enjoy a weekend together, without him having to think about work. Instead, he had left on the Thursday, and treated himself to three days of ignoring phone calls, refusing to even consider reading an email and in general, forgetting the world outside of his front door as he savoured the time he spent with his children.

For the whole weekend, thoughts of anything serious had been banned from the house. News channels were forbidden and only movies and cartoons were allowed. The four of them had spent the days in their pyjamas, watching the likes of *Shrek* and *Spider-Man*, and playing board games, completely oblivious to the government announcements that were being made with regards to a flu epidemic that was sweeping into the country.

He could have taken longer, but seventy-two hours of pretending to still be in love his wife, was more than enough to renew his appreciation of having a workplace where he could hide from her. Besides, thoughts of Michelle and the delights she had to offer were becoming more frequent in his lusting mind.

He needed his fix.

He had not heard from her for the whole time he had taken off and the absence of communication and the lack of the provocative picture messages that she normally sent to him during their time apart, were making him begin to feel needy.

The building seemed strangely quiet, just as the journey to work had done. The streets were empty, compared to how he usually found them on a Monday morning. His drive to the office had been easy, stress free, and he had not felt the urge to scream at anyone for their lack of consideration on the road.

He had begun to doubt himself at one point, needing to pull over and check his diary, making sure that it was not a Bank Holiday.

Now, in his office building, it too seemed devoid of most of the people he expected to see on a daily basis. Office doors normally open with the sounds of phones ringing and voices speaking loudly, were closed and silent.

Familiar faces that he would normally pass on the way to his office, were absent and more and more of the workspaces that he passed by, were abandoned, their usual occupants, nowhere to be seen.

Is there a big meeting that I didn't know about? He wondered.

He turned the final corner before his office, still whistling and hoping to see the teasing smoky eyes of his assistant.

Instead, he was met with a pale withdrawn face that looked exhausted and about to collapse at her desk. Michelle's eyes were rimmed red, looking sore and barely able to focus while her hair looked lank and hung over her face in unkempt strands. Her nose, normally slender with a very slight upturn at the tip, seemed bulbous and glowing a deep pink.

The extremely attractive woman had been replaced by an apparition.

She looked up at him as he swaggered along the corridor, the smile rapidly evaporating from his lips, and being replaced with a look of alarm. His confident walk changed to a hesitant shuffle as he stared in disbelief, unable to relate the ghostly vision to the woman that he spent so much of his time thirsting over.

"Jesus, Michelle," he gasped, "are you okay?"

"Do I look it?" She replied hoarsely with annoyance and immediately began to sputter with a rattle that emitted from her chest.

Matthew stopped, subconsciously keeping a healthy distance from her desk and sheepishly looked down at his shoes.

"Well, no, not really. What is it?"

"Flu, I think," she replied, paying him no particular interest and giving him the impression that she was in no mood to talk to him.

Matthew got the picture just from her body language, but he did not want to leave it at just that. In the ten years he had known her, he had never seen her in such an ill state and he felt genuine concern for her.

"Michelle, you should go home. Seriously, you look like you're at death's door."

"Thanks, Matt," she replied sarcastically, still looking at the screen in front of her and avoiding his eyes. "You look great."

Again, he realised that he was not approaching or handling things in a particularly skilful manner. He knew that he would need to be more sensitive, but his mind was still filled with other thoughts, and he was having to slowly but surely push them aside and make room for other feelings that did not involve them both having a quick sex session in the stationary room and away from prying eyes.

"Sorry," he replied finally after a moment of awkward silence. "I just think that you shouldn't be here and should be at home, tucked up in bed. I read something last week about a particularly nasty African strain of flu going about, and to be honest, I worry about you. I could drop by after work and bring you whatever you need, if you like?"

Finally, she gave him a faint smile.

"It's okay, honestly. I've been in bed all weekend, trying to sleep it off. I think I'm over the worst of it. I'll manage."

He stepped forward, suddenly feeling the urge to show her a degree of affection that would not result in sex. He reached across and placed his hand on hers.

Her skin, although glistening with feverish sweats, was cold to the touch. He instantly wanted to withdraw his hand but fought against it and forced himself to remain in 'sensitivity mode' for the sake of harmony within their relationship.

"Well, if you feel like you need to, let me know and I will take you home. I could get that ginger haired freak, young Scott, to bring your car to your house for you. Saves you having to worry about driving it yourself."

With her insisting that she looked much worse than she actually felt, Matthew headed to his office, feeling pleased with himself that he had shown her a little more than just lust, for a change.

As he sat there, with the TV on, drinking his morning coffee, whilst reading the paper with his feet up on his desk, the news reporters seemed to be speaking of nothing but war, famine, and disease.

Every story seemed to be showing riots and chaos.

He considered switching it over and maybe watching the all-female talk show panel as they discussed current affairs, but in reality, he would really be watching in the hope of catching a glimpse of the host's shapely legs and behind.

Oh Carol, he smiled to himself as his mind drifted into a particularly pleasant fantasy about the extremely attractive middle-aged female host.

Then, the screen changed and he saw the face of the Prime Minister, looking grave and dishevelled. He was no fan of the Premier and considered him a man unfit even to be a Member of Parliament, never mind the leader of the country, but something told Matthew not to change the channel.

For the next few minutes, he watched and listened, all the while his mouth slowly falling open, wider and wider, as the country's most senior politician told them of something that was beyond believable.

When the announcement was over, Matthew found himself unable to move from his office chair. He was frozen in time, gaping at the large screen mounted to the far wall and staring at the images of crowds of people rampaging through cities all over the world.

He had heard the Prime Minister's speech, but his mind was refusing to accept it. It was as though the words, in the context in which they were spoken, were being refused entry into his brain.

As the reality slowly fought its way through the fog within his skull, he blinked, bringing himself out from the trance he had slipped into. Wiping the drool that spilled from his open mouth on the sleeve of his pristine suit jacket, he sat up and reached for his phone.

He scrolled through his contacts list and found his wife's number. Standing up on unsteady legs and beginning to pace the room, he hit the 'call' button.

While the phone rang against his ear, he stepped over to the interior window that looked out over the office floor. Carefully, he parted one of the horizontal blinds with his thumb and forefinger.

Michelle remained at her desk, wearing her thick coat, shivering and sputtering and surrounded by a pile of used tissues.

She has that fucking flu, he concluded to himself.

He looked down at his hand, the one that he had placed on hers, trying to comfort her.

"Fuck," he exclaimed in a sudden panic and rushed back to his desk.

From the top drawer, he pulled a small bottle of disinfectant hand wash and clasping his mobile phone between his head and shoulder, pressing it to his ear, began to pour the entire contents into the palms of his hands. As he vigorously scrubbed, hoping to kill and remove any trace of the virus, his wife's phone continued to ring.

By now, he had broken into a sweat and began to feel light headed. He could feel his fear creeping through his body, making its way up his legs and travelling along his spine. He shivered then gritted his teeth, giving himself and emotional shake as he fought to keep his feelings under control.

Get home, get safe, then you can have your mental breakdown, he heard a voice say within the walls of his own head.

"For fuck sake, Emily, answer your fucking phone," he growled in frustration.

Finally, after what seemed a lifetime, she answered.

She sounded sleepy, probably not long since out of bed and having overslept, *again*, causing the children to be late for school, *again*.

He checked his watch. It was coming up to eight-thirty. William and Paula were due to be in school at nine o'clock, and for once, he was grateful that his wife had a habit of repeatedly hitting the 'snooze' button on her alarm clock.

"Emily," he said with relief. "Thank Christ you're in. Please tell me that the kids haven't gone to school yet."

They had not.

"Right, listen to me. Stay in the house and don't go outside for any reason, okay? For *any* reason. Do you hear me?"

He paused, allowing her sleepy mind, slowly becoming alarmed at the tone of his voice, to take in what he was instructing her to do.

"Keep the kids in and don't send them to school. Do you understand?"

She answered that she did and began to ask a number of questions.

"I don't have time to explain, darling. I'll be home soon. Turn the telly on and watch the news. Stay inside and keep the doors locked until I get there."

He hung up and hastily looked around his office, searching for something he could use as a weapon. On the news reels, he had seen and heard how the infected were attacking and killing people.

The announcement of dead people returning to life was still battering away at his stubborn mind, unable to seep in, and at the moment, his thoughts were filled with violent living sick people, attacking anyone that they saw, and not reanimated corpses.

It would be a while before the full reality of the situation would finally hit home.

He picked up a stapler and immediately dropped it to the floor, wondering why he would even consider using it as a weapon in the first place.

Dick-head, he thought.

Finally, his eyes fell upon the old-fashioned wooden hat-stand by the door. He grabbed it and placed it so that it was leaning against the wall at a forty-five degree angle with its base on the floor. He took a step back and raised his leg, his aiming mark being the centre of the stand. With one forceful kick, it snapped in two with a loud crunch.

He grabbed the lower half and planting his feet on the base of the stand, pulled and twisted until it was separated from the lower part of the broken hat-stand. He raised the length of smooth varnished wood up in front of him and inspected it, judging it on its ability to act as a club.

It was heavy and long enough for him to swing and remain out of arms reach of anyone who came near him. It was as good a weapon as he was going to get from the meagre pickings within an office building.

He suddenly remembered that Dave, one of his friends from the opposite side of the building, had a decorative Samurai sword mounted on his wall. The thought was quickly dismissed from his mind. He doubted that it was real and was probably incapable of cutting its way through a wet paper bag.

Also, he did not want to be running about, searching through offices. He wanted to get out, and get home as quickly as possible.

Grabbing his keys from his desk, he then stooped to pick up his briefcase. Years of habit, ensuring that he never left it behind, was hard to break. He hesitated, then pulled his hand away from the handle, leaving it where it was, sitting at the side of his desk.

"Fuck it," he grumbled.

If things were as bad as the television was saying, he would need to have both of his hands free to wield his club.

He stepped back over to the interior window and again, peeked through the blinds. Everything appeared as it had just a few minutes earlier. He looked down at Michelle, still typing at her keyboard and struggling on like the trooper she was.

Does she not know what's happening? He asked himself.

Does she not know about the flu and that people are dying?

He then remembered Michelle told him that she had been in bed for the whole weekend, suffering and attempting to shake the illness off.

Matthew was beginning to feel sick from nerves. He knew what he needed to do, and the streets, if they were still like anything they had been when he was on the way to work, would be easy enough to travel through. But, all of a sudden, in his mind, they were filled with monsters, all out to get him, and only him.

He formed a plan in his head. He would have to run through the building and out to the car park as quickly as he could. From there, it was five miles to his house, on the outer reaches of the city.

Thankfully, the small private estate where he and his wife and children lived was separated from the rest of the suburbs by a motorway, flanked with high hedgerows and the only way there, was across the bridge that spanned the road.

The house where he lived had only been completed two years earlier. The estate was modern and styled similar to the large suburban housing developments seen in movies set in the United

States. The houses were spacious, with long lawns and driveways stretching out to their front, joining onto the wide road that dissected the main street.

If he could get home, he was confident that their location and the layout of the estate would help to protect them.

What if I can't get to my car?

In his younger days, he had been an amateur athlete, running the London Marathon, twice, when he was in his mid-twenties, and at a respectable time. In his prime, he had always worked hard at his fitness and physique, taking pride in his ability to continue to outperform most of the men around him.

However, as the years passed by and his body needing to work harder to gain the results he wanted, coupled with his increased workload as he climbed up the corporate ladder, his priorities had changed and his interest in physical activity had taken a nosedive.

Now, in his late thirties, and having not even thought about training of any sort for the past decade, he doubted that he could run and fight his way through the building, let alone the five miles it would take him to reach safety if he had to attempt it on foot.

He glanced down at himself and without realising he was doing it, pinched at his stomach with two of his fingers.

I'm in decent shape, actually. These shoes won't get me very far though.

He continued to watch Michelle for a moment.

She was oblivious of what was happening to the world around her, just as he had been five minutes earlier. Now, he was in the know and once again, had the advantage over her.

Matthew shook his head, whipping all thoughts of such matters from his mind.

The game is over, Matt. It no longer matters whether you have information that she doesn't. She's dying there, and so is the rest of the planet.

His plan was clear and with a deep breath, he approached the door. As he clutched his club in his right hand, he reached for the handle with his left. The lock released silently and he pulled the door open and stepped out from his office.

Michelle had not noticed him and remained facing the monitor of her computer, wheezing and sniffing back the mucus that threatened to flood from her sinuses.

The fear inside him doubled its efforts to consume him and again, he began to feel nauseous, forcing him to swallow hard and take a deep breath in an attempt to remain in control. He hesitated for a moment, feeling the trickles of sweat that coursed along his spine and began soaking through his shirt.

"Uh, Michelle?" He stuttered.

"What?" Came the reply without her bothering to turn and face him.

He crept forward, inching his way towards the corridor that began on the other side of her desk. Passing in close proximity to her was something that he was not looking forward to. He could almost see the virus lingering in the air around her.

"I'm uh," he mumbled, "I'm going down to the canteen to get a brew."

"Yeah, okay," she replied, and began pushing her seat back, slowly turning her head towards him. "I'll join you."

With an icy hand of terror squeezing his throat, fearing that she was about to stand up and approach him, he let out an involuntary yelp.

Before he knew what was happening, he swung his club, striking her squarely on the back of her head. He felt the vibrations of the impact travel along his arm and heard the crack of her skull as he watched her upper body, propelled forwards from the force of the blow, crash into her workstation and her face smash down onto the keyboard.

Suddenly, he was sprinting along the corridor with tears streaming down his cheeks as his heavy footfalls echoed all around him.

Whimpering with panic filled gasps as he ran, he headed for the double doors that led into the stairwell.

14

Bull stood by the door, holding the bouquet of flowers close to his chest and unsure whether he truly wanted to enter the room. They were lilies, her favourite, and their strong scent reminded him deeply of her.

He stared at the bed and the motionless shape in the centre of it. He scanned the room and his eyes fell upon the multitude of wires and tubes running into the machines by the bedside that continually monitored her condition.

Her heart rate, blood pressure and respiratory systems were being displayed on the screens with a number of readouts, accompanied by a steady beep that sounded with each beat of her weakened heart.

She looked peaceful.

He stepped back from the private hospital room and peered in both directions along the corridor. The hospital was noisy, more so than usual, with doctors and nurses rushing from one room to the next. A never-ending stream of porters dressed in blue coveralls and wearing surgical masks and gloves pushed gurneys through the wards, collecting the bodies of the deceased and hurriedly sweeping them away towards the mortuary.

To Bull, the hospital no longer bore the pristine appearance of a highly organised and disinfected facility.

Instead, it looked more like a clinic from Africa, or the Middle East. Machines and equipment lay scattered about, pushed to the side, out of service and unattended. Dark stains smeared the usually polished floors and walls, left to fester until the inundated cleaning staff got around to washing them away while soiled dressings littered the hallways, piled high in the corners, awaiting collection and taken to the incinerators. However, the furnaces and the crews that worked them were now working overtime with more immediate and desperate matters.

The passageways that criss-crossed through the building, resonated with the sound of the sick and dying, and the suffering lament of the wounded. Sobs drifted through the hospital, often accompanied with sudden screams and cries of alarm. Panicked voices, barking orders or calling for help, reverberated from within every ward and operating theatre while the telephones rang incessantly with no one to answer them.

Nobody seemed to care anymore about keeping the conditions sterile and free of bacteria. The hospital staff, running on their reserves and pushed to the point of exhaustion, wore the same uniforms for days on end, covered with the blood and bile of their patients. They drifted through the building with dark rings around their bloodshot eyes, looking dishevelled and ready to collapse.

More and more of the much needed doctors, nurses, care workers and support staff, failed to turn into work anymore, putting extra pressure on the dwindling number that remained at their stations throughout the crisis, hoping that things would be brought under control. Each day, more of them slipped away and deserted their unattainable positions, believing, *realising*, that the situation was hopeless.

Everything appeared to be rapidly breaking down.

In the weeks since their return from Sierra Leone, Bull and the rest of the team had watched as the virus steadily spread, jumping from one country to the next at an extreme rate and soon, it was no longer isolated just to the southern hemisphere.

There had been breakouts reported in every major city in Europe and the United States.

Cities, towns and even once quiet little villages were put under quarantine with special units being brought in to *clean* them up, but the scale of the problem was severely underestimated and most of the people sent in, were never seen again. As the catastrophe spread, communications, law and order, were steadily breaking down on a global scale.

Already, India, Mexico, and a host of African countries had gone dark, with no more information being received from within their borders or from their governments. More and more cities in Europe and the west were following suit, being overrun and written off.

Germany had already began using firebombs on the most infested areas in an attempt to cleanse them of the infection. In many of the so-called, civilised countries, riots were commonplace, with looting, rape, and murders, forcing many states in America and even

Russia, to declare martial law as the deadly flu spread from one person to the next.

Confusion reigned and it was only when the virus had gone airborne that the scientists at the World Health Organisation and the world leaders acknowledged the problem and went public, confirming the thousands of unofficial reports on the internet, and informing the world's population that the dead were indeed, rising and attacking the living.

Information was sketchy, at best, and facts often became confused with fiction. Hundreds of thousands of people fell victim to the flu and the infected without knowing what was actually happening, forcing the WHO and world leaders to announce;

"All recently deceased human beings with an intact brain, regardless of the cause of death, will reanimate and attack anything living."

Even then, as the world was told, it was still a number of days before it was reported that the bites of the infected were deadly, and anyone bitten, would die and reanimate in the same way. The final announcements and acknowledgements coming from the western leaders in a personal address to their respective countries. Too little was done too late to stem the spread and by the time that the army and police forces were brought in to tackle the situation, things were already hopelessly beyond repair.

Bull had watched the broadcasts with Bobby. They had listened to the details about the flu and the different strains and the mortality rates. They had looked on as the scientists had informed them of the aggressive behaviour of some of the infected and how their bites were deadly. Then they had listened as the same scientists had revealed how a bite from someone carrying the infection would cause the victim to die and reanimate.

They saw how the British Prime Minister stumbled on his words and struggled to say what he needed to tell the public. Normally, they were used to seeing him stare at the camera, playing the part of the strong statesman who understood the people he led, sharing in their hardships and concerns, but during the announcement, he looked little different from one of the dead himself. He appeared uncomfortable, unsure of himself, and for a change, not in control of the situation.

The announcements did not come as a surprise to Bull and the rest of the men. Unknowingly, they had seen it in Syria and had fought against it in Sierra Leone. Then, they had watched as one of their own had been infected and turned into one of the reanimated corpses.

Bull blinked as his thoughts drifted back to Nick.

It was still hard to comprehend what was happening, but since they had seen and dealt with the dead first hand, they were better prepared to face the problem. However, he knew that the general population of the world did not have their insight, or ability.

The war is already lost, he thought to himself as he looked about the corridors and saw the confusion and anarchy.

He stepped into the room and quietly closed the door behind him, pressing the catch in the centre of the handle and ensuring that the door was locked. Next, he stepped over to the viewing window and pulled the curtain across, giving them complete privacy from the rest of the hospital.

He tentatively approached the bed, watching his mother as she lay sleeping. Her skin was ashen and her features looked sunken and frail. He felt a sudden pang of guilt and had to look away in shame, inadvertently raising the bright flowers up towards his face to shield his features as he stared out through the window across the rooftops of the city.

He took a deep breath and walked towards the bed.

"Mum," he whispered, gazing down at her withdrawn face and placing his hand on hers.

Her flesh was warm but her slender hands felt too delicate beneath his, and he pulled his arm away, afraid that he was about to crush her brittle bones.

"I've brought you some flowers, mum. Your favourites. I know you can't hear me, but I will leave them here, beside the bed."

He fell silent for a moment, still watching the fragile figure of his mother as she lay inert and snuggly tucked into the starched hospital sheets and blankets. His eyes began to sting, and a flood of emotion began to build up inside him, lodging in his throat like a hard slab of rock and causing him to struggle with swallowing.

His whole life, he had never known his parents. He had grown up in confusion and wondering why he had been abandoned, and what it was that he had done that was so terrible that his mother had deserted him for it. For much of his life, he had felt angry and unwanted, rejected by his family and cast out into the world before he had been given a chance to survive it.

Throughout his childhood, he had bounced from one foster home to the next, never really allowing himself to feel anything for the people around him or to settle into his surroundings. Attachment was something that he had naturally avoided, fearing that anything he grew fond of, would eventually be snatched away from him.

Love was an emotion he had never experienced, but three years earlier, it had all changed.

While collecting information on a target that had dropped from the radar and they needed to find, he accidently stumbled upon a way of tracking down his parents.

Initially, his anger had returned. He had wanted to find them and confront them, but when he arrived at her door, with teeth and fists clenched, he had been immediately disarmed at the sight of his mother. Although he had never known her, his love for her bubbled inside him and forced its way past all the negative emotions he had been harbouring.

As she explained to him her reasons for what she had done and how sorry she was, Bull's hard exterior had crumbled to reveal a soft mushy centre. He soon learned that she had spent years searching for him, wracked with grief and regret and unable to feel true happiness, knowing that her boy was out there, somewhere, but no matter how hard she looked or how deep she delved, the trail always went cold, forcing her to begin her search over again.

From there, their relationship had flourished and he spent much of his spare time visiting her and taking her out on trips to the country. They had even discovered a mutual love of Bingo together, and he secretly indulged himself, surrounded by aged men and women in the local Gala hall, enjoying the thrill he felt when one of them won a prize. Normally, it was something along the lines of a kettle or a toaster, but none of that mattered to him.

What *did* matter was seeing his mother smile and feeling the love radiate between them.

Bull finally had the mother he had always wanted, *needed*, but unfortunately, their relationship was short lived. Three months earlier, she had revealed to him that her heart was failing. The news hit him hard, leaving him feeling deflated and lost, even cursed.

Then, as Bull was wrestling to come to terms with the inevitable loss, a stroke had left her in a completely unresponsive state.

As he had always feared, the love that he had finally allowed himself to feel for once in his life, painfully burned a hole through his heart as his mother was mercilessly torn away from him.

Now, she lay in the hospital, waiting for the end.

A blood curdling scream rang out from somewhere deep within the building, snapping Bull from his thoughts. More screams followed, accompanied by the sound of running feet racing through the corridors in all directions.

Things were falling apart.

He glanced at the door and then back at his mother who seemed to be completely oblivious to everything that was going on nearby. Again, Bull thought how peaceful she looked and he thanked his stars that she did not have to worry about what was happening. He could not bear the thought of her fretting and being scared about the events that were currently taking place across the world. He wanted her to remain at peace, without worry and concern.

It was time.

He raised himself to his feet and picked up the flowers, pausing for a moment to breathe in their scent and see the angelic smile of his mother in his thoughts. Carefully, he tucked them into her hands, resting the bouquet against her chest.

He looked down at her and placed his hand on her cheek.

"I love you, mum," he whispered softly as a tear began to well up in his eye.

He smiled fleetingly and brushed his large fingers through her wispy white hair. He leaned forward, careful not to crush her, and kissed her forehead.

"I love you, mum," he repeated in her ear, and he was certain that a smile had briefly creased the corners of her lips.

Bull breathed deeply, fighting with his inner being and struggling with his thoughts and feelings. He knew what he needed to do, and that it was the right thing, but it was still an immense battle that raged within him. His emotions tore at his core, causing him a pain that he could not describe as his eyes welled to the point where his vision began to blur.

He reached his hand around his back, using his large body to shield his mother's view. He knew that she could not see anything, but he felt urged to keep his actions concealed from her. His heart pounded and his hands shook as he unsheathed the long thin blade from his waist belt. He leaned in close to her again, trembling throughout his whole body as he placed his arm behind her neck and gently pulled her close to him so that his cheek rested against hers.

With his other hand, he brought the knife across the bed and paused, the tip of the cold steel just centimetres from her head.

"I'm sorry, mum," he whimpered as the tears began to cascade. "I love you, mum, and I'm so sorry, but this will bring you peace."

He pushed the blade deep.

As gently as he could, but with great speed to prevent her from feeling anything, the knife was thrust into her ear canal. It was over in less than a second as the sharp point sliced through and scrambled that portion of her brain.

A faint gasp escaped from her throat and Bull felt her final breath brush against his face as he withdrew the long shaft, throwing it with disgust into the corner of the room where it clattered against the wall and dropped to the floor.

The rhythmic beeps of the ECG machine suddenly stopped and emitted a high-pitched squeal, as the monitor showed a flat-line, indicating that her heart had ceased.

He kept a tight grip on her, holding her close and not wanting to let go. He was overwhelmed with grief. He sobbed and rocked gently as her limp body, feeling more delicate than ever, was pressed to him in their final embrace.

He had never felt this kind of pain. It was stronger and more debilitating than anything he had known. He struggled to form his thoughts, even breathe, and his once strong and powerful body, suddenly felt weak and feeble.

He had killed many people during his life, some deserving, some not, but he had never felt anything towards it. He had lost many friends and truly suffered their loss and mourned them, but he had never had to be the one to take the life of someone that he loved.

The feeling of guilt and loss was so powerful that he was afraid to stand upright, fearing that his legs would collapse from under him and he would never be able to get up again.

For a long while, as the screams continued throughout the hospital and the moans of the dead grew in volume and number, he remained huddling his mother, stroking her hair and kissing her still warm cheek. He whispered to her endlessly as he cradled her in his arms, rocking back and forth while his tears soaked into her hair and the bed sheets.

Finally, he gently lay her down, resting her head against the pillow, where she would remain for eternity, still clutching the lilies in her hands.

His heart pounded and his knees shook as the tears continued to break through their barriers, but he knew that he could not stay there any longer. He stepped away from the bed and gritted his teeth, swallowing hard, and with it, the pain that was threatening to overwhelm him and leave him trapped in the hospital. Wiping his eyes, he forced himself to gather his strength and regain his composure.

He said goodbye to Eileen Crawford, the mother he had only known briefly but had loved a lifetime, and gave her a final kiss on the forehead before turning towards the door.

He needed to leave before it was too late.

The hospital was clearly overrun. It sounded like a riot had broken out within the wards and from what he could hear, the living were rapidly losing the battle. He stepped over to the corner and picked up the knife. Unable to look at the blood stained blade, he wiped it against a towel and gripped it in his left hand with the blade running upwards along his forearm.

With his other hand, he reached down through his jacket and pulled out the Browning pistol he had tucked into the front of his jeans. He checked the chamber and released the safety catch then, ensured that the three extra magazines were still secure in his pocket.

He stared at the handle of the door. Hell was beyond the thick wooden barrier, and he needed to be ready to take it on. He took a deep breath and shrugged his shoulders in a circular motion. At the same time, he shook his arms and legs, limbering himself up and increasing the blood flow to his limbs.

"Okay," he muttered to himself through gritted teeth.

His mind was clear and his pain had been converted into anger and a burning hatred that he would unleash upon anyone who stood in his way.

"Let's get this done."

He glanced back at his mother one last time. She still looked at peace, embracing the vibrant lilies.

Bull smiled sadly, and then reached for the handle.

The corridor was empty. Sounds of panic and terror still echoed through the wards, but the immediate vicinity was clear from the infected. The place appeared like a tornado had ripped through the building. Tables, chairs, and equipment lay strewn and overturned in every direction he looked.

Slowly, avoiding making any sound, he pulled the door closed behind him, leaving his mother in the room and protected from view.

Holding the pistol at waist level, with his elbow tucked in, he began to edge his way along the hallway. The strip lighting above him flickered, causing the long passageway to disappear before him, and then reappear a moment later. With each power short, he expected to see a horde of the infected in the corridor ahead of him.

He continued forward, his brow soaked with sweat and his palms moist as he kept a tight hold on the knife and pistol. His eyes darted in every direction, scrutinising every corner and shadow, checking that they were clear before passing them and moving further on.

A lingering scream reverberated from an adjacent corridor. It was the voice of a woman. She continued to cry out for a long while, the sound of her pain and fear evident in the howls she emitted. As her shrieks faded, deathly silence filled the void left behind.

The hospital was overrun. Anyone that could get out had already done so, deserting the frail and wounded, the vulnerable and defenceless, and choosing to save themselves as their survival instincts took control and forced them to flee. Now, the infected roamed the corridors, feasting on the sick and dying that had been left behind.

Bull was alone and surrounded.

At each junction in the long hallway, he paused, pressing himself close to the wall and carefully checking in all directions along the intersections before quickly crossing. He had another two junctions to navigate and at least four flights of stairs, and then he would be at the main reception area, through the large glass doors, and out into the open. It was a long way and he doubted that he could remain unseen the whole time.

Ahead of him, the floor of the corridor was awash with blood. A large puddle of bright crimson stretched from one wall to the next, turning black in the moments when the lighting failed. A long smear of the precious red liquid stretched along the hall and then veered off into a room on the right.

Bull paused and glanced back the way he had come, wondering whether it would be worth turning around and finding an alternative route. He did not know the hospital, and it would be easy for him to become lost within the rabbit's warren of wards and twisting corridors. If the power finally failed completely, he would never find his way back. He was three storeys above ground level, so the option of going out through a window was not viable.

"Stick to the proven route," he whispered to himself, dismissing the voice from the other side of his consciousness that urged him to turn back.

At the pool of blood, he stopped again and pressed his back to the wall. Carefully, he took a long stride to his left, straddling the puddle and trying hard to avoid getting any of it on his feet. With wet shoes, he could slip or at the very least, make noise as he walked and in the otherwise silent hallways. The sound would carry and attract the unwanted attention of every infected in the area.

He kept the smear of blood to his right as he advanced, keeping his pistol aimed to his front and the dark open doorway where the blood trail led into. There was no light or sound coming from the room and Bull squinted, fighting to see past the frame and distinguish any sign of movement in the gloom beyond. It was impossible to see, especially from the angle and distance. Instead, he decided to rely on his ears, hoping that they would warn him of any danger long before it became an immediate threat.

He was just a few metres away from the door now, moving extremely slow, placing each step with deliberation, holding his breath and keeping his eyes locked on the entrance to the dark room. The Browning pistol remained tucked in close to his body, with the muzzle pointed at the threshold.

Bull drew level with the ominous black rectangle set into the wall of the corridor. The darkness inside was complete, giving no indication of what lay beyond the doorframe. It loomed at him like a cavernous maw, wanting to swallow him up. As he passed, he imagined a hundred ravenous eyes watching him from the shadows, but nothing stirred from within.

He breathed again, as he left the doorway behind him and continued along the corridor. He was approaching the final junction before the stairway. The lights flicked out again, but this time, they did not come back on.

Shit.

Further along, he could see the shafts of light that penetrated the large glass panes of the tall stairwell. They illuminated the final section of the corridor with the sun's rays, giving the impression that everything was okay in that small section of the hospital as it was protected by the brightness, but the light did not penetrate far, and for a long stretch, Bull could see nothing but the inky blackness.

Unable to see, he carried on forward, sensing his way and keeping his right shoulder in contact with the wall. After a few more paces, the wall disappeared and he immediately realised that he had reached and stepped past the final intersection.

A noise came from his left. It was a scrape, like the sound of something being dragged along a rough surface. In that instant, the lights suddenly flooded the hallway with an intensity that almost blinded him.

The powerful glow from the ceiling lights, though they dazzled him, did not prevent him from seeing what had caused the noise he had heard.

The corridor was packed with the infected. They were crammed in, spanning from one wall to the next, and they were all facing in his direction. As the light had returned, the living man had been bathed in a brilliant whiteness, making it impossible for them *not* to see him.

The crowd instantly swarmed towards him as he turned to sprint towards the stairs. He was no longer attempting to remain undetected, using stealth to make his way to safety. Now, he was running for his life, hearing the moans and cries of the reanimated corpses as they chased after him along the corridor.

"Fuck," he hissed to himself as his heavy feet pounded against the smooth floor beneath him, echoing through the building like a jack-hammer.

"Fuck."

Halfway to the stairwell, the lights went out again, leaving him sprinting through the pitch-black and towards the light at the end of the corridor, with the sound of the horde of infected close on his heels.

Suddenly, he burst out from the shadows and into the brilliance of the stairwell, bathed in sunlight. Without slowing his pace, he reached out for the wooden bannister and pivoted himself around and on to the top rung of the first flight. He bounded down the steps, taking four of them at a time and quickly reached the U-turn for the next flight. Again, he swung his body around without losing any momentum, and more importantly, his footing.

Higher up to his right, his pursuers had reached the stairs and pounded down the steps after him. Many of them, in their haste, lost their balance and tumbled down the hard steps. The sound of their bones snapping and shattering could be heard over the din they made as they continued to howl, the sight of the fleeing man driving them to fever pitch.

Directly above him, as he continued down the next flight, Bull caught sight of the landing and the bars and bannister running out from the wall of the corridor he had run along, leading on to the first flight. More of the infected were coming from that direction.

Suddenly, with a sickening slap, a body landed on the steps in front of him. It was quickly followed by another, then another as the infected hurled themselves over the railing and dropped through the air for ten metres before smashing into the concrete steps. With the impacts, some of them almost exploded as their heads were split open and ribcages were crushed. Blood spattered the walls while the stomach-churning thumps continued as the bodies stubbornly fell from the floor above.

Bull side stepped a number of mangled corpses as they hit and continued to roll downwards, never slowing his pace and relying on his fast reactions to traverse the bloodied organic hazards that rained down around him.

At the next turn, he skidded to a halt. The stairs below him were filled with hundreds of mutilated figures, headed upwards towards him. He needed to think fast and with a quick glance to his rear, he saw the infected closing on him from the flight above.

He had no choice but to turn into one of the corridors running off from the stairwell. He did not have time to consider which direction to turn, so he sprinted into the nearest passageway. As with the floors above, this one was also in darkness, confirming that the power grid for the hospital had failed, and more than likely, would not return.

The deeper he went, the less he could see, but the sounds from behind him kept him moving forward. Fear of the unknown, was less terrifying than what he *knew* was following him.

His feet slipped in something wet, which he assumed was blood, and he barely managed to remain upright as he twisted and pivoted to keep his balance. His shoulder crashed into something he could not see. It was soft and cold and gave way against his weight. It released a grunt with the impact and Bull sensed it slip through the viscous liquid and fall to the floor with a thud and a splat.

Shit, he thought as he ploughed forward, *they're in front of me.*

More bodies crashed into him and were sent flying in all directions, as the heavily built Bull charged and smashed his way through. He felt their hands blindly grasping at him, fighting for grip as he slipped away from them and continued to force his way forward.

He was running blind, hoping for the best, but he could feel that the crowd in front of him was getting thicker. He raised his pistol and fired ahead of him. For an instant, as the crack of the bullet boomed through the building, rattling windows and causing his ears to ring, the flash of the muzzle momentarily illuminated his surroundings like the flash from a camera. Bull saw the mass of gaunt and pale faces around him, imprinted on his retina like a haunting memory. Beyond them, he glimpsed the silhouettes of many more.

The way ahead was blocked.

Without hesitation, he stepped to his right and shoulder barged the door he had subconsciously seen in the split second flash of light from his gun. The lock snapped instantly as his immense weight and strength was slammed against it, forcing it to fly open and crash against the interior wall with a resounding clang.

Bull jumped inside and saw daylight.

The room was being dimly lit from a number of small frosted windows set into the wall where it met the high ceiling. Below each of them, was a cubicle. He was in the hospital's public toilets and the windows were far too small for him even to contemplate squeezing his bulk through.

The sound of the crowd spilling in through the door behind him confirmed to him that he could not turn back either. He was trapped and could not see any other doors or windows in the murky room.

More bodies stumbled in and Bull desperately searched around him for a place to hide. He eyed the end cubical and moved towards it, knowing that he would not be able to remain undetected for long, but he had no choice. He did not have enough ammunition to fight his way out, or even thin the crowd that filled the corridor outside.

The infected were piling up behind him, tripping over one another and getting themselves wedged in the doorframe as they fought to get inside, allowing Bull the chance to consider his next move. They clambered and dragged themselves into the room, crawling over one another and towards the large meal that they sought.

As he headed towards the end cubical, Bull looked up and saw the network of large pipes that ran the length of the room, suspended on brackets from the ceiling. Realising that he now had a better option than barricading himself into a flimsy plywood box with a feeble lock to hold back the ravenous creatures, he vaulted himself up on to one of the sinks, silently preying that the pipes were strong enough to hold his weight.

He heard a metallic clatter and looked down to see that the knife had slipped from his waistband and landed on the tiled floor, skidding out of his reach. Already, the bodies of the infected were clambering towards him. They were too close, and the knife would need to stay where it had fallen.

Under his bulk, the sink struggled to remain seated to the wall and threatened to collapse underneath him. Before it was torn away from its fixtures, Bull reached up and gripped on to the thickest of the conduits, allowing it to take his weight for a split-second before hauling himself upward and to safety.

He threw his legs up and sprawled himself along the length of pipes, facing down into the room below him. Just a metre beneath him, the infected packed themselves into the room, snarling and swiping at the air in a vain attempt to reach their prey.

Bull exhaled and rolled onto his back, staring up at the ceiling.

He tucked the pistol back into the waistband of his jeans and reached into his pocket for his phone. He watched in horror and helplessness as the signal bars in the top right hand corner of the screen dwindled, then disappeared.

"Bollocks…"

15

Everybody had been called in at short notice and told to be ready for a new task. One by one, the men had arrived separately, having dropped whatever they were doing, and rushed back to the bunker. No information had been given to them on what the job was, only that they were to prepare for a conventional style operation as normal soldiers. There was no need for their covert abilities this time, and whatever it was they were going to be doing, they would be doing it loud.

The spacious store room was stacked from floor to ceiling with steel shelves, lockers, and large black boxes where the men of the team kept their personal operations equipment. Each man had a number of boxes, and depending on what the task was, depended on which container he opened.

Marty grabbed the heavy tin of machinegun ammunition and placed it on the bench in front of him. It thudded and rattled lightly as its weight dropped against the wooden planks and the bullets shifted inside. He pulled the long belt out from the container and eyed the links and rounds, checking that they were fitted correctly and unlikely to cause a stoppage. Satisfied that they were in good order, he slid them into one of the large pouches of his vest. The two-hundred spare rounds of 5.56mm linked ammunition would be his to carry, until they found themselves in a position where the gunners needed resupplying. Every man in the team would be carrying spare, along with their own assault rifles and ammunition, while the two gunners would be loaded with fifteen-hundred rounds each, giving the team a heavy amount of fire support, should they need it.

Marty looked to his left and saw the unopened boxes and the unoccupied space at the bench beside him. He looked to his right and then around at the rest of the men in the room, making a mental note of who was there.

"Where's Bull?" he asked in bewilderment when he suddenly realised that the one person that could not be missed, was actually missing.

Subconsciously, he had known that there was something absent from the atmosphere of the crammed room, but it had not registered in his mind because he had been too concerned with his own equipment.

As the group pulled on their clothing, secured their armour and vests, and began their checks, readying themselves for the briefing and the subsequent operation, Marty had noticed the silence, but then again, he had not.

The loud booming voice of Bull, as he tore into someone, ridiculing them for one reason or another, or complaining about his equipment or the lack of time off, was deficient from the air around them. In its place, a hush of preoccupation had settled over the six men as they busied themselves with their own thoughts and preparations.

Stan shrugged as he secured the straps and clips of his tactical assault vest and began rotating his shoulders, checking for ease of movement in the bulky kit before reaching down to pick up his M4 rifle and the stack of loaded magazines beside it.

"I've tried calling him, but it keeps going to his answering machine," he said as he loaded his ammunition into the pouches of his vest. "He should've received the same call-back that we did, but he's the only one that hasn't arrived. I was going to go and check with Sam, once I was ready, to see if she had comms with him."

"It's been two days since *I* last saw him," Brian added.

"Yeah," Taff said as he lit a cigarette, "me too."

"Screw the nut, Taff, and put that fag out," Danny demanded from the corner. "I'm not into breathing your toxic shit."

"What does it matter?" Taff retorted as he puffed away. "Haven't you heard? We're all likely to get eaten by dead people in the near future anyway."

As the rest of the men continued to don their equipment, check their weapons and ammunition, and of course, argue, Marty and Stan exchanged a knowing glance. Neither of them knew where Bull was, but they were sure they knew who he would be with.

They left the store room, leaving the others to continue, and headed through the rabbit's warren, towards the Operation's Room.

"Put it out, Taff," demanded a voice from down the corridor behind them.

"Bollocks," came the reply and then a sudden crash as the sound of boxes and bodies hitting the floor rumbled along the passageway.

"That twat, Bull; he had better not be off having a picnic somewhere," Stan grumbled as they walked through the gloomy corridors.

Marty shook his head.

"I highly doubt it, Stan. Something must be up."

They entered into the dark void of the command centre and immediately caught sight of Samantha, standing by a computer console and reading through a thick wad of paper attached to a clipboard.

She saw the two men enter and noticed the look of concern in Marty's face. They remained by the door, out of sight and earshot of anyone else in the room, staring at her and waiting for her to approach.

She placed the clipboard on the desk and made her way towards them. She was already feeling annoyed because she knew that there would be a problem needing her attention.

She came to a halt and rolled her eyes, holding her hand out in front of her as she butted in before Stan could speak.

"What have you clowns done now that you need me to fix? Honestly, it's like looking after school kids with you lot and I don't know why we bother with you. You're more hassle than you're worth."

Marty glanced to his left and grinned at Stan.

"I told you she would be in a bad mood and would bite our heads off." He turned to Samantha, still smiling broadly. "You don't get much these days, do you, Sam?"

"That's none of your business, Martin, and never will be," she snarled back at him. "Now, what is it?"

"Bull has failed to show up," Stan answered without hesitation. "Have you had comms with him, or know where he is?"

"That big stupid lump? He's probably drunk somewhere, or locked up," she replied in a derogative tone as she folded her arms across her chest.

"Yeah," Stan agreed, "but he has never failed to show up before. None of us have, for that matter. Something must be wrong and we need you to turn his bio-tracker on."

She was about to retort with more insults about their friend but she stopped when she saw the seriousness in Stan's eyes. It was true that the men of the team were a wild bunch to deal with when they were off duty, but she had never known them to be anything but professional and one-hundred percent reliable when it came to their job.

She sighed heavily.

"Alright, Stan, but you know I'm not supposed to do this unless you're on ops, or it's an emergency."

She turned and began to walk to the far side of the room, towards another bank of computer screens.

"This *is* an emergency, Sam," Marty added as they walked.

She glanced back over her shoulder and nodded.

"Yeah, that may well be, but if it's not, then Bull's location will be up on all the screens of Whitehall, for all to see. If it turns out that he is pissed out of his face and propping up a bar somewhere, there will be a lot of flak headed this way and I'm not taking it for you."

Marty patted her on the shoulder as she reached the workstation and pulled up her chair, then began hitting a number of login passwords on the keyboard.

"You *never* take the flak for us," he spoke reassuringly, "Gerry does."

A moment later, on the screen of the monitor in front of her, a small red dot pulsed, overlaid onto a satellite image of the country. Samantha began to zoom in onto the area of the beacon, roughly forty kilometres to the west of the bunker.

"What the fuck is he doing there?" Stan asked in confusion as he watched the details of streets, roads, and buildings come into focus.

"Is he moving at all, Sam?" Marty leaned forward, staring at the screen and reading out the coordinates of Bull's location. "Is he alive?"

Samantha hit a key and a separate screen appeared, sliding in from the right hand side of the monitor with a number of readouts on Bull's status.

"This is from over forty-eight hours ago. If he is inside the hospital, the signal may not have been updated, but he was alive at the time of the last ping."

A few seconds later, and after punching in another set of commands, a new image flashed up on the screen to the left of them, showing real-time aerial footage of the city from orbit. With great accuracy, Samantha zoomed in to the area of the hospital, where Bull's red beacon hovered, unchanged for more than two days. Although the picture was grainy, they could clearly make out the slow moving figures that swarmed through the hospital grounds, like thousands of ants crawling over a detailed model.

Marty stepped back and looked at Stan. Neither of them said anything, but they both had the same thoughts. Bull could very possibly be dead and Marty shuddered at the vision of his friend walking about as one of the reanimated *undead.*

"Is the whole hospital overrun?" Stan asked as he squinted at the screen.

"Can't be sure," Samantha replied as she began scrolling the images and scrutinizing them. "This thing is spreading like wild fire. Whole cities and towns are falling to the infected at a rapid rate and we can't keep up. That's why we called you all back."

"Called us all back?" Stan asked.

She turned in her seat and looked up at him.

"We're evacuating," she replied, staring back at Stan. "The government is about to write off the mainland and we're going to be transferred across to the Isle of Wight. Other units from the army, navy and air force, are being sent to the Hebrides, Isle of Man, and the Channel Isles. They have managed to keep it quiet, up until now, but a lot of units have been decimated by this thing."

"Evacuating...," Marty considered, still staring at the screen.

Stan leaned forward, bracing his arms against the desk and lowering his head so that he was just a few centimetres away from Samantha.

"How bad is this thing, Sam? We've seen the news and had plenty of intelligence updates from you lot. We've even seen it ourselves, here, on the streets of London over the last couple of weeks, steadily getting worse. The army and police are out in force and it looks as though chaos is winning the battle. So, don't bullshit us, Sam."

He paused, looking deep into her without blinking.

"How bad?"

She had no intention of lying to him, or trying to play down the situation.

"It's bad enough for the MoD to begin considering nuclear strikes on the most heavily affected areas."

She paused, watching their reactions.

"Airstrikes have been planned for Edinburgh and Glasgow, once the army have cleared out the civilian population, and fortresses are being thrown up all around the country to act as Forward Operating Bases. When the government and military forces have regrouped, they will begin an offensive that will, supposedly, reclaim the mainland."

"There'll be nothing left to reclaim. What about the average 'Joe-Public'? Where are they going?"

Samantha looked down at her feet, feeling a strong sense of shame and despair.

"Only essential personnel will be evacuated," she mumbled before turning her face back up towards Stan's piercing eyes. "They're being left to their own devices, Stan. This thing has spread too fast and too far, and no one was prepared for it."

Stan stood up straight and took a step back.

"Fucking hell," he whispered. "Will the government announce anything about the evac?"

She shook her head.

"How can they? What would they say; *'sorry folks, but we're off now and leaving you to get on with it'*?"

"So what's our part in this?" Marty asked.

She turned to him.

"You've a special mission to do before you join the evacuation."

"What's the mission?"

"I'm not sure of the full details. General Thompson will be briefing you up personally."

Stan turned and looked at Marty, then brought his attention back to Samantha.

"It can wait," he stated in a decisive tone. "We're off to get Bull first."

Samantha was about to say something, but Stan cut her short. He reached over and hit the print tab on the computer screen. Somewhere to their left, within the gloom of the command centre, a machine sprang to life and began churning out sheets of paper with the printed satellite imagery of the hospital in fine detail.

"Don't bother, just get the heli ready. We go and get Bull, then crack on from there. Get the orders for the flight crew changed, or falsify them if you have to, but have them standing by. We'll be 'wheels up' in twenty minutes."

Stan grabbed the mapping and satellite images, and headed for the doors with Marty close on his heels.

Samantha watched after them, feeling a warmth swell inside her stomach. Though she could not show it, she was glad that Stan had made the decision that he had. Of course, outwardly, she would need to show a degree of protest against such actions, but she knew the men well and had worked with them for a long time. Secretly, she had the greatest admiration and respect for them, though they were never allowed to see it from her.

She smiled and shook her head slightly.

"Bull, it's *always* him."

16

"Another one of those bio-hazard trucks has just pulled up," Emily said as she turned from the window to face him.

Matthew remained seated on the couch and did not bother to look up from the television as he flicked through the news reports.

"Who's it for this time?" He asked in a detached voice.

His wife, still wearing her nightgown, looked back out through the window and craned her neck, attempting to see further along the street and identify the house where the van had pulled up in front of.

"Oh no," she muttered, placing a hand over her mouth. "I think they've gone to Mr Hardy's house. His wife is a teacher at the kids' school."

That bit of information was enough to grab Matthew's attention and force him to get up, move towards the window, and stand beside his wife.

"Are you sure?" He asked rhetorically, leaning forward into the windowsill, trying to see further along the road for himself.

It was early evening and beginning to get dark, but he could clearly make out the brake lights on the back of the truck.

"Yeah, she teaches English, I think."

Matthew shook his head with annoyance.

"No, you silly bitch. I meant, are you sure that it's their house that the bio-hazard truck has gone to?"

"Oh," Emily replied, looking down at herself and feeling embarrassed and more than a little worthless at the way he had spoken to her.

For as long as she could remember, he had gone through phases of speaking to her in a disrespectful manner. Now, was obviously one of those phases.

No matter what she did, or how hard she tried, he always seemed to be cold and distant towards her, rarely showing her any affection. On occasion, he would suddenly appear warm and loving, but she could never tell when that was likely to be.

Even when he seemed to be happy, there would still be a distance between them and to Emily, they seemed to be just drifting through the motions of marriage. The spark was gone and their relationship had become stagnant.

But no matter how hard she tried not to, she loved him still.

She continued to look down at the floor and herself.

Below the nightgown, she knew that she was no longer the woman that she had once been, at least in a physical sense. Giving birth to two children, and leading the life of a bored housewife had taken their toll on her.

She had become disinterested in looking after her appearance and rarely felt sexy. Emily was well aware of how important that side of the relationship was to her husband, but was unable to reignite the fire that had once glowed within her.

Over the years, she had tried to change things, but never had the stamina to completely turn the situation around. She knew that she was in a rut, but could never seem to climb out from it, no matter how badly she wanted to. Especially when her husband had given up ever trying to make her feel special a long time ago.

She blamed herself for the decline of their marriage, despite knowing deep down that there were two sides to every coin. Over the years, through endless arguments, she had become convinced that any downfall would be her own doing.

She remained silent, standing there and feeling insignificant and inferior to her husband.

Matthew, noticing that his wife had taken a step away from the window and realising how quiet she was, turned to look at her. She refused to meet his gaze, and although he could not see her eyes and expression, he could feel the tension and upset, and knew he had been wrong to speak to her in the way he had.

He *always* knew.

Sometimes, he would hear the words flowing from his mouth, screaming inside his own head to stop, but he could not stem their flow and before he could bring himself under control, the damage was done and his frustrations had been vented upon his wife with venom spat from the bitter half of his mind.

"Sorry," he said, moving towards Emily and putting his arms around her.

He pulled her close and kissed her cheek.

"Sorry, darling. I didn't mean to speak to you like that. I'm just worried about all this, and I'm worried for you and the kids, too."

She nodded her head against his chest, accepting his apology, as she always did, and sniffed back the tears that threatened to flood out from beyond their seals.

They were all scared and stressed. The latest news had shook them to their cores and was hard to accept. However, Matthew also had a large chunk of guilt planted firmly in his mind, and it was growing tentacles through his conscience.

After clubbing Michelle, and probably killing her, he had fled from the office.

Sprinting from the scene of his horrific and cowardly crime, he tore his way down the stairs. Descending through the floors of the building, panicking and crying as he ran, he finally made it to his car. He was barely able to control his shaking hands as he attempted to push the key into the ignition and his tear filled eyes refused to focus. Eventually, he opened the driver's door, leaned out into the street, and began to vomit uncontrollably until there was nothing left in his stomach to bring up.

The streets were much busier than they had been earlier in the morning. Everything had changed since the Prime Minister had announced that the dead were getting up and eating the living.

It seemed that the entire city was on the move. People ran in panic, grabbing their loved ones and what belongings they could. Every car in the area was filled with terrified faces, all trying to get out from the built up area.

Within thirty minutes, the whole city had come to a standstill. Businesses closed their doors and many of the people responsible for the smooth flow of the metropolis, deserted their posts, all headed for home.

Soon, the streets were gridlocked.

Horns blew and angry voices cried out. A lot of people, overcome with fear, began to hear screams that were not there, leading to many cars, unable to move, being suddenly abandoned as their owners took to their feet and ran from the impending doom that they imagined was approaching them, leaving the road system almost impossible to negotiate.

It took Matthew the better part of three hours to travel the five miles from his office to his home. As he pushed his way along the packed roads, he looked on in shocked silence, unable to comprehend how quickly things could fall apart within such a short space of time.

By the time he got through the front door, he was shaking uncontrollably and almost collapsed in the hallway. Emily had propped him up, guided him into the living room, and placed his quivering body on the couch.

She had seen the news shortly after Matthew had phoned her in a panic from the office, and was up to speed on current events. Although she was terrified and still not sure whether or not to believe what she was hearing and seeing, she took the lead and began to organise things within their home.

Something had clicked inside of her. Being confronted with a global scale disaster and a horror that she could never have imagined, had awakened with a kick, a survival gene that she was unaware she even had.

Coupled with her husband being almost catatonic, she had no choice but to step up to the mark and take control.

The children were brought down from their rooms, being forbidden to move anywhere without her, even if they needed to use the toilet. She began checking all the windows and doors of the house and even taking stock of the food they had.

Bags were packed with essentials and left close to hand in case the situation arose were they would need to consider fleeing. Water was stored, anticipating possible utility failures and candles, torches, and batteries were dug out from beneath the kitchen sink and the store cupboard under the stairs.

For most of that day, she ran from one room to the next, organising and double-checking their preparations, not allowing herself too much time to begin pondering what the government had announced and its ramifications. She had not even allowed herself the time to see to her own needs, remaining unwashed and still in her bed clothes.

All the while, Matthew had remained frozen to the couch, having not spoken a word since he arrived through the door. He sat there, staring blankly ahead of him. His mind was a tangle of thoughts, mixed in with fear and remorse.

Michelle.

He pictured her lifeless body lying there, being forgotten and left to rot, after all the intimacy that they had shared over the past ten years.

She deserved better, he thought to himself. *What if it was just a cold that she had, and I murdered her?*

No matter how hard he tried, he was unable to shake the memory of her gruesome death from his mind. He could still feel the club in his hand, and hear the sickening thwack, as he smashed the life from her body, and the dull thump of her face crashing into the desk.

He shuddered internally.

It was a number of hours before he had begun to react to his surroundings again, and finally, swallowing his guilt down into his stomach, to deal with on another day, had forced himself to become a functional member of the family again.

Three days had passed and since that morning, they had all remained within the house, not daring to venture outside its protective walls.

Standing by the window, still holding on to Emily, he made his promises to her; that all would be okay and they would make it through the catastrophe together, as a family.

Finally, they released one another.

At that moment, their daughter, Paula, entered the room.

"Mum…?" She croaked.

"What is it, honey?"

Emily and Matthew turned to see her standing by the doorway, appearing unsteady on her feet and rubbing the palm of her hand against the side of her head. At first, they thought that she had just woken up and was slowly coming to, but they soon realised that their assumptions were misplaced.

Even through the semi-darkness and from the other side of the room, Matthew and Emily could both see how pale she had suddenly become. Her eyes looked swollen and her brow glistened with sweat from fever as she swayed from side to side.

She coughed, her chest sounding phlegmy and her throat rasping.

Matthew and Emily looked at one another with horrified eyes, feeling their throats tighten and their hearts become heavy as tendrils of dread began to creep through their nervous system.

“I don’t feel well,” Paula replied, weakly.

17

"Shut up," he growled into his forearm as he lay on his back, shielding his eyes and nose, and trying to ignore the endlessly shifting and moaning infected in the room below him.

"Fucking shut up, you puss filled walking piles of shit."

Every muttered demand, or movement that he made, regardless of how slight, was answered with dozens of shrieking excited voices. For a while, he had attempted to remain still and silent, in the hope that they would lose interest and go away, but they remained, crammed into the open area between the cubicles and sinks of the hospital's public toilet. Their attention focussed solely on the pipes above their heads.

He was tired, dehydrated, and starved. Most of all, he was battling with despair. It felt like he had been trapped there for weeks, abandoned and forgotten, but it had been two days. Intermittent screams still rang out through the building as survivors were discovered, and set upon by the meandering bodies staggering through the corridors in search of fresh victims within the wards.

There was nothing he could do to aid the people he heard, crying out in agony and pleading for help. He was just as trapped, desperate and forsaken, as they were. It was only a matter of time before they would finally get him too.

He lay on his makeshift mattress, on top of the pipes that ran the length of the ceiling, and attempted to sleep. It was no use. Sleep had only come to him in fits and starts and for extremely short periods. No sooner had he drifted off, he would awake, startled, after only closing his eyes for a few minutes. Despite his exhaustion, sleep was evading him and his body and mind were beginning to suffer.

On the first day of his ordeal, within hours of finding himself stranded, a low rumble had vibrated along the conduit that acted as his island of safety above a sea of snapping teeth and haunting eyes. Soon, the pipes had begun to heat up, carrying boiling high pressure water and steam through the maze of the hospital. His howls of pain and anger, as the flesh of his hands and knees suffered from the extreme temperatures, fell on unsympathetic ears and only fed the exhilaration of the swarm below him.

For four hours, he had endured the agonising pain brought on by the scalding steel and iron pipes, searing his palms and the skin of his legs as he continually shifted his weight in an attempt to prevent his flesh from melting. When it had abated and the building's automated heating systems had clicked on to 'standby', Bull vowed to himself that he would never undergo such torture again, at least from something as inanimate as a water pipe.

"Right, you horrible bastards," he sneered as he hooked his legs around one of the supports that fixed the ducts to the wall and ceiling and carefully lowered his upper body down into the room.

"Who wants to join me up here, and keep me company?"

The crowd below, a collage of pale and grey faces, smeared in blood and bearing ghastly wounds, erupted with wails as they reached up for the warm meal that hovered just above their heads. They surged, pushing and pulling at one another, their fingers digging deep into the tissue of the bodies around them as they fought to get closer.

Bull watched them for a while, carefully measuring each one of them up and choosing his target.

"You'll do nicely," he announced as he singled one of them out.

He reached behind him and grabbed his jacket, having already prepared it to form a noose. He checked the knots, tugging at them and making sure that they could take the strain. Directly below him, a man's torn face snarled up at him. His right eye was missing, as was the flesh from most of that side of his face and neck, and exposing the glistening white bone of his skull. The image reminded Bull of an album cover from a Heavy Rock group he had once seen. The man was big, broad shouldered and thick set, and almost a head taller than all the others. Perfect for Bull's needs.

Carefully aiming his jacket noose, Bull lowered it over the man's head. It was a relatively easy task, because no matter how hard the bodies around him pushed and jostled against one another and his massive frame, he remained rooted to the spot, like a stubborn old oak tree.

Once it was in position, Bull gave the jacket a quick jerk, causing the knot to tighten around the man's neck. Immediately, he began to struggle and pull at the material, thrashing his arms and shaking his head in an attempt to break free, but Bull's grip was too strong and he remained snared and at his captor's mercy.

With all of his might, Bull heaved, lifting the body from the ground and hanging from the noose. Adjusting his grip and reaching further down the sleeve of his jacket, Bull began to drag the dead man up towards him.

He growled and grunted with the strain. The muscles in his arms and shoulders bulged, threatening to split the skin, as more oxygenated blood was pumped into them. His back screamed at him as it bore the sudden weight increase of the struggling body on the end of the improvised rope. As his biceps and deltoids burned with the build-up of lactic acid, the supports and brackets of the pipes groaned and juddered in protest against the rusted bolts that held them in place.

Bull could feel the increased blood pressure rushing to his brain, forcing the veins in his neck to protrude from below the flesh, his face began to burn as his vision blurred, and his head swam. He clenched his jaw muscles and screwed his eyes shut to prevent them from popping out from their sockets.

With a long growl, through teeth that were gritted so tightly that it felt as though they were about to shatter, Bull heaved again.

The man in his grasp continued to squirm and pull at the noose, but Bull had no intention of releasing him. Despite the fact that his shoulder joints were close to dislocating and his back was screaming at him to let go, he tightened his grip.

"Come on, you big bastard," he gasped.

By now, it felt as though his spinal column was about to break in two. With one eye, he risked a glance down and saw that the man's face was now just below the ducts. Bull shifted his weight, allowing the excess of the jacket to become wedged beneath him and enabling him to release his grip with one hand. He pressed his body against the pipes, ensuring that the majority of the jacket was secure beneath him and unable to slip.

Next, with his free hand, he pulled his Browning pistol from his waistband and raised it above his head.

"Okay," he huffed, looking down into the pale flat eyes of the reanimated corpse. "Keep still for a minute, please."

He steadied the jacket with his left hand, just centimetres away from the man's chin and gnashing teeth. With all the power that he could rally, he smacked the man with the pistol. The magazine housing smashed down against the bone of the skull, and even above the racket of the bodies below, Bull heard an audible crack as the cranium split.

For a moment, the dead man's face stared back at him, bewildered, then as the thick dark blood began to seep from the large gash in his head and down over his face, he renewed his efforts to break free from the noose and reach for the man above him.

Again, Bull brought the weapon down, feeling the impact vibrate along his arm and causing the joint in his shoulder to jolt. More blood spattered outwards, splashing on to his hands and forearm, smearing the butt of his pistol in the glistening deep red fluid. A dark fissure appeared as the man's skull split further, opening up like an overripe watermelon being dropped on to a hard surface.

The man fell limp and Bull began to heave him upwards again. It seemed to take forever to get the upper part of the corpse onto the pipes and allow Bull to take a moment to catch his breath and let his heart slow down to a rate that was not on the verge of causing it to explode through the walls of his chest.

As he sat back, panting and sucking in all the air that he could, stars began to float through his vision. Every muscle in his body throbbed and he became dizzy, causing him almost to lose his balance and the grip on the body that he had fought so hard to keep.

"Fuck me," he gasped, "I hope this works."

With renewed effort, he pulled the dead man the rest of the way on to the conduit. He paused for a moment and studied the pistol in his hand.

It would have been so much easier just to shoot him, he thought, but he wanted to save his ammunition for when he really needed it.

With the carcass sprawled out, flat on its back, Bull took rough mental measurements of the gap between the man's chest and the ceiling of the room.

"It'll be a bit of a squeeze," he concluded after a minute or two. "Looks like I'll need to flatten you out a little, mate."

He rose to his knees, stooping over with his own head just millimetres from the ceiling, and leaned over the body with the mangled face head between his thighs. From that position, he had a good deal of leverage and a stable platform to work from with minimal risk of losing his balance and falling from the ducts.

He lowered both his hands to the corpse's chest and locked the fingers of both his hands together to form a single fist. Again, he checked his position and looked across at the brackets holding the network of pipes to the wall. Somehow, despite the added weight, they remained tight and secure.

Bull took a deep breath and raised both his arms together, up over his head. At full stretch, he paused for a moment, steadying his aim then, forced his shoulders around and brought his arms down with all the power he could bring to bear. His fists crashed against the man's sternum and Bull felt the bone shatter beneath the blow. He raised his arms again, this time, aiming for the ribs on the right hand side of the man's chest. Again, all of his weight and strength were thrown into the impact, crushing and snapping the bones as he continued to rain down blow after blow along the entire midriff of the cadaver.

The ribs splintered and crumbled under his assault. Some exploded beneath the flesh, slicing their way through the tissue and protruding up through the torn skin. Bull was careful with his aim and maintained his self-control, observing the area of each impact and avoiding crashing his own hands into the jagged shards of ribcage that would splinter into his own flesh.

He still did not know much about the infection, but he was pretty sure that allowing their blood to mix with his own bodily fluids through a cut, would be deadly.

He continued to pummel away at the carcass. It shook under each blow and the pipes beneath them vibrated noisily. Again and again, he smashed his fists at the torso of the dead man, until, every bone from the shoulders to the waist, was broken and crushed.

Finally, with blood dripping from his aching fists and spattering his clothing, Bull sat back and studied his workmanship.

Again, he took mental measurements.

"Good," he nodded to himself with satisfaction and an air of pride at his own ingenuity. "Good. I think that will just about do it."

The body was a mess. Its arms hung limply from either side of its mutilated torso and dangled from over the pipes, dripping with blood and fragments of bone, but Bull paid no attention to that. He viewed the grotesque scene with a different eye.

"Right then," he announced as he crawled forward, sweeping the largest pools of blood from the man's chest with his hands. "Let's give you a try, then."

He untied the knots from his jacket and laid it out over the body.

Within seconds, he was sprawled out on top of the mutilated corpse, facing up towards the ceiling and grinding his hips as he adjusted his position. His head rested on the area of the pelvis, using its natural shape as a cradle, and his legs were stretched out along either side of the pulverised skull.

"Oh yeah," he groaned, "this should be bob-on."

He paused for a moment, considering his actions and current predicament. After some reflection, he burst into laughter. It was uncontrollable and no matter how hard he tried, he could not stop.

"Fucking hell," he howled, his voice echoing through the room and out into the vast corridors of the hospital. "I'm using a dead man as a fucking mattress."

Through the sound of his own laughter, he failed to notice the distant rumble, but a minute later, he felt the vibrations as the pipes beneath him began to carry their boiling hot cargo from one end of the building to the other.

Bull's hilarity subsided and he stared up at the ceiling, concentrating on whether or not he could feel any heat through his crude and monstrous organic mattress. He could feel a degree of warmth, radiating through the cold lifeless corpse beneath him, but the searing heat was gone. He waited for another twenty minutes, praying that the high temperature would be countered by the cool flesh of the dead man.

Eventually, Bull began to find the experience quite pleasant, to a degree. The body did not get too hot, and the pipes prevented it from cooling too much and reminding him that he was lying on top of a corpse. With a little effort, he was able to push it from his mind and forget what his makeshift cot was made from.

"I reckon," he suddenly announced to his dead audience, speaking to them as though they had been eagerly awaiting for his verdict on the matter. "That if this thing gets any worse, and you lot down there, end up taking over the world, I'll patent this idea. It's better than an electric blanket."

Again, he erupted into laughter.

All that had happened within the first ten hours of his ordeal. By the next morning, he was desperately thirsty. He could feel his lips beginning to crack and his tongue swell inside his mouth.

Climbing down and getting a drink from one of the taps was out of the question. With the amount of infected packed into the room, he would not make it as far as the first sink. He desperately needed water. He knew that he could go without food for much longer than he could without fluid. His body alone contained enough reserves to sustain him for a long while, but without water, he would dehydrate, become incoherent, disoriented and eventually, if he had not already fallen from the pipes in a delirious state, would slip into a coma and die.

He needed a new plan.

For the moment, he was trapped. He knew that, but he was clinging to the hope that a way out would eventually present itself, or at least, the crowd below him would thin out enough for him to attempt a breakout. Until then, he would need to look after himself. He had mitigated the slow roasting of the pipes, and now, he needed to stay hydrated.

Within minutes, he had formed his strategy.

He removed the socks from the dead man, and then his own. Next, he took off his t-shirt and began tying them all together to form a new rope. One that he hoped would be absorbent enough.

He looked down over the side of the piping and as he expected, saw a blanket of haggard snarling faces looking back at him. Their eyes never left him and each time he exposed his head over the side, a ripple of excitement swept through the throng of bodies, even out into the corridor as their adjuration spread from one to the next.

Luckily for Bull, the pipes ran directly over the last stall in the line of toilet cubicles. It was the only one he could reach without having to climb down from his vantage point.

He began to crawl along the ducts towards his target, holding the bundle of dirty underwear in his hand. The pipes were cool to the touch and by his reckoning, he probably had another hour or so before they would begin to heat up for the first time that day. However, he could not be sure, and could only guess.

As he approached the cubicle, he began to whisper to himself.

"Please don't let there be a shit floating in there. Please don't let there be a shit floating in there."

If he *did* get there, and indeed, there *was* an unpleasant gift waiting for him, he would have no choice but to continue with the plan. He would die of thirst before anything that he caught from the bacteria in the faeces killed him.

He was having to use a rotting corpse as a bed, so he felt that he deserved at least one small mercy in the form of a clean toilet.

The infected people below him followed his every move, shifting as the living man made his way along the network of pipes above them. Their pale eyes remained locked on him and their mouths gaped with anticipation. Many of them watched in silence, as though waiting for, willing him to fall into their ravenous throats. Others groaned or hissed quietly, but in all, the room was relatively silent.

Bull could almost feel their tension, if they had any that is.

Before he reached the end stall, he stopped and pulled out the long narrow piece of copper pipe he had ripped from the side of the ducts. Carefully, he tied the skirt of his t-shirt around one end, making what appeared to be an odd-looking fishing rod.

He remained where he was, knowing that if he ventured any further, the door to the cubicle would swing open the moment that a body leaned its weight against it. Instead, he would need to reach across with his rod, lower the socks into the toilet bowl, and hopefully soak up enough *clean* water to rehydrate him.

From his position, he could see little more than the top of the cistern and the flushing handle. He could see nothing of the bowl, or what was in it.

"Please, God, don't let there be a floater," he muttered in prayer.

He lowered the socks, gently, and with as much accuracy as he could summon from the quivering rod, he fought to keep it steady. The weight on the end of the pole changed, and he guessed that the material of the socks had touched down on the water. Carefully, he allowed the tip of the rod to dip a little more, hoping to absorb enough water so that it would not have all dripped away by the time he retrieved it again.

He raised the long pipe and in the sunlight that filtered in through the small frosted windows above the cubicle, he could see that the spongy sports socks were sodden, and still clean. Or as clean as they could be after being pulled from a dead man.

He smiled ruefully as he began to pull in his catch.

As it came closer, he inspected the material for signs of having come into contact with anything unpleasant left behind in the toilet bowl. He saw none, and continued to draw the dripping white socks towards him. Finally, they were within his reach and he licked his cracked lips in anticipation.

One final inspection of the textile revealed nothing at first, but then he saw it.

His eyes blinked and he squinted, trying to see more clearly in order to identify the mark that he was sure had not been there before he had gone fishing.

It was unmistakable.

The offending smear was dark brown in colour and Bull felt his heart sink. The mercy that he had believed he had earned was not meant to be, and he now had to content himself with drinking unflushed toilet water, as well as sleeping with a dead man.

"Bollocks," he snapped as his shoulders drooped.

With a sower face, and a sombre mood, he took in the fluids that he greatly needed then placed his water collection device to the side. For the remainder of the day, he remained still and quiet, nestled on top of the bed he had constructed from flesh and bone, listening to the sounds of the infected below and along the corridors.

They grunted and snorted incessantly, and from time to time, a yearning moan would drift in through the door, coming from deep within the building as one of the dead sang out. Often, as though communicating to one another, the loan voice would receive a number of wailing replies that would linger in the still air of the hospital walkways.

Just their wretched cries were enough to drive most men to despair and break down with fear. Their voices were haunting, like a signature to the pain that they had suffered in their final moments of life and now clung to them in death.

Other noises reverberated through the corridors.

The clatter of equipment being flung to the floor and the crash of furniture being overturned and doors forced open. From time to time, a terror filled scream accompanied the sounds, but they were becoming less frequent now and Bull believed that he was probably the only person left, still alive, within the walls of the building.

He shook his head, attempting to sweep away the sounds of the dead hospital.

As he lay there, with his hands placed behind his head, he began to think about his mother. On the floor above him and along the corridor into the next ward, she lay dead, and never to return. His emotions were mixed, and despite his efforts, he could not force his mind to think of anything else.

He was torn between feeling glad that he had ended her suffering and ensured that she would not come back to be one of the mindless rotting shells, like the ones below him, but he was also filled with shame, regret and huge sense of loss.

He had loved his mother. There was no doubting that. The short time that they had spent together had been the happiest of his life. Finally, he had felt a true sense of belonging. Now, as the world slowly fell apart, he had found himself in a position where he had to be the one to end his mother's life.

Bull's thoughts flitted eternally, from feeling positive about his actions, to being ashamed and wondering whether or not he deserved to make it out of his current situation in one piece. He had never experienced those feelings before, especially so long after the fact. Still pondering his actions, forty-eight hours after they had occurred, was a completely new experience for him and he worried that they would plague him for the remainder of his life.

For the rest of the day, he remained motionless and out of sight. His mind wandered and he drifted in and out of sleep that never seemed to last for more than a minute or two. He had endured sleep deprivation on numerous occasions throughout his life, sometimes going for as long as a week without rest. Now, however, it was his own mind that was keeping him awake and he struggled to keep himself from losing his temper and screaming at the ceiling, demanding that he be allowed to sleep.

As he wrestled with himself internally, he did not notice that the sun had begun to set. The room slowly fell into darkness, the shadows created by the sinking sun stretching out and creeping across the walls. Finally, there was nothing but blackness and the sounds of the dead within the darkness.

Bull remained stationary for the remainder of the night, listening and staring through the gloom. Though he was curious, he did not risk showing his face over the side of the pipes to steel a glimpse of the room below him. He could hear them moving about, their feet scuffing against the tiled floor, and did not want to risk drawing their attention. He hoped that because he had remained hidden from view, the swarm beneath him would disperse a little and give him the chance to escape.

It was a long and sleepless night, with an avalanche of thoughts, worries and emotions smothering him.

As the sun's rays began to strike the frosted glass and slowly illuminate the room, Bull's thirst returned. He knew that he would need to make his way across to the end cubicle and drink the filthy water again.

For a while, he stayed where he was, delaying the unsavoury task for as long as possible, but by mid-morning, he was at the stage where it hurt his throat to swallow.

Let's get on with it, then, he thought, and slowly began to turn himself over on to his stomach in order to begin the crawl towards his water source.

With a tremendous amount of effort and concentration, he pulled his way along the still warm pipes, careful not to make any noise or cause the ducts to move. He wanted to remain unnoticed and forgotten by the infected.

Even if their numbers *had* reduced, it could still be a hard fight to get out of the hospital and he would need to have fluids in him. Dehydrated, he could begin suffering from cramps and muscle spasms. Worse still, as his brain began to shrink through dehydration, he could begin struggling to think logically and make correct decisions.

Centimetre by centimetre, he pulled his way along, taking more than an hour to get himself into a position where he could begin the water collection process again. Once he was in range, he pulled the long staff from his side and gently unravelled the bundle of socks and t-shirt from around the rod.

Before his next move, he risked a quick peek over the edge of the pipes.

To his delight, the room had indeed become less packed, but there were still at least twenty of the things spread out between the cubicles and sinks. None of them, however, seemed to be paying much attention to what was above them anymore. Instead, they seemed to have fallen into a trance, standing motionless and their unseeing eyes staring straight ahead of them, or at the floor as their heads lolled towards their chests.

He made his decision.

He would quench his thirst, wait another hour, in the hope that more of them would leave, and then begin his flight to freedom.

All was going well. He steadily inched his rod out towards the area directly above the toilet bowl and then began to lower the tip.

Unknown to Bull, a pair of eyes had taken note. The pale misted irises, set within the sunken dark sockets of a deathly white face, had caught sight of the strange contraption, slowly extending out from the pipes above. They watched for a while, and when the radiant fleshy face had briefly appeared over the edge, the reanimated corpse of the young doctor shuffled her feet towards the cubicle at the far end of the room.

Bull continued, oblivious to the fact that he had been seen. He was beginning to feel positive about the new day, even confident, and that he would soon be out of the death trap he had found himself in.

As he was about to raise his rod, he heard a crash beneath him. He looked over the pipes, just in time to see the body of blonde haired woman wearing a blood smeared set of green surgical scrubs, barge into the toilet cubicle and reach for the t-shirt suspended below the copper pipe. Her fingers closed around the garment as she lunged forward, ripping the clothing from the shaft as she tumbled, smashing her head against the water tank.

The noise was thunderous in the silence and as he watched his only means of hydration slip from his fingers, Bull instantly became enraged.

"You fucking bitch," he roared as the body of the woman attempted to correct herself and climb back to her feet, still clutching the t-shirt and socks in her withered hands.

Bull reached for his pistol, pulling back the hammer as he brought it into the aim. His face was red and his head throbbed from fury and thirst, but his aim was true. The gun jerked in his hand, forcing his forearm up slightly from the recoil as the bullet blasted out from the barrel in a bright flash and an ear-shattering bang.

The woman's face folded in on itself as the round and the shockwave that followed close behind the copper slug, ploughed through the bridge of her nose. The bone disintegrated and imploded, being dragged along in the vacuum caused by the velocity of the projectile and erupted from the back of her head in a spray of broken skull and pulped brain matter, all mixed together within a mist of deep red congealed blood.

The body fell backwards, landing on the lavatory and settling into a seated position, as if intentionally using the convenience, while the contents of her head coated the white tiled walls behind her.

In his fury, Bull had undone all the hard work he had accomplished in remaining unseen and allowing the room to become less densely packed. The sound of the shot had alerted every infected person within the grounds of the hospital, and the bodies within the public toilets had been snapped out of their inertia. Now, they were all back to clambering for position below the living man, and more were spilling in through the door.

"Fuck this," Bull grunted, grabbing his jacket from the body of the dead man and throwing it over his shoulders.

He raised his pistol again and began to fire into the faces of the bodies closest to him. They fell into one another as the bullets mashed through their brains, creating a pile of flailing arms and legs as they tumbled to the ground, dragging the nearest infected with them.

As Bull changed his magazine, he began to hear a new noise. It was faint at first, but over the slowly subsiding echo of his gunfire and the cries of the dead, he could hear the unmistakable whirling thump of a helicopter's rotor blades.

They were getting louder and from what he could tell, circling the hospital. As the pitch of its blades grew in volume, he was even able to recognise the type of aircraft.

It was unmistakably a Black Hawk.

Without another thought, Bull jumped down into the room, landing on the pile of bodies that he had created and immediately bringing his Browning back into the aim and loosing off another volley of shots at a rapid rate. With a skill that had become second nature to him, through years of practice and real experience, each round found its mark, punching a hole through the head of an infected corpse and dropping them like a house of cards in a sudden draft.

They tumbled to the left and to the right, spilling their thick, almost black blood over the walls and floor of the room.

Bull began to move forward, headed for the doorway and out into the corridor. Soon, he needed to change magazines again. Keeping the weapon raised and pointed towards the entrance, he released the empty clip with his thumb and allowed it to drop. It hit the floor with a clatter as he reached with his left hand for a fresh one. He slid the loaded magazine into the pistol grip and pushed down on the bolt-release catch with his right thumb, chambering a round and continuing to fire.

More infected fell under his accurate and rapid rate of fire.

By the time he reached the door and stepped through into the hallway, he was having to change magazines again, making a mental note of how much ammunition he had left.

One mag left, he heard himself whisper in his own head.

At the door, he turned left, firing his way through the throng of bodies that converged on him. With each squeeze of the trigger, the muzzle let out a blinding flash, lasting for just a fraction of a second. There were dozens of them around him in the dark corridor, all reaching out towards him as they charged forward, but were dropped by the bullets that thumped through their faces.

Bull hunched his shoulders, dropping his head to his chest and tucking his arms in close to his abdomen. He began to sprint along the corridor, barging through the grasping claw like hands all around him, and trampling the bodies that rebounded from his powerful frame as he hurtled through them, headed for the stairway.

He roared and screamed as he drove himself onward, seeing nothing of his surroundings except the bright sunlight ahead of him, bathing the stairway in its brilliance. He barely noticed the impacts of the infected around him, as he slammed into them and sent them scattering in all directions and smashing into the walls with heavy thuds.

He was focussed solely on getting into the radiant light that was just a few more metres ahead of him.

As he reached the stairwell, he could hear the sound of the helicopter more clearly. It was loud and constant and from what he could tell, had landed on the rooftop of the hospital. The din of its motors echoed down through the wide staircase, blotting out all other noise and filling him with a huge sense of hope, knowing that living people and a means of escape were just above his head.

Although he was only two floors above ground level, he decided to climb the steps towards the sound of the aircraft. As he ascended, more of the infected charged for him from the upper floors as they caught sight of the large animated form of the living man, racing up towards them.

There was nothing going to stop him from reaching the roof, and he shot, kicked, and barged his way through anything that fell into his path as he climbed the four flights of stairs towards freedom.

His pistol ceased firing and he only needed a quick glance to see that the top-slide was locked to the rear, giving him a view of the inside of the chamber. The magazine was empty and he had no more ammunition. Instead, the Browning became a part of his fist, being smashed into the faces of the bodies that assaulted him as he continued his ascent.

By now, he was howling like a wild animal, feeling his determination rise inside of him and drawing on all the reserves that his body could produce to keep him moving forwards and upwards. His powerful legs worked like pistons, springing him up from one step to the next, as his shoulders barged the infected out of his way and ploughed the road ahead.

As he reached the final turn, he heard voices up above him, quickly followed by thundering gunshots that caused the air pressure in the stairwell suddenly to increase and push against his eardrums.

He saw more corpses fall and tumble down the hard steps ahead of him, leaving trails of blood in their wake.

"Check your fire," he screamed up towards the rooftop without slowing his pace. "Check your fire. Live man coming through."

The gunfire continued, but none of the rounds came close to him as he surged forward, trusting the men above him in their skill and accuracy. All the time, he continued to call to them, making them aware of his location and that he was on his way.

More rounds snapped and thumped over his head, shattering the windows behind him and showering him with broken plaster from the walls.

Half way up the final flight, a small form turned and hurled itself towards him. It was the body of a child, no older than ten or eleven, Bull guessed. Her hospital gown was covered with blood, and in the split-second that it took for her to close on him, he saw the hideous wounds that had killed her, and subsequently brought her back.

Her throat and chest were splayed open, revealing the bones of her ribs, chest plate and spinal column. Her long dark hair was matted with the coagulated blood that was smeared over her face. Her mouth opened incredibly wide as she leapt for him, reaching out with her grasping fingers.

Bull swept her aside with the back of his fist. The blow landed against the side of her face, snapping the bones of her neck and sending her over the bannister to the floor below, where she landed with a wet smack.

He raced up the last steps through the falling bodies, with his head down and arms tucked into his sides.

Suddenly, he felt like he was floating.

His body seemed to become weightless and he glided upwards with ease, as though being transported on an escalator while his legs continued to scale the stairs effortlessly. Then he noticed the pressure he was suddenly feeling on his shoulders and upper arms and looked up to see the faces of two men, pulling him up the final few steps as others gave them fire support and continued to drop the infected around them.

"About time you lot showed up," Bull hollered over the racket of the guns and helicopter. "I thought you'd forgotten me. Wankers…"

"Better late than never," Marty screamed back at him with a grin, dragging him through the doorway and out on to the roof, towards the waiting helicopter.

The bright sunlight and clean air assaulted his eyes and lungs. Forcing him to cough and sputter after being stranded in the dead hospital for so long.

Bull's body became heavy.

His legs were like lead and his energy seemed completely to desert him. His head began to spin and his heart raced, but he smiled broadly and could not stop smiling as his friends bundled him into the waiting aircraft.

He collapsed in a heap, gasping for breath, but still grinning from ear to ear and roaring with laughter.

Stan appeared over him, staring down into his face.

"Are you okay, dick-head?" He shouted as the pitch of the engine behind them rose.

Bull could not reply. He felt too weak and the laughter that he could not abate seemed to be using every ounce of energy he had left.

"Bull, listen to me," Stan called, slapping his friend across the face. "Are you okay? Have you been bitten?"

Bull stared back at him, his face still creased with hilarity and spattered with blood. He shook his head, unable to speak.

"You really are a dick-head, Bull," Stan screamed into his face, "but it's good to see you're still in one piece."

As the Black Hawk took off, Bull's head sank back against the bulkhead and within seconds, sleep snatched him away into a deep black pit.

18

Samantha had been informed that the team was on their way back and had rushed to meet them, but before reaching the command centre, she had been summoned in to see General Thompson with the utmost urgency.

General Thompson, though she had never had cause to fear him personally, terrified her. She had seen him reduce men and women to bumbling wrecks, just by the manner in which he spoke to them. Should anyone incur his wrath, it was rare to see the offender walk away from the man without being on the brink of a nervous breakdown. His appearance alone was enough to scare most people, and even the mighty Bull avoided him like the plague and made every excuse not to have to face him.

The only person that she knew who seemed to be completely immune to the General's fearsome staring eyes, deep harsh voice, and haunting features, was Stan. They had both known each other for a long time and rumour had it, Thompson had once been Stan's Platoon Commander when he was a young private soldier, having just arrived from the recruit depot, but no one knew for sure.

After a half-hearted dressing down from the high-ranking officer, who was well aware of the situation and the team's actions, Samantha had been sent on her way with a warning of serious consequences if flight-plans and orders were ever changed again without his written authorisation.

As she left his office, eager to see if the men had all made it back, unharmed, The Prince of Darkness called her back.

"Oh, Captain Tyler," his gruff voice growled after her, making the hair on her neck stand up and goose bumps to form on her flesh.

"Yes, sir?" She asked as she turned, bringing her body into the position of attention with her arms pulled into the sides, knees braced, and eyes staring at the wall behind the General's head.

Suddenly, she felt like she was about to experience his rage first hand and that she had not gotten off lightly after all.

The General smiled slightly, causing his gaunt features to crease, creating deep shadows, and making him appear sinister and ghoulish.

If there was ever a man that was not supposed to smile, it was General Thompson, she could not help thinking to herself.

"Give my regards to Stan and his boys."

Samantha paused at the door to the Operation's Room and gathered her composure, breathing deeply and concentrating on trying to appear casual, even indifferent. She did not want them to see her flustered or excited. That would open up a huge chink in the emotional armour that she had fought so hard to maintain over the years.

She brushed her hair back from her face and rubbed her sweating palms against the material of her trousers. With a final deep breath, she pushed the heavy door and entered into the command centre.

Her eyes immediately fell upon Stan and his men, still wearing their equipment and carrying their weapons, reloaded and resupplied, ready for their new task. Her face twitched as she stiffened the muscles of her cheeks and clenched her jaw, holding back the smile of relief that threatened to burst through to the surface. Her gaze fell on each one of them in turn, and she prayed that her elation did not show in her expressions.

In the Operation's Room, Samantha could see that all the team were now accounted for. The only person missing was Nick. Her heart gave a resounding thump against her chest wall at the memory of the jovial northerner, and about what had happened to him.

Bull was standing by the refreshments table that was used to sustain the operation's staff in their caffeine addiction. Already, there was a pile of empty water bottles piling up around his feet, mixed in with the discarded wrappers of chocolate bars and energy snacks. He stood there, oblivious to everything around him, cramming as much chocolate into his face as his mouth would hold and washing it down with large gulps of fluid.

He let out a large belch that echoed up to the ceiling, unseen somewhere high above them in the darkness and turned to see that there were no bottles of fresh water left. Instead, he switched his attention to the cartons of fruit juice in his mission to quench his thirst and replenish his body of their vital fluids and nutrients.

"I'll never turn my nose up at Cranberry juice again," he gasped after sucking dry the second carton and tearing into another.

"You finally with us, Bull, or have you got to go off doing your own thing, again?" Samantha asked, sarcastically.

She watched him as he assaulted the refreshments, like an ogre from a fairy-tale at the dinner table. She knew her remarks were about to be retorted, but he would not be the man he was if he did not fire back with something. She thought highly of Bull, despite his insensitivity and brash mannerisms. In fact, his personality was what she loved about him, but again, as far as Bull was concerned, she viewed him with disdain.

Stan and his men were like brothers to her. They fought and argued incessantly, but she loved them all dearly.

"Lick the back of my balls, Sam," Bull replied between gulps and without looking in her direction.

"He's been drinking shitty water for the past few days," Brian said, in way of an explanation to Samantha for Bull's lack of manners and uncouth response.

However, they all knew very well that the large man did not need to be stranded for a number of days, drinking toilet water and surrounded by dead people, to be the way he was. Bull was naturally rough around his edges.

"I'll tell you this," Bull finally gasped, seemingly having had his fill and wiping his mouth on the back of his sleeve. "There are some right inconsiderate arseholes out there. No matter what is going on around you, you can at least flush the chain. Dirty bastards. *And* it was the ladies toilets."

Bob saw an opportunity to cross examine his friend and show everyone a glimpse into the inner workings of Bull's mind.

"So, the whole building is suddenly overrun with dead people that have come back to life and would like nothing better than to eat you, but before they made a run for it, they should've flushed? Is that what you're saying?"

Bull pondered the question for a moment, and then nodded with absolute sincerity.

"It only takes a second to yank the chain," he grunted.

Bobby was grinning broadly as he spoke, always finding Bull's reasoning a great source of amusement.

"So, if it was you sitting there, and you had a choice between wiping and flushing, what would it be?"

"Flush. No one will see your shitty arse, but they won't miss the big dump you left behind for them."

Danny began to laugh, unable to hold it back any longer.

"What would it matter? No one is going to see it, or even care."

Bull turned to him and fixed him with a harsh stare.

"*I* saw it, and *I* cared. I had to drink that water, Danny."

"What's the matter, Bull?" Brian added. "You never been camping?"

"Obviously, not the way that *you* like to go camping, you heathen."

"What if it was a stubborn one and refused to go on the first flush?" Bobby continued, wanting to gain as much entertainment from the conversation that he could before the briefing began and their serious heads were donned.

"I'd wait," Bull nodded.

"You'd wait for the cistern to refill, while reanimated dead people are banging at the door, and then flush the toilet to make sure that no one is offended by a turd?"

"Hey, you have your principles, and I have mine," Bull stated passionately as he ripped open another chocolate bar and stuffed the entire thing it into his mouth, signalling that the debate had come to a close.

Five minutes later, the doors of the Operation's Room were flung open and in walked the General, cast in shadow and looking ominous as two smaller officers walked on either side of him. Bobby watched the scene and in his mind, compared it to the entrance of a bad guy from a movie, when he appears on screen for the first time.

He wondered to himself, if that was the actual intention of General Thompson, to command the room with his presence, without even saying a word. Or, whether he really *was* the Prince of Darkness.

Bobby smiled at the thought.

As the General moved to the centre of the room and turned to face the assembled team and operation's staff, everybody focussed their attention upon him. He was easily a head and shoulders above most of the people around him, and his extremely slender frame made him appear even taller. With everyone seated, he seemed to tower up into the dark recesses of the ceiling.

"Stan," Thompson began in his rumbling voice and staring down at the team commander. "Are you and your men ready?"

Stan nodded, and that was the extent of the formalities. Thompson did not need any more information than that, and Stan knew that he did not need to give any. They were both men of action, and they liked to be straight to the point.

"Okay, ladies and gentlemen, I will keep this very brief. The situation of enemy forces is this virus has gone global. I'm sure you're all well aware of that, but what some of you may not know, is that whatever it is that is making the dead reanimate, is in the air. No matter how they die, all bodies of the recently dead will return and attack *anything* that is living."

A number of people shifted in their seats at the revelation about the virus and their lack of ability to escape it.

"Nowhere on the planet is faring well and the US, especially, is having trouble trying to contain the problem. Much of the southern hemisphere is now in the dark and Europe and North America is following close behind."

Thompson cleared his throat before moving on to the next heading of the briefing process.

"Situation friendly forces, as some of you are already aware, the mainland is being evacuated of all necessary personnel that are vital to the continued war against this *plague*.

"To be blunt, we're losing and as a result, making a strategic withdrawal to regroup and lick our wounds. Our armed forces, fighting in the Middle East and Asia, have been ordered to pull out and return to the UK. Until they arrive, we have to make do with what we have and hold our positions until reinforced."

General Thompson paused to allow his words to sink in.

A few heads turned to look at one another in surprise, but for the majority, they either had prior knowledge, or they had seen the writing on the wall for themselves and were not surprised that the government had come to the decision they had.

"Most of the cabinet," General Thompson continued, eyeing everyone in the seats in front of him, "has already left, and the majority of land, sea and air forces have either withdrawn, or are in the process of withdrawing. Within the next forty-eight hours, the mainland will be clear of all essential personnel.

"Some small units will stay behind within specially erected fortresses to keep the pilot-light on, providing us with intelligence updates and acting as collection centres for any survivors. Ships and aircraft, under the command of the newly created MJOC, Mainland Joint Operations Command, have begun evacuating as many of the civilian population as they can, but do not be in any doubt, millions will be left to fend for themselves on the mainland. A tragedy that could've been avoided if those politicians had heeded our advice from the very beginning, before things were out of control.

"So, this is how it is, and that is the general outline of the current situation."

He took a few paces to the side, his hands placed on his hips and staring at the floor, waiting for any comments or questions from the group.

No one spoke.

"All staff members are instructed to gather their family members and report back here before nineteen-hundred hours, the day after tomorrow. If you don't arrive, we will assume that you're dead. It's as simple as that.

"This is a war, people, be sure of that," he growled, pointing one of his long bony fingers towards the door. "Not the sort that we expected, but nevertheless, we are facing a real enemy. One that is more dangerous than anything we have ever faced before."

Gerry stepped out from the shadows by the door, carrying a piece of paper in his hand and began to read off a list of names.

"You are dismissed. Go to your homes and gather what you need. You are to report back here before nineteen-hundred hours on the twelfth, ready for evacuation."

The majority of the assembled rose to their feet and exited the room. Left behind, were Gerry, Samantha, and two other staff members, along with the team.

Stan sat up in his seat.

"What's our role in all of this, General?"

Thompson immediately focussed his attention on him, understanding that the men were anxious to know what their task would be.

"Stan," he began, "before you join us on the Isle of Wight, you have a special task to carry out. Gerry will fill you in on the service and support side of things, but you and your team will be travelling north immediately after this briefing."

19

As the Black Hawk transported the team north, evidence of the breakdown of civilisation and the spread of the virus was apparent for all to see. Flying at two-thousand feet above ground level, the men had a bird's eye view of the destruction, and they could literally see the world and its inhabitants crumbling beneath them.

It was survival of the fittest and in many cases, the wealthiest.

In spite of the global situation, greed was still a driving force behind many human beings and corporations attempted to cash in on people's desire to survive. The huge amounts of money the big firms made in the final months of mankind's dominance on the planet, unbeknown to them, would be worth nothing in the new world that would follow the fall of humanity. A world spawned from the deaths of the very people that the governments and large firms failed to help, because the average person could not afford to pay the high prices placed on rescue and survival.

The cost of food, fresh water, and fuel, sky rocketed, increasing up to ten times their normal prices, creating anger and public unrest as people took matters into their own hands. Riots broke out and murder became a common occurrence on the streets of the UK as people fought to protect themselves and what they had.

The sky was filled with aircraft. Commercial passenger planes and small private aircraft were taking to the air, fleeing from the mainland while their holds were stuffed with valued supplies and personal treasures, and their passenger compartments, crammed to bursting point with wealthy refugees that had parted with extortionate amounts of money and precious jewels to secure themselves a seat on any flight to safety.

Below the helicopter, fires burned in the towns and cities, engulfing entire districts and incinerating the buildings and people to piles of ash. Explosions erupted, shooting fireballs high into the air above the buildings, as gas pipes burst under the extreme heat and fuel tanks ruptured. The flames spread from one structure to the next, unchecked by the emergency services that had collapsed under the strain.

A deep grey haze had formed over the built-up areas, as the plumes of smoke was carried into the atmosphere, where it hung ominously, like a death-shroud, waiting for the remains of the population to be consumed, then it would collapse back down over the charred buildings and skeletal remains of the population.

The streets and roads were crammed with traffic, all hoping to flee from the urban areas and escape the walking dead and rampaging infected that were growing in numbers by the hour. For most of the vehicles, packed bumper to bumper on the chaotic highways, it would be their final resting place for all eternity. Many of their occupants too, would never make it out and become entombed.

Swarms of the dead, looking like masses of tiny insects, flowed through the streets, ripping their way through barricades and strongholds and devouring the living, adding them to their ranks. Some of the reanimated ambled through the detritus, while others, forming themselves into hunting packs, stormed through the streets, seeking out anything that was still living, tearing people and animals, limb from limb in their lust for blood and warm flesh.

The faltering army units, fighting alongside the crumbling police force, battled hard to retake the cities from the dead, but one by one, they were overwhelmed. Entire regiments were swallowed up and wiped from the map boards of operation's centres. On the ground, it was not as simple as removing their names from the list of available manpower. Instead, the massacred soldiers and police officers had crossed over to the enemy's side as the dead infestation continued to grow.

It was anarchy, and things were rapidly falling apart at the seams.

Soon, the helicopter was clear of the large cities in the south. They headed up through the Midlands, following the network of roads and features towards the north and flying through the plumes of acrid smoke that rose up from all around as the mass funeral pyres continued around the clock, burning the dead and undead that was unceremoniously dumped at their locations by the collection teams.

In the countryside, the infected were less densely packed, but they were still present in great numbers, scattered through the fields and lanes, pouring through villages and towns. Since it was revealed that the virus had mutated and become airborne, it seemed that no matter where the people ran to, the threat of the plague was everywhere.

Entire communities were on the move, fleeing from the advance of the infected. Others transformed their areas into fortresses, barricading the roads, boarding up their houses and throwing up miles of fencing and wire in the hope of keeping their attackers at bay. Some fared better than others, and the Black Hawk past over many small communities that had attempted to stand their ground but had collapsed under the onslaught.

The bodies of the victims, some still struggling for their lives in pools of their own blood, were torn to pieces and feasted on by the crowds of dead that had smashed their way through the feeble defences. Cars filled with terrified families attempting to flee the massacre, became bogged down and trapped as the infected closed in around them. Houses, their windows and doors nailed shut, proved no barrier against the unfeeling corpses that relentlessly battered at their barricades.

Stan and his men observed the ruins of their country in silence, watching it drift by beneath them like a reel of film from a horror movie.

The team's mission was a rescue operation.

A middle ranking member of the Royal Family, along with his wife and children, had fled the cities and found themselves trapped at their country manner, situated in the borderlands between England and Scotland. A call for help had been sent out and although a helicopter had been despatched from a nearby RAF base, nothing had been heard from them since and the base had reported that their aircraft had never returned.

As the base too was under siege, and preparing for their own evacuation, the Wing Commander had refused to send out anymore of his men or machines to help in what he considered a pointless operation.

As the Black Hawk approached the target, climbing over a large wooded feature, the country estate came into view. The old mansion was visible from a great distance, seated in the centre of a large expanse of grasslands, containing a number of smaller buildings on the outer fringes and surrounded with thick forests.

The house was huge and grand in its design. It had stood for hundreds of years, being passed down from generation to generation. Around the outside, immaculate lawns and blooming flowers and trees gave way to an expanse of grasslands and woods that would be filled with pheasant, hare and deer and even from that distance and altitude, it was easy to see the flocks of white sheep roaming the fields.

Stan leaned forward into the cockpit, poking his head between the pilot's shoulders and watching for any sign of the trapped Earl and his family. The area around the house was free of movement, but he could tell that something had happened there and began to wonder whether they were wise to land at all.

The place looked deserted and Stan indicated to the pilot to conduct a sweep of the area, to give him a complete picture of what they were going into.

"Give us a full three-sixty, Mac," Stan instructed through his headset. "Come in close to the house then sweep us over the treeline. I want to make sure we're not landing in the middle of a gang-fuck."

The pilot nodded and skilfully complied with the team commander's orders, gliding the machine over the grounds and giving the team a clear view.

Having completed its circle of the large mansion and its surroundings, the aircraft began to slow and angle its nose upwards, losing altitude and coming in to land on the wide open space, one-hundred metres to the rear of the house. The downwash from the rotors scattered any loose debris in all directions, flinging paper, clothing and garden furniture out across the lawn and tumbling away from the centre of the landing site.

The men were ready, and the doors had already been opened, creating a whirlwind within the interior of the Black Hawk. As they descended, the team moved up towards the hatches on either side, ready to jump down and allow the aircraft to take off again and provide them with air reconnaissance.

"Stand-by," Stan hollered as he squatted, leaning his body against the door frame for support and eyeing the ground and the buildings for any sign of movement.

The wheels touched down with a bump and immediately, the seven men sprung from the fuselage, dropping down onto the soft lawn and bringing their weapons to bear, moving with a grace and speed that defied their heavy loads.

Immediately, they fanned out, pushing forward to form a perimeter that encircled the Black Hawk, covering their arcs and studying the area for anything they conceived to be a threat.

They needed to be ready, physically and mentally, for a sudden attack and with the noise of the aircraft, and the abrupt change in environment, they were at their most vulnerable.

Each of them took up firing positions with their weapons at the ready, their safety catches removed and their fingers running along the side of their triggers.

Stan turned and gave the pilot a thumb's up, signalling that they were complete and that he was to take off again while the team remained in their positions, allowing for a soak period while they adjusted to their new surroundings.

As the Black Hawk took to the air, just seconds after landing, the crescendo of its motors faded to the point where the men could communicate verbally, without having to shout or use hand signals.

"Taff, take your team up towards the right and cover the outside," Stan ordered through his radio. "I'll take my team in through the south-west corner and begin our clearance, pushing north through the building from there."

Taff acknowledged the command with a double click of his radio and moved off, roughly fifty metres away with Brian and Bobby, on to a small rise in the ground that gave them a good view of the east, south and west of the house. Once in position, Brian flipped down the bipod legs of his machinegun and snuggled in behind it, adjusting his firing position and checking that he had a clear line of fire, ready to give support to the others.

"That's us in position, Stan. We have eyes on the front of the house. All clear."

"Roger that, Taff." Stan's voice was barely a whisper. *"Moving now."*

Stan, Bull, Marty, and Danny, fanned out into a line and silently patrolled towards the rear of the building, taking fast but careful steps and sweeping the area with the barrels of their weapons.

Already, they could see the damage to the entrances and windows of the ground floor. Shards of glass and splintered wood littered the granite paving that stretched out from the patio. A number of bodies crawling with flies and larvae lay close by, their heads either smashed open or completely missing.

"Looks like someone used his prize shotgun on them," Danny noted, more to himself than anyone else in the group.

As they drew closer, they were able to see into the interior through the large openings that had been left from the broken doors and shattered panes. Inside, they could see the piles of furniture that had been thrust up as barricades, scattered and pushed to the side.

Another two bodies lay amongst the wreckage.

At the smashed doorframe, they paused, studying the room beyond the threshold for movement and listening for any noise from within. After a moment, Stan nodded to Danny, directing him to enter into the house.

Inside, they spread out, covering the entrances and checking that the bodies, sprawled out on the floor with grisly head wounds, were down for good.

"Looks like they put up a good fight," Danny commented, rising to his feet after studying the wounds of the nearest corpse.

"If this room is anything to go by though, I don't think it did them much good," Marty replied pessimistically.

"Taff, we're at black-green, south-western entrance and into the first room," Stan informed his second-in-command.

Taff had a mental picture of exactly where they were and the layout of the room that Stan and his team had entered. They had been given a full briefing of the design of the house and shown diagrams of the floor plan.

As per their Standard Operating Procedures, SOPs, they had colour coded the different points of the building for ease of communication and navigation. The front, where the main doors were, was designated as white. The rear was black and the left and right, were green and red, respectively.

For a building of that size and under the circumstances, it would be difficult to clear with just four of them conducting the search. If they were attacked, it would be hard to maintain an accurate picture of exactly where they were, and it would be down to the professionalism of the men inside, keeping a cool head and remembering exactly where they were in relation to the colour code system they were using.

Taff would need to have complete trust in their ability to give him accurate updates on their locations in order for him to give effective fire support. If they got the colour code wrong, Taff could end up directing his fire into the wrong room, even killing, or severely wounding one of his own men.

"Sierra-one-zero, this is Hotel-one, over," the pilot called through the radio, high above the mansion and watching the surrounding landscape.

"Send," Stan's voice sounded distant and faint due to his location inside the house through the VHF communications each of the men carried.

"We're down to our reserves here. Our recce of the area is complete. Nothing seen. We suggest moving to the airbase to refuel."

"Roger that, Hotel-one. We'll continue our sweep and then go static and hold until you make comms again."

The helicopter flew a final circle of the area, and then headed off to the east, the sound of its engines fading as it crossed the high ground and dropped into the valley beyond. The team was now on their own, and the silence was suddenly oppressive.

Bull and Marty, working as a pair, systematically cleared each room along the right hand side of the corridor, while Danny and Stan concentrated on the left. According to the diagrams they had been shown, and judging by the standard of the furnishings, they were still in the staff quarters, where the butler, cleaners and cooks would have been housed.

Apart from the large dining room where they had entered, this side of the house appeared to be relatively untouched. Then, they came to a large pool of blood that had spilled out from the final room on the right.

Bull and Marty approached silently and cautiously, gently taking up the first pressure on their triggers. Bull remained upright as Marty, taking the lead, moved into a crouch, keeping himself clear of his friend's line of fire and preparing to enter the room.

With a grunt, Bull indicated that he was ready.

Marty took a wide step to avoid slipping in the blood beneath his feet, and jumped through the doorframe, sweeping his rifle across to the right and scanning every inch of his side of the room.

Bull checked the left.

The bedroom was relatively small, in respect to the grandness of the house. A single bed sat tucked under the window on the far wall, with a double wardrobe on the right. The small bedside cabinet completed the entirety of the furnishings and comforts, presenting a rather Spartan room.

Then there was the mutilated remains that sat in the centre of the blood soaked hard wooden floor.

"Room clear, one body," Bull hissed into his radio.

The carcass could hardly be described as human and was impossible to identify whether it had been male or female, let alone *who* it had been. The head and arms were missing and all that remained of the legs was the left femur, stripped of flesh and clinging to the pelvis by a few strands of sinew. The ribcage, mangled and wrenched open, was empty of the organs it had once nestled and protected, and appeared more like something expected to be seen on a butcher's meat hook.

"Fuck me," Marty mumbled as he stared at the blood coating the walls and floor.

At the end of the passageway, they entered into the large kitchen. All around them, food, appliances and utensils lay strewn across the tiled floor and work surfaces. A multitude of bloodied footprints, leading from the room containing the corpse, continued through the kitchen, all headed in the same direction towards the heavy wooden door that entered into the main part of the house.

In the far corner, to the right of the large mirrored fridge, lay a rounded object that seemed to be moving. On closer inspection, it became clear that it was a severed head, and probably once belonging to the remains they had found in the servant's bedroom. Much of the skin and muscle had been eaten away from its face, along with the ears, but the eyes remained, flat and lifeless and watching the men as they moved past, silently flexing its jaw.

Bull and Marty exchanged silent words, glancing at one another and then back at the severed head.

Stan nodded across to Danny and indicated the door while Bull and Marty took up cover positions, ready to unleash a hail of fire at anything that came towards them from the other side.

Danny looked back, checking that everyone was in position. Then, he gripped the handle and twisted, pulling the heavy oak barrier towards him and revealing a short corridor that opened up into a wide reception room, decorated with ornate fittings and paintings with a large staircase in the centre.

More doors led into the north wing on the far side of the entrance hall.

"Okay, Taff, we're at white-centre, in the main reception of the house. Any sign of movement out there?"

"Nothing," came the reply. *"It looks like whatever happened here, we missed it and they're all long gone."*

"Roger that," Stan replied, stepping forward and looking up on to the upper floor balcony, searching for any sign of movement or danger from above.

"Keep your eyes open. We're about to cross into the north wing, heading towards red."

Behind them, in the main entrance hall, the large double doors lay open, pushed back against their hinges. The solid wooden frames were twisted and broken, the doors having been smashed open from a sustained assault from the outside. Another body lay sprawled at the entry point, blood and remains of brain and bone spattering the white wall above it. A number of large holes had been punched into the plaster around the entrance and at least ten empty shotgun shells lay scattered across the marble floor.

Bull looked up at the large pictures that decorated the reception hall. Portraits of unsmiling regal looking figures, in all manner of styles of dress from different eras, judgingly stared down upon him.

A gentle breeze that blew in through the doorway, created a light moan and whistle as it drifted up along the grand staircase and towards the upper storey of the house.

Bull felt the hairs on his neck stand to attention. After his ordeal at the hospital, he did not relish the idea of having to deal with the infected in a confined environment again, even with his teammates and the fire power they carried.

He gritted his teeth and mentally checked himself, giving his mind a shake.

Each room they came to was strewn with debris. Broken furniture and glass covered the floors. Large pools of blood had soaked into the thick carpets of the corridor and study, but there were no more bodies to be found on the ground level. Ten minutes later, after searching their way through the wreckage of the lower rooms, the four of them were ready to make their way up the stairs.

"Heading towards white-one, Taff."

"Roger."

Outside, Brian remained tucked in behind his gun, watching the windows of the upper floor of the house.

The light behind one of the panes of glass shimmered for a moment, immediately catching his attention.

"Movement on green-one, Taff," he said, keeping his eyes locked on the building and the barrel of his machinegun pointed into the room where he had seen the change in light.

Taff came up beside him, hoping to receive a target indication from the gunner.

"What have we got, mate?"

Brian squinted, looking over the weapon and along the barrel, trying to identify what he had seen, but it had gone. He shook his head, annoyed with himself for not being able to confirm exactly what it was.

"Not sure," he replied, "but I definitely saw something move past the window of the end room on green-one."

Taff did not need to hear anything more. If Brian was sure that there was something there, then he was satisfied.

"Stan," he said into his radio, "be aware, possible movement on the upper floor, towards green-one."

Bull and Marty were in front, taking one step at a time while Stan and Danny covered their ascent to the landing of the staircase. Half way up, a step creaked loudly in the cavernous staircase beneath Marty's boot. Everybody froze to the spot, holding their breath and tensing their muscles as they expected a horde of bloodthirsty infected to come charging out from the upper floor.

Nothing.

At the top, Bull and Marty covered the approaches to the left and right, with their weapons pointed along the corridors that led towards the bedrooms as Stan and Danny moved up into position behind them.

Once they were complete, Bull and Marty continued towards the south wing, stealthily moving along the passageway and hugging the walls on either side. More paintings, showing landscapes and impressions of people that were long dead, but remained as part of the history of the house and family, covered the walls along the corridor.

At the far end, a door lay ajar, revealing a slither of light emitting from the room beyond. From what they had seen on the blueprints, the room was another large study that spanned across the gable end of that side of the house and with large bay windows looking out over the grounds to the south.

Just a few metres away, both Marty and Bull began to hear faint noises, coming from beyond the door of the study. They were the sounds of footsteps, lightly treading against the floor, as though creeping and trying to avoid detection.

Marty turned his body slightly and without looking back, knowing that Stan would be watching his men intently, pointed to his ear and then made a chopping motion with the side of his hand towards the door ahead of him, indicating that they had heard something originating from that particular room.

Stan replied with a double click of his radio, acknowledging that he understood. He turned and tapped Danny on the shoulder, then pointed to his own eyes with two fingers, then down the corridor of the north wing.

Danny nodded, understanding that Stan was going to move up into position behind the others and that he was to remain where he was, protecting their rear.

Bull could see the damage done to the door and its frame. It had been forced open. The lock had been secured, but was unable to withstand the load that had pushed against it, revealing the white pulp of the wood from beneath the layers of antique dark varnish, where it had cracked and splayed open. However, the large thick, solid oak door was still very much intact; a testament to its age-old strength.

Marty crept forward. He could hear his own heartbeat as his blood raced through his veins, pumping a surge of adrenaline through his system. With his left hand, while his right hand remained firmly gripping his rifle, he gently pushed against the heavy wooden door.

Expecting it to creek and alert anyone inside to his presence, he immediately stepped back, clutching his M4 with both hands again.

The door glided slowly and silently against its hinges, revealing more of the room and allowing more light beaming in through the floor to ceiling windows to flow over the entrance and spill into the corridor.

There was still no sign of the origin of the sounds that they could still hear, but an odour had joined the rays of sunshine that were almost blinding in the gloom of the passageway that led up from the staircase.

Bull's nose twitched as he noticed the aroma. It smelled tangy, almost metallic. He recognised it instantly. It was the smell of blood, lots of it, and he could soon taste it at the back of his throat.

"Taff," Stan whispered, keeping his eyes locked on the brightly lit doorway, "hold your fire on green-one. Entering now."

Marty rushed forward and stepped through the door, swinging his assault rifle around to the left to clear the corners as he crossed the threshold. Bull was a fraction of a second behind him and together, they swept the room with their weapons.

Body parts, caked in dried blood and tatters of meat still clinging to the bones, lay festering all around the room. The floor was awash with the deep red lifeblood of numerous bodies, squelching beneath the men's boots as they tread on the thick spongy carped.

A black cloud of bloated flies took to the air as the men rushed in, disturbing them from their feast and causing a droning swarm as they swirled through the large open area.

At the far end, seated close to a large antique desk, a young boy of no more than four years old, sat on a lavishly embroidered rug, clutching what appeared to be a toy robot in his hand. All around him, swathes of encrusted blood covered the surfaces of the furniture, walls and floors. Handprints, footprints and smears indicated the struggle that had ensued as the infected had poured in through the broken door and the victims, with nowhere to flee to, had been torn apart and picked clean by the dead, their body parts then discarded in all directions.

The child looked up at the men as they entered but for now, remained where he was, just watching the two strangers standing in front of him.

Marty snorted and took a step back, lowering his rifle slightly and observing the horrific scene. His right heel crunched down of what was left of somebody's spinal column, but he took no notice.

His attention was fixed on the boy.

Stan entered behind them and looked around, seeing the butchery that had taken place and smelling the early stages of decomposition. The rich aroma of rotting meat, mingled with the sharp scent of blood struck his senses immediately. He had experienced the smell a thousand times before, but it still never failed to make him want to take shallow breaths.

He too saw the boy.

The small figure still had not moved. His hair was matted and standing out in all directions and his t-shirt and shorts were stained to a deep mottled brown. He sat there, looking from each man to the next, clutching his toy, as if unsure of what to do. His opaque eyes, set in a pale grey face, studied the large figures standing in front of him, seemingly making his mind up on his course of action.

Finally, the young boy clumsily rose to his feet, dropping his toy robot, and on rickety legs that had a number of large bloodied tears ripped from the soft flesh, exposing his shin bones and the network of tendons and veins running along them, began to stagger towards the closest man.

Bull, being the nearest, took a hesitant step backward as the dead child approached him. He glanced from the corner of his eye nervously.

The boy gurgled, causing a river of clotted blood to spill from his withered lips, cascading down over his chin and splashing onto the floor in large globs.

Stan moved forward, nudging past the inert Bull.

"Here," he grunted.

With one hand, he reached down, grabbed the small gargling figure by the throat, and pulled him upwards, lifting him off the floor and bringing him up to eye level. The boy writhed and clawed at Stan's forearm, attempting to dig his small delicate fingers through the material of the team commander's jacket, snarling and snapping his teeth at the warm body that held him in a tight grip.

For a moment, Stan studied the boy, trying to identify him, but it was impossible to tell who he was. The child's face was too withdrawn, having lost all of its plumpness through lack of blood pressure. The eyes, which were normally an easy way to recognise a person, were no longer human. They were flat and sunken back into their sockets, with a milky film coating the large dark spot of the dilated pupil, giving no indication of colour or shape.

Finally, Stan took a step forward, still gripping the boy by the throat and slammed his small body down on the antique desk. Pinned, and unable to struggle free of Stan's overwhelming strength, the child continued to squirm.

With his free hand, Stan pulled out his knife from the scabbard attached to his harness. With the precision of a surgeon, the blade glided up towards the gaunt face of the child and with lightning fast movement, was thrust through the boy's left eye, driving deep into his frontal lobe and all the way to the back of his skull.

The body fell limp and the arms dropped to the table with a gentle thud. Stan withdrew his blade and released his grip around the boy's throat. He stepped back and watched the body for a few seconds then turned away, wiping his blade on the back of his trousers before sheathing it again.

"It's not one of the Earl's kids," Stan finally remarked with indifference. "I don't think so anyway, judging by the cheap brand labels in his clothing."

The sound of thunder struck them from further down the hall, close to the stairway. Stan turned and sprinted through the door, just in time to see the body tumble at the far end as Danny's shots hit their mark.

"Contact rear," Danny cried over his shoulder as he watched for more targets.

"What's happening, Danny?" Stan hollered as he bounded along the corridor.

"Last room on the left at red-one," Danny replied.

They waited for a minute, allowing Stan to inform the support group of their situation, before venturing down the north corridor and towards the room where the infected man had come from.

Danny and Stan led the way, while Bull kept an eye on the staircase and the main entrance to the house. Although they had not seen anyone on the outside of the stately home or in the surrounding area, it did not mean that they were not there, lurking in the shadows or in one of the many other buildings of the estate.

The room was empty.

A flimsy chest of drawers had been used as a barricade to seal the door and now sat toppled over, scattering clothing and other items across the carpet. The large ornate bed, situated in the centre of the room took up most of the space available, leaving just a narrow walkway around the perimeter.

Danny stepped across and walked to the far side of the room, stepping into the beams of light coming in through the window and checked down the far side of the bed.

"Got another one here," he said in a hushed voice, "looks dead."

"This is the Earl," Stan informed him from outside, in the hallway.

"How can you tell?" Marty asked, looking down at the corpse that had landed in a slump against the wall. "Danny blew his face off."

Stan stood up from the body, holding a wallet in his hand and sifting through its contents, pulling out cards of all colours and designs. He handed one of them across to Marty, showing the man's picture and personal details.

"This must've been his wife then," Danny added, glancing at the body of the woman on the floor beside the bed and then noticing the shotgun, its breach sitting open and empty, on the satin sheets of the bed. "Looks like the Earl did the honours on his wife before running out of ammo for himself. The top of her head is missing."

It was clear that their mission had come to an end. The Earl and his family were dead and Stan immediately decided that it was pointless to continue with any further search. The house had been cleared and they had found nothing but corpses. With the Earl's body identified, their task was over.

"Taff, mission complete. All family members are dead. Inform Gerry and get comms with the heli. Tell them we're ready for pick up then close in to our location."

A couple of minutes later, Stan and his group moved back down towards the ground floor, and headed for the kitchen.

"First things first, Bull," Stan said with a sigh as he placed his rifle down on the work surface. "Check the gas is still working and get the kettle on."

As Bull and Marty began ransacking the cupboards, looking for tea and coffee, Taff arrived with his group from the same entry point that the search team had come through.

"Looks like it was a bit of a bloodbath in here, lads," Bobby noted, looking around at his surroundings.

"HQ informed, Stan, but no comms with the pilot," Taff said gravely.

Stan nodded.

"Have you tried the HF?" Danny asked, and instantly regretted his question.

"No, I've been sitting on the lawn, drinking Martini's and my finger shoved right up my arse, Danny," Taff snapped.

"Keep trying," Stan ordered, then turned to Marty. "You and Bull go across to the garage on the north end and see if there's anything we can use. If the heli is lost, then we may have to make our own way home."

Bobby spotted the meaty lump, sitting in the corner by the fridge. At first, he was unable to make out exactly what it was, but after a moment, as his eyes focussed and his mind accepted the truth, he realised that it was a head. He walked across and reached down, grabbing a fistful of its hair and lifting it from the pool of sticky blood. The dead eyes locked on his as he turned the shredded face around, studying it with curiosity but remaining wary of where he placed his fingers as the mouth continued to open and shut.

"I don't get it."

"You don't get what?" Brian asked.

Bobby turned to him, frowning intently and lowering his arm, casually holding the decapitated head by his side like any other household item.

"This," he said, shaking the head slightly in his hand, indicating what it was that he was struggling to understand.

"I don't get *this*. How can dead people still be moving about? I know the scientists are trying to figure it all out, but I can't see how it could be happening. It makes no sense."

"Well, yeah, it *is* pretty fucked up, but what does it matter? It's happening and we have to deal with it."

"Are you serious?" Bobby gasped. "You're supposed to be an intelligent bloke and here we are; dead people, with no blood pressure or pulse or, *anything*, that helps *us* to move about. How's it happening?"

"Bobby," Brian began in a voice that said he was tired of thinking too much, "I'm sick of trying to work it out. There's no explanation for it, as yet. So why should I lie awake at night, pondering walking dead people when much smarter men than me still can't come up with an answer? If you're so interested, *you* work it out. Maybe you should even look at it from a religious sense if you want to take the easy option? I'm past caring and just want to survive this thing. When the clever people doing all the tests and experiments work it out, then I will happily take an interest again. Until then, I'm shoving my head as far up my own arse as it will go."

Bobby shook his head and turned his attention back to studying the head with a renewed interest.

"I don't fucking get any of it," he mumbled.

Stan picked up the saucepan as the water began to bubble. He poured the boiling liquid into a cup and lifted it to his lips. He sipped, grimaced at the temperature and then passed it across to Taff, who gladly accepted it.

"Did you send the sit-rep to Ops?"

Taff nodded.

"Yeah, I told them about losing comms with the heli as well."

"And?"

Taff placed the cup on the side and turned to face Stan.

"They said nothing. They just acknowledged that they had understood the report. They'll be bugging out soon, and if the heli is gone, then we won't make it for the evac."

Stan shrugged and began to chew his lip.

"They'll leave us here to rot. You know how these things go, Stan."

Bobby slung the decapitated head back into the corner where it rolled across the kitchen tiles and came to an abrupt stop when it hit the wall.

"Yeah, and with every aircraft needed, they're not going to waste any fuel picking *us* up. They'll be nice and safe in their cosy beds and won't need a bunch of dick-heads like us anymore."

Stan looked back at him, deep in thought.

"Try the heli again. If they don't answer up within the next hour, we'll have to make our own way out."

Bull and Marty arrived a few minutes later. The rest of the team turned to them, waiting for them to report on what they had found at the garage.

"We found one of the security guys," Marty informed them as Bull snatched up the cup from Taff and emptied it in one gulp. "Dead from a gunshot wound to the head. Looks like they bugged out and left the Earl and his family to face things alone."

"What about vehicles?" Stan asked.

"One," Bull replied, smacking his lips and setting about making a fresh cup. "A VW Camper van. In good condition too."

Stan nodded. It would have to do. He turned and looked out through the kitchen window and over the long garden, leading on to the sprawling fields surrounding the house. He then glanced up at the sky and realised that they were approaching the late afternoon.

"It'll be getting dark soon," he said quietly to himself as he contemplated what they were to do next.

He turned around and faced Taff.

"We'll stay here for the night. Keep trying to get comms with the pilots and inform ops of our intentions. At first light, we'll head for the airfield, on the off chance that they're just having comms problems and been delayed for whatever reason."

Taff nodded.

"No worries, Stan, but you know yourself that it won't be the case."

Stan nodded gravely.

"Yeah, I know, but we have to be sure. Otherwise, it's a long drive to get to our new home. We'll take a look, anyway."

Taff and the others set about securing their location, blocking off the entrances with furniture and anything heavy that would cause a problem for anyone, or anything trying to get into the house.

Bobby made the call to the Operation's Room with the Iridium phone.

The voice of the Operation's Room operator came through clearly.

"That's us going static at our current location, report-line, Alpha-One. Lost comms with Hotel-one and moving to report-line, Alpha-Two at first light by alternate means."

"Roger that," came the almost robotic reply from the man on the other end. *"No aircraft available at this time. We have your bio-transponders up on the tapestry, and will remain on over-watch until your next comms."*

Bobby finished the call and looked up at their commander.

Stan shrugged.

"Typical, the RAF don't want to come and pick us up."

"Either that, or we've been written off," Danny remarked.

"Well, I guess we will soon see on that one. In the meantime, let's get some food and rest. Bull, is the van good to go?"

"Yeah, Stan, full tank and like I said, in good order," Bull replied. "If we're staying here for the night, I'm going to try out one of those four-poster beds upstairs. I've not slept for three days and I'm on my chin-strap. Could do with a clean up as well."

Stan looked over at him. He was still dressed in the same, bloodstained jeans he had been wearing during his time trapped in the hospital.

"Good idea," Bobby agreed, indicating the state of Bull's clothing. "You look like you've been hanging about with Hannibal Lecter on his annual 'rude person's' all you can eat buffet."

20

She continued to call out for help from the bedroom window overlooking the street, but no one came to her aid. She pleaded into the night, her terror filled words echoing through the small private estate and falling upon deaf ears.

Everyone was scared. Those who could hear her, pretended that they could not, burying their heads in their hands or beneath pillows, trying desperately to blot her plight from their guilt filled minds.

"Please," she whimpered as her voice began to falter from hours of entreating, *"I'm trapped. Please help me and my baby. Someone help us."*

He could clearly see her, silhouetted from the dim light behind her. She clung tightly to her child, keeping him close and doing all she could to protect him.

Below, a small crowd had formed on her lawn, clambering at the entrances and windows. The thumping continued as they hammered at her door, their noise joining her beseeching cries that lingered in the deathly silent streets.

Earlier in the evening, as the dark of night had begun slowly to spread across the sky, the first of them had shown up. A lone figure, its shoes scuffing against the hard surface of the road, ambled along the street. Its movements were clumsy and it twitched and jerked, as though invisible strings were pulling at its limbs. Nobody knew where it had come from, but it was soon accompanied by others. The houses that remained occupied, extinguished their lights and their owners hid themselves from sight.

The ghostly figures had sauntered along, bumping into parked vehicles and knocking over dustbins and garden ornaments, creating a commotion that attracted more of their kind from the surrounding area. They prowled through the housing estate like a pack of hungry wolves, grunting and growling at their reflections in windows while searching for their prey.

Before long, there were at least twenty of them, scattered along the road, their dark silhouettes standing out against the bright moonlight. At first, it seemed that the infected would continue through the street, passing by the houses and on to wherever they were going.

Then, the sound of a baby's cries stopped them in their tracks. As though someone had pressed a button on a remote control unit, they froze, cocking their heads, listening for where the noises were coming from. Finally, one of them had let out a bone-chilling howl and sprinted towards the house where the woman and her baby lived. The rest, seeing their ghoulish comrade move, followed and began their assault against the walls.

That was seven hours ago, and still, no one had attempted to help the poor woman and her child in any sort of way.

He stepped back and allowed the small gap in the blinds to close as the vertical sheets of material fell back into place.

"Are they those dead people that were on the news?" She asked from behind him, afraid to move too close to the window.

He shrugged, taking a further step back, still staring at the blinds.

"I can't tell if they're dead or sick," he replied. "I don't think it matters, though."

"What should we do?" Emily asked, looking back at him, pleadingly.

Matthew turned to her, barely able to see the left side of her in the darkness while her right, was illuminated by the moon that shone brightly from the street beyond their window.

"There's nothing we *can* do," Matthew whispered back. "There are too many of them out there and it won't take much for them to turn their attention on us."

Emily shook her head, glaring at her husband and unable to accept that her friend, Catherine and her baby, Thomas, would be left to the mercy of the infected.

"We have to do *something*."

"Listen," Matthew hissed, stepping towards her and placing his hands on her shoulders.

His words were filled with belligerence and desperation in his attempt to make her understand what he was about to say.

"We will do *nothing*, Emily. Do you understand? Paula is sick, and we don't know what with. William is scared, and we can't risk putting their lives in danger for the sake of your fucking mate. Do you get what I am saying to you? My heart goes out to Catherine and her baby, it really does, but we need to look after ourselves and forget everyone else. We will do sweet fuck all, Emily."

She turned away from him, understanding some of his reasoning, but baffled by his indifference towards a woman that they had both known for a long time. Just two years before, Catherine and her husband had gone with them on a holiday to southern France, but now, it was as if he could not care less for the stranded and terrified woman.

Emily sat down on the couch, leaning forward with her head in her hands as Catherine's wavering pleas continued to resonate from beyond their windows.

"Her husband was killed a year ago," she said quietly. "Do you remember?"

"Yes, I remember. I went to the funeral, in case you've forgotten. Killed in Afghanistan when his truck was blown up."

Emily nodded as a tear escaped along her cheek.

"Yeah, and now, she's all alone, Matt. She has no one to help her and they will both die over there."

He nodded and sat down beside her, placing his arm over her shoulder, changing his approach to one of understanding and tenderness.

"I know, Emily, and I am very sorry for her and her son, but Paula is sick and we need to look after our own kids without risking them, *or* ourselves. Believe me, if there was anything we could do, I would do it."

Emily suddenly felt her blood begin to surge. An anger that she had not felt in a long time began to rise up within her, screaming at her from inside her own mind.

There's a lot we could do.

"Spineless wanker," she spat through closed teeth as she pulled herself away from him and jumped up from the sofa.

Leaving him sitting there in the dark, stunned and unable to react, she stormed out from the room and into the hallway. She scooped up the cricket bat she had placed by the porch and began hurriedly to remove the chains and locks from their front door.

She worked frantically, unsure whether or not to believe that it was really her that was in control of her body and mind. She did not feel the same. Usually, anything that her husband said or decided would be the final word and the course of action that they would stick to. Now, over the past few days, she had felt different, stronger in her thinking and her actions. Faced with impending danger and knowing that Matthew was unwilling to do what was necessary, or right, she took matters into her own hands.

Finally recovering from his wife's unexpected outburst, Matthew heard the sounds of the chains being released. Realising what was happening, he sprang from the couch and burst into the hallway, seeing his wife about to open their home up to the infected.

"Emily," he cried hoarsely, trying to gain her attention but remain inaudible to the world outside. "What the fuck are you doing?"

She did not turn to speak to him, or even interrupt herself from turning the final key, releasing the bottom dead-bolt in the frame of the door, then reaching for the handle with the cricket bat held tightly in her right hand.

"Something that you don't have the balls to do," she uttered over her shoulder.

Matthew felt panicked. He could see that she was determined to go out there and help her friend, but he could not let her. She would be killed and they would all probably suffer the same fate, shortly after.

He ran forward and grabbed her by the sleeve of her jacket, pulling her away from the door, causing her to lose her grip on the handle before she could turn it.

"Get the fuck off me, Matthew," she growled, shrugging her shoulders and breaking free from his grasp.

She reached for the handle again, her mind set on helping her friend across the street.

Rattled by the sudden change in his wife and her actions, Matthew felt he was about to lose control of her. Unable to stop himself, he grabbed her again and spun her around to face him. Before he knew what he was going to do, his fist shot up from his side and landed against the side of her cheek with a sickening smack.

Her head shot backwards from the force of the blow, straining against the muscles and bones in her neck. She felt her brain clatter within her skull, as though suddenly being knocked free from its foundations. Emily fell back, crashing into the wall of the hallway. Her legs buckled as her eyes rolled upwards in their sockets as darkness took her. Her body went limp and slid down towards the floor.

Matthew stepped back, his fist still clenched at his side and his body shaking uncontrollably. Despite all his faults, he had never hit her before and seeing his wife, unconscious at his feet through his actions, terrified him.

Realising what he had done, he dropped to his knees and began to sob.

"Emily," he pleaded, "I'm sorry, darling. I didn't mean to…"

She groaned, rolling her head, but still oblivious to the world around her.

"I'm sorry," he continued, racked with regret and shame. "I'm sorry, Emily. It was an accident. I would never hurt you, Emily. You must believe me."

He reached out to her and began stroking her hair. Even in the low light, he could see the swelling of her face and the bruise that had already begun to form.

Her head continued to move but her eyes remained firmly shut. As her mind slowly focussed, her features became contorted with pain, feeling the throbbing ache of her cheekbone. She raised her hand towards her face and immediately pulled it away, wincing with agony.

"What…" she mumbled distantly, "what happened?"

Matthew, still sobbing, saw his chance to carry out a degree of damage limitation, attempting to reason with her and justify his actions.

"You were out of control, Emily. You were going to open the door and let those things in. I had to stop you. I…"

Her eyes opened fully and focussed on his. Again, she raised her hand to her swollen cheek and glared back at her snivelling husband as he sobbed over her.

"You hit me," she exclaimed. "You hit me, you bastard."

Even after him knocking her to the floor, she was still aggressive and assertive, unlike the demure woman he was used to.

Again, he stalled in his actions and stumbled on his words while his wife, came to and stole his dominance away from him.

"You fucking bastard," she hissed, climbing to her feet and pushing his arm away as he tried to help her stand. "You hit me, you fucking coward."

Matthew felt his shame begin to ebb away and become replaced with rage. She was speaking to him in a way he had never experienced from her, and it scared him. Subconsciously, he knew that he was physically stronger, but already, she was proving to be the better person, psychologically. His grip on the household was being snatched away from him, at a time when he needed to feel confident in himself and assert his claim to supremacy.

His wife, half his size and a fraction of his strength, was ripping off his testicles and throwing them on to the rubbish pile.

Emily saw his hand form itself into a fist again as she reached her feet and turned to face him square on. She could see his face, creased with anger and turning red as his blood boiled within his veins.

"Go on," she growled up at him with wild eyes that burned deep into his. "Hit me again, and I'll stick a fucking knife through your throat when you're asleep."

He could see that she meant every word and knew that he needed to do something to put his wife back in her place. What he was about to do, he did not know, but a noise from within the house snatched their attention away from one another.

The door to the cupboard beneath the stairs juddered, accompanied with muffled screams. They both turned to look in the direction of the thumps and stared at the lock as the frame struggled to hold it in place.

Paula, gagged and restrained, was assaulting the door from the inside, trying to get out.

21

It was still dark when Stan awoke.

Lying still for a moment, waiting for his brain to catch up with his eyes after fighting its way through the fog of sleep, he stared up at the ceiling. The house was deathly quiet, and with all the holes in the windows and doors, the temperature had dropped considerably. He exhaled, watching his breath form into a mist and disappear into the dark air.

He checked his watch. It was coming up to five o'clock in the morning and still another hour until first light, but he knew that there was no chance of him getting back to sleep. His brain was now fully awake, and already going over the options, they had discussed in detail the night before.

All had agreed that the RAF base was their best option. If the place had been overrun, then they may still be able to find something of use to help them with their journey south. HQ had told them that there were no aircraft available at that time, but they could read between the lines and were all far too long in the tooth to think that, with everything else that was going on, another precious helicopter would be sent to get them.

They were also aware that a number of other military airfields were still in operation in the northern regions of England, but all had agreed that the airbases could be more hassle than they were worth. With the infected running riot across the country and all available military personnel and assets being pulled out, the airfields would be well defended, and as a group of heavily armed men with no identification, they could end up being shot as deserters or a rogue unit, before they even got close.

Instead, they had all decided that they should head for Manchester. The airport to be precise. At that moment, it was being used as a refugee collection centre and Forward Operating Base for the units that would be acting as a rear guard. Thousands of civilians were flocking to Manchester Airport and as the army fought hard to maintain the perimeter, commandeered commercial airliners were flying the refugees out.

There, Stan and his men hoped they would be able to get themselves onto a flight to the Isle of Wight and join in with the rest of the evacuation and the preparations for the counter offensive. Staying on the mainland, they all concurred, would be a death sentence.

He peeled himself from the large couch he had been sprawled across. A faint metallic click echoed through the room as his M4, securely fastened to his tactical vest and held at his side, shifted position and knocked against the butt of the pistol on his hip. Everyone slept with their kit on and their boots still firmly attached to their feet, ready for anything.

He sat up, ran his fingers through his hair and yawned widely, stretching his arms out and releasing the tension from the muscles in his back and shoulders. He winced with the pleasure/pain that he felt as they contracted back into position.

"I'm getting too old for this," he grumbled as he stood up and made his way out through the door.

He crossed the entrance hall and checked the makeshift barricade that they had thrown up to block off the main doors. It looked secure enough and anything trying to get in would be stalled and the men would be alerted in the process.

In the kitchen, he found Brian, sitting on a wooden chair with his feet up on the large table that seemed to fill a good portion of the room.

"Morning, mate," Brian greeted him cheerfully as he stepped through the door and pulled up a seat for himself.

Stan grunted and rubbed his eyes.

"Here."

He looked up and saw Brian leaning across the table and grinning at him, holding out a cup for him to take.

"Get some brew down you. Bloody good coffee, that is."

Stan shrugged as he sipped at the steaming black liquid.

"These people were Royalty, what did you expect…Nescafe?" Stan asked, his voice sounding hollow as he spoke from behind the cup.

Brian chuckled, leaning back on his chair and folding his arms across his chest. They both sat in silence for a moment, savouring the stillness of the night.

Brian looked out and up at the dark sky through the kitchen window and saw the bright white moon glowing against a cloudless backdrop of twinkling stars.

"Looks like it's going to be one of those mornings were the sun and moon are in the sky together," he stated, feeling the urge to say something and shattering the tranquillity.

Stan glanced out and shrugged his shoulders with disinterest.

"What do you think of all this, Stan?" Brian asked, forcing the team commander to contemplate putting his brain into gear.

Stan knew exactly what Brian was referring to. He could have said nothing, or told him that he was not interested in thinking about it right now, but that would have been a lie. Since the day when he had seen a crowd of dead people staring back at him at the destroyed village in Syria, it had played on his mind. Of course, at the time, he had not known what he was looking at, but after Sierra Leone and Nick, he had not been able to think about much else.

Now, everybody knew, and it was everywhere.

"I thought you weren't interested in pondering the whole thing?"

"I've slept since then," Brian replied. "Besides, Bobby is a great bloke and all, but not the sort that I would usually have deep and meaningful conversations with."

"But I am?" Stan asked, placing his cup onto the table and nodding at Brian, informing him that it was empty and needed refilling. "Who do I look like…, Jeremy Kyle?"

Brian shook his head and smiled. With his feet still resting on the kitchen table, he leaned further back on his chair, balancing on the two rear legs. He reached over, stretching his arm out to the stove. With the equilibrium and grace of an acrobat, he scooped up the old-fashioned tin kettle and skilfully shifted his weight, bringing all four chair legs back into contact with the kitchen floor.

"We've known each other for a long time, Stan," he said as he began to refill the cup with hot expensive coffee. "Since the late eighties when you saved me from getting a bullet through my head from the IRA."

Stan nodded. He remembered the operation well.

Brian, born in Belfast, had grown up during the height of the troubles in Northern Ireland. At the age of eighteen, he joined the

British Army and eventually, was recruited into 14 Intelligence Company, also known as 'The Det'.

In the mid-1980s, Brian infiltrated an IRA terrorist cell that was operating in South Armagh, close to the border with the Republic of Ireland. For three years, he remained undetected, helping to smuggle people and weapons across from the south, and organise attacks against security forces in the north.

All the time, he relayed his information back to 'The Det' and in turn, they conducted their own operations based on the intelligence that he had given them.

An extremely covert and complex system of counter terrorism operations, surveillance, disinformation and intricate back stories, were put into place and built up around Brian to give his cover a great deal of depth.

Any operation planned by his cell, or any other cell that he had information about, was thwarted before it could be put into practice and 'The Det', were always careful to conceal any knowledge of the attack from the suspicions of the IRA.

They had to make it appear that bad luck and equipment failure were always to blame, and not the fact that the British and RUC were wise to their plans and allowing them to think for one minute that someone was operating against them from within their own ranks.

At one point, they went to the extent of using a flock of sheep to trigger an explosive device that had been planted beneath a culvert, intended for a British patrol that was due to pass through the area. On another occasion, a careless bulldozer operator, who was actually a member of the SAS, accidentally crashed into the car that had a boot full of explosives and was parked close to a police station. Its heavy thick steel bucket dropped on top of the rear of the vehicle and absorbed most of the blast, resulting in no casualties.

Brian's mission was to remain within the cell and gradually become close to the commander of the South Armagh Brigade. An event that finally took place in 1987.

Over the next twelve months, British Intelligence slowly built their file on the man responsible for all the attacks, kidnappings, murders and other IRA linked crimes in the turbulent county that was known as Bandit Country.

What nobody knew, was that the IRA had begun to suspect that there was an informant within their midst, and that Brian had been singled out. When they began to investigate him further, with their own secret network of information gathering and informants, Brian's cover was removed, layer by layer.

The IRA walked him into their trap like a lamb to the slaughter. As they launched a diversionary strike, intended to draw away the security forces that protected him from afar, they closed in on Brian.

At the time, Stan had been part of the counter terrorist team with the SAS and was the commander of the reaction force, ready to move at a moment's notice to either help their principle, Brian, or act on his intelligence.

As the bombs began to detonate in the town of Markethill, more and more of the reaction force were siphoned off to help with the carnage and the follow up operations. Stan and his team, suspecting the intentions of the IRA, refused to allow themselves to be drawn in and kept their vigil on Brian.

When Stan's gut instincts began to scream at him that something was wrong and that they needed to act, they moved. Disobeying all orders to stand down and allow Brian's cover to remain intact, they jumped into the two Ford Cortina's assigned to them. They raced to the safe house they had seen Brian enter, accompanied by a number of known high ranking and particularly ruthless and sadistic IRA players.

The four of them stormed the building, killing eight terrorists, including the Brigade Commander with a well-placed shot through his mouth before he was able to pull the trigger of the pistol that was being held to Brian's temple.

When he had recovered from the torture he had received at the hands of his captors, Brian repaid Stan in the only way he knew how. Having heard a rumour that Stan had become particularly attached to it, Brian stole the Cortina that had been used by the team during the raid. From there, he smuggled it across the Irish Sea and drove it down to Hereford, presenting it to his emotionally retarded rescuer at Sterling Lines.

Stan had kept and drove the car until the point when the wheels were virtually falling from the chassis.

His face showed no sign, but Stan smiled internally with nostalgia, remembering the old Ford with fondness.

"And now you want to talk about current events?" Stan asked with a slight smirk that Brian could not see in the gloom of the kitchen.

"I'm just curious to know how you see things going. Better than just sitting here in the dark for the next hour, don't you think?"

Stan sighed and shifted in his seat.

"It's clear to see how things are going, Brian. The mainland is lost. How it managed to get that way, is beyond me, but it's gone. If the bulk of our forces manage to get back from the Middle and Far East, then we can recapture it, but until then, it's every man for himself and the majority of people..." he paused and leant forward slightly, nodding with confidence in what he was saying, "will die."

Brian nodded in return, agreeing with Stan's opinion.

"Do you think our forces will get back on time, or even make it back at all?"

Stan shrugged.

"It'll be difficult. They were already bogged down as it was and now, they have to disengage from an enemy who will probably seize the initiative against our weakened forces as they begin to withdraw."

"You think that will happen?" Brian replied with scepticism.

"It's what *I* would do."

"The world's fucked, really, isn't it?" Brian drained the last of the coffee and slammed the cup down on the table.

"Fucking politicians and bleeding hearts. If they had dealt with this properly from the beginning, recognising it for what it was and not pussy-footing about with public opinion and sensitivities, we wouldn't be in this mess."

"Now it's up to the likes of us; the black sheep of society and the kind of people that the world likes to pretend don't exist, to save their arses," Stan added, reading the mind of his friend seated on the opposite side of the table.

"Exactly," Brian concurred.

They both fell silent for a while.

"Do you think *we'll* make it?" Brian finally asked in an indifferent tone, staring out through the window at the black sky.

Stan said nothing.

With everyone packed into the VW van, Marty shifted the engine into gear. He pressed down on the accelerator and the old, but well maintained, vehicle gradually pulled out from the garage.

Struggling beneath the weight of seven men carrying a large amount of weapons and ammunition, the van, excruciatingly slowly, began to gather speed.

"We're not going to get far in this bucket, are we?" Stan commented from the passenger seat and began to fiddle with the old-fashioned analogue radio fitted into the dashboard, turning the dials through a mass of hissing frequencies.

"These things run forever, Stan," Marty replied with a hint of affection for the VW Camper. "I've always wanted one."

"Well, we're not keeping it, and we're not going camping," Bull added from the seat behind him, reaching across and slapping his shoulder. "As soon as we find a tank, I'm cross-decking into that, thanks."

Stan finally give up on the radio, realising that either the aerial was damaged, or all the stations had shut down. Not even the emergency broadcasts were running anymore.

The wheels crunched against the gravel of the courtyard, slipping and struggling to maintain traction. Finally, reaching more compacted ground, the tyres gripped and they headed away from the house.

Taff looked back over his shoulder, watching the old mansion shrink from view as they drove towards the treeline. Fleetingly, he wondered how many years it would take before the building crumbled to dust or was reclaimed by the wild nature around it.

A narrow road led them into a gap in the trees, where the dark shadows of the woods swallowed the path and cast it into gloom. Unable to see more than a few metres ahead of the bumper, Marty flicked on the headlights. They knew that the track snaked through the dense woodland for at least two kilometres, leading out through large iron gates that spanned the entrance to the estate.

In the beams of light that pierced the murkiness, Marty caught a glimpse of something up ahead. In the centre of the track, stood a solitary figure. It was impossible to see any detail from that distance and low light, but as Marty eased off the pedals and reduced his speed, the shape moved.

It began to charge towards them, and even above the chugging engine, they could hear the shriek that it released into the cold air beneath the trees.

"Floor it," Stan ordered, watching the infected body close the gap towards them. "The engine is in the rear, Marty. Run the bastard over."

Marty complied, dropping the vehicle into a lower gear and pressing his foot all the way down to the floor. The engine growled from behind them in the passenger compartment and the revolutions shot into the red on the dashboard as the van continued forward, struggling to increase its momentum.

The figure was still closing, now just thirty metres away.

Stan pulled his pistol from the holster on his hip and thumped off the safety catch.

"For fuck sake," he grumbled, realising that at their current speed, the infected person was unlikely even to notice the impact.

He began frantically to turn the handle for the window, watching it slide down slowly into its housing within the door and willing it to open faster. He leaned out, exposing just his head and shoulders from the passenger door and raised his weapon.

Taking aim at the approaching figure, compensating for the movement of the Camper van, he increased the pressure on the trigger…

Without warning, something crashed into him from the left side of the vehicle, forcing his head to clash with the door frame and knocking the sense out of him for a moment. Suddenly, his body felt heavy and he could feel himself being pulled from the window. His eyes focussed on the ground rushing by below the van and he quickly realised that something was holding on to him.

Clutching the material of his jacket, a pair of hands stubbornly clung from his arm. Its weight hindered him from using the pistol he still held in his hand as he tried to prevent himself from slipping through the open window.

At the end of the clutching hands that gripped so tightly they had begun to pierce his skin through his jacket, he could see a dimly lit face. Its lips were curled back as its teeth snapped up at him and its vacant eyes stared into his own. Its legs, being dragged along the road and battered against the hard surface, slowly began to disintegrate as the tarmac took its toll on the flesh and bone. The woman, her attention focussed solely on reaching up to take a bite from Stan, was completely oblivious to the destruction of her lower limbs.

Another impact, and Stan was vaguely aware of a second body coming around from his right as the hood of the vehicle smashed into the sprinting figure on the road. As it hit the van, it spun and was sent hurtling around towards Stan who was still unable to pull himself back inside.

Before the second infected was able to collide with him, it smashed into the wing mirror with its head and its legs were swept beneath the chassis. In the process, it was rammed into the face of the woman, causing her to lose her grip as they were both pulled beneath the rear wheels that crushed their bodies into the track with an audible squelch.

Finally, Stan was able to pull himself back inside and began to wind the window back up, blowing out a sigh of relief and rolling up his sleeve to inspect the area where her hands had gripped onto him.

"In the future, Marty, we'll just stick to ramming them," Stan said in resignation as he rubbed his wrist. "Saves on ammunition too."

A couple of hours later, after skirting around a small town to the east, they approached the area of the RAF base.

Danny knew the airfield and advised them to approach from the north, towards the rear gate that was less likely to be as heavily defended, or worse, surrounded by infected. A kilometre short, they stopped and Bull, Danny and Taff moved forward to conduct a reconnaissance of the road leading in and the gate itself.

"The place looks deserted, Stan," Taff reported on his return. "The gate is still intact and secure and we saw no sign of anyone in the immediate area of the northern part of the airfield, but we could see smoke and vehicles further to the south. I think it's worth a look."

They broke in through the gate, leaving it open should they need to make a rapid retreat from the base.

They went static for a while as Stan viewed the base through his binoculars. He could see the control tower and the hangers, but was unable to distinguish any details. He could also see the faint columns of smoke drifting up from numerous points around the airfield and further inside the base behind the hangers, where the barracks, facilities, living quarters and administration buildings were.

"Keep it tight, boys," he ordered as he lowered his binoculars. "I don't think we're going to find anyone alive in here."

Driving along one of the runways, they were soon able to see that the base had completely fallen to the infected. The buildings, many of them having lost their windows and doors, lay in ruins, peppered with bullet holes and the black scars of fire. A number of vehicles sat abandoned, some, burned to their frames and the wrecked and ravaged bodies of dozens of people lay scattered all around.

The majority of the dead were wearing civilian clothing, but there were a few that were dressed in the remains of military uniforms, having been brought down by the hordes of infected that had somehow breeched their defences.

The Camper came to a halt in front of one of the large hangers that appeared to remain untouched by the fires that had burned most of the buildings beyond use. The men debussed and as Taff and his team pushed out to provide an over-watch on the area, Stan moved forward with his group.

The air was thick with the smell of aviation fuel, burning rubber and the distinctive stench of decaying flesh. The men felt their bodies stiffen and their grips tighten on their weapons as they moved, their eyes scanning every inch of ground around them and watching the shadows of the buildings and destroyed vehicles for movement.

The huge hanger doors were open slightly, leaving a two-metre gap in the centre. Beyond the threshold, nothing but blackness could be seen. The dark chasm loomed out at the men like the gaping mouth of a giant steel monster as they approached. With their weapons held at the ready and their fingers resting lightly against the triggers, they moved towards the foreboding black void in the doorway.

They took up position at the side of the opening and Stan began to edge his way forward towards the cavernous maw. At the edge of the door, he paused then pushed his head into the gap, just enough to allow him to see inside without silhouetting his body against the light from the outside.

The sharp tang of rotting blood and festering innards struck his nostrils immediately. A second later, his eyes adjusted to the change in the light and he was able to see the carnage that had taken place inside.

The large space of the hanger echoed with strange and haunting noises. Some sounded like a mournful wind blowing in through the entrance, becoming trapped within the walls of the building and drifting through the ceiling rafters. Other sounds were comparable to the lament of a tortured soul, moaning in protest. More noises, resonating across the hard concrete of the hanger floor, appeared beastly and filled with unthinkable horror and pain. They grunted aggressively, growling in the darkness, accompanied with the crack of bones and the ripping of flesh.

Stan pulled his head back, having seen enough and not wanting to remain exposed for too long in case one of them decided to look up.

He looked across to his left and nodded at Marty.

"The place is packed with them," he whispered.

Inside, Stan had seen hundreds of the infected, scattered throughout the hanger. They were obscured by shadow but, in the dim light, he was able to see them glistening with the blood that coated their bodies and the ground all around them as they fought and squabbled over the scraps of human remains.

"What do we do?" Marty asked.

Stan stepped out, moved towards the far end of the doors, and began to inspect the closing mechanism.

"I think the power is out, but we can still get it shut by hand," he whispered to the others as they fell into position behind him.

They looked up at the thick chains, attached to pulleys and wheels that would allow them to seal the doors.

"We'll have to be quick," Bull grunted, understanding what Stan had in mind. "As soon as those doors begin to move, it'll be like a dinner bell to those fuckers."

"Agreed," Stan nodded then keyed his radio. "Taff, we're sealing the doors. The hanger is full of them, so be ready to slot anything that makes it through. We don't know if there are more in the area so don't fire unless you really need to."

"Roger that," Taff replied.

"Why don't we just leave it and fuck off?" Danny asked, glancing back at the ominous gap in the doors.

"If one of those things suddenly decides to take a walk in the sun, they'll see us and we won't exactly make a rapid getaway in that hippy-wagon, will we?" Bull pointed out to him. "Besides, there might be some useful kit around here we could use."

As Stan counted down from three, they positioned themselves on the chains, ready to begin heaving the door closed.

Together, they pulled with all their combined strength, yanking on the chains, releasing their grip and reaching higher to begin the process over again. The heavy steel of the shutters began painfully to rumble along their runners, squealing and grinding as they moved.

As Stan and his men worked feverishly on the chains, Brian watched from his position by the VW Camper. The gap in the heavy doors was closing, but nowhere near fast enough for his liking. He could hear the grating noise of the wheels as they screeched their way along their rails, struggling against the efforts of the men and the corrosion that fought to hold them in place. The clangs of the hangers doors as they jostled in their frames, echoed out across the open space of the airfield, sounding like the beating of a steel drum.

"Come on, you bastard, close," he growled between his teeth as he tightened his grip on his machinegun, pulling it tighter into his shoulder. "Come on…"

With just half a metre to go, a figure suddenly appeared at the entrance and stumbled out from the darkness and into the bright light of day. It looked around in confusion, unsure of what to do at first as the doors continued to shut behind it. Then, it caught sight of the four men to its left, struggling with the chains to force the door through its final few centimetres.

With no time to warn the others, Brian took off towards the hanger, intending to intercept the creature before it reached Stan and his men. The infected man also launched itself into a sprint, silently speeding its way along beside the hanger doors, its arms outstretched and its eyes fixed on its target.

As he closed in, Brian saw the reason for the man's silence. He ran, with his head thrown back and his windpipe and trachea hanging down to his chest. His lower jaw, attached to his face by strands of torn flesh, swayed as he ran, leaving his long bloated and blood soaked tongue hanging out from his ruined mouth.

With a loud bang, the doors finally closed. The huge heavy shutters shuddered as they began to settle into position and already, the sound of pounding fists could be heard from within the hanger, accompanied with the cries and wails of the infected.

Brian flung himself forward, his feet leaving the ground and his shoulder aimed for the body of the man as he continued to run towards the others. He slammed into the side of the infected corpse, launching it into the air and crashing into the hanger wall. The body hit with a wet slap, spattering thick congealed blood in all directions as the impact caused the body partially to explode.

With the momentum of his assault, Brian continued forward, unable to change his direction in mid-flight. He hit the same spot that his target had whacked against, just a spilt second earlier, smashing his head into the hard steel of the hanger door and falling into the putrid remains of the infected man.

He blacked out.

Bull raced across to Brian's aid, reaching his friend just as the diseased creature had managed to crawl on top of him. With a heavy kick, Bull virtually removed the thing's head, snapping the spinal column and sending it sprawling backwards and bouncing into the shutters again.

Marty joined him and helped to drag Brian's limp body away from the danger. They knew that their friend could have sustained serious neck and head injuries, but they needed to get him away from further harm. Together, they hauled him back towards the Camper, where Bobby and Taff lay him out in the back and began to check him over.

The rest of the men pulled back from the hanger, watching the buildings and doorways for any more of the infected.

"How is he, Bobby?" Stan asked, leaning in through the side door and looking down at Brian's bloodied face.

Bobby shook his head, still examining the unconscious man.

"I can't see any blood coming from his ears or anything. His heart rate, breathing, and blood pressure seem normal, so I don't think he has a skull fracture and I can't feel any damage to his spine, but in these conditions, I can't be sure."

"What about internal bleeding?"

"Again, I can't be sure, Stan, but his blood pressure is fine. All we can do is make him comfortable and keep an eye on him, for now."

Stan nodded and turned back to Taff.

"Search in pairs. Check for vehicles, ammunition and anything that could be useful. Don't venture into the main base area. We don't know if there are more of them about."

"You can bet your left bollock that there will be, Stan," Taff commented as he turned to Danny. "Youngster, you're with me. Bull, Marty, check the other hangers."

"Make it quick. We need to get Brian taken care of."

Stan watched as his men set about scouring the area. If there was anything of use, he was sure that they would find it. He stepped back and looked at their Camper van.

"Would be nice to get something a little more robust that this tub," he said, sticking his head back inside and watching Bobby as he worked on Brian.

Bobby nodded, his attention focussed solely on his patient.

"Aye, Stan, it would be even better to have a heli come in and pick us up. We've only gone a few miles, and already, we're a man down."

After a while, Taff returned, empty-handed.

"We found our Black Hawk," he reported to his commander. "Looks like the shit hit the fan while they were in the middle of refuelling. The whole thing, including the two pilots, are burnt to a crisp over the far end at the fuel point. We were only able to recognise it from the serial number stencilled on the tail."

Stan nodded.

"What about vehicles?"

"Nothing," Danny shook his head. "Everything we came across was virtually destroyed. Looks like they bugged out in good order, grabbing everything that could still roll or fly. The place has been picked clean, Stan."

"Where's those two fuckwits? Have they been back yet?" Taff asked, looking around for Bull and Marty.

Stan shook his head and turned to look in the direction he had last seen the pair as they went off to forage.

"You two are the first to get back."

Taff was about to say something, but the sound of gunfire in the distance and coming from between the hangers, stopped him before he could speak. Everybody froze and looked at one another, then turned to see if they could identify where the shots had come from.

"Get in the driver's seat, Taff," Stan ordered with urgency as he caught a glimpse of movement from between two buildings on the right hand side of the hanger they had sealed the doors on earlier.

Danny jumped into the rear, carefully hopping over Brian and side stepping past Bobby who remained at his post as the medic.

"Go, Taff," Stan cried, pointing his hand towards the hanger. "That way. Put your fucking foot down, Taff."

As he forced the vehicle into gear, Taff looked across to where Stan was pointing. Another burst of rapid shots rang out. He saw the movement, but there were too many of them to be able to distinguish individuals. A second glance revealed the two men, Bull and Marty, sprinting for their lives ahead of the crowd that was close on their heels.

Taff, pressing hard on the accelerator and allowing the revolutions to reach their maximum before changing up through the gears, screamed at the dashboard, pleading with it to give him more speed.

"Come on, you bastard. Come on."

The Camper headed for the mass of bodies and the two men racing towards the van. By now, Stan could see the faces of Bull and Marty, sucking in all the air they could and forcing their legs to drive them forward at top speed.

The infected that followed were showing no signs of letting up on their pace and from what Stan could see, they seemed to be closing the gap.

"Don't stop, Taff," Stan shouted. "Keep going, and don't stop or we'll never get enough speed up to get going again."

Taff aimed the old vehicle towards their friends and gunned the engine.

"Stand by on the door, Danny," Stan called over his shoulder as he kept an eye on the two advancing men and the hungry swarm behind them.

By now, the cries and moans of the infected could be heard over the rattling engine of the old Volkswagen. A mass of screaming voices rose up into the air, seemingly filled with excitement and rage as they chased after the men that fled from them.

Bull was running flat out, keeping a tight grip on his machinegun and panting for breath, feeling his fear rising by the second. Marty, being much lighter and more athletic than his friend, had taken the lead and a gap of a few metres had opened between them as they headed for the van that was closing in.

The Camper suddenly spun to its left.

Its wheels screeched and its engine howled as it turned in a circle that was far too tight for what it had been designed to do. Smoke poured out from behind its tyres and as it completed the manoeuvre, momentarily balancing on the two right hand wheels, it almost toppled over onto its side.

A volley of shots snapped through the air, whizzing by Bull as he continued in his run. They cracked the air around him as they slammed into the bodies directly behind, dropping them to the floor and dragging others with them. The mass fall allowed Bull to gain a metre or two, but they still relentlessly charged in his wake.

Marty reached the van and was pulled in by Danny and Bobby, and hurled to the back as they continued to fire at the bodies behind Bull.

The Camper was still moving and beginning to pull out from its tight circle, ready to gather speed. Taff could not allow them to slow any more than they had done already and hoped that Bull still had the stamina to catch up.

Even over the screaming of the infected, Marty could hear Bull's heavy feet slapping against the tarmac and his wheezing breath. As the van turned away from his friend, Marty raised the butt of his rifle and smashed it through the glass of the rear window. It shattered into a million pieces, scattering tiny beads across the asphalt of the runway.

The open door was turned at a forty-five degree angle from Bull, just a few metres beyond his reach. It was turning slowly, and soon, if he did not catch up, would be headed away from him. He could hear the snorts and growls behind him, but he could not afford himself even the most fleeting of glances backwards. It would slow his pace, only slightly, but worse still, he could trip and fall.

"Come on, Bull," Marty encouraged from the rear window, hollering over the noise of his M4 as he ripped off a number of shots in rapid succession. "Move your fucking arse, mate. They're right on top of you."

In his mind's eye, Bull pictured the pale and withered hands of the plague-ridden monsters reaching out behind him, their fingers just centimetres away from his collar, ready to grab him and drag him down into their midst.

With a panic filled gasp as his body surged with fear and adrenalin, Bull felt his legs begin to increase their pace. He reached out for Danny, their hands almost touching as the hot fumes of the vehicle's exhaust brushed against his face.

Another clatter of fire erupted close to his head as Marty continued to empty his magazine into the advancing throng of rampaging snapping teeth.

Bull heard them fall heavily against the runway, their bones smashing as they crashed to the floor and were subsequently trampled by the others as they raced over them.

His fingers came into contact with Danny's, and they closed around one another. With the forward motion of the vehicle and Danny heaving with all his strength, Bull was carried along, his feet barely touching the ground beneath him. Allowing his weapon to hang free, crashing against his blood filled thigh muscles, Bull reached out with his other hand and gripped onto the doorframe.

As the Camper gathered speed, Bull vaulted into the rear compartment.

The crowd continued to give chase, but Taff was able steadily to pull away from them, watching them in his rear view mirror as they began to fall behind. He blew out a loud sigh of relief, blinking the nervous perspiration from his eyes as it poured down over his forehead.

Marty and Bull collapsed to the floor of the passenger area, gasping and screwing their eyes tight from the pain in their legs and chests as the lactic acid began to disperse and their bodies screamed out for oxygen.

"Jesus," Marty panted, leaning back and breathing deeply through his nose as he attempted to bring his exhausted and shaking body back under his control. "They came from the hanger. Fucking hundreds of them."

"Yeah," Bull confirmed, coughing and sputtering between words. "We forgot to check the side door, didn't we?"

Taff drove the van in a wide arc, manoeuvring the vehicle through a one-hundred and eighty degree turn, careful not to allow the speed to drop and giving a wide birth to the mass of bodies that continued to head for them. They passed them by, with twenty-metres to spare from the closest of the infected.

Bull rolled over, coughing uncontrollably and almost vomiting.

"I'm sick of this. That's twice now, I've had to run like a lunatic with those things chasing me," he complained, wiping the bile that dripped from his mouth on the back of his hand.

"What now then, Stan?" Taff asked from behind the wheel.

"We head for Manchester."

"We'll need to find some fuel though, at some point," Bobby added, leaning forward from the rear and peering over Taff's shoulder at the fuel gauge.

Taff steered the Camper towards the exit, headed for the northern gate where they had come through earlier.

"We'll find something," Stan mumbled.

He watched the road ahead, noticing that the sun was beginning to dip towards the horizon and the shadows of the trees stretching out across the ground.

"It'll be dark soon," he said thoughtfully.

22

"Captain Tyler," a voice called out to her from across the room.

She looked up and turned around from her desk, and saw Gerry entering into the Operations Room and making a beeline for her. A young woman, possibly in her late twenties, with dark hair tied up into a neat bun at the back, walked at his side.

Samantha instantly recognised the American Air Force uniform that the new arrival was wearing, but there was something different about it. It looked darker than usual. Normally, the US military were pristine in their appearance, their uniforms crisp and spotless. The woman walking beside Gerry, however, looked bedraggled, and as though her uniform had not been cleaned in weeks.

As they drew closer, Samantha was able to distinguish that the dark patches covering the young woman's clothing, was actually blood.

"Samantha," Gerry said, sounding pleased to have found her and smiling with relief as he shook her hand, "are you ready to go?"

She looked at each of them in turn, feeling confused and caught off guard. She could see in Gerry's eyes what it was that he was referring to, but she could not believe that he was actually expecting her to join the evacuation.

"What are you talking about?" She gasped. "Our lads are still out there, trying to get themselves back here. We can't leave yet."

He shook his head.

"I'm sorry, Sam, I really am, but we can't wait any longer. London has fallen."

He glanced up at the ceiling, as though he was able to penetrate the layers of rock and dirt and see into the infested streets, high above them on the surface.

"So has most of the country for that matter. The whole of our infrastructure is collapsing. The last of the choppers are pulling out, and they won't be back to pick up any stragglers."

"I don't fucking care," Samantha snapped, not having the patience or desire to remain diplomatic. "Stan and his team are headed south towards Manchester as we speak. Brian is hurt and we don't know how badly. They need us to do all we can to pull them out from the shit that *we* dropped them into."

She paused for a moment and Gerry took it as an opportunity to press his argument and continue trying to convince her that she needed to leave. Before he could speak, she raised her hand, pointing a long slender finger at his chest. Her face changed shape and colour, glowing red and contorted with anger.

"Don't bother, Gerry, because I don't want to hear it. Our boys are out there, and as soon as we shut down, they're on their own and we won't have a clue what's happening to them. The mobile networks are crumbling fast and they are unreliable at best. Sat-comms are overwhelmed, but at least here, we have eyes on their progress.

"If, and this is a big fucking *if*, Gerry, by some miracle, a helicopter becomes available, I will know where to send it and still be in comms with them. Running off to the Isle of Wight will leave them cut off. You may be able to toss them away that easily, but *I* see them as more than just a disposable asset."

"No one has a choice in this, Sam. These are orders from Thompson," Gerry protested, trying his best to disassociate himself with the command to leave the team to their own devices. "All personnel are to join the evacuation, immediately."

She shook her head, stubbornly standing her ground.

"What can they do?" She asked with a defiant smile. "Court-martial me? They can go ahead, but I'm not going anywhere until I know we have done everything we can to help the men, and you're a cunt for even contemplating that I would even consider deserting them and leaving them to rot, Gerry."

Her last comment made him blink, and his words become lodged in his throat, unsure if he had heard her correctly. He could see that she was adamant in her decision. Nothing would persuade her to do otherwise and he wished that General Thompson were still there to reinforce his orders and have Samantha dragged to the helicopters if necessary.

Gerry, as the Operations Officer, was the most senior rank left on station, the others having already been evacuated.

"Sam, please," he implored her, "as soon as we get to the other end, we can re-establish comms and see what we can do."

“Save it, Gerry,” she spat, holding up her hand and then turning away from him. “I know how much of a gang-fuck it will be and it will be too late by the time we have our systems up and running again.”

He sighed heavily, feeling his control slipping from his fingers and knowing that he was beating his head against the hardest stone wall on the planet. Samantha was a strong-willed and extremely loyal woman. The sense of duty she felt towards Stan and his men, was surpassed only by her efforts to make them believe that she did not care.

“Okay,” he finally succumbed, speaking in a defeated tone as his shoulders dropped and his body physically deflated as he realised he had lost. “Do what you think you need to do, Sam, but can I ask just one favour?”

She turned back to him, her arms folded tightly across her chest and a scowl carved into her features. Her defences were up and Gerry knew that there was no way through or around them. Only a complete surrender of his own convictions would bring a cease-fire at that moment and he would need to compromise.

“What is it?” She asked, unwilling to show any cooperation or sign that she was prepared to negotiate.

“When I get to the island, I’ll do my best to get the Ops up and running as soon as I get there. Hopefully, within the next twenty-four hours, we will have comms and a full over-watch on Stan and the lads. Once we’ve established comms, will you drag your stubborn arse out of here and join us?”

A smile, both of victory and satisfaction, threatened to crease her lips, but Samantha fought against it and managed to keep her poker face intact.

“Once you’re up and running, Gerry, but not a moment before,” she nodded.

“Great,” Gerry answered, feeling relieved that they had reached a settlement. “I’ll cover for you and if The Prince of Darkness asks, I’ll tell him you’ve gone sight-seeing around the island, or something like that.”

Samantha finally smiled.

“In the meantime,” Gerry continued, turning his body slightly and indicating the woman standing beside him. “I’d like to introduce you to Lieutenant Frakes. She is your pilot and the poor soul you have just stitched up to stay in this hell-hole with you. I'm sure she'll be pleased about that."

Samantha suddenly felt a pang of guilt. She reached out, shook the American pilot's hand, and smiled apologetically, unsure of how to react or what to say.

"Melanie, please call me Melanie," the pilot replied in a distinct New York accent. "I don't see the point in using rank with all that's going on."

Samantha looked at them both with concern.

"No, you should leave. Honestly, I'll be fine here. Jonesy and Emma have already said that they won't leave until I do. You should join the evac, Lieutenant."

She paused and corrected herself.

"Sorry, I mean, Melanie. We have weapons and can take care of things. There's no need to risk anyone else."

Gerry shook his head resolutely.

"No chance, Sam. If this place falls, you need a way out. The Lieutenant will stay, ready to pull you out at a moment's notice. I'm not leaving you stranded and me having to face Thompson, being forced to explain why his favourite captain was left to rot. That's a rock and a hard place that I don't want to find myself wedged into."

Samantha almost blushed. She had no idea that General Thompson thought so highly of her, but it would explain why he was always more understanding and lenient to her rebellious moments.

"Okay," she finally nodded and turned to Melanie, "I'm really sorry to drag you into this. It's not what I wanted."

The Lieutenant smiled back at her sympathetically and looked down at the state of her own uniform.

"Don't worry about it. It will give me the chance to clean up a little. Besides, it's good to meet someone who cares what happens to their troops. You're tenacious, I'll give you that."

She reached up and began to untie her hair, sighing with relief as she felt the tension ease from her scalp. She ran her fingers through the knots that had formed in her long brown locks, massaging them with the tips of her fingers.

"We were the last to make it out from Lakenheath. The place fell pretty quickly once the perimeter was breached. Our commanders; they either died in the fighting, or fled. Most of our people never made it."

Again, she looked down at the encrusted blood stains, smeared all over her grey and dark blue camouflage patterned uniform.

Her voice became hollow, and filled with sadness.

"Me and my crew, we had to fight our way through hundreds of our friends. They had turned and were attacking us. When we finally made it to our aircraft, there was only me and the co-pilot left."

The three of them remained silent for a moment, seeing that the young woman was vividly remembering the events that had brought her there.

"You sound like you could do with a brew," Samantha finally said, making light of the atmosphere and encouraging a smile from Melanie. "We British folk can deal with *anything*, as long as we have a cup in our hand."

"Right then," Gerry began as he took a step forward and grabbed Samantha by the hand. "Twenty-four hours, Sam. It's time for me to leave, but I promise that I'll get the Ops up and running as quickly as I can. Good luck."

"You too, Gerry."

He turned away and headed out through the door where his security team waited for him on the other side, ready to escort him to his aircraft and to join the evacuation.

Samantha walked away and returned a few minutes later, placing a plastic cup, filled with coffee, on to the desk where Melanie had taken a seat. She paused for a moment, considering her approach then, began asking the questions that she had been fighting the urge to bombard her with while Gerry was still lurking within earshot.

"What kind of aircraft is it? How much fuel do you have?"

"It's a CH-47, a Chinook," Melanie replied. "Not much in the way of fuel though, I'm afraid. Just enough to get us to the Isle of Wight, hopefully."

She looked up and watched the response of Samantha as she took a sip from the cup. She could see that the captain was working something out in her head and Melanie believed that she knew exactly what she was contemplating.

"I know what you're thinking, but we won't make it. The helo is pretty banged up as it is, and with our current fuel levels, we wouldn't be able to reach your guys and make it back. We would end up having to ditch somewhere."

"Shit," Samantha hissed.

That was her plan scuttled before it could even be seriously considered, never mind put into practice. She suddenly felt deflated and sighed heavily.

"Where's your co-pilot?"

"On the landing pad with the Chinook," Melanie replied, motioning towards the door with a slight cock of her head. "He'll stay there until we're ready to leave. Gerry was kind enough to supply us with a couple of guys to fill the gaps in our aircrew. They'll act as our door gunners if need be. We have plenty of weapons and ammo, but only dregs in terms of fuel and I don't know of anywhere else to get any."

Samantha pictured the aircraft in her mind's eye. She knew where the landing pad was; along one of the tunnels and up into the basement of one of the high-rise office blocks. To get to the roof, they would need to climb the stairs behind the service elevator of the offices. All in all, it would probably take them at least seven minutes to get there, and that was on a good day, without the added threat of dead people chasing them.

She reached under her desk and pulled out a green canvas satchel. A number of metallic clunks resonated from within the bag as she placed it onto the table. Next, she pulled out her rifle, a British Army issued SA80-A2.

She pulled back the cocking lever, checked the chamber and then proceeded to slide in a full magazine that she took from the canvas 'grab-bag'. Next, she chambered a round. The sound of the working parts slamming forward, echoed loudly through the high ceilinged room, both unnerving and reassuring in the same instance. She checked the safety catch then slung the weapon over her shoulder.

"I'll be keeping this close," she said with a smile, looking down at the young blood spattered pilot.

"I don't blame you," Melanie smiled back at her and patted the pistol that was secured in the drop holster attached to her thigh.

"That's Jonesy, over there," Samantha said, stepping away from her desk and pointing over her shoulder to a young red haired man who was barely visible in the dimly lit Operation's Room. "He's our comms guru."

She turned and directed her attention at him.

"You're a proper nerd aren't you, Jonesy?"

"Why?" The man asked without looking up from his post. "Just because I know how to turn on a computer and like to play World of Warcraft?"

"Well that's two steps closer to being a nerd than most people, I suppose," Melanie added quietly with a grin.

Samantha nodded her agreement and smiled. Already, she was warming to the young American, seeing that despite the horror she had obviously been through, her character refused to be broken.

"That over there," she said, indicating another shadowy figure who had begun to move towards the coffee machine. "That's Emma."

The woman waved, only fleetingly giving Samantha and the Chinook pilot her attention, then continuing on with what she was doing. Melanie was barely able to make out any details of her in the darkness, but the one thing that she could clearly identify, was the dull glint of gun metal from the rifle that she too, carried slung over her shoulder.

"What happened at Lakenheath?" Samantha asked, turning her attention back to Melanie.

She was curious to know how such a strongly defended base could crumble into complete anarchy so easily.

Melanie shook her head.

"I really don't know," she replied in confusion. "We had been out for almost twenty-four hours, running rescue missions and supporting the ground units that were being forced back and getting overrun. We were exhausted and trying to get some rest, then the alarms went off and the guns started."

She hesitated for a moment.

"It was total chaos. People were running everywhere. The base was full of refugees and I think that's how they got in. No one knew what was happening and people were being caught in the crossfire.

"We had to run," she added with a hint of shame. "There was nothing we could do, so we ran. Mike, my co-pilot and I were the only ones to get out from our unit. The rest of them..." she shuddered at the memory and screwed her eyes shut. "They were killed and...eaten by those things out there."

Samantha nodded sympathetically, clearly seeing the grief and terror that her new friend was going through.

"Now you're stuck here because of me? I'm sorry, Melanie."

The Lieutenant looked up, wiped the tear from her eye, and forced a smile.

"Hey, don't worry about it, Sam," she said in a breaking voice but trying her best to sound upbeat. "It's our duty. The world may be screwed up, but we still have a job to do. You want to help your guys, and *I* want to help *you*."

For the next couple of hours, Samantha ran through their operation with Melanie, telling her about the team make-up and what their mission had been. She showed her the bio readouts of the team and how they were overlaid onto real-time satellite imagery. She explained how Jonesy was keeping track of their movements and staying in communications with them, while Emma kept her eyes on the countrywide events that could possibly have an impact on the progress of Stan and his men.

Emma pointed to the screen in front of her, showing a digital map of the country with various colours, indicating the status of the different cities and towns. Even the road systems, airports and harbours were highlighted, and depending on their colour, they were listed as safe, under attack, or overrun.

Melanie gasped as she leaned forward and stared in disbelief at the monitor. There were more patches of red than there were of any other colour, and as she continued to look, a flashing amber light turned to a constant red.

She squinted and read the name of the city.

"Liverpool," she said aloud.

Emma nodded.

"There's more and more of them falling by the minute. Yesterday morning, the greens outnumbered the reds and ambers. Now, there are only a few places left that are considered safe. London fell this afternoon."

Emma tapped the screen with the tip of her half chewed pen, indicating a blue dot that pulsed within the area of London. The entire city and its outlying districts were swathed in red and the roads leading out, were the same deep crimson, looking like a bloody splat that had been dropped on the capital of the United Kingdom.

"That's us," Emma said with a heavy sigh and raising the pen back to her mouth. "An island of blue, in an ocean of red."

"My God," Melanie gulped, "how long do you think it will be until the whole country is overrun?"

"Hours, days," Jonesy shrugged from his desk. "Who knows? The only thing we *do* know is that it will definitely fall."

On his screen, Melanie saw the seven red dots of Stan and the others. At the side, she saw the bio-readouts of each of them. Every few seconds, the dots changed their position on the map, having been updated from their satellite trackers.

"They're heading south," Jonesy began, feeling a responsibility to give the newcomer a brief outline of what was happening. "At the moment, they're about a hundred miles north of Manchester. They're heading for the airport and one of the last places in the north-west that is still securely in our hands."

He pointed to the airport and Melanie glanced at the city to the left of the screen.

"But Manchester has fallen, it's all red," she noted. "And the area of the airport is flashing amber…"

Samantha nodded.

"Yeah, they're under siege. The infected have completely surrounded them but the perimeter is holding, for now."

"How will your men make it through?"

"Stan and his boys are the best at what they do, Melanie," she smiled proudly. "They could get into the Queen's underwear drawer, sit there for a week and no one would know they were there. If there's a way through, they'll find it."

Now, there was nothing left to do, but wait.

Jonesy kept in regular communications with the team through the satellite communications, and Emma passed on any updates on the routes they were taking and any large concentrations of infected.

By midnight, Stan had informed the Operation's Room that they were going to try to find a place to hole up for the night and hopefully, find fuel.

"You should try and get some rest too," Samantha suggested to her new friend.

"Yeah," Melanie replied, brushing her hands down over her uniform and grimacing in disgust as she inspected her palms. "I think I'll get that clean up I've been promising myself. Is there anything around here that I could change into?"

Samantha was about to answer. Then, the lights went out.

The room was cast into complete darkness. Everybody froze in position, gripped by terror as the cold blackness enveloped them.

"*Shit*," someone hissed.

"What is it? What's happening?" Melanie's American accent, filled with anxiety, was distinct as she called out.

"The main grid. I think the main power-grid has failed," Jonesy replied from somewhere deep within the room.

A bright shaft of light suddenly breached the darkness, silhouetting Jonesy's body as he clasped the torch between his teeth and illuminated the control panel attached to the wall that he had set about inspecting.

Another beam of light joined the first as Samantha began checking the computers and screens that had gone blank when the power failed.

"What about back-up generators? Don't you have them?" Melanie asked as she drew her pistol, suddenly feeling afraid of what may be lurking in the dark.

"Yes, we do," Emma replied, "but they're not kicking in. They should've automatically come on by now."

"All systems are down," Samantha announced as she stepped back from the computers. "We're completely blind."

She looked down at the Iridium phone in her hand and saw on the glowing yellow screen that the signal was gone. With the power out, the antenna, which was fixed to the office buildings above ground, was not able to transmit of receive and they would not have communications again until they were on the surface. Without a line-of-site signal to the communications satellites, orbiting high above the earth's atmosphere, they were in a dead spot.

“Fuck,” Samantha growled.

Without the Iridium, contact with the team was impossible without them exposing themselves above ground.

“Do you think the power will come back on?” Emma asked optimistically, as she stepped up behind Jonesy and took over control of the saliva smeared torch he had been gripping between his teeth.

“I doubt it,” he replied as he continued to stare at the blank control panel. “The whole thing is dead and there’s nothing we can do from down here.”

“What do we do?” Emma asked. Her voice had begun to break.

“How the fuck should *I* know?” Jonesy snapped back at her, turning away from the control panel and picking up his light. “Ask Captain Tyler. She’s the one in charge here, not me. I’m just the fucking nerd, remember?”

Emma turned and headed for the captain. Half way across the room, she stopped dead in her tracks.

From beyond the door, and somewhere high above them, they heard the distinct sound of gunfire. Shots, fired in rapid succession, boomed through the darkness, carried along the narrow corridors and down through the tight stairwells.

Other noises soon joined in with the cracks of the guns.

They were the sounds of people dying. Screams from the men and women who had still not been evacuated, rang out in blood curdling cries. The thudding crashes and bangs as doors gave way and defences crumbled, reached the ears of the people in the Operation’s Room, confirming that the bunker had fallen to the infected.

“Shit,” Samantha said quietly, staring up at the dark ceiling, “they’re inside.”

23

Banks of thick grey clouds had drifted in across the night sky, obscuring the moon and preventing its light from penetrating through to the land below. As a result, the small private estate had become a jumble of long dark shadows and blackened buildings, and any detail had become impossible to distinguish.

In the house across the road, Catherine and her baby had long since fallen silent. The infected had finally managed to break in through the door and for a while, her screams had filled the night air. Even then, no one had rushed to help her.

The houses lining either side of the road remained dark and still as their owners hid behind their protective walls and doors, cowering in the shadows and hoping that they would not be detected by the creatures that stalked their way through the outside world.

In the silence, even the slightest noise seemed to echo like the reverberations of ringing church bells. Throughout the nights, crashes and bangs were carried for miles on the wind and the sounds of agony and terror rang out as people were set upon by the dead.

Everyone had heard Catherine's cries, but they were scared, terrified of stepping outside.

Matthew, standing by the window and peeping through the gap in the blinds, watched the dark figure with curiosity as it made its way along the gloomy street.

It was different from any of the others he had seen. It moved with purpose and coordination, creeping between the parked cars, pausing at each one for a few moments before moving on to the next.

He could not see any details of the figure, only the dark outline, but it was clear that whoever it was, they were alive, and not one of the infected bodies that lurched through the estate, searching for living flesh.

"Emily," he whispered, not wanting to take his eyes from the street and instead, vigorously waving his hand behind him to get her attention.

The low soft rumble of his wife's gentle snoring came as her reply.

"Emily," he hissed, louder and more urgently than before.

He reached out with his foot and kicked at the bed, his toes just about reaching the mattress and able to make it shift beneath her.

"Wake up, Emily."

With the sudden movement of the springs below her, she woke with a start, forcing her body upright and her eyes darting about the room with shock and dread, trying to identify the threat before it was too late.

"What, what is it?" She asked, searching through the darkness for her husband, her eyes still adjusting to the dimness. "Where are you, Matt? What's happening?"

Matthew remained quiet for a moment, an invisible smile stretching his lips as he watched the confused and distressed reaction of his wife.

"It's okay, Emily, I'm here."

He waved to her from the side of the window, hoping that his hand movements would be easier for her to see against the faint ambient light that managed to penetrate into the room from the outside.

She crawled across the bed and stepped over to join him where he stood hidden by the long thick curtains. Instinctively, she pressed herself close to him, needing to feel his body in close proximity to hers.

She still hated him for hitting her, but under the circumstances, she understood what had driven him to do it. He was afraid, just as she was. Remembering the incident, she subconsciously raised her hand to her face and gently pressed at her swollen cheek.

He had never laid a finger on her before, and with all that was going on, she was able to forgive his reactions, to a degree.

However, she had vowed to herself, if he ever did anything like that again, regardless of the circumstances, she would make good on her promise and drive a knife through his throat while he slept.

"What's happening?" She whispered.

"Take a look," Matthew replied in a hushed voice, nodding down into the street. "There's someone out there. Someone living."

She looked along the road and saw the shadows of the infected, lurking around a number of houses, trampling across lawns and staggering along the curb-side. At first, she was unable to see what

Matthew was looking at, but then she caught a glimpse of movement from the corner of her eye. It was fast and deliberate movement. Motion that was only capable from someone that was uninfected by the virus.

She looked closer and focussed. There, she saw the silhouette of a man, making his way towards them, bounding between the static vehicles, carefully and silently, and passing through the infested estate.

"He's alive," she stated.

She was about to turn to her husband, but something else caught her attention. There was more movement, further along the street. A dark shape was following the man's progress, noiselessly travelling along in the middle of the road.

By now, the living man was just a few houses away, still hopping from vehicle to vehicle and the bulky object gliding along behind him.

"Oh my God," Emily gasped, "he has a van following him."

Matthew screwed his face in confusion, wondering if he had heard his wife correctly, or if she had seen something he had missed. Making a separate gap in the blinds, he peered out to see for himself.

Emily had not been mistaken at all.

A van, an old style Volkswagen Camper from what he could tell, was quietly gliding along in the man's wake. On closer inspection, Matthew realised that there were more men at the rear of the vehicle, pushing it from behind, while one of them remained inside to steer.

"Jesus," he said, his breath misting against the cold glass as he leaned closer to the window to get a better view. "What are they doing?"

The first man was now directly in front of their house. He stopped at the side of a car and then suddenly stood up and signalled to the others with the van. Slowly, and without making the slightest sound, the Camper pulled up alongside of him and came to a complete stop. Two of them remained in the area between the two vehicles while the others fanned out into a circle, crouching down behind other static cars and intently watching the area.

Matthew strained to see what the two men were doing in the gap between the Camper and the estate car that they had stopped beside of. Then, he realised what was happening.

"They're siphoning fuel, I think," he whispered to Emily, watching the scene, totally absorbed in the events taking place outside of their house.

"Holy shit, and they have guns," he exclaimed, pointing to the nearest of the men and the long slender object he carried in his hands. "They must be soldiers, or police, or something like that, but they're definitely armed."

In his excitement, Matthew had caused the blinds to move, attracting the attention of the closest of the men. Remaining in cover, crouched behind the next door neighbour's people carrier, the man swivelled and brought his rifle around, aiming it at Emily and Matthew as they peered down at him through the window.

Both of them froze to the spot, inhaling a silent gasp as they waited for a torrent of gunfire to burst through their bedroom window that would end their lives.

After a couple of seconds without the expected projectiles ploughing through their window and bodies, Matthew peeked through his half-closed eyelids.

The man had already turned his attention elsewhere, having realised that there was no threat and continuing to cover the street.

Matthew, his heart beating loudly in his ears and his knees suddenly feeling weak, pivoted away from the window and pressed himself against the hard cover of the wall. He blew out the long gusting breath that he had been holding and felt his body begin to tremble.

"Fucking hell," he gasped, "I thought he was going to shoot us."

Emily had not moved. She remained at the blinds, watching what the men outside were doing and following their progress.

Silently, she cursed her husband for his cowardly and self-preserving reaction.

A muffled shriek erupted from down the stairs and was soon accompanied by loud crashes and bangs that were deafening in the silent night.

Once again, Paula was assaulting the door of her cell beneath the stairs, barging her body at the barrier to get out and screaming that awful pain filled and hateful wail beyond the gag that appeared to be slipping from position around her mouth.

Matthew and Emily looked at one another, their eyes blazing with terror and grief as they listened to their daughter and the horrifying sounds that emitted from her. Never in their lives had they heard such a noise and the fact that it was coming from their precious little girl, was more distressing to them as they pictured Paula causing herself all sorts of harm while she viciously attacked the solid door of the cupboard.

Emily reached up and clasped her hands over her ears, shaking her head and crying, trying to blot out the heartrending pain that the wails of her daughter caused her.

Matthew, realising that the noise could probably be heard in the street, stepped back to the window.

The men below were moving, turning their bodies and pointing their weapons in all directions. At first, he wondered if they could hear Paula and were looking for where the noise was coming from, then he saw the multitude of figures that were closing in from the peripherals, headed towards the epicentre of the sound and inadvertently, closing in on the seven men in the street below.

As the racket of Paula's assault continued to haunt their souls, tearing at their hearts and their minds, Matthew looked on as the circle of death slowly tightened around the soldiers. The closest of them looked up at the window again, feeling no need to raise his rifle this time. He turned around, and Matthew believed that he was saying something to the others. A few more heads swivelled and glanced in his direction.

By now, Matthew could no longer hear his daughter. He had managed to blot her from his thoughts as he became more concerned with what the heavily armed men, just metres from their front door, were intending to do next.

Two of them stood up from their positions behind the cars and stepped out on to the pavement. Together, moving with stealth, they headed for the house and within seconds, Matthew could no longer see them due to the downward angle.

"Shit," he whimpered, "they're at the door."

Emily still had her hands covering her ears, shaking and sobbing uncontrollably. He grabbed her and shook her vigorously, attempting to snap her attention back to reality and focus on the present situation.

She looked up at him, her eyes glowing red with anguish and glistening with tears. Her face was pale in the low light that shone through the window, and even in the semi-darkness, Matthew could see her lips quivering uncontrollably.

"Emily," he began sternly, "darling, you must keep it together. Those men outside, they're on their way here. They have guns, Emily, and I don't think we will be able to stop them from coming in."

A sound at the entrance to their bedroom made them both spin around with fright. William was clearly shaken by the stifled wails of his sister and they could hear him whimpering, even above the screams and thumps from below the stairs.

Matthew turned back to look into the street.

The ring of infected were closer, zeroing in on the noise coming from Paula, but they did not seem to have noticed the men, as yet. The rest of the soldiers were also moving, headed to join the other two at the porch.

One of them, he noticed, looked hurt and was being half carried by one of the others, his arm wrapped around the neck of his teammate for support as he hobbled and staggered towards the house.

"Open the door," a calm and toneless voice suddenly called out through the darkened hallway, drifting along up the stairs and into the bedroom where Matthew and his family stood shaking with fear.

Matthew felt his blood freeze in his veins and stared down at his wife and son, unable to form his thoughts or even respond to the man's words.

Again, the voice called up to them.

"We know you're in there. Now open the door."

Still, the man sounded calm, despite the multitude of flesh eating ghouls that were converging on his location.

"Listen, mate, we know that you're in there, so you have two choices; either come down and let us in, or we kick our way in."

The man paused for a moment, then with unmistakable malice in his tone, called out to the occupants again.

"Now, open the fucking door."

"We've no choice. We have to let them in," Matthew said to his wife as he stepped out onto the landing and leaned over the bannister, staring down at the shadows that moved beyond the frosted glass panels.

"But," she began to protest, stammering her words, "but, they might shoot us."

Matthew shook his head as he began to descend the stairs.

"If they were going to shoot us, I think they would've already done it. But if we *don't* let them in, then there's a chance they *will* shoot us."

He reached the entrance to their home and paused for a moment, steeling a deep breath as he stretched his arm up for the first lock at the top. Paula continued to hammer away from inside the cupboard behind him, screaming so loudly that his ears buzzed and pressed inwards against the sides of his head.

It was clear now that the material they had secured over her mouth, had completely slipped from its position.

He could see the movement of the men outside and hear their anxious whispers as they identified the closing threats to one another. From what Matthew could tell, they were getting ready to force their way into the house.

"Wait," he called out through the glass, "wait, I'll let you in."

With shaking hands, he set to work on releasing the locks and dead bolts that held the door firmly in place against the frame. Finally, there was just the handle left. He twisted it and as the lock slipped from its housing, the barrier suddenly sprang open, crashing against his left temple and sending a blinding flash across his vision. He stumbled backwards; distantly aware of the bulky shapes beginning to pour into the hallway.

With a thud, the entrance was sealed.

As his senses drifted back to him, Matthew found himself looking back up the stairs at his wife and son as they remained on the landing, fearfully watching the new arrivals as their large dark frames filled the area at the bottom of the stairs.

Matthew turned around and saw nothing but blackness. For a split second, his mind spun with confusion but quickly realised that he was staring at the massive back and shoulders of a man that must have weighed twice as much as he did.

With nowhere else to go, he had no choice but to step back up onto the bottom rung of the stairs. From there, he was able to see the men that had entered into his home. At the moment, they paid him no attention as they stood in a tight circle, deep in a hushed discussion.

Paula's screams suddenly abated and the clatter of the door faded to a half-hearted thump. The men fell silent and looked in the direction of the space beneath the staircase.

Still, they remained oblivious to Matthew.

Finally, feeling the urge to gain their attention, he let out a low grumbling cough. The seven heads, blackened by shadow, turned to look up at him. For a long moment, they just stared at him, not moving and saying nothing. Then, they turned away and continued their whispered group conference.

Behind them, dark shapes began to flutter across the glass of the door and soon, the first of the fists clashed against the heavy frame. The door shook, and Matthew suddenly felt panicked, realising that he had not locked it tight after the men had piled in over the threshold.

"It's alright," said the same calm voice that had called up to them from the letterbox. "We locked it while you were busy dancing about the hallway. It'll take them a while before they can get in. The porch is too narrow for them to combine their weight and at a bad angle to the driveway for them to get any leverage."

"Yeah," another hushed voice agreed mockingly. "Thank fuck you're a keen gardener and planted those bushes so close to your door."

"Aye," another of the men concurred, "they bloom lovely during the summer, Bobby."

Together, the seven men moved away from the hall and headed to the rear of the house and into the kitchen. Matthew followed and Emily and William gingerly crept down the stairs, hesitating at the bottom as they watched the ghostly shadows that beat at the entrance to their home. They moaned incessantly, but gone was the vigour in their efforts and the aggression in their voices. Since Paula had ceased her assault, there was no more noise to stimulate their excitement.

In the kitchen, Matthew watched the men as they set about searching through the cupboards, scouring with their pinpointed LED lights and rummaging through the family's food stocks. He did not protest, afraid of provoking them, but he felt that he needed to say something, *anything*, to get them to acknowledge his existence.

He felt someone move behind him and turned to see his wife and son standing in the doorway, glaring back at him with uncertainty. He could see their fear filled eyes shining in the gloom. They stared at him, turning to him to protect them from the band of armed and frightening men that had invaded their home.

"I'm Matthew, and this is my wife and son, Emily and William," he stated, in a voice that held more than a hint of trepidation.

One of the men stopped and handed the carton of orange juice that he had been glugging from, to the man standing next to him. He gasped and let out a stifled burp, then wiped his mouth on the back of his gloved hand.

"Pleased to meet you," he said, without bothering to introduce himself.

Matthew, once again, recognised the voice as the calm mannered, but intimidating man who had called to them to let him in. Already, Matthew was scared of him. He had seen nothing of his features and heard only a few of his words, but the man had an aura of terror about him and it chilled him to the bone.

Another of them stepped forward. In the beams of light that flitted about the room, Matthew was able to see the camouflaged patterned vest that he wore and the multitude of pouches attached to it, stuffed with rifle magazines. His face, covered with grime and sweat, did not appear threatening. Although he did not smile as such, his eyes did not convey any malicious intent.

"I'm Bobby," he said and then turned to his left, indicating the man with the frightening voice who had gone back to draining the last of the orange juice. "And that scary old bastard is our leader, Stan. He's a big teddy-bear once you get to know him."

"I'm Matthew," he nodded in return.

"Yes," Bobby replied, "you've already told us that."

A number of flashes emitted from the rear of the room, and shortly afterwards, an orange glow lit the kitchen. One of the men had found a large candle and placed it onto the kitchen work surface, illuminating him from below and making his hard features dance with the flickering flames.

"That's better," his gruff voice snorted, clearly pleased with the difference that the dim light from the candle had made. "Now I can see what I'm eating. I just threw a fucking Oxo cube down my neck, thinking it was chocolate."

Matthew recognised the man as the huge bulk he had found himself wedged behind and pressed up against the wall by when they entered.

Bobby took another step closer, his face shrouded with shadow and nothing but blackness. He shone his light over the three family members and paused when he saw Emily.

"Looks like someone was talking, when they should've been listening, eh?"

Emily raised her hand and covered the large bruise on her cheek bone and turned away from the scrutinising eyes of the soldier standing before her.

Bobby turned his light to her husband and glared at him accusingly. Matthew, feeling ashamed and afraid, looked down at his feet.

"You have an infected in the house. A loved-one, I presume?"

Matthew turned to him, suddenly feeling defensive.

"Yes," he nodded, "my daughter, Paula. She's sick."

"Sick? Is that what you think this thing is? She has a cold or something?" Someone asked sarcastically from the rear of the room.

"She's infected, Matthew," Bobby continued. "Believe me, there is no cure for this, and she won't get better. You saw the news?"

He nodded, feeling his throat tighten and the atmosphere in the room change from one of indifference to one of impending danger.

"This virus is like nothing the world has seen, mate. Believe me, because I've seen most of them. How long ago did she become *sick*?"

"Two days ago," he croaked, stepping back and reaching out for his wife's hand for support. "She got sick two days ago. She became uncontrollable, so we tied her up and locked her in the space beneath the stairs."

Bobby glanced at their group leader.

Stan nodded, giving a silent command.

"Okay," Bobby began with a sigh, "now listen. You've seen the broadcasts, but probably refuse to believe them, right?"

He did not wait for a reply and instead, nodded towards the door leading into the hallway, indicating the outside world.

"Those people, out on the street, they're dead. They're not sick, and they won't get better. Believe me, we've seen enough of it to know and we've already lost one of our guys to those things."

"Paula's not dead," William said protectively, his voice breaking with despair as he clung to his mother's waist, "she's just very ill and when this is all over, she'll be okay."

Bobby shook his head.

"I'm really sorry, little man, but you need to understand."

He looked back at Matthew.

"You *all* need to understand. This won't be over. This thing is worldwide and even the big and powerful countries like the US and Russia are crumbling. Anyone that catches the virus, will die. Anyone coming into contact with the people carrying the virus, will die. Your daughter, *isn't* your daughter anymore. Anything that she ever was, died with her, and now she is just like those things out there."

"I understand that it's hard to accept, but it's the truth and you *need* to accept it, or you won't survive this," another voice offered from the darkness of the kitchen.

Emily began to sob and buried her face against her husband's chest, feeling her legs weaken as what she had already known, was spelled out to her. She had watched the broadcasts and listened to the doctors, but when Paula had fallen ill, she refused to believe that her little girl could be taken away from her and become one of the monsters that were attacking people and spreading their infection across the world.

Matthew could see the change in the attitude of the men. They had gone from one of apathy towards the family, to becoming completely focussed on them. He began to fear that they were being viewed as a hindrance, or even a threat.

"What are you going to do?" He asked, swallowing hard as a tall slender figure stepped forward from the rear of the group.

"I'm sorry," Bobby continued sympathetically. "Our only form of transport is stuck in the road. We managed to get some fuel siphoned, but those things are stopping us from reaching it. You saw how your daughter's screams attracted every one of them from the surrounding area. Right now, she's quiet, and hopefully, those things will lose interest and go away, but we can't risk her making more noise and bringing them back. Plus, she's too dangerous to keep in the house. If she got loose, she could infect us all."

Matthew stared back at them, watching the tall man approach and then, saw the glint of the knife he held in his hand. Shaking his head, he stepped back into the doorway, shielding his wife and son behind him.

"No," he pleaded, "no, please. You can't."

The men followed and closed in on them. In a flash, two of them had forced the family members into the rear dining room and blocked the door with their bodies. Matthew, suddenly feeling like an animal backed into a corner by a hungry predator, charged forward.

Before he reached his target, a hand shot up and caught him, stopping him in his tracks and gripping him by the throat. Immediately, he became completely helpless as the fingers closed around his windpipe, squeezing him like a vice for a moment, and then tossing him back towards his family.

"Don't," the voice growled down at him, "I'll kill you if I have to."

The three of them huddled together, cowering beneath the menacing shadow of the huge man standing over them.

Bobby pushed his way through into the room and struck the man shaped mountain across the chest with the back of his hand.

"Fucking hell, Bull," he snarled, "you're scaring the shit out of them."

"Sorry, I just didn't want them to see." Bull replied innocently.

Bobby reached down and grabbed William from his parents, picking him up in his arms and seating him against his hip as he pulled out a chair from the dining table.

"Here," he said as he sat down with him across his lap, "do you want to see something really cool, William?"

The boy nodded.

Bobby angled his LED light and shone it into his own face. His lips parted and he stretched his head backwards as he pointed the light inside, illuminating the interior of his mouth.

"You see that?" He asked, pointing to the rear molar on the right with his tongue.

William looked, stooping his head to get a better view, curious to see what Bobby was trying to show him.

"It's a silver tooth," he announced, thinking that he had seen all there was to see and feeling disappointed.

"Nope," Bobby replied with a smile, knowing that the child would not have the slightest idea of what he was looking at. "It's titanium, the strongest metal in the world. Can you guess why I have a tooth made from titanium, William?"

The boy shook his head.

"I have a titanium tooth in my head because…, and this is the really cool bit…, underneath it, there's a little bomb."

William's eyes grew with intrigue and doubt as he pulled away, smiling and shaking his head, looking to his parents for them to confirm that the man was lying.

"Honestly, it's a little bomb," Bobby continued with sincerity, "I flick off the titanium casing and then bite down on the primer. We all have one."

He looked over to Bull, who in turn, replied with an enthusiastic nod.

"Why would you have a bomb under your tooth?" William asked with scepticism.

Bobby smiled and leaned in close to him, patting him on the back and making it seem as though he was about to share something of extreme importance with him.

"So that if the bad guys catch me, they can't make me tell them all my secrets," he answered in a loud whisper.

"Actually, that *is* really cool." William concluded. "Are you guys like…, Call of Duty: Black Ops, or something?"

"Yeah, something like that."

Outside, in the hallway, while William was too busy being distracted by Bobby and his 'cool tooth', Matthew and his wife heard the door to the cupboard beneath the stairs being opened.

Immediately, there were a number of grunts, growls and snorts, joined with the sound of a struggle.

They knew what was happening, but something held them in place, stopping them from doing anything against the men around them. It was not fear of the soldiers, or what they would do to them. It was acceptance. They had even considered doing something similar, the day before when Paula's body had become lifeless, knowing what would happen to her as the virus moved into its next stage. However, despite their knowledge of what was coming, the love they felt for the little girl who they had cherished and watched with pride and joy as she grew, prevented them from doing what was necessary.

Although their hearts were breaking as they listened to the unholy growls of Paula, gnashing her teeth as she struggled against the men who held her down, they knew that it would soon be over and she would be saved from her misery.

A few seconds later, the noise ceased and a heavy thud echoed into the dining room from the hallway.

Emily felt her heart become heavy in her chest, like a lead weight sitting inside her ribcage, and her stomach began to knot. Her shoulders slumped and her head sagged as her vision blurred with an ocean of tears.

"I knew she was dead," she said quietly in a quivering voice and staring down at the floor. "She became ill two days ago, and by yesterday afternoon, she wasn't breathing. We knew then that she was gone. I just didn't want to believe it."

Unable to do anything else, she broke down, sobbing for her daughter.

Stan stepped into the room and approached the mother of the young girl he had just helped to kill. He stopped and looked down at her, studying her for a while. Finally, he squatted, bringing his face down so that it was level with hers.

Reaching out, he lifted her chin with the tips of his fingers, showing a tenderness that no one else in the team had ever witnessed from him before.

"I'm sorry, Emily," he said softly, causing the men around him to glance at one another with raised eyebrows and shrugging shoulders.

"We had to do it. It's done and her suffering is over."

24

"Okay," Samantha said decisively, "we're leaving. There's nothing we can do for Stan and his team without power."

She snatched up the Iridium phone and shone her light across to the opposite side of the table where Lieutenant Frakes stood, her pistol clutched tightly in her hand.

"Melanie, are you ready to go?"

She did not need to be asked twice, and she quickly fell into line behind Samantha as she made her way towards the door.

"Do you have comms with your co-pilot? Do they know what's happening and that we're on our way?"

Melanie shook her head, immediately realising that Samantha could not see her.

"They're not answering, but it could be because of the layers of rock between us and them."

"I really hope that's all it is," Samantha replied pessimistically.

She reached back, handing the torch to Melanie and freeing up both of her hands so that she could manipulate her rifle with better effect.

"Here, hold this."

As Jonesy and Emma brought up the rear, the four of them silently crept out into the hallway. The entire bunker was in darkness and not even the back-up system indicator lights, usually glowing red, showed on any of the panels that they began to pass.

Above them, the gunfire had ceased. It had not lasted long and it was clear that the fight was lost. The infected were in, and the survivors could hear the footfalls of the rampaging dead making their way through the dark, wailing and moaning, and crashing into objects as they continued their blind search for their next victims.

"Stay close. Don't get separated and for fuck sake, keep quiet," Samantha whispered over her shoulder as she began to gingerly make her way along the corridor, keeping her body close to the cold damp wall on her left.

Another cry of pain and fear rang out from high above them. It lingered in the moist air and shook the four survivors to their cores as it rattled through their ears and clawed at their nerves. All of them knew that, eventually, the infected would find their way down the stairs, either deliberately, or by accident. It did not matter which. They just hoped that they could get out before it happened.

Somehow, their defences had been breached. Either they had succumbed to the combined weight of the swarming mass pressing against the blast doors on the top level, or someone had deliberately allowed them into the bunker.

Samantha knew that the doors would not fail due to the power shortage and she felt confident that even a million people pushing against the two inches of steel plating, could not force them to buckle out from their hinges.

She shuddered at the thought of someone deliberately compromising the integrity of their subterranean shelter.

What if they're still here?

Their lights glimmered against the concrete walls, glistening against the tiny rivulets of water that seeped in due to their position below the Thames waterline. Patches of moss that were growing in the cracks stood out sharply, their vibrant greens contrasting distinctly against the dull grey of the skimmed walls.

A cool breeze, heavy with the smell of mould and decay, blew towards them from the far end of the corridor, confirming that somewhere high above them, the bunker doors lay open to the outside world.

Finally, as they slowly made their way through the oppressive darkness, surrounded by flickering shadows and the echoes of dripping water and crashing footsteps from the upper levels, Melanie's light bounced from something that reflected dully up ahead of them. With a second sweep of the torch, they were able to see the metal railings of the staircase at the far end of the passageway.

Samantha paused and studied the steps for a moment. They were grated steel, running up for a short flight and abruptly turning back on themselves as they reached up towards the next level in the bunker. On the second level up and further along the corridor, they would find the tunnel that would lead them to the helicopter landing pad.

However, getting there would be a different matter.

As she reached the bottom of the stairwell, Samantha could already hear the metallic clangs of dozens of feet stomping their way down the steel treads, descending from the upper floors. They echoed through the stairway, becoming louder and accompanied by the increasing symphony of vivacious growls and snorts from the infected as they drew nearer. More and more were joining in on the hunt, pounding their way down the staircase.

"Shit," Samantha fizzed, her attention focussed on the stairs above them as she began to ascend. "They're coming down. Keep it tight. We need to make it up to the next level before they cut us off."

Melanie's torch beam bounced from the walls as she raced up the stairwell behind Samantha. Jonesy and Emma were close behind her and she could hear their heavy breathing as they battled with their fear. The noise above them was growing louder by the second, heralding the approach of the infected. Melanie began to panic, believing that their escape would be blocked if they did not move faster.

"Come on, Sam," she encouraged from behind, "we need to move."

Samantha, almost blind to what was in front of her, was climbing the stairs as quickly as she could. Already, she had misplaced her footing a number of times, her boots slipping from the edge of the steps and almost sending her crashing into the hard steel plates. If she was not careful, she could very easily slip on the damp grating and find herself stranded with a broken ankle or worse, unconscious.

She reached the top of the first flight and turned the bend. She brought her rifle up, ready to fire at anything that came at her from the floor above them. For a moment, she was greeted with a wall of blackness, as Melanie had not yet turned the corner and illuminated the passageway for her.

Samantha moved forward through the darkness, taking small steps and feeling with the toes of her boots before placing each foot. It was impossible to see anything ahead of her and instead, she relied heavily on her hearing.

From what she could tell, the blood thirsty horde was still a couple of levels above them, but they were close and within the next minute or so, they would be on top of them.

Her knee made contact with something at the foot of the next flight and her throat instantly tightened up. She gasped and instinctively took a step back, already beginning to squeeze the trigger on her rifle.

Melanie's light suddenly illuminated the area in front of her, having caught up from the turn in the stairs. At her feet, Samantha saw the pile canvass sacks that had been left behind. She let out a loud gasp of relief and stepped to the side of the discarded bags. She had almost fired into them.

She anxiously checked over her shoulder to see that the others had caught up and were following. Without wasting any more time and throwing caution to the wind, they began to pound their way up the next set of steps.

Melanie reached out and held onto the back of Samantha's shirt, making sure that she stayed closely tucked in behind her and they did not become separated again.

The infected were close. Their smell had already filled the entire stairwell, accompanied by their thundering footsteps and ghostly wails. Samantha's nose twitched at the scent of decaying bodies, the sickly sweet tang making her want to cover her mouth and nose, but she fought the urge, opting to keep both hands on her rifle.

She was just a few steps from the top of the final flight and the entrance to the corridor that led into the tunnels. She looked up, and a few metres above them, in the flickering light of the torch beams from Jonesy and Melanie, she caught a glimpse of the dark shadows that were descending upon them.

As the light shifted, she saw the first of the infected, halfway down the final flight of steps above. The light from behind her drifted from the blood coated white shirt and illuminated the pale eyes and blackened face of a corpse, staring back at her.

Instinctively, she raised her rifle and fired.

In the confines of the staircase, the report of the discharging rounds sounded like the crack of thunder, clapping at their ears and threatening to implode their skulls. The flash was blinding, shooting out from the muzzle like a volcano of brilliant white.

The body fell as a number of bullets ripped through its chest, splattering blood and bone into the air around it. The infected man toppled forward and bounced down the stairs, smashing against each rung as Samantha raised her aim again and fired into the lunging figures that followed close behind.

"Run," she screamed down at the others as she stood in the doorway leading into the corridor, holding off the advance of the dead.

"Fucking run. Get to the tunnel."

As Melanie reached the top of the steps, she was momentarily blinded in the muzzle flash from the rifle that jerked in Samantha's hands. Her head buzzed with the echoing blasts that announced the demise of yet another of the infected. With each flash, she caught a glimpse of the contorted and hate filled face of Samantha as she continued to dispatch the creatures that had begun to pile up at the foot of the stairs.

"Go," she screamed, as she stood her ground.

Melanie jumped through the doorway and spun around, raising her light in her left hand and illuminating the cramped staircase. With her right hand, she took aim with her pistol and joined Samantha in the melee. Their weapons roared together, hammering at the falling bodies as they began to choke up the stairwell.

Jonesy was through and into the corridor but in the narrow confines, he was unable to bring his rifle to bare and support Melanie and Samantha.

"Stoppage," Samantha screamed out, hitting the release catch and reaching for a fresh magazine.

She ducked, keeping herself below Melanie's line of fire and stepped into the corridor as she slammed her cocking lever forward and chambered a round. Within seconds, she began firing again and continued to pour a hail of projectiles back at their attackers.

"Emma," Melanie cried out, seeing the final member in their group as she reached the top step and the body that dropped from between the bannister, landing on top of her and knocking her flat to the ground.

She turned her pistol and fired, hitting the squirming body in the shoulder, but it had no effect. In the next instant, as Samantha's rifle continued to blast away beside her, Melanie heard the blood curdling screams of Emma, as the teeth of the infected closed over the soft tissue between her shoulder and neck, tearing a huge hole out from the muscle, which instantly began to pour with a river of blood.

Melanie made to take a step forward as Samantha's rifle roared again. The discharge was close to the side of her head and forced her to instinctively duck and pivot on her heel, jumping to the side to get out of the line of fire. Her head buzzed and her vision danced as the torch slipped from her hand and clattered against the floor, rolling away from her and casting its beams across every surface, illuminating the infected and the living, freezing them in instants of light like the separate frames in a roll of film. The light trundled away and finally went dark as it smashed against the wall, leaving only Jonesy with a means of countering the blackness that threatened to swallow them up.

As she cleared Samantha's arcs, Melanie felt a body land nearby and a cold hand reach out and close around her ankle, gripping her tightly and trying to pull her downwards. She could feel the body squirming at her feet as it attempted to climb up to her, tugging and jerking at her clothing. She kicked and pulled, trying to break free, but the first hand was quickly joined by a second and the grip tightened.

Raising her pistol, she screamed out as she repeatedly pulled the trigger, emptying the remainder of the magazine into her attacker. As the final round exploded from the chamber and the top slide locked in the rear position, she saw the snarling face below her implode in the instant of the final muzzle flash. A cold splash of sticky liquid hit her cheek as the hands lost their grip and slipped away from her lower leg, allowing her to step free.

As Emma's shrieks continued and Samantha's rifle boomed over and over again, Melanie began to change out her empty magazine, frantically reaching for a full one and almost dropping it from her shaking hands.

"Back, get back," Samantha cried out, grabbing the young pilot by the arm and forcing her to the rear. "Move back."

She reached into the satchel slung over her shoulder and pulled out a High Explosive grenade. It was the only one she had, but now was the time to use it. The stairwell was now packed with the infected, tumbling over one another in the dark and piling through into the corridor as the three survivors began to retreat.

She knew that they could do nothing to help Emma as she was swallowed up by the mob. Her cries for help and howls of agony continued to echo through the corridor, but it was impossible to reach her.

As Jonesy and Melanie fell back and began to fire into the advancing black mass, Samantha pulled the pin on the grenade, keeping the 'fly-off' lever clutched against her palm. Stepping backwards, she tried to judge where exactly Emma was within the throng of bodies, but there were so many of them, pulling and tearing at her, that her position seemed to have changed a number of times.

Still, she screamed out in desperation, her voice filled with pain.

"Bastards," Samantha spat with rage and threw the grenade into the area where she believed her friend to be.

She heard the heavy grenade land with a thud and turned to run through the wall of fire that Melanie and Jonesy had thrown up, feeling the displacement of air and hearing the ear-splitting snaps as their rounds whizzed through the darkness around her, covering her withdrawal.

"Run," Samantha screamed at them as she reached their position.

Behind them, a blinding flash lit up the corridor. A deafening thump, sounding like an enormous steel weight had just been dropped on to the stairwell from high above, crashed against their ears, joined with a shockwave that pushed at their backs and hurtled them forward. The increased air pressure in the corridor squeezed their bodies, threatening to collapse their lungs and burst their eyes out from their sockets.

The earth stood still for a moment as the concussion of the exploding grenade stole their breath and senses away. They seemed to drift through time and space, being carried through the passageway by an enormous invisible hand. Then, as the sound of the blast faded and with ringing ears and bursting lungs, the three of them were slammed into the floor, feeling their bodies being pressed into the hard concrete as the shockwave raced along the narrow hallway, looking for a way out.

Jonesy was the first of them to reach his feet again. Staggering and unable to see clearly, he grabbed for the torch that had fallen from his hand and spun around, shining it back down the corridor towards the entrance into the stairwell. It was hard for the light to penetrate the thick cloud of smoke and dust, but nothing came out from the swirling debris. It appeared that Samantha's grenade had bought them a few precious seconds.

"Come on, Sam, get up," he grunted, unsteady on his feet as his vision continued to dance in the gloom.

He grabbed hold of Samantha and Melanie and began to drag them by their shirts along the corridor.

"Up, get up. We need to move," he screamed at them.

Groggily, they both climbed to their feet, disoriented and unable to walk without leaning against one another for support. They groaned and sputtered from the effects of the blast and the dust that lingered in the air.

Behind them, the infected had begun to recover from the explosion. Bodies, cut in half by the flying shrapnel and shockwave, dragged themselves along the corridor, spilling their entrails out over the cold concrete in their wake. Others, still descending from the floors above, crashed down the steel steps and trampled over the fallen.

Samantha, vaguely cognisant of her surroundings, became aware that something was no longer in her position. It was not her rifle. That was still firmly in her grasp. She reached down to the map pocket on her trousers and realised that she had lost the Iridium phone, her only means of contacting Stan and his men.

"Shit," she cursed hoarsely as she began to feel about her in the dark.

"The sat-phone. I've lost the fucking sat-phone."

"Leave it," Jonesy shouted, still pulling at her arm. "Leave it, Sam. It's too late for that now. We need to go."

The three survivors forced themselves into a stumbling run, hobbling along the passageway on unsteady legs, still holding onto one another and constantly under threat from toppling forward as their lack of balance caused them to struggle to remain upright.

They could hear the sounds of the dead behind them, tearing their way through the darkness in hot pursuit. They moaned and howled, hundreds of voices crying out together and creating a sound that clawed at the bones of the living.

"Keep going," Jonesy encouraged, "we're nearly there."

Up ahead, his torch light flashed across a door set into a thick steel frame. It was the entrance into the tunnel.

Timing his run, he threw out his leg and hit the door with a forceful kick. Instantly, his body was stopped dead in its tracks. The crack was audible within the bang of the impact as the bones in his ankle shattered.

Jonesy crumpled to the ground and yelped, feeling a pain like nothing he had experienced before, shooting up from his leg and into his brain, completely overwhelming him. The agony burned brightly before his eyes, blinding him for an instant as he reached down towards his wrecked ankle.

Samantha, feeling Jonesy drop from her side, almost tripped over him as she reached forward for the handle. She pulled down and the door swung open, forcing a backdraft of cool air into the smoke and dust filled corridor.

Melanie snatched up Jonesy's rifle and turned to face the rear, pointing in the direction they had come.

"Grab him," she shouted to Samantha nodding down at the injured man. "Get him out of here. I'm right behind you."

"Stay close, Melanie," Samantha called back to her, "we're counting on you to fly us out of here."

As Samantha scooped up the screaming Jonesy from the ground and began to drag him into the tunnel, Melanie began to pour a heavy weight of fire into the corridor behind them, screaming as she did so from fear and anger.

The three of them, limping and firing as they fled, made slow progress through the catacombs of the underground bunker. The dead were closing in. Unaffected by the damage they had sustained from the gunshots and exploding grenade, they were gaining ground.

Melanie emptied her magazine and turned to catch up to the bouncing light of the torch in Samantha's hand.

"How far," she wheezed, reaching into the satchel hanging from the Captain's neck and feeling for a fresh magazine.

Finally finding what she was looking for, she slammed it into place and forced the cocking leaver forward again.

"About a hundred metres, I think," Samantha groaned back at her, struggling with the weight of Jonesy as she helped him to leap along on his remaining good leg.

He was howling with pain and frustration with each step and begging Samantha not to leave him behind.

Something moved up ahead of them in the tunnel. In the instant that she saw it in the torch beam, it was impossible for her to recognise. She stopped, dropping Jonesy to the floor and raising her rifle. She could hear the commotion behind her, as their pursuers continued the hunt, but now, the threat was also in front of them.

Her heart, already beating rapidly, began to skip beats. Her body was exhausted and her mind was beginning to lose its grip, giving in to fear and panic. They were cut off from their escape. Somehow, the infected had got ahead of them, and now, they had no way out. Her finger pressed against the trigger as she waited for her target to show itself again.

"Don't shoot," a voice called out to her from within the inky blackness.

As the pounding footsteps got louder up ahead, drawing nearer and the voice became clearer, Melanie recognised the man approaching them.

"Mike," she gasped, turning for a moment to look over her shoulder, and then firing another volley into the invisible snarling mass that was following them.

He came to a halt in front of them, and in the glow of the light in her hand, Samantha saw the look of horror and alarm in his face as he stared back down the tunnel and heard the dead approaching.

Another man, one of the aircrew on loan from Gerry, stepped forward and helped to carry Jonesy, slinging him over his shoulder and turning to head back into the pitch-black of the tunnel.

"Come on," Mike encouraged, grabbing hold of Melanie and pushing Samantha ahead of him.

"The chopper is ready to go. We just need *you* to fly it, Mel."

At the far end of the shaft, they reached the stairs leading up from the basement of the office block. From there, hauling their wounded and struggling up the endless flights, they forced themselves through the darkness and up onto the roof, the infected close behind and refusing to give up the chase.

As they barged through the fire exit at the top of the stairs, they were hit by a blast of cold air and a thunderous roar, as the huge engines of the Chinook howled beneath the rotors. At the rear ramp, a man stepped out, shouting something through the racket of the aircraft and anxiously waving them forward, and then disappeared again into the body of the huge machine.

A drumbeat of low rumbling concussions, barely audible over the noise of the helicopter, rang out from the forward part of the fuselage, accompanied by a number of bright flashes in rapid succession of each other. In her exhaustion, Samantha struggled to understand what was happening, but a rearward glance clarified things for her.

The infected had reached the top of the stairs and had made it through the door. She saw them fall, their heads imploding and limbs being ripped from their bodies. Jets of asphalt and splinters of masonry, mixed in with blood and bone, shot up like fountains all around them as the 0.5 inch calibre rounds from the heavy machinegun chewed up anything that followed the survivors out onto the rooftop.

The aircrew were manning their guns, hammering away at the infected as they piled through the fire escape.

Moments later, the remnants of the bunker personnel were sprawled out on the floor of the passenger compartment, close to collapse and grimacing from the exertion and pain threatening to overwhelm their worn bodies and minds.

Melanie could not afford to rest and forced herself forward and into the cockpit where she took control of the machine.

Soon, as the pitch of the engine grew and the rotors changed angle and increased their speed, the wheels of the CH-47 lifted off from the asphalt roof of the building. As the helicopter rose up a few metres, the crew manning the guns ceased firing, opting to conserve their ammunition for when they really needed it.

The infected, no longer being held back by the heavy rounds that smashed their bodies to pulp, spewed out through the disfigured and crumbling doorway and raced towards the aircraft, hovering just beyond their reach.

Gripping the cyclic, Melanie yawed the Chinook to the right and into the open space beyond the rooftop's edge. The infected, determined in their assault, blindly followed the escaping helicopter.

Many of them, unaware of the danger to their existence, launched themselves from the building and out into thin air, plummeting to the ground below and crashing into the hard pavement where they exploded like bags of offal.

The sun had risen on the new day. Its dazzling rays shone from above the horizon and reached out over the rooftops of London, blinding in their brilliance. Below, a new world had been born. One where the living fear the dead and death, was no longer final.

It was time for Samantha and the others to join in with the evacuation. They set a bearing for the Isle of Wight and headed away from the bunker, over the dying land and out towards the English Channel.

25

The old VW Camper snaked its way through the network of roads leading south. It was still dark when they had finally been able to leave the house, the infected having lost interest and wandering off to search for other victims elsewhere. Now, three hours into their journey, the sun was slowly fighting its way up towards the horizon, turning the sky in the east to a deep pink.

"What's your name?" William asked inquisitively, turning in his seat and staring over the back-rest at the man sitting behind him.

"Brian," he replied groggily, struggling to see through his swollen eyes.

"What happened to your face?"

"I fell."

"How did you fall?"

"I wasn't looking where I was going." Brian tried to force a smile, but the pain in his head prevented the muscles in his face from moving into the positions he wanted and instead, he grimaced.

"Why weren't you looking where you were going?" William continued to force the conversation, despite Brian's clear discomfort and injuries.

"Because I was too busy saving *their* arses," he grunted, nodding to the other men cramped into the Camper van around him.

"How did you save them?"

"William, that's your name, right?" He was beginning to lose patience.

The boy nodded back at him.

"Do you always ask so many questions, William?"

"He's always been a curious one," Emily replied in a flat and distant voice without turning to face him.

She remained pressed up against the window, seated next to her husband and with their son wedged between them. She stared out at the landscape, watching the dark hills and trees as they rolled by, barely noticing them as her thoughts remained elsewhere, with her daughter, Paula.

As the soldiers slept, she had sat with the body of her child, wrapped in a blanket and tucked into her bed. For hours, she had held her, sobbing endlessly and talking to the lifeless form. For twelve years, she had loved her child and did all she could to protect and care for her, but the virus had taken Paula away from her, turning her into one of the monsters that were sweeping the globe and feasting on the living.

It was not fair. Paula had done nothing to deserve her cruel punishment that their vengeful God had dealt out to her. She was young and full of innocence.

Despite her grief, she was grateful to the soldiers for having done what she and her husband could not. At first, she had wanted to hate them, but she was incapable of holding them responsible for her daughter's death. Paula was already dead. She knew that, and accepted it now. What Stan and his men had done was a mercy, saving the little girl the unearthly suffering of remaining as one of the plague's victims.

Her eyes were bright red from the tears that had unceasingly cascaded down from them. Her body was weak from the anguish she suffered and her chest hurt from the heartache she felt. Try as she did, she could not shake the thought of Paula, still lying in her bed, left behind in the home they had made together as a family.

At least she will remain there, she thought.

She raised her hand to her mouth and pursed her lips against the tips of her fingers, then pressed them to the window, sending out a final kiss to the daughter that had been snatched away from her at only twelve years of age.

"Sleep tight, Paula," she whispered.

They continued south, picking their way through the detritus left on the roads, weaving between the broken down vehicles and having to crash their way through clusters of the infected. Many other people were also still travelling the highways, some by car and others, on foot. They were all heading in different directions, making their own way towards what they considered to be a safe place for them to hide.

The one thing that they all had in common was the fact that they had been left to their own devices. The long columns of military and police trucks had gone. The soldiers and police had either been pulled out, or they had deserted, leaving the roads to fall into chaos and the refugees to fend for themselves. The sky, only a day or two before, being blackened with the amount of aircraft flying in and out from the country, was now empty and clear of anything that was manmade.

Marty, driving the van, picked his way through the still moving traffic that remained, pushing forward and cutting people up at every opportunity. Horns blasted and people shouted in anger and frustration, but he paid them no attention. His mind was solely focussed on reaching Manchester, headed for the airport and their way out.

"Anything?" Taff asked, leaning forward between the two front seats.

Stan, sitting in the passenger seat, stared at the screen of his Iridium phone, as once again, it informed him that the number he was trying to reach, was out of service.

"Nothing," he replied, shaking his head, "I've heard nothing from them since their last update, saying that the airport was still amber. That was six hours ago." He turned and looked back at Taff. "For all we know, the place could be overrun by now."

"We can still take a look, though."

Stan looked back into the passenger area behind him, squinted at the family of civilians and then back up at Taff.

"Yeah, we can, but I'm not sure about our excess baggage back there. We may need to fight our way through, or out," he whispered.

Taff took a quick glance over his shoulder.

Emily was still staring out the window, Matthew was asleep with his head thrown back, and lolling from side to side with the motion of the Camper, while William was still busy grilling Brian.

"We couldn't leave them there, Stan. You agreed yourself that they should tag along and be taken to the airport."

Stan bit his lip.

"Yeah, I suppose so," he said in agreement, remembering how lost the family had appeared when they were getting ready to leave after the infected had meandered away from the house.

"The moment they become a burden though, we ditch them."

Taff nodded and sat back down in his seat next to Bobby who continued to snore loudly with his face pressed up against the window, a river of drool flowing down from his mouth and over the glass.

Hours later, after having to continuously take detours around the impassable roads, travelling along tracks, country lanes and through empty villages, they reached the motorway that would lead them in towards Manchester Airport.

It was daylight now and in the distance, they could see a hive of activity in the sky above the airfield. Planes were taking off constantly and helicopters buzzed around above the buildings, looking like black flies circling over a meal that had been left unattended.

Everyone was now awake and alert, checking their weapons and ammunition, ready to take the fight to the enemy, dead or living.

Bobby turned to Emily and Matthew.

"We're almost there. Stay close and don't let go of each other. Do you understand?"

They both nodded back to him, their eyes bursting with fear and their pale drawn faces, glistening with beads of sweat.

Neither of them spoke.

"Good," Bobby continued, "we don't know what we're going into, so be ready to move. Run when I say and stop when I say. Keep a tight grip on William because we're not here to babysit for you, and don't do *anything*, unless I tell you, okay?"

Again, they nodded their response, terrified of what was to come and wishing it to be over as quickly as possible. Matthew reached up, grabbed hold of the endlessly chattering William, and dragged him back into his seat, planting him between himself and his mother and placing his arm across him so that he could not move from his seat.

"Be quiet now, Will. The soldiers need to concentrate on what they're doing and don't need you getting in the way."

Twenty minutes later, they reached the slip road that led them up towards the main terminals. On the final leg of their journey, there had been no signs of life. The road was packed with vehicles, but they were all empty and burned to virtually nothing, with thousands of charred bodies littering the ground around them. Huge craters pockmarked the embankments, tarmac lanes and even a number of bridges had collapsed.

It was clear that the air force had made a last-ditch effort to clear the area of the dead, running bombing and strafing missions along the choked roads around the airport, destroying countless infected and living people.

Now, Stan and his men sat staring at the terminal buildings, just five-hundred metres ahead of them. In front, the army had hastily erected huge four metre high concrete T-walls that, as far as they could tell, encompassed the whole of Terminal-One.

On the outside of the T-walls, a dark bubbling mass, looking like a smear of brown and black, swathed the length of the walls. It was the infected, thousands of them, all pressed up close to one another as they pounded their bodies against the hard concrete, clambering at the impenetrable barrier.

It was impossible to see a way through.

"Looks like we may have to look for an alternate way in," Marty grumbled as he leaned forward against the wheel, staring at the wall of bodies.

Stan sat up and watched for a moment, studying the crowd and searching for any indication of a weak point in the legion of infected.

"The whole place is probably like this," he concluded.

A high pitched rumble filled the air outside of the van as a huge black shadow rose up from the rear of the terminal and soared into the sky. The men recognised it instantly. It was a C-130 Hercules military transport, probably having brought in ammunition and reinforcements and now, evacuating civilians on its return journey to wherever it was headed.

As the C-130 took off, the bodies all around the perimeter erupted with excitement, reaching up for the immense black monster that sailed gracefully over their heads. A ripple flowed through the crowd and the mass swarmed to the right, following the aircraft as it climbed higher and further beyond their reach, leaving a large portion of the wall free from obstruction.

Not all of the infected chased after the plane. Many were left behind, writhing on the floor with smashed limbs or staggering with injuries that left them incapable of anything other than an uncoordinated stagger.

Stan, seeing an opportunity decided that there was no point in waiting and trying to find another way in. He watched how the sea of bodies moved off, futilely chasing after the plane that they had no chance of reaching.

They moved en-masse, fighting and trampling one another as they blindly raced away from the walls and took off along the access road to the main terminal.

"Marty," Stan growled, winding down his window and placing his rifle into a position where he could fire from. "Go for it."

Marty gunned the engine, forcing the revolutions in to the red before carefully releasing the clutch. The wheels spun for a moment, and then the Camper lurched forward, headed down the gentle slope that led up to the front of Terminal-One.

With two-hundred metres to go, Stan was able to identify the gate that had been fitted into the walls. It was made from thick steel, he guessed, and spanned a gap of about five metres. Above the entrance, he could see a number of gun emplacements and the bobbing heads of the soldiers as they began to take notice of the approaching vehicle.

Two the right, between the terminal and the multi-storey car park, the swarm of infected had stopped. Having lost sight of the Hercules, they had come to a halt and turned their attention back towards the terminal building.

"Shit," Stan grunted, "they've seen us."

Marty nodded and aimed the vehicle for the gate.

"There's no way they'll open up for us now."

"Well, we can't turn back," Stan pointed out, taking aim with his M4 at one of the bodies that had already began to charge towards them. "This tub won't make the turn."

Committed to their course of action, with nothing else in the way of options, Marty raced towards the heavy gate, praying that the soldiers above would not treat them as a threat and convert their VW into a tangled mess with their heavy weaponry.

With just fifty metres to go, the first of the infected crashed into the front of the vehicle, bouncing to the side and being dragged beneath the wheels. The van lurched and swayed, throwing the passengers about within the interior as more and more bodies hurled themselves at the struggling old Camper.

Stan's rifle rattled, dropping numerous targets with an accuracy that only a veteran of his years and skill could accomplish. A number of cracks rang out from the interior as Bull and Danny began smashing their weapons through the side windows, and soon, Stan's rifle was joined with the clattering staccato of their weapons.

Bull was hammering away with short bursts from his machinegun, sending glowing red tracer rounds smashing into the bodies of the infected as they converged on the vehicle racing towards the entrance of the airport. Hundreds of rounds were fired within a short space of time, dropping dozens of the infected, but in spite of the heavy fire and their severe losses, they kept on coming.

It was impossible for the men to make even the smallest of dents in their mass ranks.

"We're not going to make it," Matthew was screaming from the rear, holding his hands over his ears and staring out at the dark wall of death closing in on them.

"We're not going to make it. They'll get us."

Brian reached forward and grabbed Matthew by the neck, tearing his attention away from the window for a moment and pushing his snarling swollen face up close to the panic stricken man who was shaking in his grasp.

"Shut the fuck up and hold on to your wife and kid. Say another word, and *you*, won't fucking make it. Now get a grip of yourself."

He released the man and went back to picking off targets as they approached to within a distance where he was able to see clearly through his slatted eyes.

From outside, they heard the steady heavy beat of a Browning 0.5 Heavy Machinegun. All around them, the crowd was being churned into minced-meat as the soldiers manning the defences gave fire support for the little van and its occupants.

With the added help from the troops, and seeing the sea of infected fall in their droves and their advance slowed, the team felt a glimmer of hope.

Marty swung the wheel around and brought them to a screeching halt, directly in front of the steel gates. Seeing the crowd swarm towards them and begin to envelop their vehicle, he leaned back in his seat and began to kick out the windscreen. Stan, realising what Marty was doing, joined him and together, they created a means of escape from the surrounded Camper as the glass was pushed out from its frame.

They scrambled forward, pulling themselves through the window, feeling dozens of cold hands reaching up for them as they fought their way out and up on to the roof.

Above, the defenders of the airport continued to provide cover as they brought their rifles to bare and began shooting downwards, directly into the sea of infected faces that crowded around the survivors.

By now, the VW van had become a tiny island within an ocean of infected and it was under serious threat of being swept away.

"Up," Bobby screamed, dragging Matthew to his feet as the interior resounded with the thumps and moans of thousands of bodies attacking the vehicle.

"Get up and get onto the roof. Move it, Matthew, move."

William and his parents were terrified, unable to move and clasping their hands over their ears, screaming over the sound of the gunfire and the raucous cries of the blood thirsty figures pressed up against the windows. Everywhere they looked, all they could see were ghastly faces with pale eyes and gaping mouths, staring back at them and snapping their teeth.

Bobby had to physically push them forward and over the front seats where Stan and Marty reached down from the roof with waiting arms. All around them, the infected tumbled. Blood spattered in all directions as the countless rounds ploughed through their bodies, but still, they pressed forwards with their assault.

Bull and Danny, struggling to squeeze their bulky bodies through the narrow opening, climbed out through the rear window and up onto the Camper. Standing with their feet firmly planted, they began to pour all their fire into the infected around the front of the van, covering Stan and Marty as they helped the three remaining members of the family.

William was the first to be passed up.

Marty hauled him through and turned to his left, lifting the little boy high above his head and up towards the grasping hands of the brave soldiers reaching down over the gate.

Two of them caught him by his wrists and lifted him to safety.

Next, Matthew squirmed through the gaping window. He saw the men on the walls, holding their hands out to him, but before he was able to reach them, he lost his footing and slipped. He hit the hard surface of the van's roof, cracking his head and seeing a shower of stars cascading through his vision.

Climbing to his feet and struggling with his senses, he began to make his move again.

From the rear, at the top of the wall, a deafening bang, mixed with an almighty whoosh and a bright flash, caused him to stumble again. A split second later, as he tumbled across the van, trying to steady himself, the detonation of the missile rocked the vehicle from side to side. The blast wave and ear-splitting concussion caused him to fall backwards over the side of the vehicle, tumbling into the waiting arms of the infected.

Emily, unaware of what had happened and still reeling from the shock of the explosion and the heavy gunfire, was oblivious to the screams of her husband as he was swallowed up by the ravenous horde.

Under the cover of heavy fire, Bull was the last to be hoisted to safety, taking five men to lift his huge weight up and over the blockade.

On the other side, as the infected continued to tear the VW Camper to pieces and pound their hands and faces against the steel gate, Emily looked around for her husband. She began to panic, fearing that he had been left in the van.

"Where is he?" She screamed over and over, turning to begin climbing the steps to the top of the barriers again.

Bobby grabbed her and pulled her back. She fought against him, tearing at his hands and forcing him to tighten his grasp on her as he held her by the arms.

"I'm sorry, Emily, but he's gone," he shouted into her face, struggling to be heard over the noise of battle and the unearthly shrieks from outside.

"No," she cried, "we can't leave him. We have to go back."

Bobby took hold of her by the collar and began to drag her along, following after the others as they headed for the main building. All the while, she fought against him, kicking, screaming, and trying to pull away from him.

"He's gone, Emily. He's dead."

Inside the terminal, they were greeted by thousands of eyes staring back at them. Everywhere they looked, people sat or stood in clusters, holding on to one another with what remained of their belongings stuffed into the bags at their feet. Some were crying and others talked, but most, just sat in terrified silence, staring back at the newcomers who had just arrived.

Bobby dragged Emily in through the doors. She was becoming more and more incoherent with each step from the shock and grief of losing her husband and daughter within the space of twenty-four hours.

She sobbed and cried and Bobby knew that if he let go of her, she would fall to the ground and would not get back up.

Danny was holding William by the hand, speaking words of encouragement to him and doing his best to stop him from realising that his father had not arrived with the rest of them. The traumatised boy looked about him with bulging eyes, watching the crowds of shell-shocked refugees.

Staying close together as a group, they began to push their way through the throng of people and deeper into the terminal. There was no security or smiling airline attendants anymore, ready to help and facilitate the commuters. Now, it was just a free-for-all, with soldiers, police and civilians, cramming themselves into whatever space they could find, waiting patiently for their turn to be flown out.

"Fuck me," Bull huffed, "it's like the retreat from Stalingrad in here."

Outside, the guns continued, but the sound was no longer so harsh on their ears. They seemed to be coming from far away, from somewhere else, the thick panes of glass that spanned the length of the front of the terminal, stretching from the floor to the ceiling, buffeting the endless crack of the exploding rounds.

All around them, Stan noticed the people were paying very little attention to the battle that raged beyond the huge glass walls. Their eyes stared blankly, as though having seen enough horror to last a thousand lifetimes, becoming numbed to the sound of gunfire and the moans of the infected.

The group gathered at the foot of a stalled escalator, wondering where to go next. There did not seem to be anyone taking command of the airport and no matter where they turned, they were met with indifference from the soldiers, slumped with exhaustion, trying to gain some rest before their turn on the barricades came around again.

"What do..." Brian's question was cut short.

The thick glass stretching along the length of the terminal building's entrance burst inwards, exploding into a million pieces and sending shards of razor sharp shrapnel flying in all directions as a ball of fire and debris from outside blasted its way into the building.

In the instant before he was hurled into the air, Stan watched in slow motion as Brian's head was torn open, a large chunk of glass slicing its way through his scalp and severing the upper part of his skull. His blood and brains were spattered in all directions, striking Stan in the face as the shockwave lifted him from his feet and threw him several metres across the terminal. He landed amongst a tangle of bodies and limbs from other survivors who had been caught in the explosion.

The concussion of the detonation knocked the wind from his body and sent his senses spiralling into a black abyss, but the shocked expression on Brian's face at the moment of his grisly death, stayed imprinted at the forefront of his mind.

The building was roaring with the frightened screams of the wounded and fleeing refugees. The rumble of the explosion was still echoing through the terminal as the smoke and dust began to pour in through the gaping holes in the windows.

Stan, unable to stand, began to crawl towards the body of his friend, slithering through the blood and entrails that coated the floor beneath him. His head buzzed and his ears rang, but he could clearly see Brian's lifeless corpse, lying on his back and staring up at the ceiling high above them.

"Brian," Stan heard someone shouting through the chaos.

The voice sounded distant, as though it was travelling from miles away.

"Brian..."

As the voice continued to cry out, he realised that the words were coming from his own mouth while he dragged himself forward, reaching out towards his old friend and calling for him to get up.

A pair of hands suddenly yanked him from the floor and hurled him to his feet. His legs were weak and his body struggled to remain upright. He looked back down at Brian's mutilated body and made to reach out for him.

He stumbled, barely catching his balance and felt a wetness seeping through his own clothing, running down along his spine. His head swam and as his vision turned red with the blood pouring from the wound in his head. He began to sway.

Stan collapsed into darkness, vaguely aware of someone lifting him off his feet and charging through the echoing screams.

The sounds of voices brought him to.

He could hear and feel movement all around him and as his eyes slowly opened, his head threatened to burst from the pain. His face was still covered with blood and his sight was tinged with crimson.

"Stan," a voice hovering over him gasped with relief, *"Stan, can you hear me?"*

He let out a groan, incapable of forming any words.

"Get some water, quick," the voice ordered urgently.

Moments later, he felt the cold splash against his lips and feeling it revitalise him slightly, reached up with his remaining good hand, grabbed the bottle and began to drink greedily.

"Easy, Stan," the voice coaxed, *"take it easy, mate."*

Blinking heavily as the cool liquid cascaded over his face, washing some of the blood from his eyes, he looked up and saw Danny leaning over him, cradling his head in his arms as he held the bottle to his lips.

"Where," his throat hurt as he attempted to speak, "where are we? What happened?"

"They got in," Danny replied, updating his team commander on the events that had occurred after the gates had been blown wide open.

"Fuck knows what happened, but they got in. It was pandemonium down there, Stan."

"The others, what about the others?"

"We're here, Stan," Taff said reassuringly from his side then turned to look at Danny.

With a nod of approval from the others, Taff continued.

"Brian's dead, Stan. He was killed in the blast."

The face of Brian loomed at him from deep within his mind. At first, it was one of him smiling, from days gone by, but then, it quickly changed to the mangled face of his friend, his brains pouring from the opening in his skull and his lifeless eyes staring back at him.

Stan screwed his eyes shut.

"Where are we?"

"In the control-tower," Bull's straining voice informed him from the other side of the room where he was busy piling anything he could get his hands on up against the doors.

"There's a fucking million of them out there."

Stan was badly hurt, but he was determined not to allow his wounds to incapacitate him. He had a large gash across his scalp and a wound in his neck that Bobby had managed to stop from bleeding. His arm, lacerated with deep cuts that reached to the bone, severing muscles and tendons, was virtually useless, and the slither of steel that had sliced through his back, had been just millimetres away from severing his spinal column.

He tried to sit up, but Danny pushed him back.

"Easy, Stan. Take it easy."

"You fucking take it easy," he grunted back, swiping Danny's hands away and hauling himself upwards.

Wincing with pain and feeling the fresh blood clots around his wounds open up again he looked about the room, making his own appreciation of their situation.

There were a number of faces that he did not recognise staring back at him with horror filled eyes. Some were in military uniform and others were clearly civilian.

William sat huddled with his mother beneath one of the desks built into the wall of the circular room.

On the far side, was the entrance and to the left, was a steel ladder leading up through a hatch in the ceiling.

From beyond the doors, the pounding continued as Bull and Marty attempted to fortify their position. By now, they had ripped out most of the fittings, furniture and computers, adding them to the ever increasing pile in an effort to stop the infected from breaking in.

Stan, even in his weakened and wounded state, could see that the barricade would not hold for long. Already, the doors were shuddering beneath the onslaught, threatening to burst out from their frames and collapse into the main room of the control tower.

"The ladder," Stan groaned, climbing to his feet and using his rifle as a crutch to help him up.

"Get up onto the roof."

After a brief argument between Stan and Taff, the commander finally relented and allowed himself to be hoisted up onto the top of the control tower by Bull and Marty as they hung down through the trap door.

One by one, the survivors, fifteen of them in total, climbed the ladder and pull themselves through the hatch and onto the roof.

Outside, planes were frantically pulling away from their ramps and heading for the runway. Jet engines roared all around as the pilots pushed their machines to the limit in order to escape the doomed airport.

Some aircraft had been slow to react, and from their vantage point above the control tower, the survivors watched as hundreds of infected smashed their way in and tore through the trapped passengers.

After a few minutes, Bobby and Taff were the only remaining people inside the control room. The door was beginning to give way and they turned to see the first of the infected faces pushing itself through the small gap.

They paused, looking at the ladder and quickly realised that it was fixed in place with a number of bolts in the floor and ceiling. They did not need to say anything. They knew that they would have to destroy the fixtures before they could think about saving themselves.

Bobby looked at Taff and shrugged, resigning himself to the task.

"Cunts," Taff roared.

He turned and ran towards the door. Reaching across the barricade, he raised his M4 and smashed the butt against the face of the snarling man. The bone of the skull cracked and imploded, and the dead face slid down through the gap and crashed into the floor with a wet smack.

Together, Taff and Bobby began to hammer at the bolts, shouting with frustration as they saw their efforts yield no results. Above them, the others continued to shout down into the control room, demanding that they begin to climb.

The doors began to splinter and the barricade shifted.

Bobby stepped back and fired off a whole magazine into the floor around the bolts, ripping up tufts of the carpeting and splinters of the hard concrete as ricochets whizzed and zipped in all directions.

"For fuck sake," Bobby roared, "come on, you bastard."

The pair of them kicked and kicked at the frame, throwing all their weight into the assault until slowly, it began to move. Sensing victory, they barged their bodies against it and forced the ladder back against its fittings in the ceiling. With a loud creaking noise, it buckled against the brackets, dislodging it and rendering it impossible to be climbed.

Taff turned and fired into the first of the bodies that had squeezed their way through the gap and began scrambling over the barricade. He watched them crumple with multiple hits as his rifle shook in his hands and switched his aim to the heads of the next.

To his left, he sensed Bobby's frenzied movements and turned to see him unravelling a hosepipe from a red container on the wall. Without any explanation, Bobby raised his rifle and fired into the windows that overlooked the runway. They splintered and shattered, bursting out into the open air and without waiting for the glass to cease falling, Bobby charged forward, gripping the fire hose tightly in his hands.

"Follow me, Taff," he yelled over his shoulder as he disappeared through the opening in the tower window.

Taff hesitated, glued to the spot.

He looked on in shock, his mouth agape, unsure whether he had really seen what his eyes relayed to him. He had just witnessed his friend hurl himself through a window with nothing but a hosepipe to stall his decent and shouting words encouragement for him to do the same as he dropped from sight.

Beside him, the hose rolled out rapidly and came to an abrupt halt as it reached the limit of its length and snapped taut. A loud grinding noise rose up from behind and Taff turned just in time to sidestep the steel bracket that the fire hose had been wrapped around. Torn from its mounting on the wall, it shot out through the window in Bobby's wake.

Even over the sound of bodies crashing against the door behind him, Taff was sure that he heard a wet splat and heavy thud from outside on the runway.

He looked up and saw the stunned expression on Bull's face staring back down at him through the hatch. Neither of them said anything but a loud crunch forced Taff from his daze. He turned and saw the doors being forced open, away from their frame and a tide of mottled flesh begin to flood into the tower.

Bull was too high for him to reach and faced with the choice of being devoured by the snapping jaws of the infected, or following Bobby to a quick death, he chose the latter.

As the first of the grasping hands reached to within just centimetres from his back, Taff rocketed himself forward towards the gaping hole in the window frame. Bellowing at the top of his lungs as he launched himself upwards, his momentum carrying him forwards towards his target, he sailed through the air and out to join Bobby.

He became weightless.

He could feel his innards become displaced within his body as he hurtled towards the hard tarmac of the runway beneath the tower. He fell, seemingly for hours, through the still air, hearing nothing but the sound of his own heartbeat and the voices of his memories as they flooded into his mind from all throughout his life.

His body twisted, his arms flailed, and finally, he spun upright, his feet plummeting towards the ground.

Shit, oh shit, he heard his own mind screaming out, over and over.

In the final moments, he saw the vibrant green of the grass verge around the control tower, racing up to meet him.

Fuck, this is going to hurt.

26

Bobby was dragging him, shouting at him to move under his own steam, but the pain in his legs prevented him from little more than a hobble. After landing, Taff had crumpled into a heap, feeling his ankles and knees buckle beneath the impact. He was certain that, at the very least, his right ankle was broken and his left knee had popped out of position. His hips and back also screamed at him, sending convulsions of agony through his entire body, making him suspect he had slipped a disc and fractured his pelvis.

Bobby continued to force him to move.

Bobby too was hurt. He had felt his back crack during his fall and was sure that it was broken along with a number of his ribs. However, his fear of becoming a feast for the infected compelled him to keep going.

Limping across the runway, with the tower receding into the distance behind them, they headed for the nearest of the small private hangers, far to the south of the terminal. Out to their right, a number of aircraft, military and commercial planes, were hurriedly making their way into position to begin take-off and make their escape. There was no way that the two wounded men could catch them now, and even if they did, it was unlikely that the pilots would stop to pick them up. The airport had fallen and to wait any longer, left them at risk of never being able to take off again as the infected were already pouring onto the runways and racing towards the taxying planes.

"Where are we going, Bobby?" Taff wheezed as his body threatened to give up on him.

"Just keep going," Bobby grunted, still holding onto his friends harness, pulling and dragging him along.

In danger of their injuries engulfing them and leaving them incapable of continuing, they reached the first of the hangers.

Inside, they found nothing but emptiness, forcing them to persist with their search. Far behind them, they could hear the terminal as it fell into chaos. The agonizing moans of the infected drifted out onto the airfield, carried along on the cool air, and the shattering screams of living people, being eaten alive, rasped at their ears.

In the hangers that they passed, they watched for signs of movement, both of them fully aware that if they were attacked, there was very little that either of them could do in their present condition. They limped along, gritting their teeth and swallowing down their pain as their speed was reduced to little more than a shuffle.

They were forced to search further and further along the airfield, all the while, their bodies threatening to succumb to their injuries. Taff could feel his ankle swelling against the interior of his boot and already, his knee was stretching the material of his trousers as it became bloated to twice its normal size. Each step sent an excruciating pain through his nervous system, wracking his body and blurring his vision, making his head spin and his mind tumble.

Reaching the final hanger, Taff collapsed against the door, unable to walk any further on his crippled limbs.

"I'm done. I'm fucked," he groaned, sinking to the floor as Bobby continued on into the shadowy building.

A moment later, he reappeared, smiling broadly at him and began helping him up again, pulling him by the arm.

"We're in luck," he panted.

Taff stared back at him.

Bobby's pain contorted face looked as exhausted as Taff felt and he wondered how the man was still going after all they had been through. With great difficulty, he climbed to his feet and conceded that he would allow his aching body to be dragged just a little further.

Inside, leaning against one another for support as they staggered deeper into the wide open space of the building, Bobby pointed to something in the far corner.

Taff was expecting to see a car, or truck, but instead, he saw an airplane.

He turned to Bobby, wanting to hit him, but he did not have the strength, and instead, he just drooled and slurred his anger filled words.

"A fucking Cessna?" He grunted. "*I* don't know how to fly a fucking plane."

Bobby grunted and turned away from him, continuing to drag himself along, his foot scraping across the concrete as he hobbled towards the little aircraft, drawing on his reserves of endurance and determination.

"Well, we're lucky that *I* know how to fly one, aren't we?"

Inside the cockpit, Taff collapsed into the co-pilots seat as Bobby began his checks before starting up the engine.

"Will this thing start? How much fuel do we have?"

Bobby ignored the questions.

As he flicked switches and checked dials and readouts, Taff watched, understanding nothing of what his friend was doing. A few minutes later, with the prop turning at full revolutions and the tiny airplane racing down the runway, bumping along and swaying from side to side, Bobby turned to him, an insane looking grin etched across his face.

"Fuel isn't the problem, mate."

Taff, close to unconsciousness and with his eyes beginning to roll, stared up at him from his slumped position in the co-pilot's seat.

"So, what *is* the problem then?" He shouted over the din of the engine, delving deep into his own energy reserves to remain conscious and make himself heard.

Bobby shifted his position and began to pull back on the control yoke, feeling the wheels begin gently to bounce against the tarmac. The nose angled upwards and the plane was suddenly airborne, rapidly gaining altitude and soaring away from the terminal.

Bobby let out a laugh that sounded close to madness, amazed at the fact that he had actually managed to take off. Still hooting, he checked over his shoulder and looked back down at the ground, seeing it receding fast below the tiny Cessna.

"We did it," he roared, "we made it."

Far below them, they were able to see the gaggle of survivors that crowded the roof of the control tower. With a couple of sharp movements of the centre-stick, Bobby forced the wings of the Cessna to alternately dip, hoping that their friends noticed and recognised the signal.

He turned back to Taff who was still staring up at him.

"Landing," he shouted as loudly as he could.

"What about landing?" Taff hollered back, forgetting their earlier conversation.

“Landing,” Bobby repeated matter-of-factly, “fuel isn’t the problem, Taff; landing is.”

“Why?”

“I’ve never done it,” Bobby confessed with a shrug. “I’ve only had four lessons.”

27

The streets of London were flowing red with blood. The infection had seized control and anyone lucky enough to remain alive, had been forced to flee, abandoning the British capital and leaving it to rot along with its new populace.

Samantha watched through the window, seeing the crowds of monsters that flowed through the streets like flood waters from a river that had burst its banks. Smoke was rising from almost every structure in the city as the fires swept through entire districts and explosions obliterated buildings, reducing them to smouldering rubble.

She was no fool, and did not try to convince herself that everyone had managed to escape. She knew that there would still be hundreds, if not thousands, of people trapped within the city, terrified and huddled together, waiting to die.

On the outskirts, a few cars were still desperately trying to pick their way through the gridlocked roads, smashing their way through the debris and infected. Some of them made it, but most became bogged down, unable to move and their occupants remaining trapped inside, waiting for the windows to finally give way as swarms of pale faces clustered around and beat their bodies and hands against the glass.

She closed her eyes and bit down on her lip, fighting with her feelings, knowing that she was being lifted to safety, while so many other people had been left to die.

An hour or so later, after cutting their way through the sky over the south of England, they passed over Portsmouth. It was the last built-up area before they were out over the Channel for the short skip across The Solent and onto the Isle of Wight.

At just a few hundred feet above the city, Samantha could clearly see the chaos on the ground below. Just as London had been, it was given up to the dead.

At the harbour, she looked on at the sea of people fighting to get a place on the ships that were hastily throwing off their lines and attempting to put some distance between them and the harbour wall.

On closer inspection, she was able to see why the ships were so keen to set sail.

The perimeters around the harbour had collapsed.

Thousands of the dead were pouring in, spreading like locusts through the quayside and attacking the fleeing people, who all instinctively headed for the docks.

"My God," Samantha whispered, watching the scene as it unfolded, unable to comprehend the speed at which the infected could overwhelm an entire city.

Within minutes, the dockside was nothing but a seething mass of bodies, impossible to distinguish between the living and the dead.

The last ship, a large Channel ferry, cast off and rapidly made its way from the dock wall and out into the middle of the harbour, attempting to reach deeper water and head for sea. Suddenly, she made a sharp turn to starboard, quickly accompanied by a bright flash that shot up from the area of the stern. Debris and parts of the vessel's superstructure flew into the air and within seconds, flames and black clouds of billowing smoke began to engulf the ship.

Even from the altitude, it was easy to make out the hundreds of figures that ran in all directions along the decks, hurling themselves into the water as another explosion ripped through the hull, and tore a hole in the bow.

The ship quickly began to list to port and as their aircraft continued onwards, Samantha's final view of the ferry was one of it capsizing and beginning to sink, dragging thousands of refugees into the depths along with it.

"All those poor souls," she shuddered, turning away and wiping a tear from her eye, "we left them to die."

She felt helpless and ashamed, knowing that so many people had been left behind and abandoned. She buried her face in her hands and began to cry soundlessly within the howling interior of the Chinook.

Outside, in the cold morning air, other aircraft had taken flight. *All* of them were headed away from the British Isles.

A short while later, they were over the Isle of Wight.

Hundreds of ships and boats lay at anchor around her coast and the sky over the island, buzzed with helicopters and fighter jets. Amongst the vessels, sat a number of destroyers and an aircraft carrier, the remains of the Royal Navy's fleet in the area around the British Isles.

As the CH-47 began its approach, Samantha caught site of something coming towards them from the north. She looked closer and saw the small white object, a hundred feet below them to their rear, clearly struggling to maintain its altitude. Its wings were swaying, and the tail continued to yaw to the right, being buffeted by the side winds that threatened to push the small single propped airplane off course and spiralling into the earth.

Curiously, she eyed the aircraft, realising that it was headed for the island but wondering where it was intending to land. As far as she knew, the engineers and construction workers had not yet finished the runway and the only planes and helicopters allowed to approach within a kilometre of the HMS Illustrious, were military aircraft. If the tiny Cessna even appeared to head for the aircraft carrier, it would be blown out of the sky.

By now, the flimsy airplane had passed beneath their fuselage and Samantha, feeling drawn to continue her vigilance on its progress, jumped from her seat in the rear and raced up towards the cock-pit.

"Do you have comms with that plane?" She called into Melanie's ear and pointed out through the window.

Melanie shook her head.

"We've already tried. They're not answering up."

They were now over Northwood, heading deeper into the island and soaring over the patchwork landscape of the rural areas.

Something was tugging at Samantha, and she could not understand what, or why. She felt drawn to the little Cessna, keen to see what it did and where it went.

She *had* to know what would become of it and if they made it down safely.

"Stay with them," she shouted and patted Lieutenant Frakes on her shoulder, "don't let them out of your sight."

Curious, but unwilling to question why, Melanie complied and kept a safe distance behind the unbalanced and seemingly random flight plan of the Cessna.

Samantha stayed beside her, watching its progress intently and willing them to make a successful landing. She noticed that she had begun to sweat, and her nails had been digging into her palms so deeply that they had broken the skin.

It was clear that the pilot was intending to land, but the ground below was a freshly ploughed field and uneven, at best. Worse still, they were descending far too rapidly and Samantha quickly realised that it could only be an amateur behind the controls as it began to reduce its airspeed and dip towards the fields.

"What the fuck is this lunatic doing?" Mike gasped from the co-pilot's seat beside Melanie in the cockpit.

Melanie, her mouth agape, shook her head as she looked on in disbelief.

When the small plane was just twenty-five metres from the ground, the pilot clearly pulled back too far on the control yoke. With its speed reduced, the nose flared upwards and the tail dipped sharply towards the ground.

The people in the Chinook watched in horror as the Cessna's engine stalled and the undercarriage plummeted towards the churned mud below.

It crashed into the earth with a 'belly-flop', sending thick clumps of soil and parts of the aircraft flying through the air in all directions as the remains of the Cessna slid and rolled through the squelching mire, finally coming to a dead stop in a hedge with smoke pluming from its tattered fuselage and engine.

Melanie slowed the Chinook to a hover and eyed the wreckage.

Nothing moved from within the cockpit of the downed aircraft, and Samantha felt her stomach churn.

"Get me down there," she ordered Lieutenant Frakes with urgency. "I need to know."

END

http://www.lukeduffybooks.com/

Also By Luke Duffy

Made in the USA
Lexington, KY
17 February 2016